MISTRESS OF THE GAME

BOOKS BY SIDNEY SHELDON

Are You Afraid of the Dark?

The Sky Is Falling

Tell Me Your Dreams

The Best Laid Plans

Morning, Noon & Night

Nothing Lasts Forever

The Stars Shine Down

The Doomsday Conspiracy

Memories of Midnight

The Sands of Time

Windmills of the Gods

If Tomorrow Comes

Master of the Game

Rage of Angels

Bloodline

A Stranger in the Mirror

The Other Side of Midnight

The Naked Face

SIDNEY SHELDON'S
MISTRESS
OF THE GAME

Tilly Bagshawe

WILLIAM MORROW
An Imprint of HarperCollins*Publishers*

Bug

For Alexandra Sheldon,
with love and thanks

MISTRESS OF THE GAME. Copyright © 2009 by Sheldon Family Limited Partnership, successor to the rights and interests of Sidney Sheldon. All rights reserved. Printed in the United States of America. No part of this book may be used or reproduced in any manner whatsoever without written permission except in the case of brief quotations embodied in critical articles and reviews. For information address HarperCollins Publishers, 10 East 53rd Street, New York, NY 10022.

HarperCollins books may be purchased for educational, business, or sales promotional use. For information please write: Special Markets Department, HarperCollins Publishers, 10 East 53rd Street, New York, NY 10022.

FIRST EDITION

Library of Congress Cataloging-in-Publication Data has been applied for.

ISBN 978-0-06-172838-9

09 10 11 12 13   WBC/RRD   10 9 8 7 6 5 4 3 2 1

PROLOGUE

LEXI TEMPLETON'S HANDS TREMBLED AS SHE READ THE letter. Sitting on the bed in her wedding dress, in what had once been her great-grandmother's bedroom, her quick mind began to race.

Think. You don't have much time.

What would Kate Blackwell have done?

At forty-one, Lexi Templeton was still a beautiful woman. Her lustrous blond hair was untouched by gray and her slim, petite figure showed no sign of her recent pregnancy. She'd been determined to get her killer body back before her wedding. She wanted to do justice to her vintage Monique Lhullier gown, a clinging column of the finest ivory-white lace. And she had.

Earlier, the hundred or so wedding guests gathered at Cedar Hill House, the Blackwell family's legendary Maine estate, had gasped when Lexi Templeton appeared on the lawn arm in arm with her father. Talk about Beauty and the Beast. Peter Templeton, Lexi's father, once an eminent psychiatrist and one of New York's most eligible bachelors, was now an old man. Frail, bent almost double with age and grief, Peter Templeton led his beautiful daughter toward the rose-covered altar.

He thought: *I can go now. I can go to join my darling Alexandra. Our little girl is happy at last.*

He was right. Lexi Templeton *was* happy. She knew she looked radiant. She was marrying the man she loved, surrounded by family and friends. Only one person was missing. That person would never witness another of Lexi's triumphs. He would never delight in another of her failures. His life and Lexi's had been intertwined since birth, like the tangled roots of a great tree. But now he was gone, never to return. Despite everything that had happened, Lexi missed him.

Can you see me, Max, darling? Are you watching? Are you sorry now?

For a moment, Lexi Templeton felt a pang of loss. Then she laid eyes on her husband-to-be, and all her regrets evaporated. Today was going to be perfect. The cliché. The fairy tale. The happiest day of her life.

The president of the United States was unable to make the wedding. There was a small matter of a war in the Middle East. But he sent a congratulatory telegram, which Lexi's brother, Robbie, read aloud when the newlyweds cut the cake. And everybody else was there. Captains of industry, prime ministers, kings, movie stars. As chairwoman of the mighty Kruger-Brent, Ltd., Lexi Templeton was American royalty. She looked like a queen because she was one. She had it all: great beauty, immense wealth and power that stretched to the four corners of the globe. Now, thanks to her new husband, she had love, too.

But she also had enemies. Powerful enemies. One of whom was determined to destroy her, even from beyond the grave.

Lexi read the letter again.

I know what you've done. I know everything.

The net was closing in. Lexi felt the fear churn in her stomach like curdled milk.

There must be a way out of this. There's always a way. I will not go to prison. I will not lose Kruger-Brent. I will not lose my family. Think!

A few hours earlier, the governor of Maine made a speech about Lexi at the reception.

". . . a remarkable woman, from a remarkable family. Lexi Templeton's personal courage and integrity are known to all of us. Her spirit, her determination, her business acumen, her honesty . . ."

Honesty? If only they knew!

". . . these make up the public face of Lexi Templeton. But today, we're here to celebrate something else. A very private joy. A very private love. And a love that those of us who know Lexi know she so richly deserves."

Lexi thought: *None of you know me. Not even my husband. I don't "deserve" his love. But I fought for it, and I won it, and I'm damned if I'm going to let anyone take it away from me. Least of all you.*

Now most of the guests had gone. Lexi's brother, Robbie and his partner were still downstairs. So was Lexi's baby daughter, Maxine, and the nanny. Any moment now Lexi's husband would come looking for her. It was time to leave for their honeymoon.

It was time . . .

Lexi Templeton walked over to the window. Beyond the formal lawns of Cedar Hill House she could see the closely huddled white roofs of Dark Harbor, and behind them the dark, brooding sea. This evening the roiling water looked unusually ominous.

It's waiting. One day it will swallow the island whole. A big wave will come and wipe everything out. As if none of this ever existed.

Two men in suits got out of a car and approached the security gate. Even before they pulled out their badges, Lexi Templeton knew who they were. It was just like it said in the letter: *The police are on their way. You have no way out, Alexandra. Not this time.*

Tears stung the back of Lexi's eyes. She could hear her aunt Eve's voice as clearly as if she were still alive, taunting her, laden with spite. Was she right? Was this really it? The end of the game? After all Lexi's struggles? She remembered a Dylan Thomas poem she'd learned at school: "Do not go gentle into that good night. Rage, rage against the dying of the light."

Damn right I'll rage. I'll not let that old witch beat me without a fight.

The cops were through the gate now. They were almost at the door.

Lexi Templeton took a deep breath and went downstairs to meet them.

 BOOK ONE

ONE

DARK HARBOR, MAINE. 1984

DANNY CORRETTI LOOKED DOWN THROUGH THE branches at the swirling mass of people below and felt gripped by a wave of vertigo.

"What the hell are we doing here?"

Closing his eyes, he tightened his grip around the ancient yew tree, making sure both he and his camera remained concealed in the thick green foliage.

"Making money," his companion whispered excitedly. "Look, there she is!"

"Where?"

Following his friend's line of vision, Danny Corretti trained his zoom lens on a figure huddled in the very center of the crowd of mourners. Dressed head to toe in black, with a thick, floor-length lace mantilla covering her immaculately cut Dior suit, it was impossible to make out her face. She could have been anyone. But she wasn't anyone.

"Are you kidding me?" Danny Corretti frowned. Below him the churchyard seemed to lurch ominously, the ancient graves rising and falling like horses on a ghoulish carousel. "I can't see shit. Are you sure it's her? It could be Johnny Carson under all that lace."

His companion grinned. "Not with that ass it couldn't. It's her all right."

From the tree to his left, Danny Corretti heard the low *whir, whir, click* of a rival camera. Refocusing his zoom, he began to shoot.

Come on, baby. Give Daddy a smile.

A clear shot of Eve Blackwell's face would be worth a cool hundred grand to whichever photographer got there first. Anyone skilled enough to capture her elusive baby bump could expect to earn twice that.

Two hundred grand!

Not a lot of money to the Blackwells perhaps, heirs to multibillion-dollar Kruger-Brent, Ltd., the diamond empire turned vast, multinational conglomerate that had made them the richest family in America; but a fortune to Danny Corretti. It was the Blackwells who had brought Danny and his fellow paparazzi to St. Stephen's churchyard on this chill February morning. They had come to bury their matriarch, Kate Blackwell, dead at last at the grand old age of ninety-two.

Look at them. Like bloated blackflies, swarming around the old lady's corpse. Revolting.

Danny Corretti felt his nausea return, but tried not to think about it, or about the excruciating pain in his back from being stuck up a tree for six straight hours. He longed to stretch out, but didn't dare move a muscle, in case he alerted the Kruger-Brent security guards to his presence. Watching the dour, black-clad figures pace the perimeter of the churchyard, pistols clutched like security blankets to their ex–Marine Corps chests, Danny Corretti felt a stab of fear. He doubted Kate Blackwell had hired any of them for their sense of humor.

You'll be okay. Just get the shot and get out of here. Come on, Eve, baby. Say cheese.

Danny Corretti wasn't really cut out for this sort of covert work. A tall, skinny man with preternaturally long legs and an unexpected shock of white-blond hair above his Italian olive complexion, there weren't too many hiding places in the Maine churchyard that could accommodate his lanky, six-foot-two frame. The yew tree had been his best option, but he'd had to arrive ludicrously early this morning to beat his rivals to such a coveted vantage point. As he clung to the upper branches now, every sinew of his body felt like it was on fire, despite the numbing cold of the day. He gritted his teeth, cursing his long legs to the heavens.

Just think of the money.

Ironically, if it weren't for his long legs, Danny wouldn't have been on this crazy job in the first place.

If it hadn't been for Danny's long legs, his mistress's husband would never have noticed his size-twelve feet sticking out from under the marital bed.

Ah, Carla. God, she was beautiful! Those breasts, as soft and succulent as two ripe peaches. No man could resist her. If only that neanderthal she married hadn't punched out early . . .

It was Danny's long legs that had gotten him beaten to a pulp and landed him (uninsured) in the local hospital. Thanks to his long legs, his wife, Loretta, had discovered his affair, divorced him, and taken the house. Now, thanks to his long legs, Loretta's rat-faced lawyer was demanding that Danny pay alimony to the tune of a thousand bucks a month.

A thousand bucks? Who did they think he was, Donald friggin' Trump?

Yes, Danny blamed his long legs entirely for his current predicament. Why else would he be spending his Sunday morning bent double and freezing his ass off in a four-hundred-year-old tree above a graveyard, risking his neck for one lousy picture of the woman the tabloids had dubbed "The Beast of the Blackwells"?

Danny Corretti's long legs had a lot to answer for.

He was gonna get that shot of Eve Blackwell if it killed him.

The priest's voice rang out through the February chill, deep and strong and powerful.

"Merciful God, you know the anguish of the sorrowful . . ."

Behind her thick veil, Eve Blackwell sneered. *Sorrowful? To see that old witch dead and buried? Please. If I were ten years younger I'd be doing cartwheels.*

Today Eve was burying one of her enemies. But she would not rest until she had buried them all.

One down, three to go.

"You are attentive to the prayers of the humble . . ."

Eve Blackwell glanced around at the small group of family and friends who had come to bid her grandmother Kate farewell and wondered if any of them could be described as humble.

There was her identical twin sister, Alexandra. At thirty-four, Alexandra was still a great beauty with her high cheekbones, mane of buttermilk hair and the striking gray eyes she had inherited from her great-grandfather, Kruger-Brent's founder, Jamie McGregor.

Eve's eyes narrowed with hatred. The same hatred she had felt for her twin since the day they emerged from the womb.

How dare she! How dare my sister still look beautiful.

Alexandra was weeping openly, clutching tightly to her son Robert's hand. Blond, delicate and sweet-natured, ten-year-old Robert was a carbon copy of his mother. A gifted pianist, he had been Kate Blackwell's favorite, and Kruger-Brent's heir apparent.

Not for much longer, thought Eve. *Let's see how long the boy lasts without Kate around to protect him.*

Eve Blackwell felt her chest tighten. How she loathed the pair of them, mother and son and their crocodile tears! If only it were Alexandra's body being lowered into the gaping, frozen earth today. Then Eve's happiness would truly be complete.

Beside Alexandra hovered her husband, the eminent psychiatrist Peter Templeton. Tall, dark, handsome and blue-eyed, Peter Templeton looked more like a quarterback than a psychiatrist. He and Alex made a handsome couple. Peter had once been arrogant enough to think he understood Eve. He believed he'd seen through her, through to the molten core of hatred that bubbled deep within. Alexandra, in her goodness, had never been able to see how much her twin sister hated her. But her husband knew better.

Eve smiled.

Vain fool. He thinks he knows me, but he's barely scratched the surface.

No, the priest would find no humility in Peter Templeton.

What about her own husband, the eminent plastic surgeon Keith Webster? Many people thought of Keith Webster as humble. Eve could hear his grateful patients now: "Dear Dr. Webster, such a gifted surgeon, but so shy and unassuming about his talents." Eve felt her flesh creep as Keith wrapped a protective, conjugal arm around her shoulder.

Protective? He's not protective. He's possessive. And psychotic. He blackmailed me into marriage, then deliberately destroyed my face, carving up my beautiful features and turning me into this grotesque, this creature from a carnival freak show. All so that I wouldn't leave him.

One day I'll make that bastard pay for what he's done.

Eve Blackwell was many things, but she was not stupid. She knew that the trees and bushes around St. Stephen's Church were alive with photographers, and she knew why: they all wanted a picture of her hideously ravaged face.

Well, they could go to hell, the lot of them. From behind, you could still make out Eve's perfect, womanly figure. But her front side was completely concealed. No lens on earth could penetrate the thick, handwoven lace of her veil. Eve had made sure of it.

Once a renowned beauty, in recent years Eve Blackwell had become a virtual recluse in her Manhattan penthouse, terrified of showing her monstrously scarred face to the world. Indeed, she had not been seen in public for two years. The last time was at her grandmother's ninetieth birthday party at Cedar Hill House, the Blackwell family's private Camelot, just yards from where the old woman was now being laid to rest.

Kate Blackwell was the lucky one. She'd gone to join her beloved ghosts: Jamie, Margaret, Banda, David, the spirits of Kruger-Brent's long and violent African past. But there was to be no such rest for Eve. With rumors already flying about her pregnancy—Eve and Alexandra Blackwell were both expecting, but the family had refused to confirm this to the press—Eve was well aware that the price on her head had doubled. There wasn't a tabloid editor in America who wouldn't sell his soul for a half-decent picture of the Beast of the Blackwells *with child*.

And to think, they call me *a monster* . . .

"Lord, hear Your people, who cry out to You in their need . . ."

Eve watched silently as Kate Blackwell's coffin was lowered into the freshly dug grave. Brad Rogers, Kate's number two at Kruger-Brent for three decades, stifled a sob. Now a very old man himself, his hair as white and thin as the dusting of February snow beneath his feet, Brad Rogers had been all but broken by Kate's death. Secretly he had loved her for years. But it was a love she could never return.

How tiny she is! thought Eve in wonder as the pathetic wooden box disappeared into the bowels of the earth. Kate Blackwell, who had loomed so large in life, feted by presidents and kings. How insignificant she was, in the end.

Not much of a feast for the worms of your beloved Dark Harbor, are you, Granny?

For years, Kate Blackwell had been Eve's nemesis. She'd done everything in her power to prevent her wicked granddaughter from achieving her life's ambition—taking control of the family firm, the mighty Kruger-Brent.

But now Kate Blackwell was gone.

"Eternal rest grant to her, O Lord, and may perpetual light shine upon her."

Good riddance, you vengeful old bitch. I hope you rot in hell.

"May she rest in peace."

Danny Corretti looked miserably at the negatives in front of him. His back was still killing him after this morning, and now he felt a migraine coming on.

"You get anything?"

His friend tried to sound hopeful. But he already knew the answer.

None of them had gotten the two-hundred-thousand-dollar picture.

Eve Blackwell had outsmarted them all.

TWO

IN THE MATERNITY UNIT AT NEW YORK'S MOUNT SINAI Medical Center, Nurse Gaynor Matthews watched the handsome, middle-aged father take his newborn child in his arms for the first time.

He was gazing at the baby girl, oblivious to everything around him. Nurse Matthews thought: *He's thinking how beautiful she is.*

Nurse Matthews was pleasantly plump, with a round, open face and a ready smile that accentuated the twin fans of lines around her eyes. A midwife for more than a decade, she'd seen this moment played out thousands of times—hundreds of them in this very room—but she never tired of it. Besotted dads, their eyes lighting up with love, the purest love they would ever know. Moments like these made midwifery worthwhile. Worth the grinding hours. Worth the crappy pay. Worth the patronizing male obstetricians who thought of themselves as gods just because they had a medical degree and a penis.

Worth the rare moments of tragedy.

The father gently caressed his baby's cheek. He was a beautiful man, Nurse Matthews decided. Tall, dark, broad-shouldered, a classic jock. Just the way she liked them.

She blushed. What on earth was she doing? She had no right to think such things. Not at a time like this.

The father thought: *Jesus Christ. She's so like her mother.*

It was true. The little girl's skin was the same delicate, translucent peach as the girl he'd fallen in love with all those years ago. Her big, inquisitive eyes were the same pale gray, like dawn mist rolling off the ocean. Even her dimpled chin was her mother in miniature. For a split second, the father's heart leaped at the sight of her, an involuntary smile playing around his lips.

His daughter. *Their* daughter. So tiny. So perfect.

Then he looked down at the blood on his hands.

And screamed.

Alex had been so excited that morning when Peter drove her to the hospital.

"Can you believe that in a few short hours she'll be here?"

She was still in her pajamas, her long blond hair tangled after a fitful night's sleep, but he didn't think she'd ever looked more luminous. She wore a grin wider than the Lincoln Tunnel, and if she was nervous, she didn't show it.

"We're finally going to meet her!"

"Or him." He reached over to the passenger seat and squeezed his wife's hand.

"Uh-uh. No way. It's a girl. I know it."

She'd woken up around six with fairly mild contractions and insisted on waiting another two hours before she would let him drive her to Mount Sinai. Two hours in which Peter Templeton had walked up and down the stairs of their West Village brownstone sixteen times, made four unwanted cups of coffee, burned three slices of toast and yelled at his son, Robert, for not being ready for school on time, before being reminded by the housekeeper that it was in fact mid-July, and school had been out for the last five weeks.

Even at the hospital Peter flapped around uselessly like a mother hen.

"Can I get you anything? A hot towel?"

"I'm fine."

"Water?"

"No thanks."

"Crushed ice cubes?"

"Peter . . ."

"What about that meditation music you're always playing? That's calming, right? I could run to the car and get the tape?"

Alex laughed. She was astonishingly calm.

"I think you need it more than I do. Honestly, darling, you must try to relax. I'm having a baby. Women do this every day. I'll be fine."

I'll be fine.

The first problems began about an hour later. The midwife frowned at one of the monitors. Its green line had begun rising in sudden, jagged leaps.

"Stand back please, Dr. Templeton."

Peter searched the woman's face for clues, like a nervous airline passenger watching the flight attendant during turbulence . . . if she was still smiling and handing out gin-and-tonics, no one was gonna die, right? But Nurse Matthews would have made a first-class poker player. As she moved surely and confidently around the room, a professional smile of reassurance for Alex, a brusque nod of command to an orderly—*fetch Dr. Farrar immediately*—her doughlike features gave nothing away.

"What is it? What's the problem?"

Peter struggled to keep the panic out of his voice, for Alex's sake. Her own mother had died giving birth to her and Eve, a snippet of Blackwell family history that had always terrified Peter. He loved Alexandra so much. If anything should happen to her . . .

"Your wife's blood pressure is somewhat elevated, Dr. Templeton. There's no need for alarm at this stage. I've asked Dr. Farrar to come and assess the situation."

For the first time, Alexandra's face clouded with anxiety.

"What about the baby? Is she all right? Is she in distress?"

It was typical Alex. Never a thought for herself, only for the child. She'd been exactly the same with Robert. Since the day their son was born, ten years ago now, he'd been the center of his mother's universe. Had Peter Templeton been a different sort of man, a lesser man, he might have felt jealous. As it was, the bond between mother and son filled him with joy, a delight so intense that at times he could barely contain it.

It was impossible to imagine a more devoted, selfless, adoring mother than Alexandra. Peter would never forget the time Robert came down with chicken pox, a particularly nasty case. He was five years old, and Alex had sat by his bedside for forty-eight hours straight, so engrossed in her son's needs that she had forgotten to take so much as a sip of water for herself. When Peter came home from work, he'd found her passed out cold on the floor. She was so dehydrated she'd had to be hospitalized and placed on a drip.

The midwife's voice brought him back to the present with a jolt.

"The baby's fine, Mrs. Templeton. Worst-case scenario, we'll speed things up and do a cesarean."

Alex went white.

"A cesarean?"

"Try not to worry. It probably won't come to that. Right now the heartbeat looks terrific. Your baby's as strong as an ox."

Nurse Matthews had even risked a smile.

Peter would remember that smile as long as he lived. It was to be the last image of his old, happy life.

After the smile, reality and nightmare began to blur. Time lost all meaning. The obstetrician was there, Dr. Farrar, a tall, forbidding man in his sixties with a pinched face and glasses that seemed in permanent, imminent danger of toppling off the end of his long, shrewlike nose. The green line on the monitor took on a life of its own, some unseen hand pulling it higher, higher until it looked like a fluorescent etching of the north face of the Eiger. Peter had never seen anything quite so ugly. Then came the beeping. First one machine, then two, then three, louder, louder, screeching and screaming at him, and the screams turned into Alex's voice, *Peter! Peter!* and he reached out his hand for hers, and it was their wedding day, and his hands were trembling.

Do you take this woman?

I do.

I do! I'm here, Alex! I'm here, my darling.

The doctor's voice: *"For Christ's sake, someone get him out of here."*

Peter was being pushed, and he pushed back, and something fell to the floor with a crash. Then suddenly the sounds were gone, and everything was color. First white: white coats, white lights, so strong Peter was almost blinded. Then red, the red of Alex's blood, blood everywhere, rivers and rivers of blood so livid and ketchup-bright it looked fake, like a prop from a movie set. And finally black, as the movie screen faded, and Peter was falling into a well, down, down, deep into the darkness, pictures of his darling Alex flickering briefly in front of him like ghosts as he fell:

Flash!

The day they first met, in Peter's psychiatrist's office, back when Alexandra was still married to that psychopath George Mellis.

Flash!

Her smile, lit from within as she walked up the aisle to marry him, an angel in white.

Flash!

Robert's first birthday. Alex beaming, with chocolate cake smeared all over her face.

Flash!

This morning in the car.

We're finally going to meet her!

Dr. Templeton? Dr. Templeton, can you hear me?

We're losing him. He's blacking out.

Quick! Someone catch him!

No more flashes. Only silence and darkness.

The ghosts had gone.

Reality did not return until he heard his baby cry.

He'd been awake for almost half an hour, listening to the doctor and the hospital staff, even signing forms. But none of that was real.

"You must understand, the level of hemorrhaging, Dr. Templeton . . ."

"The speed of the blood loss . . ."

"Highly unusual . . . perhaps her family history?"

"After a certain point, heart failure cannot be prevented."

"Deeply sorry for your loss."

And Peter had nodded, yes, yes, he understood, of course, they'd done all they could. He'd watched them wheel Alex away, her ashen face covered with a bloodstained hospital sheet. He stood there, breathing in and out. But of course it wasn't real. How could it be? His Alex wasn't dead. The whole thing was preposterous. Women didn't die in childbirth, for God's sake, not in this day and age. This was 1984. This was New York City.

The shrill, plaintive cry seemed to come out of nowhere. Even in his profound state of shock, some primal instinct would not allow Peter to ignore it. Suddenly someone was handing him a tiny swaddled bundle, and the next thing Peter knew, he was gazing into his daughter's eyes. In an instant, every last brick of the protective wall he'd been building around his heart crumbled to dust. For one blissful moment, his heart swelled with pure love.

Then it shattered.

Wrenching the baby out of his arms, Nurse Matthews thrust her at an orderly.

"Take her to the nursery. And get a psych up here, right now. He's losing it."

Nurse Matthews was good in a crisis. But inside she was riddled with guilt. She should never have let him hold the child. What was she thinking? After what that poor man had just been through? He might have killed her.

In her defense, though, Peter had seemed so *stable*. Fifteen minutes ago he was signing forms and talking to Dr. Farrar and . . .

Peter's screams grew louder. Outside in the corridor, visitors exchanged worried glances and craned their necks to get a better view through the glass window of the delivery room.

Hands were on him again. Peter felt the sharp prick of a needle in his arm. As he lost consciousness, he knew that the peaceful blackness of the well would never return to him.

This wasn't a nightmare. It was real.

His beloved Alex was gone.

The press had a field day.

ALEXANDRA BLACKWELL DIES IN CHILDBIRTH!

To the public she would always be Alexandra Blackwell, just as Eve was forever known by her maiden name. "Templeton" and "Webster" simply didn't have the same cachet.

KRUGER-BRENT HEIRESS DEAD AT 34

AMERICA'S FIRST FAMILY STRUGGLES TO COPE WITH LOSS

The national fascination with the Blackwells was well into its fifth decade, but not since Eve Blackwell's surgical "mishap" had the papers been thrown such a juicy bone. Rumors were rife.

There was no baby: Alexandra had died of AIDS.

Her handsome husband, Peter Templeton, was having an affair and had somehow contrived to end his wife's life.

It was a government plot, designed to bring down Kruger-Brent's share price and limit the company's enormous power on the world stage.

Like Peter Templeton, no one could quite believe that a healthy, wealthy young woman could be admitted into New York's finest maternity hospital in the summer of 1984 and wind up twenty-four hours later on a slab in the morgue.

The rumors were fueled by a stony silence from both the family and the Kruger-Brent public-relations office. Brad Rogers, acting chairman since Kate Blackwell's death, had appeared just once in front of the cameras. Looking even older than his eighty-eight years, a white-haired apparition, his papery hands trembled as he read a terse statement:

"Alexandra Templeton's tragic and untimely death is entirely a private matter. Mrs. Templeton held no official role within Kruger-Brent, Ltd., and her passing is not pertinent to the management or future of this great company in any way. We ask that her family's request for privacy be respected at this difficult time. Thank you."

Refusing to take questions, he scurried back into the maze of the Kruger-Brent headquarters like a distressed beetle searching for the safety of its nest. Nothing had been heard from him since.

Undeterred by the lack of official information, perhaps even encouraged by it, the tabloids felt free to start making the story up themselves. Soon the rumor mill had taken on a life of its own. But by then it was too late for the family or anyone else to stop it.

"We must do something about these press reports."

Peter Templeton was in his study at home. With its tatty Persian rugs, antique Victorian upright piano, walnut paneling, and bookcases crammed to bursting with first editions, it had been one of Alex's favorite rooms, a place to retreat to after the stresses of the day. Now Peter paced it furiously like a caged tiger, shaking the newspaper in his hands.

"I mean this is the *New York Times,* for God's sake, not some supermarket rag." The disdain in his voice was palpable as he read aloud: "*'Alexandra Blackwell is believed to have been suffering from complications of the immune system for some time.'* Believed by whom? Where do they get this nonsense?"

Dr. Barnabus Hunt, a fat Santa Claus of a man with a crown of white hair around his bald spot and permanently ruddy cheeks, took a contemplative draw on his pipe. A fellow psychiatrist, and Peter Templeton's lifelong friend, he had been a frequent visitor to the house since Alex's death.

"Does it matter where they get it? You know my advice, Peter. Don't read this rubbish. Rise above it."

"That's easy for you to say, Barney. But what about Robbie? He's hearing this kind of poison day and night, poor kid."

It was the first time in weeks that Peter had expressed concern for his son's feelings. Barney Hunt thought: *That's a good sign.*

"As if his mother were some kind of prostitute," Peter raged on, "or a homosexual or a . . . a drug addict! I mean, anyone less likely to have AIDS than Alexandra . . ."

Under other circumstances, Barney Hunt would have gently challenged his friend's assumptions. As a medical man, Peter should know better than to give any credence to the pernicious idea that AIDS was some sort of righteous punishment for sinners. That was another thing the press should be blamed for: whipping the entire country into such a frenzy of HIV terror that gay men were being attacked in the streets, refused employment and even housing. As if the dreaded disease could be spread by association. It was a bad year to be gay in New York City—something Barney Hunt knew a lot more about than his friend Peter Templeton would ever have suspected.

But now was not the time to raise these issues. Six weeks after Alex's death and Peter's grief was still as raw as an open wound. His office at Kruger-Brent headquarters remained empty. Not that he'd ever done much there anyway. When Peter first married Alexandra, he'd insisted to Kate Blackwell that he would never go into the family business.

"I'll stick with my psychiatry practice, Mrs. Blackwell, if that's okay with you. I'm a doctor, not a businessman."

But in the years that followed, the old woman had ground him down. Kate Blackwell expected the men in her family to contribute to "the firm," as she called it. And what Kate Blackwell wanted, Kate Blackwell always got in the end.

But now Kate, like Alexandra, was gone. There was no one to stop Peter from spending entire days holed up in his study with the phone unplugged, staring mindlessly out of the window.

The true tragedy of Alexandra's death, however, was not Peter's retreat from life. It was the wedge that it had driven between Peter and his son, Robert.

Robbie Templeton was Barney Hunt's godson. Having known him since birth, Barney had seen firsthand the unusually close bond between Robbie and Alexandra. As a psychiatrist, he knew better than most how devastating it could be for a boy of ten to lose his mother. If not handled correctly, it was the sort of event that could fatally alter someone's personality. Dead mothers and estranged fathers: two of the key ingredients for psychopathic behavior. This was the stuff that serial killers, rapists and suicide bombers were made of. The danger for Robbie was very real. But Peter point-blank refused to see it. "He's fine, Barney. Leave it alone."

Barney's theory was that because the child had internalized his grief (Robbie hadn't cried once since Alex's death, an immensely worrying sign), Peter had convinced himself that his son was okay. Of course, the psychiatrist in him knew better. But Peter Templeton the Psychiatrist seemed to have shut down for the moment, overwhelmed by the pain of Peter Templeton the Man.

Barney Hunt, on the other hand, was still very much a psychiatrist and he could see the truth all too clearly. Robbie was screaming out for his father. Screaming for help, for love, for comfort.

Unfortunately his screams were silent.

While Peter and Robbie drifted past each other like two ruined ghosts, one member of the Templeton household provided a tiny, flickering light of hope. Named Alexandra, after her mother, but referred to from the start as Lexi, the baby that Alex had lost her life delivering was already an utter delight.

No one had told Lexi she was supposed to be in mourning for her mother. As a result, she yelled, gurgled, smiled and shook her little fists with happy abandon, blissfully ignorant of the tragic events surrounding her arrival into the world. Barney Hunt had never been big on babies—a confirmed bachelor, and closet homosexual, psychiatry was his life—but he made an exception for Lexi. She was quite the sunniest creature he had ever encountered. Blond-haired and fine-featured even at six weeks, with her mother's searching gray eyes, she "smiled whene'er you passed her," like Robert Browning's "Last Duchess," as content to be held by strangers as by her doting nurse.

She reserved her broadest grins for her brother, however. Robbie was entranced by his baby sister from the moment she arrived home from the hospital, rushing to greet her as soon as he got back from school, irritating the maternity nurse by dashing straight to her crib whenever she cried, even in the middle of the night.

"You mustn't panic so, Master Robert."

The nurse tried to be patient. The boy had just lost his mother, after all.

"Babies cry. It doesn't mean there's anything wrong with her."

Robbie scowled at the woman, full of contempt.

"Oh, really? How do *you* know?"

Peeling back the soft cashmere blankets, he lifted his sister to his chest, rocking her softly till her cries subsided. It was two in the morning, and outside the nursery window a full moon illuminated the Manhattan sky.

Are you out there, Mom? Can you see me? Can you see how good I'm taking care of her?

Everyone, including Barney, had been worried that Robbie might have very conflicted feelings toward the baby. He might even become violent toward her, "blaming" Lexi in some simple, childish way for their mother's death. But Robbie had confounded them all with an outpouring of brotherly love that was as unexpected as it was clearly genuine.

Lexi was Robbie's therapy—Lexi and his beloved piano. Whenever he felt the smooth, cool ivory beneath his fingers, Robbie was transported to another time and place. Every other sense shut down and he became one with the instrument, body and soul. At those times he knew his mother was with him. He just knew it.

"Robert, darling, don't lurk. Come in."

The forced cheeriness in Peter's voice made Barney Hunt wince. He turned and saw his young godson hovering in the doorway.

"Uncle Barney's here. Come and say hello."

Robbie smiled nervously.

"Hi, Uncle Barney."

He never used to be nervous, thought Barney. *Who's he afraid of? His dad?*

Standing up, he clapped Robbie on the back.

"Hey, sport. How you doing?"

"Good."

Liar.

"Your dad and I were just talking about you. We were wondering how things were going at school."

Robbie looked surprised. "School?"

"Yeah, you know. Have the other kids been giving you a hard time? About the stuff in the newspapers?"

"No, not at all. School's great. I love it there."

He likes school because it's an escape from this place. An escape from grief.

"Did you want to ask me something, Robert?"

Peter's tone was tense, his speech clipped. He'd remained seated behind the desk since his son came in, rigid-backed, his whole body clenched, like a prisoner on his way to the firing squad. He wished Robbie would go away.

Peter Templeton loved his son. He was aware that he was failing him. But every time he looked at the boy, he felt overcome by a wave of anger so violent he could hardly breathe. Suddenly the bond that Robbie and Alexandra had shared in life, the love between mother and son that had once been Peter's greatest delight, left him consumed with jealous rage. It was as if Robbie had stolen those hours from him, those countless, loving moments with Alex. Now she was gone forever. And Peter wanted those moments back.

He knew it was crazy. None of this was Robbie's fault. But still the fury corroded his chest like battery acid. The irony was that Peter felt nothing but love for Lexi, the baby who had "caused" Alex's death. In his grief-addled mind, Lexi was a victim, like himself. She had never even known her mother, poor darling. But Robert? Robert was a thief. He had stolen Alexandra from Peter. Peter couldn't forgive him for that.

Even now, Peter sometimes overheard the boy talking to her.

Mommy, are you there? Mommy, it's me.

Robbie would sit at the piano, a beatific smile on his face, and Peter knew that Alex was with him, comforting him, loving him, holding him. But when Peter woke in the night, screaming Alex's name, there was nothing. Nothing but the blackness and silence of the grave.

"No, Dad." Robert's voice was barely a whisper. "I didn't want to ask anything. I . . . I was going to play the piano. But I can come back another time."

At the mention of the word *piano,* a nerve in Peter's jaw began to twitch. He'd been idly tapping a pencil on the desk. Now he gripped it so hard it snapped in his hand.

Barney Hunt frowned. "You okay?"

"I'm fine."

But Peter wasn't fine. His hand was bleeding. One by one, slow, heavy drips of blood splashed onto the polished wood of the desk.

Barney smiled reassuringly at his godson. "We won't be long. Five minutes and then I'll come and find you. We can play some catch, how's that sound?"

"Good."

Another shy smile and Robbie was gone, slipping out of the room as silently as he had arrived.

Barney took a deep breath.

"You know, Peter, the kid needs you. He's grieving, too. He—"

Peter raised his hand. "We've been through this, Barney. Robert's all right. If you want to worry about something, worry about these damn newspaper reporters. They're the damn problem, okay?"

Barney Hunt shook his head.

He felt for Robert, he really did. But there was nothing more he could do.

Eve Blackwell closed her eyes and tried to fantasize about something that would bring her to orgasm.

"Is that good, baby? Do you like that?"

Keith Webster, her husband, was drenched in sweat, pounding away at her from behind like an overexcited terrier. He'd insisted on regularly "making love," as he put it, throughout Eve's pregnancy. Now that her time was fast approaching, her belly was so vastly swollen that doggy-style sex was the only option. A small mercy for Eve, who was no longer forced to look at Keith's weak, weaselly face twisted into a mask of sexual ecstasy every time he made love to her.

If you could call it making love. Keith's dick was so small, it registered only as a mild irritant. Rather like having a badly behaved child seated behind you in a movie theater who won't stop kicking the back of your seat.

Eve faked a moan.

"That's wonderful, darling! I'm almost there!"

And suddenly she was, her mind lost in a delicious, slow-moving slide show of images from the past:

Herself as a thirteen-year-old, seducing her married English teacher, Mr. Parkinson. When she'd cried rape, she'd destroyed the pathetic little man's life. But he'd deserved it. They all did.

Fucking her way through the military academy that adjoined her and Alexandra's finishing school in Switzerland. How intoxicating sex had been back then, back when men used to throw themselves at her feet!

Stabbing George Mellis in the heart and dumping his body in the sea at Dark Harbor. Just thinking about the look of surprise on George's face as the blade tore through his flesh could sometimes bring Eve to climax.

The world knew George Mellis as Alexandra Blackwell's first husband—a footnote in the great Blackwell family history. In reality, he'd been a sadistic playboy and pathological liar who had once raped and sodomized Eve, a crime for which he ultimately paid with his life.

Of course, Alex never knew the truth about George Mellis. She never knew he was in league with her evil twin sister; never knew that Eve and George had remained lovers throughout Alex's brief marriage to him; never knew that the pair of them had intended to murder her and steal her inheritance, or that Eve had been forced to murder George instead when their plans went awry.

Alex never knew the truth. But Eve knew. Eve knew everything.

Not that Eve had minded killing George. In fact, it had been a pleasure.

Keith Webster increased the pace of his thrusts, shaking with excitement as his delicate surgeon's hands reached around for his wife's enormous, pregnancy-swollen breasts.

"Oh Christ, Eve, I love you! I'm coming, baby, I'm coming!"

He let out a sound that was half groan, half whimper. Eve pictured George Mellis at the moment of his death, then mentally substituted Keith's face for George's. She orgasmed instantly.

Keith slid off her back like a toad slipping down a wet rock. He lay back against the pillow, his eyes closed in postcoital contentment. "That was incredible. Are you okay, honey? Is the baby okay?"

Eve stroked her belly lovingly. "The baby's fine, darling. You mustn't worry."

Keith Webster had been neurotic about his wife's pregnancy from the start, but Alexandra's death a few weeks ago had heightened his anxiety tenfold. It was common knowledge that Eve and Alexandra's own mother, Marianne, had died giving birth to them. Now the same fate had befallen Alex. It was easy to imagine that Eve might be next. That some unseen genetic fault lurked in the shadows, waiting to snatch his beloved from him.

Keith Webster had loved Eve Blackwell from the moment he set eyes on her. It was true that shortly after their marriage, he had deliberately mutilated her face. Playing on Eve's innate vanity, he had persuaded her to let him perform a minor operation to erase the laughter lines around her eyes. Then, once he had her under anesthetic and utterly at his mercy, he had proceeded to destroy her beautiful features one by one.

At first Eve had been angry, of course. He'd expected that. But now she saw things clearly. He'd *had* to do it. He had no choice. As long as Eve remained so mesmerizingly, intoxicatingly beautiful, he was at risk of losing her. Losing her to other, less worthy men, men who could never love her the way he did. Men like George Mellis, who had once beaten Eve so badly she had almost died. Keith Webster had restored her looks after that attack. It was the day they met. Eve had been so deliciously grateful afterward, he'd fallen in love with her on the spot.

But what Keith Webster giveth, Keith Webster could also taketh away.

It was a lesson Eve needed to learn.

Others might find his wife's grotesquely scarred features repellent, but not Keith Webster. In his eyes, Eve would always be beautiful. The most beautiful creature on earth.

Keith Webster had no illusions about his own appearance. When he looked in the mirror, he saw a slight, shortsighted man with only a few wisps of sandy hair left clinging to his otherwise bald head, like seaweed on a bare rock. Women had never been interested in him, period, never mind women as insanely attractive as Eve Blackwell. He'd felt no compunction about blackmailing Eve into marriage (Keith knew she had murdered George Mellis and threatened to go to the police if she didn't marry him) and he felt no guilt about it now. After all, how else was he supposed to possess her? To fulfill her destiny, and his own?

Once again, Eve had given him no choice.

Resting a loving hand on her baby bump, Keith felt replete with happiness. Terrified of being photographed and ridiculed like a carnival sideshow, Eve had become a virtual prisoner in their penthouse apartment since he "re-created" her, as he liked to think of it. With nothing to do with the long, lonely hours of her existence but cater to his every whim, she had finally capitulated and given Keith the one thing he desired above all others: a baby, their baby, a living, breathing affirmation of their love.

What more could any man ask for?

She'd had a rotten pregnancy, poor thing, with violent bouts of morning sickness throughout. Although Keith knew there had never been much love lost between his wife and her twin sister, he was sure that Alexandra's sudden death must have frightened Eve.

Still, only a few weeks to go now.

Bending his head reverently, he kissed his wife's belly, murmuring endearments to his unborn child.

Soon the baby would be born. Then all their troubles would be over, the pain of the past forgotten.

Eve's labor was long and agonizing. While the press huddled like baying bloodhounds beneath her hospital window, Eve spent sixteen grueling hours feeling her body being ripped apart from within.

"Are you sure you won't consider a pain killer, Mrs. Webster? A shot of Pethidine would really take the edge off your contractions."

"My name is Blackwell," Eve hissed between clenched teeth. "And no."

Eve was adamant. No drugs. No relief. She had conceived this child to wreak her vengeance, to bring righteous suffering to her enemies and to reclaim her stolen inheritance: Kruger-Brent. It was right that he should be born from suffering. That the first sound he heard should be his mother's screams.

If she didn't despise him so intensely, Eve might almost have felt sorry for Keith Webster. The pathetic, inadequate milquetoast she'd been trapped into marrying actually believed she was *happy* to be having his child! Hovering over her like an old maid, full of pity for her morning sickness . . . except it wasn't morning sickness at all. Eve's violent bouts of vomiting were triggered by pure revulsion. The very idea of Keith's seed growing inside her was enough to make her retch.

True, she had allowed him to impregnate her. This baby was no mistake.

He thinks I conceived out of love.

Eve laughed aloud. The arrogance of Keith's madness knew no limits.

The truth was that Eve Blackwell hated her husband. Hated him with a murderous passion so strong, she was surprised the nurses couldn't smell it on her skin.

When Keith had first removed Eve's bandages and shown her her ruined face, five long years ago, she'd screamed until she passed out. In the weeks that followed, she had sobbed and raged, her emotions swinging wildly from shock to disbelief to terror. At first she'd been so desperate she had actually clung to Keith. Yes, he'd done this terrible thing, but he was all she had. Without his protection, she feared being flung to the wolves, torn to shreds like a hunted animal. As the years passed, however, Eve stopped worrying about Keith abandoning her. She realized, with amused horror, that the man was so deranged he actually still found her attractive. Keith Webster had turned Eve Blackwell into a monster: the Beast of the Blackwells. But she was *his* monster. To Keith, that was all that mattered.

"The baby's crowning, Mrs. Web—Ms. Blackwell. I can see the head!"

Eve wished the nurses would stop smiling. Didn't they realize the agony she was in? It was like being attended by a troop of giddy schoolgirls.

Thank God Keith had agreed to stay in the fathers' waiting room.

Eve had begged him: "I want you to still find me sexy, my darling. You know what they say about men who watch their wives give birth. It ruins, you know, *that*, forever."

Keith insisted that nothing could dim his passion for her. But to Eve's astonishment, he'd agreed to stay away.

"One more push! You're almost there!"

The pain was so strong Eve was surprised she hadn't lost consciousness. Like a riptide it pulled at her till she was no longer aware of anything but the sensations deep inside her womb.

She thought about Alex, realizing for the first time how physically painful and terrifying her sister's death must have been.

Good.

It was ironic. Eve thought about all the time and effort she'd put into trying to kill her twin over the years: setting her nightgown alight at their fifth birthday party; arranging riding accidents, sailing accidents and finally the whole complicated murder plot with George Mellis. (Knowing George was both penniless and psychotic, and that his rich-playboy routine was all an act, Eve had encouraged him to woo and marry her sister. The plan was for George to win Alex's trust, persuade her to make a new will that left him everything, including her controlling stake in Kruger-Brent, then get rid of her, splitting the inheritance with Eve.)

But somehow Alexandra had survived every one of Eve's elaborate schemes. The bitch was like one of those novelty birthday candles you couldn't blow out. And then *bam!* Out of nowhere, a simple act of God had come along and erased her, like the unwanted stain she was.

Alexandra Blackwell, Kruger-Brent heiress and famous beauty. Dead in childbirth at the age of thirty-four.

It was so perfect, it was almost biblical.

Eve heard a loud, feral noise. It took a moment to register that it was her own voice, screaming as the final contraction racked her body. Seconds later, she felt a warm wetness between her legs and the frenzied kicking of tiny legs. A slimy, bloody creature, covered in waxy-white vernix, slithered into the waiting arms of the midwife.

"It's a boy!"

"Congratulations, Ms. Blackwell!"

One of the nurses cut the cord. Another cleaned up the afterbirth.

Weak with exhaustion and blood loss, Eve slumped back against the sodden sheets. She watched as the nurses cleaned and examined the baby, ticking things off on a chart. Suddenly she felt choked with panic.

"What's wrong with him?" She sat bolt upright. "Why isn't he crying? Is he dead?"

The midwife smiled. *Well, how about that for a surprise?* Eve Blackwell had been so detached and hostile during the birth—quite frankly, she'd been an out-and-out bitch to the nursing team—they'd begun to suspect she didn't *want* her baby. But obviously they'd misjudged her. The concern in Eve's voice now was unmistakably genuine. *She's going to make a great mommy after all.*

"He's right as rain, Ms. Blackwell. Here, you can see for yourself."

Eve took the white bundle. When she looked down, Eve saw a small, olive-skinned face topped with a crown of glossy blue-black hair. The nose and mouth were babylike and nondescript. But the enormous, dark brown eyes with their fringe of black lashes and steady, focused gaze; those were extraordinary. The boy looked up at her, silently scanning her face. To the rest of the world, Eve was a freak. To her baby, she was the universe.

Eve thought: *He's intelligent. Cunning, like a little gypsy.*

She smiled, and though she knew it wasn't meant to be possible, she could have sworn he smiled back.

"Have you thought of a name for him yet?"

Eve didn't even look up.

"Max. His name is Max."

It was a simple name, short, but to Eve it suggested strength. The boy would need strength if he was going to fulfill his purpose and avenge his mother.

Eve had conceived Keith Webster's child for one reason and one reason only. Because she needed an accomplice. Someone she could mold in her own image, feed with her own hatred, and send out into the world to do all the things that she, a prisoner in her own home, could no longer do for herself.

Max would make Keith Webster pay for what he'd done to her.

Max would bring Kruger-Brent back to her.

Max would worship and adore and obey her, the way that men had always worshipped, adored and obeyed her, before Keith robbed her of her looks.

"Knock knock."

Keith appeared at the door, bearing a huge bouquet of roses. Handing them to a nurse, he kissed Eve perfunctorily on the top of her head before taking his son in his arms.

"He's . . . he's beautiful." His voice was choked. When he looked up, Eve saw that there were tears of joy streaming down his face. "Thank you, Eve. Thank you, my darling. You've no idea what this . . . what *he* means to me."

Eve smiled knowingly.

"You're welcome, Keith."

And she sank into a contented, dreamless sleep.

THREE

ROBBIE TEMPLETON FELT A FAMILIAR, CHURNING FEELING
in the pit of his stomach as he walked through the revolving doors of the
Kruger-Brent building on Park Avenue.

"Good morning, Mr. Robert."

"Nice to see you again, Mr. Robert."

"Is your father expecting you?"

Everybody knew him. The receptionists, in their gray-flannel company uniforms, the security guards, even José, the janitor. Robert Templeton was Kate Blackwell's great-grandson, fifteen years old, with
the world at his feet. One day he would take his place as CEO and
chairman.

So they said.

Robbie had been coming to this building with his mother since he
was a little boy. The impressive, marble-floored atrium with its six-foot
flower arrangements and walls smothered with priceless modern art, Bas-
quiats and Warhols and Lucien Freuds, was Robbie's playroom. He'd
played peekaboo in the elevators and hide-and-seek down the long, corporate corridors. He'd swung his legs and spun around in Kate Blackwell's swivel chair till he was too dizzy to stand.

All his life he'd tried to love the place. Tried to feel the passion and
pride that everyone assumed he'd been born with. But it was no good.

Walking through the familiar swing doors today felt the same as it always did: like walking through the gates of hell.

His mind wandered back to his seventh birthday. His great-grandmother Kate had promised him a birthday treat.

"Something wonderful, Robert. It'll be just the two of us."

He remembered being so overcome with excitement, he couldn't sleep the night before. *Something wonderful.* A private visit to FAO Schwarz? All he could eat at Chuck E. Cheese? Disneyland?

When Kate led him through the doors of the boring office building, he assumed she'd left something behind there. An umbrella, perhaps? Or her Mickey Mouse ears?

"No, my darling," she told him, her rheumy old eyes alight with a passion he couldn't comprehend. "*This* is your surprise. Do you know where we are?"

Robbie nodded miserably. They were at Daddy's office. He'd been here hundreds of time with Mommy, and it always made him feel weird. It was too big. And empty. When you shouted real loud, the walls threw your voice back at you. Though he couldn't have explained it, he'd always gotten the feeling that the office made his daddy sad, too. Neither of them really belonged here.

But his great-grandmother saw things differently.

"This is our kingdom, Robert! Our palace. One day, when I'm gone and you're all grown up, this will all be yours. All of it."

She squeezed his hand. Robbie wondered where she was planning on going, and how long she'd be gone. He loved his great-grandmother, even if she *did* have crazy ideas about boring old office buildings being palaces. He hoped she wouldn't be gone too long.

It was a Sunday, and the building was deserted. Leading him into the elevator, Kate pressed the button for the twentieth floor. Soon they were in her office. Installing Robbie in the leather-backed swivel chair behind her desk, Kate sank into the armchair in the corner, the one usually reserved for visiting dignitaries, ambassadors, presidents and kings.

Robbie could hear her voice now.

"Close your eyes, Robert. I'm going to tell you a tale."

It was the first time that Robbie had heard the whole story of Kruger-Brent, the company that had made his family wealthy and famous and different from everybody else's family. Even at six, Robbie Templeton knew he was different from the other kids. Even at seven, he wished with all his heart that it weren't so.

Today, of course, Robbie Templeton knew the legend of Kruger-

Brent by heart. It was as much a part of him as the blood in his veins and the hair on his head. He knew all about Jamie McGregor, Kate's father. About how he had come to South Africa from Scotland in the late 1800s, penniless but determined, and founded the most profitable diamond-mining business in the world. Jamie had been cheated by a local merchant, Salomon Van der Merwe. With the help of Van der Merwe's brave black servant, Banda, Jamie had taken his revenge; first by stealing the perfect twenty-karat diamond on which the Kruger-Brent empire was founded and then by impregnating Van der Merwe's daughter, Margaret—Kate Blackwell's mother.

The name of the company Jamie founded was a further insult to the merchant who had not only cheated him but tried to have him killed. Kruger and Brent were the names of the two Afrikaner guards who had chased Jamie and Banda as they fled for their lives, their pockets weighed down with Van der Merwe's diamonds.

Kate herself had no memories of her father, who died when she was very young. But it was clear from the hushed, reverential tones in which she spoke of him that in her eyes, Jamie McGregor was nothing short of a god. She loved to tell Robert how much he looked like his great-great-grandfather. And indeed, if the portrait of Jamie McGregor that hung in Cedar Hill House was anything to go by, the resemblance was striking.

Robbie knew his great-grandmother meant it as a compliment. But he wished she'd stop saying it all the same.

After Jamie McGregor's death, Kruger-Brent was run for two decades by his friend and right-hand man, another Scot named David Blackwell. Kate fell in love with David. Despite being twenty years her senior, and at one point engaged to another woman, David ended up marrying her. As so often in her life, Kate had seen something she wanted and refused to rest until she made it her own.

David Blackwell was the second great love of Kate's life.

The first was Kruger-Brent.

When David was killed in a mine explosion shortly after World War II, everyone had expected his young, pregnant widow to grieve for a year or so and then marry again. But it never happened. Having lost one love, Kate Blackwell devoted the rest of her long life to the other. Kruger-Brent became her sun and her moon, her lover, her obsession, her world. Under Kate's chairmanship, the company grew from being a successful, African diamond business to a global giant, with holdings in copper, steel, petrochemicals, plastics, telecoms, aerospace, real estate, software. Kruger-Brent was in every sector in every market in every corner of the globe. And still Kate Blackwell's lust for acquisition and expansion remained insatiable. Even stronger, however, was her obsession with finding an heir. Someone within the extended Blackwell clan who could carry on her good work and take the firm to even greater heights of world domination after she died.

When her own son, Tony, buckled under the pressure of his inheritance and lost his sanity, Kate transferred her ambitions to his twin daughters: Alexandra, Robbie's mother, and Eve, his scary aunt. Eve and Alexandra's mother died giving birth to them. With their father confined to a mental institution, it was left to Kate to raise the two little girls.

From the start, Kate Blackwell was determined that *one* of her granddaughters should take over Kruger-Brent when she came of age. For many years, it was going to be Eve. Eve was always the dominant twin, and her succession seemed natural. But then something terrible happened. Something so bad, it had convinced Robbie's great-grandmother to cut Eve out of her inheritance altogether.

Whatever the terrible thing was, it was a secret Kate had taken with her to the grave. Robbie would have liked to ask his aunt Eve himself what had happened all those years ago, but he was far too frightened. With her shrouded face and strange, cryptic way of talking, Aunt Eve had always given him nightmares. Even his parents seemed a little bit afraid of her, which frightened Robbie even more.

Still, he longed to know what had passed between his great-grandmother and his aunt. Because whatever it was, it was responsible for his own, unhappy position. Like his grandfather Tony before him, Robbie had dreams for a life outside of Kruger-Brent. All he'd ever wanted to do was play the piano. But Kate Blackwell had named him as her heir against his own, and his parents', express wishes. The force of her will was unstoppable, something generations of her family had learned the hard way.

Robbie smiled at Karis Brown, the head receptionist. A softly spoken brunette in her midforties with a trim figure and dancing, merry hazel eyes, Karis had the sort of face that radiated kindness. Though far less beautiful, she reminded Robbie a bit of his mother.

"Dad's not expecting me. At least, I don't think he is."

There was always the possibility that Mr. Jackson, the principal of St. Bede's, Robbie's prestigious private high school, had called ahead.

Karis Brown raised a questioning eyebrow. "Not in any trouble, I hope?"

Robbie shrugged sheepishly. "No more than usual."

"Well, in that case, I guess I'd better send you up. Good luck."

She handed him a specially coded card for the elevator that would allow him access to the twentieth floor. All of the Blackwell family's private offices were on the top two floors of the building, and security was tight.

"Thanks."

Karis Brown watched Robbie shuffle reluctantly over to the elevators, hands thrust deep in his pockets, and wondered what mischief he'd been up to this time. Like most of the Kruger-Brent staff, Karis Brown had a soft spot for Robbie. How could you not love him, with those soulful gray eyes and that mop of surfer-blond hair and the adorable way he blushed whenever you looked him in the eye? Everyone at the firm knew that Robbie Templeton was a wild child. Ever since his mom died, he'd been flying off the rails faster than an express train on black ice, poor lamb. In the last five years, he'd been expelled from more schools than Karis Brown could count. But to meet him you'd never believe it. He seemed like such a sweet, shy, gentle soul.

The elevator doors closed behind him. Karis Brown hoped Robbie's dad wouldn't be too rough on him.

"You did *whaaaaat?*"

Peter Templeton was having a bad day. He'd woken up with the daddy of all hangovers. He knew he was drinking too much lately, but the guilt only served to make his pounding headache worse. People told him his grief would lessen in time, but it was four years now since he'd lost Alex and the loneliness was as bad as ever. Evenings were the worst. During the daytime, he'd learned to busy himself with work, or with Lexi.

At four years old, Lexi was a Pandora's box of delights and surprises. Every day she came out with something new and funny that melted her father's heart. But by eight o'clock at night, the little girl was out like a light, however hard Peter tried to keep her awake. When Lexi went to bed, it was like someone switching off his life-support machine. By eight-thirty, he'd usually found the whiskey. By ten, as often as not, he was out cold.

This morning, hungover again, he'd arrived at the office to find his desk piled high with work. It was bonus time at Kruger-Brent, one of the most stressful times of the year. Other board members made most of the big decisions, but since Brad Rogers's retirement, Peter Templeton was the nominal chairman. This meant it was his job to manage the expectations of Kruger-Brent's star performers—an impossible task; good people never believed they were getting paid enough—as well as to reprimand the underachievers.

What right do I have to reprimand anyone? They all know I'm the biggest piece of deadwood in the entire company. I'm a psychiatrist, not a businessman. If only I'd been stronger with Kate Blackwell all those years ago. I don't belong at Kruger-Brent. No one knows that better than I do.

The fog in his brain had finally begun to clear. Then Robert showed up like a bad penny, announcing that they were kicking him out of St. Bede's.

"I told you what I did, Dad. I smoked a joint. Jeez. One joint. It's no big deal."

The throbbing between Peter's temples had returned with a vengeance.

"Robert. You smoked a joint *in math class.* What did you *think* was going to happen? Did you think your teacher was going to let that slide?"

Robbie stared out of the window. Normally you could see a panoramic Manhattan skyscape from his father's office, but today was so cloudy it had disappeared, smothered by an eerie rainbow of grays.

"Goddammit, Robert, I'm at my wit's end. I can't help you if you insist on sabotaging your own life like this. Don't you care about your future?"

My future? How am I supposed to care about my future when I can't figure out my present? I don't even know who I am.

"If you think you're going to spend the rest of the year lounging around at home sitting on your keister, you can forget it, buster."

Sitting on my keister? Buster? He talks like a character from a 1950s comic book. No wonder he doesn't get it.

"You're grounded. As of right now."

"I thought you said I wouldn't be lounging around at home."

"Don't talk back to me! Don't you dare!" Peter's voice was so loud the secretaries at the other end of the corridor could hear him. "You will see *no one.* You will talk to *no one.* You want to waste your life, Robert? You want to wind up in prison? Well, maybe it's time you had a taste of what prison feels like."

Robbie laughed. He knew it was the worst possible thing to do at that moment, but he couldn't help himself.

You want to give me a taste of what prison feels like? Jesus, Dad. My whole life is a prison. With no parole! Can't you see that? I'm trapped.

"You think this is funny?" Peter was shaking with rage.

Robbie turned to face him. "No. No, I don't. I—"

Wham!

The slap came out of nowhere. Peter brought his hand down across Robbie's face with such force it sent him flying backward. Losing his footing, Robbie cracked the back of his head against the glass of the window, then fell to the floor, stunned.

For a few seconds, father and son stood frozen in shocked silence. Then Peter spoke.

"I'm sorry, Robert. I shouldn't have done that."

Robbie's eyes narrowed. His cheek glowed livid red from the blow.

"No. You shouldn't have."

Scrambling to his feet, Robbie pushed past his father, head down, and stumbled toward the elevator.

"Robert! Where are you going?"

Seconds later, Robbie was back in the lobby. He pushed through the revolving doors and out into the cool, fresh air of the street. Tears streamed down his face.

God?

Mom?

Anyone?

Help me. Please, please help me!

Running blindly down Park Avenue, Robbie Templeton began to sob.

The depression had started in earnest at the age of twelve, with the onset of puberty.

Before that, Robbie remembered periods of great sadness. Times when he missed his mother so badly it registered as a physical pain, like acute, grief-induced angina. But these were only temporary interludes. By playing the piano, going for a walk, or goofing around with Lexi, he could usually shake them off.

Once he turned twelve, however, something seismic seemed to shift within him. An inner blackness took hold, and this time its presence was constant. Robbie felt as if he'd descended into a tunnel without end, and then someone had blocked off the entrance. There was nothing to do but put one foot in front of the other, hopelessly, for eternity. Voices, sweet voices tempting him to suicide, followed him everywhere. If it weren't for Lexi, he would have heeded their call years ago. As it was, he struggled for his little sister's sake to go on. On and on and on, deeper and deeper into the never-ending darkness.

Once, he'd confided to his uncle Barney about his feelings. The next day, his father came bursting into his bedroom, pressing Prozac into his hand and forcing him into sessions with a therapist three times a week. Robbie listened politely to the therapist for a year and flushed the Prozac down the toilet. He didn't know much anymore, but he knew that his father's guilt pills were not the answer to his problem.

That was the last time Robbie Templeton sought help from adults. From then on, he was alone.

As if the blackness weren't bad enough, Robbie was painfully aware that he was not "normal" in other ways either. Girls were a problem. His so-called friends, the group of kids who hung around him because he was rich and good-looking and who knew nothing of the tortured boy within, were all obsessed with girls. Specifically with their breasts, legs and vaginas.

"Did you see the tits on Rachel McPhee this semester? Those babies have, like, *tripled* over the summer."

"Annie Mathis has the sweetest, tightest little pussy in tenth grade. Talk about the Tunnel of Love!"

"If Angela Brickley doesn't wrap those lips around my dick by the end of this year, I swear to God I'm gonna kill myself."

Of course, there was a lot of bullshit being talked. A lot of bravado. Robbie knew full well that most of the boys in his class were still virgins, for all their talk about pussies and blow jobs. But that wasn't the point, or the problem. The problem was that they were all *interested* in girls. All of them.

Robbie Templeton wasn't.

He remembered how his heart had stopped a few weeks ago when Lexi announced blithely: "I know why you don't have a girlfriend."

Skipping around the kitchen in her favorite neon-pink princess dress, sipping cherry Coke through a swirly straw, she fluttered her eyelashes at Robbie like Mae West.

Four years old, and already she's better at flirting than I am.

"No you don't, Lexi."

"I do."

Did she? Was it that obvious?

Robbie tried really hard never to look at other boys in public. So hard it sometimes made his eyes ache. Certainly he never did it at school. Not because he was scared of what the other kids might say, but because he was disgusted by his own feelings, consumed with a shame he could neither understand nor express. He couldn't be gay. He *refused* to be gay. Besides, if you never did anything about your urges, if you never acted on them, then you weren't technically gay at all. You were just confused. Weren't you?

Lexi gazed up at him adoringly.

"It's because you're waiting for me to grow up so you can marry *me*. Right?"

The relief was so overwhelming, Robbie burst out laughing. Scooping his sister up into his arms, he twirled her around till she squealed with delight.

"That's right, sweetheart. That's exactly right."

"*I'm* your princess."

"Yes, Lexi. You're my princess."

Suddenly a voice yelled, "Open your eyes, moron!"

Robbie glanced up. He'd been so engrossed in his own thoughts he wasn't looking where he was going. He'd bumped into a businessman on his way to lunch, knocking him clean off his feet.

The man bellowed, "What are you, retarded or something? Freak."

"Sorry. I didn't see you."

Robbie kept walking, head down. Inside his head, the tape kept playing, over and over:

He's right. I am a freak.

He had no idea where he was going. He knew he'd have to go home eventually, but he couldn't face it right now. Walking into Grand Central station, he bought a ticket for the first train to anywhere and jumped on board.

FOUR

∞

THE GIRL WAS A REDHEAD. SHE HAD HUGE BREASTS THAT seemed to wriggle like puppies beneath her tight angora sweater. Her black leather miniskirt was so short that Robbie could see the daisy pattern on her white cotton panties.

Her name was Maureen Swanson. She was captain of the cheerleading squad, the most popular girl in school. Every guy at St. Bede's wanted to fuck her brains out.

Almost every guy.

Maureen Swanson stared at Robbie. "Don't I know you?"

Robbie looked at his shoes.

"Hey. Rain Man. I'm talking to you. *Hellooooo?*"

It was just his luck. Of all the hundreds, maybe even thousands, of trains leaving Grand Central that afternoon, he had to pick the one with Maureen the Mammary Monster on board.

"You're the Blackwell kid, aren't you?"

Robbie looked around for a means of escape but there was none. The car was packed with commuters. He was hemmed in like a sardine in a tin.

"Bobby, right? Tenth grade?"

"Robbie."

"I knew it!" Maureen couldn't have looked more triumphant if she'd just solved the riddle of the Sphinx or discovered the meaning of life. "Robbie Blackwell."

Hearing the name Blackwell, other passengers turned to look at Robbie. Some of them stared quite openly. Was he really one of *them*?

"Actually, my name is Templeton. And you don't know me. We never met."

Maureen rose to her feet, eliciting admiring glances from the more circumspect businessmen and wolf whistles from the braver ones. The women in the car glared at her.

"Well, Robbie *Templeton*." Maureen smiled lasciviously, easing herself down onto Robbie's lap. "We can soon fix that."

Robbie felt his insides liquefy. Not with desire. With fear. Why the hell hadn't he thrown himself onto the tracks when he'd had the chance? Anything would have been better than the death by smothering he was about to endure in the rift-valley of Maureen Swanson's cleavage.

"Where are you headed?"

It was a good question. Where *was* he headed? He still had no idea. The train had started to slow down. A disembodied voice informed the passengers that they were approaching Yonkers.

"Yonkers. This is my stop."

Extricating himself from Maureen's viselike embrace, he began to elbow his way through the human wall of commuters, only just making it out before the car door closed. He stood on the platform as the train pulled away.

Thank God. She's gone.

Maureen Swanson's voice rang out behind him: "What a coincidence. This is my stop, too."

Robbie's heart sank.

How had she made it off the train without him noticing? Who was she, Harriet Houdini?

Maureen Swanson was two years older than Robbie Templeton. Maureen Swanson was also a goddess. The type of girl who could have any guy she wanted. Of course, the guys Maureen Swanson wanted were college linebackers built like O. J. Simpson. Robbie was built more like Wallis Simpson. Handsome undoubtedly, but at fifteen still small and slight and looking every inch the tenth grader that he was.

On the other hand, Robbie was also the heir to the Kruger-Brent fortune. For $10 billion, it appeared, Maureen Swanson was prepared to make an exception to her usual dating criteria. Robbie Templeton might not be built like a football player, but he was worth more money than most pros.

Maureen smiled. "I know a guy who lives around here. There's always a party going on at his place. You wanna check it out?"

Robbie weighed his options. He did *not* want to check it out. He did *not* want to go to a party, especially not with Maureen Swanson. He wanted to be left alone so that he could go and kill himself somewhere, quietly, without his last memory being a pair of Dolly Parton breasts or daisy-patterned panties from JCPenney. Was that so much to ask?

And yet . . . A party meant other people. Noise. Drugs. Distractions for Maureen.

Drugs.

Robbie shrugged. *What the hell.*

"Sure, why not? I've got nothing better to do."

When Peter Templeton got home that evening, he expected to find his son waiting for him.

"Robert!"

He let the front door slam shut behind him.

"ROBERT!"

Peter Templeton no longer felt guilty about slapping Robert that afternoon. He was against physical violence generally, especially as a form of parental control. But desperate times called for desperate measures. Robert had stood in his office, laughing at him. Actually laughing. After all the trouble he'd caused the family: the expulsions, the run-ins with the police, the shoplifting. After all the money and time that Peter had personally spent trying to help him, all the therapists and vacations and hundred-dollar-an-hour piano lessons, Robert still thought of the situation as one big joke.

Well, the joke was on him this time. Peter Templeton had had enough.

Bounding up the stairs two at a time in the direction of Robbie's bedroom, Peter ran into the housekeeper, Mrs. Carter. She was standing on the landing. She looked apologetic.

"I'm afraid Master Robert's not here, sir. We haven't seen him since he left for school this morning. Is something wrong?"

Peter scowled. "Damn right something's wrong. He's gone and gotten himself kicked out of St. Bede's. I doubt there's a school left in the state of New York that would take him now. Frankly, I can't say I blame them."

"Oh dear."

Mrs. Carter wrung her hands despairingly. She adored Robbie, but he did seem to be getting himself into an awful lot of scrapes lately.

"Robbie? Is that you?"

Lexi had heard the front door slam and came running out of the nursery in her nightgown, eager to see her brother. As always, Peter's heart lifted at the sight of her.

She looked more like her mother every day. She had Alex's eyes and lips and hair. Alex's smile, half coy, half knowing, top lip slightly curled. She even walked like her mother. But in temperament she was quite different. Where Alex had been gentle and soft, Lexi was fiery and energetic. Mrs. Carter affectionately referred to her as "our little piranha." Even Peter, with his chronically rose-tinted paternal vision, could see that Lexi was not perhaps the *model* of a decorous young lady. *Spirited* was the word he used. Less partial observers tended toward *spoiled*. *Willful* was another favorite. *Totally out of control* was not unheard of.

"There's my princess." Peter kissed the top of Lexi's head. She smelled of warm cookies and talcum powder. He felt his anger melting away. "What are you doing out of bed so late?"

Lexi frowned, then pouted, her deep gray eyes welling with tears.

"Robbie!" she wailed. "I want Robbie! Where's Robbie? Where *is* he?"

Peter felt the bitterness choking him. First Alex, now Lexi. Robert had sucked away their love like a vampire, leaving Peter with nothing. Only with immense effort did he keep the emotion out of his voice.

"Robbie's not here right now, sweetie. Would you like Daddy to tuck you in? I could read that story you like. The one about Squirrel Nutkin?"

"NO!" It was a yell. "NOT Daddy! Rooooobbiiiieee!"

Mrs. Carter ushered Lexi back into her bedroom. Poor Mr. Templeton. He looked like he'd just had acid thrown in his face. He had to learn not to take things so much to heart. Mrs. Carter had four kids of her own. Like every mother, she knew that children could be spiteful and thoughtless, especially at Lexi's age. You couldn't take it personally.

Once Lexi was settled back in bed, Mrs. Carter came downstairs. She found her boss in the study.

"Is she asleep?"

Peter's voice sounded odd. Deadened and dull. Mrs. Carter noticed the tumbler of whiskey in his hand and the open bottle on the desk. The hairs on her arms began to tingle with foreboding.

"Yes, sir. Sound asleep."

Peter took a big slug of his drink. When he looked up, his eyes were glassy.

"Good. Thank you. You can go."

Suddenly Mrs. Carter didn't feel right about leaving Lexi alone in the house with her father. What if Mr. Templeton passed out cold, and something happened to the girl? She'd never forgive herself.

"It's all right, sir. I can stay for a while. At least until Master Robert gets home safely."

Mr. Carter—Mike—would be at home expecting his dinner. He was bound to make a fuss, but it couldn't be helped.

"I can fix you some supper if you like. There's leftover beef in the pantry. I could whip you up some Stroganoff."

"No. Thank you."

Peter drained his glass and immediately poured himself another.

"Go home, Mrs. Carter. I'll see you in the morning."

The words were polite, but the tone was liquid steel. The housekeeper hesitated.

She thought about Lexi and poor Master Robert. Should she leave them here, alone, with their drunken father? Probably not. But if she forced the issue and demanded to stay, she might lose her position. Where would that leave her own kids? With Mike out of work, her salary was all they had.

She reached a decision.

"Very good, sir. As long as you're sure."

The children would be all right. 'Course they would. She was blowing the whole thing out of proportion. Mike would get his precious dinner on time, and all would be right with the world.

Far be it for that lazy bastard to learn how to turn on a microwave.

Robbie sat up in bed, trying to focus.

"I know you want it. You've been staring at me all evening. What are you waiting for?"

Maureen Swanson, naked from the waist up, crawled across the bedspread toward him. Her repellent, swollen udders swung beneath her like bloated bagpipes. When she peeled off her panties to reveal a neatly trimmed rust-red bush, a pungent whiff of rotting fish assaulted Robbie's nostrils. He felt the bile rise in his throat.

What am I waiting for? I'm waiting for Scotty to fix the teleporter and beam me back to the Enterprise, *that's what I'm waiting for.*

Unbidden, an image of William Shatner in a tight green shirt and spray-on pants popped into Robbie's head. He smiled. Then Maureen came closer and the smile died on his lips.

"It's okay," she whispered huskily. "Everyone gets nervous their first time. You just relax and let Mama take care of you. Everything's gonna be sweet."

Oh God, no!

Even in his coke-fueled haze, Robbie could see the filth under Maureen's fingernails as she slipped her hand beneath the waistband of his Calvin Klein briefs.

"What the hell?"

Maureen glowered at him accusingly. In the palm of her hand she cradled his limp penis, like a useless lump of Silly Putty.

"Are you queer or something? You're not even hard."

"Of course I'm not queer." Robbie found his voice at last. "I . . . I just . . . I think I took a bad pill, you know? I don't feel so good."

Talk about an understatement. The whole evening had been a nightmare, a fitting end to one of the worst days of his life. Maureen's so-called friend turned out to be a small-time drug dealer and wannabe mafioso called Gianni Sperotto, a rat-faced Italian kid with an acne-scarred face, a nose that streamed like a faucet, and breath so putrid you could practically see it. Gianni's "apartment" was the top floor of a condemned warehouse. In a year or two, no doubt, some hotshot real-estate whiz would have developed the place into a chrome-walled bachelor pad and sold it for Park Avenue prices. Not even a shit hole like Yonkers had been immune from the development fever that had swept America in the past decade. Overnight, it seemed, an entire generation had become millionaires by the simple expedient of knocking out a few walls and rechristening crumbling industrial relics as "loft-style penthouses."

But not Gianni Sperotto. Gianni Sperotto was too busy shoveling coke *up* his nose to see the fortune right under it. His "party" consisted of a bunch of half-dead hookers and junkies shooting up on one of the scores of fetid mattresses littering the floor. The bed where Maureen had dragged Robbie was Gianni's own sleeping area, cordoned off from the rest of the room by a cardboard screen, over which their host had thrown a pair of psychedelic velour curtains, a lone shot of color in the otherwise bleak and desperate squat.

There was no music, no dancing, no other even vaguely attractive male to distract Maureen from her prey. Robbie figured his only hope was to get her so looped that she forgot about him. It was a great plan, apart from one tiny snag. In order to get Maureen high, he'd had to get high himself. Robbie got hazy after one strong joint. Maureen Swanson, by contrast, appeared to have the constitution of an ox. No, make that a team of oxen. The girl popped X like they were M&M's and vacuumed up the coke like a pig rooting for truffles. The drugs had done nothing at all to dampen her ardor.

"A bad pill, huh? We'll see about that. Lay back and close your eyes."

Too disorientated to resist, Robbie did as she asked. The next thing he felt was Maureen's warm, wet tongue between his legs. Apparently, she saw his flaccid state as some sort of challenge.

If only I could rise to it!

When the curtain was yanked aside and the men burst in, Robbie's first emotion was pure relief.

His second was panic.

"Police!" Robbie felt a rough, male hand on his arm. "Party's over, kids. Get up, stand against that wall, and put your hands on your heads. Now!"

Robbie's mind was racing. Years of Sunday nights religiously spent watching *T.J. Hooker* on TV told him that this must be a drug bust. His pants were in a heap at the foot of the bed, with three ecstasy pills tucked into the back pocket—Gianni Sperotto's version of a party favor.

Bright side: I'm a minor. The worst they can give me is juvenile detention.

Not-so-bright side: They can give me juvenile detention!

For all his bravado in his dad's office, Robbie Templeton was terrified of the thought of prison. To him it seemed far worse than suicide. Death meant peace. It meant being with his mother. But prison, even juvie, for a pretty boy like him? They'd eat him alive. And that was *before* they found out he was a Blackwell and one of the richest kids in the country.

Spread-eagled half naked against the wall, he tried to concentrate. It wasn't easy with Maureen Swanson screaming and cursing next to him like a banshee.

"You assholes lay one finger on me, and I swear to God my dad will personally slice off your balls!"

The police officer laughed. "I'd advise you not to threaten us, sweetheart."

"Great ass," added his partner. "How about you spread those legs a little wider?"

Robbie racked his brains. Did he have any ID in his jeans? Anything they could use to prove who he was? Man, it was hard to think when you were high.

Without warning, Maureen Swanson spun around and smashed her fist into the police officer's face. The cheap cocktail ring she was wearing sliced into his eyeball like a knife through butter.

"Jesus Christ, you little bitch! You blinded me!"

In the pandemonium that followed, Robbie seized his chance. Making a run for the open window, he dived through it headfirst.

A blast of cold night air hit his lower body. That's when he remembered that he was naked from the waist down. When he opened his eyes, he remembered something else:

Gianni Sperotto's bedroom was on the sixth floor.

The fall seemed to take forever. Time stretched out in serene slow motion. Robbie knew he was going to die. The thought made him smile. He'd imagined this moment countless times, wondered if he would feel fear when the time came. But now that it was actually happening, he felt suffused with a deep, rich contentment. Almost joy.

The ground rose slowly to greet him, green and gray in the moonlight.

Then everything went black.

"Dude?"

"Hey, dude? Can you hear me?"

Robbie was by a river, lying in the long grass. He was in South Africa, in the wilderness near Burgersdorp, the little Transvaal town where his mom used to take him as a small child. Once known as Klipdrift, this was the place where Jamie McGregor had made his fortune. The birthplace of Kruger-Brent, the spot where it all began. The wind was blowing softly through the acacia trees. Above him, Robbie could see his mother's face, the loveliest sight in the world. Her lips were moving. She was trying to talk to him. But her voice sounded strange. Unfamiliar.

"You are one lucky son of a bitch, man. You coulda killed yo'self."

His mother's face was fading.

Mom! Come back!

But it was too late. Alex was gone, her loving gaze replaced by the curious stares of three black strangers, kids not much older than Robbie.

He was lying on his back, sprawled across some rhododendron bushes. Their springy branches must have broken his fall. When he tried to move, the pain in his left leg was agonizing. With some help he found he was able to stand.

"You must be seriously high, bro." The oldest boy shook his head admiringly. "What'd you think, you was Superman or somethin'?"

His friends laughed loudly.

"You do realize you're buck naked? Or maybe *I'm* Superman? Maybe I got some of that Kryptonite shit, X-ray vision goin' on."

More laughter.

"P-please," Robbie stammered. "Help me. The cops . . . they'll be down here any second. One of you give me your pants."

The boys looked at one another.

"Say what? We ain't giving you our goddamn pants."

Robbie thought for a moment, then started pulling at the little finger of his left hand.

"Here. Take this." He pressed a solid-gold signet ring into the oldest boy's hand. It had once belonged to Robbie's great-great-grandfather, Jamie McGregor, and it bore the symbol of two fighting rams: Kruger-Brent's crest. "It's gold. It's worth five hundred bucks at least."

The boy looked at the ring.

"Jackson, give Clark Kent here your pants."

Jackson looked outraged. "Screw you! I ain't giving him my god-damn pants."

"I said take 'em off! Now! Here come the cops, man."

A pair of uniformed police were rushing out of Gianni's building with flashlights. Robbie thought: *They're looking for a body.*

The black kid slipped out of his jeans like a snake shedding its skin.

Robbie watched him sprint into the darkness, the Carl Lewis of Westchester County. Seeing three black figures disappearing across the scrubland, the cops gave chase. It gave Robbie a few valuable seconds in which to make his move.

He pulled on the pants. They were huge. Yanking the belt onto its tightest notch, he could just about keep them up. Slowly, he began to walk. The pain in his leg was getting worse. Shutting out everything else, he focused his mind on Lexi and his mother. He couldn't go to prison. He had to get away. Humming softly to the sound track playing in his head—Grieg's Piano Concerto in A Minor—he limped on into the darkness.

By the time Robbie got home, it was six in the morning.

Dawn had already broken over the West Village. In doorways, the homeless were starting to stir, bags of rattling bones trying to shake off the combined effects of sleep and booze and move on before the first police patrols arrived. Robbie watched them. Not for the first time he thought how ironic it was that only a few feet of brick separated these hopeless hulks of human refuse from people like him: the richest of the rich. Those bums must think he had it all. What would they say if they knew how often he lay awake at night, in feather-bedded comfort, dreaming of blowing his brains out?

He had no key. That had been in his pants, along with the ecstasy. Limping down to the basement, he punched a six-digit number into the keypad by the service door, which clicked open obligingly. *Welcome home.*

He wondered what was going on back in Yonkers. Had the cops caught up with his three black buddies? Unlikely. But that didn't mean he was out of the woods. Maureen Swanson might have spilled the beans, told the police who he was and where to find him.

Whatever. If she had, there was nothing he could do about it now.

Creeping up the kitchen stairs to the entryway, he was relieved to find the house silent and in darkness. He'd almost reached the top of the main staircase when a voice rang out behind him.

"I'm in the study, Robert."

Shit.

Robbie's heart sank, dread pooling in the pit of his stomach.

Please, please let him not have been drinking.

Peter sat on the red brocade couch. He was talking to his wife.

You know how difficult they are at this age, darling. I haven't been firm enough with him in the past, that's the problem. But it's never too late to change.

Alex was agreeing with him. Standing by the window, in the green Halston dress he'd bought her for their tenth anniversary, she nodded encouragement. Where would he be without her? Her love and support meant everything to him. They gave him the strength he needed.

If it were just the trouble at school, I could forgive him. Even the drugs. But there's Lexi to think about. He's a terrible influence on her, Alex. He's trying to take her away from me. I mean, I can't allow that, can I?

Alex shook her head: *Of course you can't, darling. But let's not waste all night talking about Robert. Do you like my dress?*

I love it. You know I do. You look so beautiful.

For you, Peter. I look beautiful for you.

"Dad?"

Peter looked up. Alex had gone. The room swayed gently, like a ship. Everything was tinted with a sepia haze. It was like being inside an old photograph of the *Titanic*. Disaster had not yet struck, but it was imminent.

Peter Templeton waited for his son's twin faces to merge into one before he spoke.

"Where have you been all night?"

Robbie shifted mutely from foot to foot.

"I asked you a question."

"With a girl."

It wasn't a lie. Not technically.

"Which girl? Where?"

There was so much anger in Peter's voice, Robbie found himself shivering.

"In Yonkers. We took a train," said Robbie, deftly answering the second question but not the first. It wouldn't help anyone to drag Maureen Swanson's name into this. "Listen, Dad, I'm sorry about what happened at school today. Really. I don't know why I do these things. Sometimes I . . ."

"Sometimes you what?"

Peter's rage was growing. He didn't want to hear apologies or explanations. He wanted Robert to admit his guilt. To acknowledge that he deserved to be punished. Punished for monopolizing Alex's affection. Punished for turning Lexi against him.

"Sometimes I just can't handle it." For the second time that day, Robbie started to cry.

Don't blubber, for Christ's sake. Be a man. You've brought this on yourself.

Behind a red brocade cushion, out of view, Peter Templeton's hand tightened around the gun.

When he took the Glock out of the safe a few hours earlier, he'd been fantasizing about killing himself. A bottle and a half of Scotch had robbed him of all rational thought and left him bitter and broken. He had failed. As a man, a husband, a father. The gun felt comforting in his hand. An escape. But then Alex had appeared; dear, sweet Alex. Peter stuffed the pistol under the cushion so as not to scare her.

Now he reached for it again. The cool metal pressed against his palm.

Robert had come home.

Robert needed to be punished.

Peter only half heard what the boy was saying.

"I'm not the same as the other kids. I don't fit in at St. Bede's. I don't fit in anywhere. Maybe it's because I miss Mom so much. Maybe . . ."

Robbie let the sentence trail away. Peter had tossed the cushion aside. He had a gun in his hand and was waving it around wildly, like a conductor's baton.

He said: "Please. Go on. This is interesting."

Cold fear gripped Robbie by the throat. He held his breath.

"Perhaps when you're done, you can explain to me why it is that my daughter doesn't want to know me anymore. Why you thought you had the right to steal Lexi from me."

Robbie was shaking so violently he didn't trust himself to speak. He'd seen his father drunk a thousand times, but until today Peter had never been violent. Maybe the slap he'd given Robbie in the office earlier had unleashed some inner monster? Like a shark who gets a taste of blood, then plunges into a feeding frenzy.

Robbie chose his next words carefully.

"Lexi has nothing to do with this."

It was exactly the wrong thing to say. When Peter responded, his voice was a roar. "Don't tell me Lexi has nothing to do with this! Don't you *dare*! She has *everything* to do with this. You're stealing her away from me, just like you stole your mother."

He fired a single shot at the ceiling above Robbie's head. Bits of plaster rained down onto the boy's shoulders.

Adrenaline pumped through Robbie's veins like rock music.

He's not just drunk. He's deranged. He's going to shoot me.

Killing himself was one thing. *Being* killed, especially by his own father, was quite another. Robbie realized in that instant with searing clarity that he did not really want to die. He was fifteen years old. He wanted to live. All he had to do now was figure out how.

The window to the street was behind him. If he turned and ran, his father could put a bullet in his back. There was no escape. His only hope was to try to reason with him.

"Dad, I never stole Mom from you. She loved you. She loved us both."

"Don't you tell me how your mother felt about me! You know nothing." Peter pointed the gun directly at Robbie's chest. "Alex and I were fine until you came along."

"Dad, please . . ."

The low whistle in Peter's head was growing louder and louder, like a boiling kettle. He clutched his temples. The room swayed again.

I'm drunk. What the hell am I doing?

He glanced at the window, willing Alex to be there. He needed her advice, now more than ever. But she was gone.

"Daddy, stop it! Stop shouting!"

Lexi appeared in the doorway clutching her favorite soft toy, a stuffed white rabbit.

The noise in Peter's head was unbearable.

He said: "It's all right, sweetheart. Come here."

Robbie watched his little sister take a trusting step toward the couch. Without thinking, Peter turned around to face Lexi. The gun was now pointing in her direction.

Robbie had to save Lexi. Instinct took over. He let out a primal, savage scream, running at his father like a maddened bull.

Peter glanced up. The expression on Robbie's face was curiously frozen, like a videotape on pause. The fear was gone. It had been replaced by something else. Determination perhaps? Or hatred? Peter wasn't sure.

He heard the housekeeper's voice.

"No!"

Mrs. Carter had had a terrible night. She hadn't slept a wink, lying awake next to her husband, Mike, tossing and turning with guilt. She should never have left Mr. Templeton alone with those kids. He was in no fit state to take care of them. By five o'clock, she could take it no longer. Leaving a snoring Mike in bed, she pulled on yesterday's clothes without even taking a shower and hurried across town. As she slipped her key into the front door, she heard a loud bang. Heart pounding, she followed the raised voices in the direction of the study. She burst in just in time to see her employer aiming a shiny black pistol directly at his four-year-old daughter's head.

Peter needed to think, but he couldn't. The whistling in his head was so loud he wanted to cry. Suddenly he *was* crying. He opened his eyes and looked at Lexi's face.

She's so like Alex.

A second shot rang out.

The whistling stopped.

FIVE

MAX WEBSTER TOOK THE SHINY RED PACKAGE FROM HIS mother and turned it over excitedly in his hands.

It was heavy. Something solid. He decided it was probably not a toy, despite the childish wrapping paper and jauntily scribbled HAPPY BIRTHDAY in gold glitter across the top.

"What is it?"

Eve Blackwell smiled at her son, her eyes dancing with anticipation.

"Open it and find out."

It was Max's eighth birthday. A striking child, with a predatory, aquiline nose, ink-black eyes to match his hair, and cheekbones most fashion models would have killed for, there was something both feminine and adult about him. Max had none of the fat-cheeked innocence of his friends. Max was knowing. He was lean. He was wild. If other little boys were puppies, Max Webster was a cougar in their midst, as dangerous as he was beautiful.

Less than an hour ago, the Fifth Avenue penthouse Max shared with his parents had been crammed to bursting with fat-cheeked, eight-year-old puppies, all eager to ingratiate themselves with their famous classmate. The party had been Max's father's idea.

Keith Webster said: "The boy needs friends, Eve. He needs to socialize. It's not normal for a kid his age to spend every minute of his free time with his mother."

Eve did not object. She simply retired to her bedroom for the duration, locking the door. The party went ahead, and Max was inundated with presents: Transformers and Skalectrix and Hornby train sets and Action Men galore. Everybody ate a lot of cake and s'mores and drank Coke till it came shooting out of their noses in frothy black torrents. Keith Webster took pictures.

Afterward Keith Webster asked his son: "So, sport, d'you have a good time?" His face beamed with love and pride.

Max nodded. *Sure, Dad. It was great.*

Max waited for Keith Webster to leave. Sunday night was Keith's regular softball game. He and some of the other surgeons from the hospital had gotten a team together to help relieve the stress of their life-and-death jobs. As soon as Max heard the click of the front door, he went in search of his mother.

"Are they gone?"

"Yes, Mommy."

"All of them?"

"Yes. It's just us now. I'm sorry it took so long."

Eve unlocked her bedroom door. Dressed in a chocolate silk kimono-style robe that fell open at the front to reveal matching lace underwear, she pulled her son close. At eight, Max was still a fairly short child. The top of his dark, gypsy head reached just above Eve's navel. Pressing his cheek against her smooth, flat stomach, she felt him inhaling her scent, a mixture of Eve's own feral smell and the Chanel perfume she had worn since girlhood.

All Max did was breathe. But Eve could feel the adoration in his small, compact body. A familiar rush of power made her flesh tingle.

"Come, sit down on Mommy's bed. You can have your special present now."

Max watched, delighted, as his mother retrieved the package from her glove drawer. *This* was what he'd been waiting for. Not some asinine party with a bunch of kids from school who'd only come over in the first place because they wanted to gawk at his mom. As if Max would ever let that happen!

He thought again about Keith Webster. His father. How he loathed him.

So, sport, d'you have fun?

Fun? With you?

Max longed for the day when Keith Webster would be gone. Then he would have his beautiful mommy all to himself. Then he could finally stop pretending.

With trembling hands, he tore at the wrapping paper. Inside he saw a glint of black metal. A train?

"Do you like it?"

Eve's voice was husky, barely a whisper. Max gazed at her face. With the outside world, his mother always went to great lengths to hide herself. But not with him. Max was special. He got to see the real Eve Blackwell, scars and all. He loved her so much it sometimes made him weep.

"Mom!" He gasped. "Is it . . . real?"

"Of course it's real. And very old. It's been in my family for a long, long time."

Lovingly, Max stroked the gun's trigger, his childish fingers caressing, exploring. Such power. And it was all his.

Eve said: "You're almost a grown man now, Max. You're too old for toys. Keith doesn't understand that, but I do."

Eve Blackwell always referred to her husband by his Christian name in front of their son, never as Dad or Daddy. In the early days, Keith had complained about it.

"I wish you'd drop the whole first-name thing. It's creepy. Max doesn't call you Eve."

But Keith's sporadic efforts to introduce the d-word into his son's vocabulary always petered out after a few weeks.

Eve would insist: "It's not me, darling, it's Max. Besides, I don't see that it's such a big deal. It's just one of his little quirks. The more you go on about it, the more he'll dig his heels in. You know what children are like."

"Does Keith know you've given it to me?" Max asked, still mesmerized by the gun. It was perfect. Like his mother.

Eve smiled. "No. It's our secret. I'll keep it in the safe for you so as not to arouse his suspicions. You may take it out whenever you wish. Just ask me and I'll get it for you."

A shocking thought suddenly occurred to Max.

"It isn't Uncle Peter's gun, is it? The one he . . . you know. When I was little?"

Four years earlier, Max's uncle, Dr. Peter Templeton, had almost shot his children in a drunken rage. No one was sure whether he'd intended to kill himself, or Lexi, or Robert. Peter himself was too drunk to remember. All anyone knew was that the housekeeper had arrived at the Templeton brownstone early one morning to the sound of shots, that she'd wrestled the gun from Uncle Peter's hands, and that in the process she'd been shot in the arm.

The woman had been paid off, of course. Max overheard Keith saying that the check was "in the millions," but evidently the money had been well spent: the story never made its way into the press. From that day on, Max's uncle Peter had not touched a drop of liquor. The gun he used had mysteriously disappeared.

Eve shook her head.

"No, darling. It's not Uncle Peter's gun. It's far more special than that. This gun once belonged to my grandfather, David Blackwell. Your great-grandfather."

Max's eight-year-old chest swelled with pride. He loved to hear his mother tell stories about her family. His family.

Max's earliest memories were of his mother's deep, sensuous voice lulling him to sleep with tales of his great-great-grandfather Jamie McGregor and the thrilling empire that he founded. Max's first word was *mama*, his second *Kruger* and his third *Brent*. While other boys dreamed about dinosaurs and Superman, Max's subconscious glittered with the stolen diamonds on which Jamie McGregor had built his fortune. *My fortune.* Max Webster had no need for fairy tales, of wronged princesses and dragons and gingerbread castles. His mother was the wronged princess. Eve had had her kingdom stolen from her and been imprisoned by his evil father in her penthouse tower. He, Max, was Eve's avenging knight. Kruger-Brent was their castle. As for the dragons to be slain, there were too many to count. Everyone Max knew was an enemy, from the despicable Keith, to the boys at school who made fun of his mother, to his Templeton cousins, Robert and Lexi.

Your cousins have stolen your inheritance, my darling. They have taken what's yours and cast you out like a serpent in the desert. Just as I was cast out.

Max's mother made their struggle sound mythical. And so it was. Eve had been cast out of the Garden of Eden. Max was the chosen one, the prophet, the messiah. It was Max who would restore the promised land to Eve.

Only by returning Kruger-Brent to his mother would Max win the greatest prize of all: her love. That was their covenant, sealed with the blood of his birth. Max thought about it constantly.

Until that day, the glorious day when he fulfilled his destiny, he must learn to survive on the scraps of love Eve tossed him. Usually his mother was cold and distant. Her constant physical presence in the apartment was like exquisite torture. Max longed for her embrace like a scorched riverbed longs for rain, but time after time he was denied. Keith Webster could touch her, with his sick, cold hands. But Max could not. On the rare occasions when his mother held him close, like today, the little boy felt he could move mountains. Pressed against her, lost in the intoxicating smell of her skin, joy coursed through his child's body like heroin.

Eve stood up. Drawing her silk robe more tightly around her, she walked over to the window.

Max sat alone on the bed. As always, he felt his mother's leaving like a physical pain. He clasped the gun, her gift, pressing it lovingly to his cheek.

"Your great-grandfather David never used that pistol. Never fired a single shot."

Eve was looking out the window. She seemed to be speaking to herself rather than to him.

"He was too much of a coward."

Max took the bait, an innocent lamb gamboling to the slaughter. "*I'm* not a coward, Mommy. *I'm* not afraid to use it."

Eve turned around.

"Is that so? And what will you use it for, my darling?"

Max didn't answer. He didn't have to.

They both knew what the gift was for.

I'll use it to kill Keith Webster.

I'll use it to kill my father.

SIX

∞

LIONEL NEUMAN LOOKED AT THE YOUNG MAN SITTING OP-
posite him and found his mind wandering back into the past.

It was 1952, a similar bright June morning. Kate Blackwell was sitting in the very same chair as the young man. Counting back, Lionel
Neuman realized with a shock that Kate must already have been sixty
at the time. The image his mind's eye had carefully filed away was of a
middle-aged but still beautiful woman: slim, impeccably dressed, and
with a full head of glossy black hair only intermittently laced with silver
threads. She was worried about her son.

*Tony isn't himself, Lionel. It's as if something has died inside. I've tried
everything I can to make him happy, but it's no use. He's determined not to
marry.*

The problem with Kate Blackwell was that although she sought
advice from time to time, from Lionel Neuman, Brad Rogers and a few
other Kruger-Brent lifers, she never took any of it. Any fool could see
what was wrong with Tony Blackwell. The boy wanted to be an artist,
and Kate wouldn't let him. Her ruthless trampling on his dreams eventually cost poor Tony his sanity. But Kate Blackwell could never see it
that way. She went to her grave believing she'd done the best for her
son. That it was *Tony* who had let *her* down.

Of course, Tony Blackwell did marry. For a few short months he was happy, blissfully happy, until his wife, Marianne, died giving birth to their twins, Eve and Alexandra.

They're all dead now. Kate, Tony, Marianne, Alexandra. But I'm still here. Same office. Same family. Same problems. What a curious thing life is.

The young man sitting opposite Lionel Neuman was Kate Blackwell's great-grandson, Robert Templeton. Had Tony *not* married, of course, young Robert wouldn't be here. Neither here in this office nor here on this earth. But Kate Blackwell had gotten her way on that as on all things. It hardly seemed possible, but the child was nineteen years old already, six feet tall in his socks and as blond and chiseled as any matinee idol.

He's not a child, though, is he? He's a man. That's the problem.

"There's nothing you can do to stop me."

Robbie's tone was surly and aggressive. He sat forward, his delicate pianist's fingers resting on his knees, and glared at the old man defiantly.

"I'm legally an adult now. This is my decision and mine alone, so show me where to sign and I'll get out of here."

"I'm afraid it's not quite as simple as that, Robert."

Lionel Neuman ran a crepey hand through his wiry, salt-and-pepper hair. He reminded Robbie of an elderly rabbit. His nose seemed to be permanently twitching, as if he could pick up nuances of legal language purely through smell. Even his office had the air of a burrow, with its dark wood, dimly lit Tiffany lamps and wine-red leather-bound legal tomes stuffed into every nook and cranny.

"Your father—"

"My father has nothing to do with this."

Robbie slammed his fist down on the desk. The top pages of Lionel Neuman's neat pile of documents fluttered in consternation, then lay still. The old man himself remained unperturbed.

I see you have your great-grandmother's hot temper. But you don't scare me, kid. I've been shouted at by more angry Blackwells than you've had hot dinners.

Such a pity. Robert had been an adorable little boy. No wonder Kate had loved him as she did. But he had grown, in Lionel Neuman's opinion anyway, into a thoroughly spoiled, thuggish young man. At nineteen, Robert Templeton already had a juvenile police record for theft and drug-related offenses. *Theft!* What on earth could the heir to Kruger-Brent possibly need to steal?

Lionel Neuman had been around long enough to know that wealth on the Blackwells' scale, obscene wealth, was often more of a curse than a blessing. Robbie Templeton showed every sign of going the same way as poor Christina Onassis, lost to drugs, booze and depression. He reminded Lionel of Shakespeare's Hamlet. Denmark's prince suffered "the slings and arrows of outrageous fortune." Robert Templeton's fortune was certainly outrageous. Come to think of it, Kruger-Brent's market cap was probably higher than the entire GDP of Denmark. As for the "slings and arrows," young Robert brought those upon himself.

Lionel Neuman blamed the boy's father. Ever since that unfortunate incident with the gun, Peter Templeton seemed to have abnegated his paternal responsibilities entirely. He was too guilt-ridden to discipline his own children.

A stint in the army, that was what Robert needed.

Nothing like a taste of war to whip a young hoodlum like him into shape.

"As chairman and a life member of the Kruger-Brent board, your father has a right to be informed of decisions that may materially affect the company."

"But he can't stop me from signing away my inheritance. He can rant and rave about it if it makes him feel better. But there's nothing he can actually *do*. Is there?"

Lionel Neuman shook his head. *So much anger. And arrogance. The arrogance of youth.*

"Ultimately, Robert, you are correct. The decision rests with you. However, as your family's attorney for more than four decades, it is my duty to inform you . . ."

Robbie wasn't listening.

Save it for someone who cares, Grandpa. I don't want Kruger-Brent. I never did. And I don't care about the goddamn family. Apart from Lexi, not one of them is worth a damn.

He'd come to a decision last night. Admittedly he'd been looped at the time, lost in a heroin and tequila haze while playing the filthy, dilapidated piano at Tommy's, a gay bar in Brooklyn.

Some older guy who'd been coming on to him all evening yelled out: "You know what, kid? You could do that shit for a living."

It was a throwaway remark. But it hit Robbie like a bullet between the eyes.

I could do this for a living. I could run away. Away from Dad, away from Kruger-Brent, away from my demons. Change my name. Play piano in some anonymous bar somewhere. Find out who I really am.

Robbie Templeton wasn't interested in Old Man Neuman's concerns and warnings and quid pro quos. He wanted out.

"Here." He grabbed a piece of paper from Lionel Neuman's blotter. Using the lawyer's pen, he scrawled two lines that were to change his life forever.

I, Robert Peter Templeton, hereby renounce all claims, entitlement and inheritance left to me by my great-grandmother, Kate Blackwell, including all rights and shareholdings in Kruger-Brent, Ltd. I transfer those claims in their entirety to my sister, Alexandra Templeton.

"It's signed and dated. And you just witnessed it."

Handing the paper to the alarmed attorney, Robbie stood up to leave. Lionel Neuman was struck again by how unusually good-looking the boy was. Truly a gilded youth. But the telltale signs of substance abuse were already beginning to show. Bloodshot eyes, sunken cheeks, bouts of uncontrolled shivering.

How long before he winds up on the street, another hopeless, helpless, faceless addict?

Six months. Tops.

"Thank you for your help, Mr. Neuman. I'll see myself out."

SEVEN

∞

LEXI TEMPLETON WAS NOT LIKE OTHER LITTLE GIRLS.

When she was five years old, her father received a phone call at the office.

"I'm afraid you're going to have to come and pick Lexi up right away."

It was Mrs. Thackeray, the principal of Lexi's kindergarten. She sounded distressed.

"Has something happened? Is Lexi okay?"

"Your daughter is fine, Mr. Templeton. It's the other children I'm worried about."

When Peter arrived at the Little Cherubs Preschool, a tearful Lexi hurtled into his arms. "I didn't do anything, Daddy! It wasn't my fault."

Mrs. Thackeray pulled Peter to one side.

"I've had to send two children to the emergency room this morning. Your daughter attacked them with scissors. One little boy was lucky not to lose an eye."

"But that's ridiculous." Peter looked at Lexi. Clinging to his legs in a yellow cotton sundress with matching yellow ribbons in her hair, she looked the picture of innocence. "Why would she do a thing like that?"

"I have no idea. My staff assures me that the attack was entirely unprovoked. I'm afraid we won't be able to have Lexi back at Little Cherubs. You must make alternative arrangements."

In the back of the limousine, Peter asked his daughter what had happened.

"It was *nothing*." Lexi swung her legs merrily, entirely unrepentant. "I don't know why they all made such a fuss. I was doing my collage. It was a picture of Kruger-Brent. You know, your big tower where you go to work?"

Peter nodded.

"It was really pretty and silvery and I did all tinfoil on it. But then Timmy Willard said my picture was 'damn stupid.' And Malcolm Malloy laughed at me."

"That was mean of them, honey. So what did you do?"

Lexi looked at him pityingly, as if to say, *What sort of a question is that?*

"I stuck up for myself, like you told me. I stabbed Timmy in his head. Don't *worry*, Daddy," she added, seeing Peter's stricken face. "He didn't get dead. Can we go to McDonald's for lunch?"

The child psychologists were all in agreement.

Lexi was highly intelligent and highly sensitive. Her behavioral problems all stemmed from the loss of her mother.

Peter asked: "But what about this vengeful streak? Her lack of moral boundaries?"

The answer was always the same.

She'll grow out of it.

"Don't let me hear your excuses! You have poisoned the queen. You will have your head chopped off straight away."

Lexi grappled with her limited-edition *Little Mermaid* Barbie doll.

"That'll teach you, you fishy-tailed crin-i-mal." She grinned triumphantly as the head came free. "Now you are absolutely DEAD!"

"Lexi!"

Mrs. Grainger, the new nanny, walked into the bedroom. A sea of decapitated dolls littered the floor. She sighed.

Again? Whatever happened to tea parties and teddy bear's picnics?

Eight-year-old girls had sure changed since her day.

In her midfifties, widowed, with no children of her own, Mrs. Grainger had been hired as a replacement to the infamous Mrs. Carter. (The Templetons' former housekeeper had made the most of her blood money, divorcing her grumpy husband, Mike, and running off to Hawaii. She was last seen on a beach in Maui having coconut oil massaged into her ample backside by a half-naked twenty-year-old called Keanu. Mrs. Grainger had never gotten along with coconut oil.)

Mrs. Grainger was fond of Lexi, but she was no pushover. Those Barbie dolls cost money. She'd scolded Lexi more times than she could remember about taking better care of them.

"What's going on?"

Lexi's mind began to whir: *Mrs. Grainger is mad. What will stop her being mad? What does she want to hear?*

"Don't worry, Mrs. G. I was just playing a game. I can easily fix them again. Look."

Retrieving Ariel's head from the far side of the room, Lexi struggled vainly to reattach it to the body. It wasn't as easy as it looked. The stump of the neck was too fat for the hole above the shoulders that seemed to have magically shrunk since she ripped the head off. Strands of red nylon hair kept getting tangled around Lexi's fingers. Sweat began to bead on her forehead.

"Honestly, I can do it. I've done it before."

"That's not the point, Lexi. You shouldn't have pulled her head off in the first place. This carpet looks like *The Night of the Living Dead.*"

"It's not *my* fault. Ariel was trying to kill the queen."

Lexi gestured toward one of the few Barbie dolls still sporting a full complement of limbs. Dressed in regal red velvet, with a string of tinsel wrapped around her head, the blond effigy lay prostrate on the extortionately overpriced "Barbie's Four-Poster" that Robbie had bought his sister last week.

Just what Lexi needed. More toys.

"She's been poisoned. See? That's why she's gone a funny color."

With a groan, Mrs. Grainger noticed that the doll's cheeks had been defaced in what could only be described as a frenzied attack with a green felt-tip pen. She prayed that Lexi hadn't gotten green ink all over her clothes and bedding as well. That stuff was murder to get out.

Lexi said solemnly: "If you poison someone, you do get your head chopped off. That is a real, true fact, Mrs. G. I learned it in history."

Her expression was so adorably earnest, it was a struggle not to laugh.

"Yes, well. I'd prefer it if history didn't repeat itself quite so often all over the bedroom floor."

The nanny's tone was stern. But Lexi knew she had won. There was mad and there was pretend mad, and she was smart enough to know the difference.

Raised adult voices drifted up from downstairs. Lexi's face clouded with anxiety.

"Daddy's shouting. You think Robbie's in trouble again?"

"I have no idea." Mrs. Grainger shut the bedroom door firmly. "If he is, it's nothing for you to worry about. Your brother's big and ugly enough to take care of himself."

Lexi looked furious. "Robbie isn't ugly. He's the handsomest brother in the entire universe in space. Everyone says so."

Mrs. Grainger sighed. She wished Lexi wouldn't take everything quite so literally. She also wished Mr. Templeton would learn to keep his voice down. He had no idea how sensitive his daughter was, or how bright. Lexi was like a tiny satellite receiver, picking up all the tension in the house and translating it into a view of the world that was becoming increasingly skewed.

Today she was chopping the heads off her dollies.

But what about tomorrow?

Pervert!... Preying on innocent children... Sickos like him should be castrated.

Peter Templeton tried to focus on his breathing. He must keep calm. He must not lose his temper with the dreadful woman standing in his drawing room, screaming obscenities at him like a crack whore.

Ludo and I could go to the police, you know.

The woman might sound like a crack whore. In fact, her name was Angelica Dellal, wife of prominent JPMorgan banker Ludo Dellal and mother of sixteen-year-old Dominic Dellal: football star, head boy at Andover and (if Peter had interpreted her potty-mouthed ranting correctly) his son Robert's homosexual lover.

Homo! Freak!

The abuse washed in and out of Peter's consciousness like a toxic tide of effluence spewing from a sewer.

In her early forties, with handsome, aristocratic features and the sort of immaculately blow-dried, highlighted hair that immediately stamped her a rich man's wife, Angelica Dellal must once have been a great beauty. But any sex appeal she might once have possessed had long since been groomed to death, buffed and manicured and Botoxed into oblivion. At this moment she looked positively ugly, mouth stretched wide, face contorted with rage, diamond-encrusted hands flailing wildly.

"So . . . ?"

With a jolt, Peter realized that she had finally exhausted herself.

"I'm sorry. What was the question?"

Angelica Dellal looked as if she might spontaneously combust with indignation.

"The *question* is what are you going to do to ensure your disgusting, perverted son stays the hell away from my boy?"

"I'll talk to Robert."

"*Talk?* Is that it? My husband caught them in the back of a car together, okay? Your kid was *sucking my kid's dick*. Are you hearing this? Am I getting through?"

She jabbed a French-polished talon at Peter. He instinctively stepped back, clutching the couch for support. *Had Robbie really?* He shuddered. It didn't bear thinking about.

"Perhaps your husband was mistaken."

His voice was a whisper. Peter knew Ludo Dellal had not been mistaken. And yet he couldn't admit it, not even to himself.

Despite years of psychiatric training and decades of practice, Peter Templeton could not accept that his son was gay. How many closet homosexuals had he counseled over the years? Scores, probably. With those poor desperate men, those tortured strangers, compassion had come easily. But with his own son, it was a different matter. He wanted, desperately, to believe that it was this horrible woman's son who had led Robert astray, and not the other way around. That it was his, Peter's, child who was going through a phase. *His* child who would grow out of it, *his* child who would go on to be a football star at Harvard and have a wife and kids, and look back at these teenage indiscretions as nothing more than a blip. As sexual teething pains.

He clung to hope like a bare-knuckle climber clutching at a rock face. Robbie wasn't remotely effeminate. Girls hung around him like fleas on a rat, pestering him for dates. Perhaps he was just shy? A late bloomer? It was possible.

Your kid was sucking my kid's dick.

Mrs. Dellal was leaving, sweeping up her fur coat and Chanel quilted purse like Cruella de Vil.

"I mean it. If I see your homo son within ten miles of our house, or Dom's school, I will call the police. And you better *pray* the cops find your boy before my husband does."

The front door slammed shut.

Silence.

"Daddy?"

Lexi stood in the doorway wearing a white muslin dress with butter-flies embroidered on the sleeves and a blue bow in her buttermilk hair.

Peter thought: *Look how innocent she is.*

"What's a pervert?"

To his great embarrassment, Peter felt himself blushing. "Gee, honey, it's, erm . . . it's a bad word."

"Yes, but what does it mean?"

"It doesn't mean anything, sweetie."

"Oh. Well, what's a homo, then?"

For God's sake. How much had she heard?

"Why don't you go on upstairs and play, Lexi. I'll come up in a few minutes and join you."

"I'm bored of playing." Lexi dropped her voice to a conspiratorial whisper. "Does pervert mean *S-E-X*?"

"Go and watch *The Jungle Book.* Tell Mrs. Grainger I said yes to TV just this once."

Lexi skipped off to the playroom with squeals of delight. Peter sank wearily onto the couch. *Oh, Alex. Why aren't you here? Why is it still so hard?* He knew he had to talk to Robbie about the Dellal boy. He just didn't know where to start.

As it turned out, he didn't have to. Robbie broached the subject himself. Rolling home at eleven o'clock, drunk as a lord, he found his dad in the kitchen.

"You'll be pleased to hear I'm gunnaway," he slurred. "Meanmy-frendom."

"You're drunk, Robert. I can't understand you."

"My *friend.*" The word rolled cruelly off Robbie's tongue. "Me and my *friend* Dom are going away. To New Orleans. I'll be out of your hair for good. Break out the champagne!"

Raising his hand, as if making a toast, he lost his balance, gashing his head against the kitchen table as he slid to the floor.

"Oops." Tears of laughter coursed down his cheeks.

"Your drinking isn't funny, Robert."

"It's not? Jeez, that's strange. Yours was always *hilarious.*" Contempt blazed in Robbie's eyes. "Maybe I should pull a gun on you? Liven things up a bit. Would that be funny, *Dad*?"

Peter felt like crying. When had the word *dad* become an insult?

"Dominic's mother was here this afternoon. Making threats. She says if you go near her son again, she'll report you to the police for proselytizing."

"Prozshele . . . *what*-le-tizing? Man, that's a new one on me. We'll have to try that some time. Dom loves to try new things."

Peter snapped. "You're revolting! Do you think this is a game? That boy is barely sixteen years old."

Robbie shrugged. "He knows what he's doing. As a matter of fact, he's damn good at it."

"His parents will prosecute. You could go to jail, Robert, you do realize that?"

"Not if they can't find us."

Robbie's head was heavy. After he left Lionel Neuman's office this afternoon he'd wandered from bar to bar, slowly drinking his way into the numbed, half-conscious state that had become a way of life for him recently. Holding a conversation was like trying to swim through thick, warm soup.

The truth was he didn't even care that much about Dom Dellal. It wasn't like they were in love or anything. But his father's disgust made him want to lash out. It reminded Robbie of all his own feelings of guilt and self-loathing.

Just my luck to be the world's first gay homophobe.

"I went to see Old Man Neuman today."

"Really."

"Yeah. Took myself outta the will." Robbie dissolved into drunken giggles. "I told him. I said, 'You can stick your money. I don' wan' Krugerfugginbren.'"

Peter sighed. "You can't simply write yourself out of the will, Robert. There are trusts . . . it's complicated."

"Not anymore it ain't. I gave it all to Lexi."

Robbie stood up. The room spun like a clothes dryer. Putting a hand to his forehead, he felt the sticky warmth of blood on his fingers.

Peter thought: *Has he really repudiated Kate's will? Can he do that?*

Out loud he said, "You're too drunk to talk sense now. We'll talk in the morning."

"I won't be here in the morning."

Robbie took an unsteady step forward, squaring up to his father. His eyes glinted with drunken, reckless rage.

Peter's stomach lurched. Robbie was so close, he could smell the stale alcohol on his breath. *I'm afraid of him. I'm afraid of my own son.*

"I'm going to New Orleans. With Dom."

"If you leave this house tonight, don't bother coming back."

The words were out of Peter's mouth before he knew they were in his head. "Don't worry. I won't. Good-bye, Dad."

"Good-bye, Robert."

Peter watched his son stagger out of the room, blood still flowing from the gash on his head. Seconds later, he heard the front door slam.

He waited for the guilt to hit him. *This is the part where I run after him. Tell him I didn't mean it.* Seconds passed. Then minutes. Peter realized that the feeling swelling inside his chest was not guilt at all.

It was relief.

Switching off the downstairs lights, he tiptoed up to Lexi's bedroom.

It'll be just the two of us now, darling. You don't need your brother. Daddy'll take care of you.

He wouldn't wake her. He'd just kneel next to the bed for a moment. Breathe in her sweet child's smell. Take comfort from her warm, sleeping, innocent body.

He pushed the bedroom door open slowly. The room was pitch-dark. Picking his way toward the bed from memory, gingerly stepping past the toy box and over the discarded clothes, Peter knelt down next to the bed and reached out a loving arm.

A gust of wind in the face caught him by surprise.

He glanced up. The bedroom window was open.

Beneath it, in the dim glow of the moonlight, he stared at the empty bed.

Lexi was gone.

EIGHT

THE FIRST THING SHE WAS AWARE OF WAS DARKNESS.

Total darkness.

Not the darkness of her bedroom. The thick, cold, suffocating darkness of the grave.

She tried to scream, but no sound came out. Something had been stuffed into her mouth, a bitter-tasting cloth. She couldn't breathe.

Where am I?

Panic began coiling its way around her heart like a snake. Was she dreaming? She sat up. Her head cracked painfully against something solid and metal.

A coffin? No! Oh God, please, no!

Daddy!

Again she screamed. Again the cloth choked her, stifling the sound in her throat. Slowly, consciously, she began to inhale through her nose.

Keep calm. You're alive. Don't panic.

Air filled her lungs. *Relax.*

Bedtime stories about her great-great-grandfather Jamie McGregor came flooding into her mind. Jamie had been brave and cunning and resourceful. He'd battled sharks and land mines, escaped shipwrecks and fought off assassins. No situation had been too hopeless for him to figure a way out of it.

She tried to think logically.

What happened? How did I get here?

It was no good. She couldn't remember. Mrs. Grainger had put her to bed, and then . . . and then . . . darkness. The fear returned like a great crashing wave.

Help me!

Lexi shivered. She realized suddenly that she was freezing cold. She was still wearing the thin cotton nightie she'd gone to bed in. Beneath her back the hard metal floor felt like sheet ice.

Bump.

What was that?

The floor was moving. It vibrated steadily, then every twenty seconds or so, it threw her body upward, like a tossed pancake. Suddenly it dawned on her: *A car. I'm in the trunk of a car. I've been kidnapped, and they're taking me somewhere. To their hideout.*

If it hadn't been happening to her, it would probably have been exciting. Kidnapping was one of Lexi's favorite games. But this was no game. This was real.

"Get out."

The man wore a mask. Not a ski mask, like bank robbers wore in the movies. A rubber Halloween mask. It made him look like a corpse.

Too consumed with fear and cold to move, Lexi froze. Her eyes widened with terror.

Another voice. "Don't just stand there, man, pick her up. Get her inside before someone shows up."

The corpse reached into the trunk and grabbed hold of Lexi's arms. On instinct, she fought him, kicking and scratching like a wildcat.

"Fuck!" The corpse clutched at his forearm. Her sharp nail had drawn blood. "Little bitch!"

Pulling back his arm, he punched her in the face so hard she blacked out.

Time passed.

She was in a room with no windows. A low-wattage lightbulb burned constantly. Days and nights became one. At first, the pain in her face where the corpse had punched her was unbearable. But gradually it began to subside.

There was a bed in one corner, an old-fashioned porcelain chamber pot and a battered cardboard box containing a few desultory books and toys. The walls were bare, the floor smooth, green linoleum. It felt more like an office than a room in a house. The toys and books were all designed for much younger children.

My kidnappers don't know much about kids.

Fear gave way to boredom. There was nothing to do, nothing to break the monotony of the endless, lonely hours. At regular intervals, a masked man would enter, empty and replace the chamber pot and bring Lexi some food. Her captors never spoke to her, or answered when she spoke to them, but occasionally she heard their dim, muffled voices through the walls.

There were three of them. A leader with a deep voice and a strange, foreign accent, and two others—the corpse and a third man who wore a variety of animal masks, sometimes a pig, sometimes a dog or a snake. It was the third man, animal man, who really frightened her.

He was standing over her bed. He had the pig mask on.

"Make a sound and I'll kill you."

No you won't. If you were going to kill me, you'd have done it by now. You need me alive.

Lexi opened her mouth to scream but it was too late. A huge, hot hand clamped over her mouth. He was on the bed, pushing her down. The weight of him squeezed the breath from her body. One hand still covered her mouth, but Lexi could feel the other clawing beneath her nightgown. *NO!* A sharp pain between her legs brought tears to her eyes. She tried to move, to struggle, but it was hopeless. She was pinned like a leaf beneath a boulder.

He made strange noises. Deep, guttural groans Lexi had never heard before. The hair on her scalp began to rise with terror. Then suddenly the weight lifted.

Voices.

"What are you doing in there, man?"

It was the leader.

"She ain't due another meal for three hours."

Lexi couldn't see the pig's face, but she could tell he was afraid.

He hissed at her. "One word and I will slit your throat. Understand?"

She nodded.

Agent Andrew Edwards looked at the stack of black-and-white photographs on the table in front of him. It was as thick as a phone book.

"Is this all of them?"

"Yes, sir. That's every warehouse, hangar and industrial facility within a fifteen-mile radius of where the car was dumped."

It was eleven days, four hours and sixteen minutes since Peter Templeton had reported his daughter missing. Agent Edwards had played the tape of Peter's desperate 911 call so many times he could recite it by heart. Nine times out of ten with these child disappearances, the parents ended up being involved. What could you say? It was a sick world. But in this case, Agent Edwards believed the father. Not only did Peter Templeton's distress seem genuine, but the ransom note left under the child's pillow bore all the hallmarks of an organized criminal operation: no fingerprints, typed on the most common Lexmark printer paper, succinct, untraceable.

The Blackwell family had two weeks to transfer $10 million to a numbered account in the Caymans. If they involved the police at any point, the girl would be killed immediately.

Agent Edwards was a Scot by birth but a New Yorker by temperament. He had pale skin, watery amber eyes and hair that couldn't quite make up its mind whether to be blond or red. He loved the Yankees, hated the street gangs and drug dealers that plagued the city and described his yearly vacation to the Jersey Shore as "traveling."

He sighed heavily.

"There must be three hundred facilities here."

"Four hundred twenty."

"Got any good news for me, Agent Jones?"

"As a matter of fact, sir, I do. *These*"—Agent Edwards's colleague handed his boss a much-thinner manila folder—"are the derelict or deserted premises."

"How many?"

"Only eighteen of 'em." Agent Jones smiled. "I can set up surveillance this afternoon, if you want."

"No. Not yet."

"But, sir, we have less than sixty hours. The deadline—"

"You think I don't know what the damn deadline is?"

Agent Edwards was pissed. What kind of idiots was the Bureau hiring these days? The last thing he wanted was to have every warehouse in New Jersey crawling with feds. If these guys got spooked, they'd kill the kid on the spot.

The Blackwell family had taken a huge risk involving the authorities at all. With their money and connections, they could easily have made the payment quietly and been done with it. Or hired their own private hit men to get these guys.

But they hadn't. They'd come to Agent Edwards with a case that would either make or break his career. Screwing up was not an option.

Finding the kidnappers' car had been a coup. Agent Edwards had matched the DNA on hairs found in the trunk to hairs from Lexi's bedroom pillow. Two voice-distorted phone calls to Peter Templeton's office were probably made from inside a large, industrial structure. The FBI's tech team had analyzed the echo, if you could believe that shit.

But it wasn't enough. Agent Edwards didn't want eighteen targets. He wanted one.

"Send a chopper up. Not too low. It needs to sound like routine air traffic."

"Yes, sir. What are they looking for, exactly?"

Agent Edwards looked at his junior witheringly.

"The Emerald City of Oz. Jesus! *Tire tracks*, shit-for-brains. They're looking for fucking tire tracks."

He never wanted to get involved.

He was in a brothel in Phuket when the call came through, enjoying the attentions of a pair of eleven-year-old twins. Pussies so tight they could have cracked hazelnuts, tongues as eager and skillful as any of the high-end hookers he used back home. Bliss.

He loved the Thais. Such an enlightened people.

"Ten million bucks, split three ways. The house has third-world security. Trust me, you'll be taking candy from a baby. Get in, get the kid, get the money, get out."

"I don't need that kind of money."

Laughter. "You don't have to *need* it. You just have to want it."

"I'm straight now, all right? Find someone else."

He closed his eyes in pleasure as the girls plundered his body with their tongues and fingers. At home, he paid prostitutes to dress up as schoolgirls. But nothing could compare to the real deal: the smooth skin; the hard, budding breasts; the hairless paradise between the legs . . .

"You know, the little girl is adorable."

The voice on the phone wasn't giving up.

"She's the spitting image of her mother. Everybody says so."

He hesitated. An image of Alexandra Blackwell in her youth popped into his mind. He remembered her well. The long, lithe legs tanned a perfect caramel. The cascade of blond hair. The trembling pale-pink lips, parting, smiling.

Hello, Rory. It's been a long time.

"How old did you say she was?"

One of the Thai twins circled her tongue around his anus. The other opened her mouth, cocooning his balls in a cave of warm, soft wetness. He moaned with pleasure.

"She's eight."

Eight years old.

The spitting image of her mother.

Everybody says so.

"All right. I'll do it. But this is the last—"

He never got to finish. The line had already gone dead.

"Have you found her?"

Peter Templeton clutched Agent Edwards's hand so tightly he nearly cut off the circulation.

Agent Edwards thought: *Poor bastard. He's aged ten years in the last two weeks.*

"We think so. Yes. A facility in Jersey, near—"

"When are you going in?"

"Tonight. As soon as it's dark."

"Can't you do it now?"

"Tonight will be better. This is the best way, sir. Trust me. We have a lot of experience with hostage situations."

Peter thought: *I hope to God he knows what he's doing.*

Agent Edwards thought: *I hope to God I know what I'm doing.*

They both thought: *What if they kill her between now and night-fall?*

"Try and get some rest, sir. As soon as we hear anything, I'll let you know."

The leader and the other man were angry with the pig. Lexi heard them fighting. She could only make out fragments.

We agreed . . . Can't control yourself . . . What if she identifies?

She won't . . . the mask, man.

Goddamn pedophile . . .

. . . How much longer? . . . I want my money.

Soon . . .

Two weeks already . . . If they were gonna pay . . .

Shut the hell up, man! You'll get your money.

Lexi pressed her face to the door of her cramped cell, straining to hear every word. Not because she was frightened. But because she was determined to glean as much information about her captors as possible. Especially the pig, the man who had hurt her, who had forced his body inside her.

My family will come for me. One day soon, they'll come. Then I'll make that pig suffer for what he did to me.

Her greatest nightmare was not that she might be killed, but that her kidnappers might somehow escape. She mustn't let that happen. They had to be punished.

"Jesus Christ. How much longer?"

Agent Edwards squatted behind an unmarked car in the gathering darkness. Next to him squatted his junior partner, Agent Jones. Behind them crouched Chuck Barclay, the commander of the special Marine Corps unit that was about to lead the rescue operation.

"Twelve minutes." Captain Barclay smiled, a flash of white teeth illuminating his tar-blackened face. He was a small, rather unprepossessing man in his midforties, with a thin wiry body and pinched face; more of a fox terrier than the mastiff that Agent Edwards had been expecting. More worryingly, Barclay's "crack squad" appeared to consist of only five young marines with night-vision goggles and standard-issue handguns. There wasn't an automatic weapon or a hand grenade in sight.

"Barclay's the best," Agent Edwards's boss had assured him.

He'd better be.

The twelve minutes felt like twelve hours. It was a warm, late-summer night, but Agent Edwards could feel the hairs on his arms and neck stand on end. Cold clammy sweat seeped from his pores. His shirt was wet. He noticed Agent Jones was also shivering. The crumbling textile mill on the hill above them was barely discernible in the darkness. Even with the roar of traffic on Route 206 in the distance, it felt like the most desolate place on earth.

Then, suddenly, a movement. Captain Barclay gave a tight nod to his men. Seconds later, as if by magic, they had dispersed across the flat landscape, dropping into the undergrowth like so many silent leaves. It was impressive.

The two FBI agents were alone.

"This is it, sir."

Agent Jones was scared of his boss. Andrews was a moody bastard at the best of times, but the Templeton kidnapping had them all on a knife's edge.

"Yes, Jones. This is it."

"It'll be okay, sir. Everybody says these guys are the best."

"Hmm."

"According to reconnaissance—"

"Shhh." Agent Edwards put his finger to his lips. "Did you hear that?"

"What, sir?"

"Gunfire."

"I didn't hear a s—"

There was a blinding flash of light. A noise like a lion's roar but hundreds, thousands of times louder, erupted around them. Instinctively both men covered their ears and dived for the ground.

"What the . . . ?" Agent Jones's ears were ringing. He could taste earth and grass and dust in his mouth.

"Bomb! Stay down!"

Another roar. Deafening, like being sucked up into a thunder cloud. Flames were visible at the top of the rise. The mill was lit up in an impromptu son et lumière. It was eerily beautiful.

Agent Edwards fumbled beneath his sodden shirt for his gun.

"Call for backup. I'm going up there."

"Sir, no! You can't. You don't know what's going on—that building might collapse at any minute."

Like my career, if I don't get that Templeton kid out of there alive.

"Just make the call!" Agent Edwards shouted over his shoulder. A third explosion swallowed his words whole. Agent Jones dived for cover again.

By the time he opened his eyes, his boss was gone.

Lexi had just finished eating when she heard the first gunshot. She knew instantly what it was.

They're here! They've come for me! I knew they would.

Thirty seconds later, the door to her room swung open. It was the leader, the foreigner. He must have had no time to grab a mask. A hastily tied scarf covered only the bottom half of his face.

"Get over here. Now!"

Curly brown hair. Brown eyes. Not many lines: he's young, younger than the pig. Pinkie ring. Small scar above the left eyebrow.

"NOW!"

Lexi stayed where she was. She pretended to be too terrified to move, but inside she felt elated. She watched the leader hesitate. The third man, the corpse who hit her in the face the day they brought her here, appeared in the doorway behind him.

"Leave her, man! I set the traps. Let's get out of here."

"Jeez, Bill, we can't just leave her. The place is gonna blow."

Bill. The corpse's name is Bill.

"You want her, you take her. I'm outta here."

Lexi saw him run away. *Good-bye, Bill.*

The leader hovered helplessly for a moment, then took a step toward her. Lexi stepped back.

He doesn't seem like much of a leader now. I can see the fear in his eyes.

"Fine. Have it your way. Stay here and burn."

He turned and ran after his friend.

Lexi waited until the sound of their footsteps faded. Then she stepped out of the room.

It was the first time she had ventured beyond her cell door since they brought her here, whenever that was. Days ago, weeks, months? She found herself standing in a narrow corridor that opened out after about ten feet into a vast, derelict space, like an airplane hangar. But she had no curiosity about her surroundings. She wasn't even looking for her rescuers.

She was looking for the pig.

Where is he? Has he gotten away already? Please don't let him escape.

Another brief volley of gunfire on the other side of the building caught her attention. Lexi turned toward it and froze. A giant fireball was hurtling toward her.

Like a comet in a bowling alley. And I'm the pin.

She was so surprised, she forgot to be afraid. After that it was all a blur.

Flames, everywhere. Glass and brick and wood falling from the ceiling. Walls folding, melting in the searing heat. Then a single, deafening *BOOM*, so loud not even the earth could contain it.

It was the last sound Lexi Templeton heard.

NINE

∞

HE WAS THE MOST FAMOUS BARRISTER IN LONDON.

As he strode down the Strand toward the Old Bailey, the city's venerable criminal court, immaculate in his Savile Row suit and polished, handmade brogues, people stared.

You know who that is, don't you? That's Gabriel McGregor. Hasn't lost a case in six years at the bar. He's a genius.

A blond-haired, gray-eyed beauty, Gabe McGregor was built like a rugby prop-forward, broad-shouldered, barrel-chested and with legs as long and strong and straight as oak trees. There was a solidity about him, a strength, in his body, his jaw, his steady, direct gaze that made juries think: *I believe this man.* Underlying his physical strength was a powerful intellect. Gabriel McGregor could judge a case's nuances in a matter of moments. He knew instinctively when to push a witness and when to hold back. When to bully, to flatter, to cajole, to frighten, to befriend. Every judge at the Bailey knew and respected him. Gabriel McGregor was a class act.

Glancing at his watch, he quickened his pace. It wouldn't do to be late to court. His long stride seemed to swallow up the yards of sidewalk effortlessly, like a whale gulping down krill. He was a colossus, a giant among men.

"Gabe, thank God. I thought you'd done a runner."

Michael Wilmott was a solicitor. Every time Gabe saw him, the same three words popped into his head. *Weak. Pathetic. Disappointed.* Michael Wilmott was overweight, overworked and overwhelmed. He wore a cheap, shiny suit with sweat patches under the arms and a permanently harassed expression. If there were such a thing as a legal A-team, Michael Wilmott was not on it, had never been on it, *could* never be on it.

"I wouldn't do that, Michael." Gabe spoke in a soft Scottish brogue. "I told you I'd be here. I never break my word."

"No. You just break innocent householders' skulls in six different places."

The words were like a glass of ice-cold water in Gabe's face. Reluctantly he stepped out of his fantasy world and back into reality.

This wasn't the Old Bailey. It was Waltham Forest Magistrates' Court.

He wasn't a hotshot lawyer. He was a nineteen-year-old drug addict, accused of burglary, assault and grievous bodily harm with intent to kill.

Michael Wilmott was all that stood between him and twenty-five years in Wormwood Scrubs Prison.

"The magistrates don't want to hear your heroic speeches, and nor do I. Keep your head down, let me do the talking and try to look like you're sorry. All right?"

Gabe nodded meekly. "Yes, sir."

Gabriel McGregor was born in the Aberdeen Royal Infirmary in Scotland in 1973. The only son of Stuart McGregor, an impoverished dockworker, and Anne, Stuart's childhood sweetheart, Gabe was a strong, handsome baby who grew into a strong, handsome boy.

Gabe couldn't remember the first time he'd heard the name Jamie McGregor. All he knew was that he had only ever heard it uttered with venom and hatred. He heard the name so often, it seemed as much a part of his childhood as the smell of ship oil, the scratchy feeling of cheap polyester clothes against his skin, and the ominous thud of the bailiff's fist on the front door of the family's run-down, tenement flat.

Jamie McGregor was the source of all their troubles.

It was Jamie McGregor's fault that they lived their lives hand-to-mouth, in crushing, soul-destroying poverty.

Jamie McGregor made Gabe's father drink and hit his mother.

Jamie McGregor made his mother cry as she tried to cover the bruises with cheap foundation from Boots.

Jamie McGregor . . .

Not until he was a teenager did Gabe piece together the truth. Jamie McGregor, the famous entrepreneur who had founded Kruger-Brent and become one of the richest men in the world, was his great-great-uncle. Jamie McGregor had had two brothers, Ian and Jed, and a sister, Mary. Ian McGregor, the eldest brother, was Gabe's great-grandfather. Ian's son, Hamish, was Gabe's grandfather. Hamish's son, Stuart, was Gabe's dad.

The rot had started with Jamie's brother, Ian, back in the early 1900s. Ian McGregor never forgave his younger brother for running off to South Africa and making a fortune.

"Who does he think he is, disappearing halfway 'round the world, leaving us to take care of Mam and Da and the farm? Sending nae money home to those as raised him?"

Ian had conveniently forgotten that he had laughed in Jamie's face when he announced his intention to sail for the diamond fields of Africa. That growing up he had beaten the boy mercilessly, frequently cheating him out of his scant share of food and giving him the toughest, most arduous jobs on the family's meager, rocky, little farm north of Aberdeen. By the time Jamie founded Kruger-Brent and made his millions, both his parents were dead, condemned to early graves by the relentless poverty of lives spent tilling the land. Jamie did send money home, to Mary, the only one of his siblings who had loved and supported him. But when she, too, died, of tuberculosis, aged only thirty, the payments dried up. Jamie had not seen or spoken to either of his brothers in over a decade. He did not feel he owed them anything.

Ian McGregor saw things differently. If he'd been tough on Jamie, it was only for his own good. He had loved the boy like a father, worked hard to provide for him, and what had been his reward? Abandonment. Betrayal. Destitution.

Ian began to drink heavily. As Jamie's fortune and reputation grew, so, too, did his brother's bitterness and envy. The years passed, and Ian passed this loathing on to his own son, Hamish, who in turn bequeathed it to Gabe's father, Stuart, like some sort of terrible genetic disease.

When Gabe was growing up, just to speak the name Jamie McGregor was to invoke the devil. Over the years, other names were added to the family's roll call of hatred. *Kate Blackwell. Tony Blackwell. Eve Blackwell. Robert Templeton.* Gabe's grandfather, Hamish, devoted his retirement years and every penny of his meager savings to a doomed lawsuit against the mighty Kruger-Brent corporation. Time after time the case was thrown out of courts from Glasgow to London to New York. Each time the judges were more scathing.

Frivolous.

Greedy.

Entirely without foundation.

Hamish McGregor died a bankrupt, bitter man. Twenty years later, the same fate befell his son, Gabe's father. Gabe was sixteen when his dad died, his mind corroded with drink and hatred, his body broken from the long, backbreaking years on the docks.

Despite everything, Gabe had loved his dad. He tried to remember the good times they'd had together. Playing on the beach at Elgin when he was three or four. Watching Celtic play at Parkhead, screaming their heads off in the terraces. Dancing around the tree at Christmas, all three of them in the front room, Mam, too, before Dad had started to hit her, before the bitterness got too much.

Two weeks after his father died, Gabe left home.

His mother was worried.

"Where will you go, son? You've nae qualifications. You'll nae find work in Aberdeen, nae now the shipyards are gone."

"I'm not staying in Scotland, Mam. There's work down south. Plenty."

"You mean *London?*"

Anne McGregor couldn't have sounded more horrified if Gabe had said he was moving to Beirut.

"I'll phone you as soon as I'm settled. Do not worry, Mam. I can take care of myself."

TEN

PETER TEMPLETON SAT IN THE PRIVATE WAITING ROOM AT
Mount Sinai Medical Center, staring at the wall. This was where he'd
lost his beloved Alex. Even the smell of the place, a mixture of disinfec-
tant and cheap vanilla candles, was gruesomely familiar.

How much more tragedy did the gods have planned for him?

When would it end?

Mindlessly, he picked up a frayed copy of *New Woman* magazine.

I don't want a new woman. I want my old woman back.

A few doors down the hall, Agent Andrew Edwards was still in surgery. The man had been a hero, according to his partner. Astonishingly
brave. After the second bomb, he'd run into the blazing building, looking for Lexi. He never gave up.

*It should have been me in that mill, not him. If he lives, I will reward him
for his courage. He can have anything he wants.*

If he lives.

Something had gone terribly wrong. The FBI believed they were taking on a small group of armed kidnappers. They'd expected a shoot-out.
Instead they stumbled into a series of sophisticated booby traps, triggering
bombs powerful enough to wipe out entire villages. Captain Barclay and

his men never stood a chance. The first explosion killed three of them outright. By the time FBI reinforcements arrived, all five were dead, entombed in what would soon be the charred wreckage of a fire so catastrophic it could be seen from fifty miles away.

Early indications were that the kidnappers themselves had escaped. In the confusion, and desperate attempts to find Lexi, valuable time had been lost. If they had gotten out, they could be anywhere by now, scattered to the wind.

If they'd gotten out. The fire was so intense, it would be weeks before a final determination was made on all the human remains. It didn't help that nobody knew exactly how many bodies they were looking for.

Peter overheard the fire chief talking to one of the surgeons.

"It's a miracle anyone made it out of there alive. Agent Edwards is a lucky guy."

Second-degree burns to eighty percent of his body, two shattered legs and severe internal bleeding? thought Peter. *I'd love to meet an unlucky guy.*

"Dr. Templeton?"

Peter looked up. A pretty woman doctor was talking to him.

"You can come in now. Your daughter is awake."

Lexi blinked, taking in her surroundings.

She was in a hospital. Even if the nurse hadn't been standing at the foot of her bed, she'd have known it instantly from the smell. She remembered it from the time she'd had her tonsils out last year. That and the fact that they let her have ice cream for breakfast. *I wonder if I'll get that this time?*

The room had been designed for children. A cheerily colorful Winnie the Pooh frieze circled the whitewashed walls, and the visitors' armchair was smothered with teddy bears. It was a comforting room, bright and pleasant. But something wasn't right.

The nurse was smiling at her. Lexi could see her lips moving.

That's strange. Why isn't she talking out loud?

Dimly, memories of her kidnap and rescue floated back to her. Nothing coherent. Fragments of fragments. The sound of gunfire. Doors opening. Blinding light. She remembered the face of the man who had scooped her into his arms. He had pale skin and kind eyes. His lips had moved, too, like the nurse's.

I wonder where he is now?

The next moment the door swung open and Peter walked in. Lexi's heart leaped for joy. He rushed to her side, wrapping his arms around her and smothering her in kisses. She could feel the warmth and strength of his body, taste the salty wetness of his tears. It was wonderful, a dream come true. And yet something was still not quite right. She felt distant. Detached. As though a part of her wasn't really there. But which part?

Oh, Daddy! I knew you'd come.

That was when it hit her.

The silence.

Her mouth was shaping words. She could feel the sound of them in her chest, feel her breath pushing them out into the room. But she couldn't hear them. With slow dawning horror, she realized that she couldn't hear anything.

Dad.

She tried the word again.

Daddy!

She started to panic. It was the same feeling of terror she had waking up in the kidnappers' car. Dizzyness, racing heart, nausea. Her mind flashed back to the mill. She was in her bed in the cell. The door creaked open. The pig! He was moving toward her.

One word and I will slit your throat.

Lexi threw back her head and screamed.

"What's happening?" Peter panicked. The noise Lexi was making was earsplitting, bloodcurdling, like nothing he'd ever heard before. Like an animal being slaughtered. "For God's sake, somebody help her!"

The woman doctor moved toward them, but Lexi wouldn't let her near, clinging to Peter like a baby chimpanzee to its mother. Her screams got louder. Her nails were digging into Peter's shoulder. Blood seeped onto his shirt.

"Do something!"

The doctor filled a syringe, but it was difficult. The child was wriggling uncontrollably. Pulling aside Lexi's hospital gown, she made a lunge, sinking the needle into her thigh.

Lexi's eyes widened with shock. Then suddenly her small body relaxed. She was a rag doll in Peter's arms.

Peter laid her down softly on the bed. He was shaking.

"What the hell was all that about?"

"It could be any number of things," the doctor explained. "Please. Sit down."

Mindlessly Peter pushed the teddies onto the floor and sank into the visitors' chair.

"We need to run some more tests. Your daughter . . . there are signs of . . . mistreatment."

Peter looked blank. He noticed that the doctor had hazel eyes that matched her hair and a smattering of freckles on the bridge of her nose.

"There's no easy way to say this, I'm afraid. But we believe Lexi may have been sexually assaulted, Dr. Templeton. In addition to the trauma of her abduction, there are signs . . ."

The doctor's voice trailed off. She may still have been speaking, but Peter heard nothing except a low ringing in his ears. The ringing turned into a rumble, then a clatter, like a train gaining speed as it hurtled down the track:

Sexual assault, sexual assault, sexual assault . . .

He put his hands over his ears.

"Dr. Templeton? Are you all right?"

"She's eight years old. She's a baby."

Tears rolled down his cheeks.

"I know it's a lot to take in." The doctor's hands were on his, warm, sympathetic. "Try to hold on to the fact that she's alive. No burns, no serious injury, other than her hearing, of course. Agent Edwards saved her life."

"Her hearing?"

"That's what I've been telling you, Dr. Templeton. We need to run some more tests. But you should try to prepare yourself for the worst. There's a strong chance that your daughter may never be able to hear again."

ELEVEN

GABE MCGREGOR HAD TOLD HIS MOTHER HE COULD TAKE care of himself. But he proved to be a poor prophet.

Although by no means stupid, Gabe was dyslexic and easily bored. As a result, he had left school at sixteen without any qualifications, despite being naturally good with numbers. He arrived in London with nothing but his good looks, optimism and fifty pounds in cash in his back pocket. Work was scarce.

"I'm a hard worker. I know I'll have to start at the bottom. What about the mail room?"

He was sitting opposite the head of human resources at May & Lorriman, an investment bank in the city.

"I'm sorry, son, but this isn't a Michael J. Fox movie. Even our mail boys have a minimum of five GCSEs—General Certificates of Secondary Education."

The head of human resources felt sorry for Gabe, but there was nothing she could do. Rules were rules. She'd only agreed to see him because he'd shown up at the office every morning for the past week, begging for an interview.

Undaunted, Gabe set off down Moorgate, determined not to leave the City, London's famous financial district, till he had a foot in the door. But it was the same story everywhere.

"You'll have to submit a written application," said Merrill Lynch.

"Three A-levels or equivalent is our minimum qualification for back office," said Goldman Sachs.

"We don't hire casual workers," said Deutsche Bank.

Gabe was baffled.

The banks all claim to want "entrepreneurs." Applicants who can "think outside the box," that's what their brochures say. But show a bit of entrepreneurial spirit and they slam the door in your face.

Next he tried the real-estate agencies. There was plenty of money in property, and at the end of the day it was a sales job. *I can do that.* Foxtons, Douglas & Gordon, Knight Frank, Allsop's. Gabe tried them all, knocking on doors, tramping the streets of London from Kensington to Kensal Rise till his feet ached and his head throbbed.

I don't need a salary. I'll work on commission.

All I'm asking for is a chance.

I'm sorry, son.

You need A-levels.

Go back to school.

Depressed and defeated, Gabe finally began looking for manual work, but even that was tough. The Irish had a stranglehold on construction in the capital and were loath to dole out work to a Scot with no friends to recommend him.

Have you worked on a site before, lad?

No.

What's your trade, jock? Electrician?

No.

Plumber?

No.

You must have some skills?

Gabe sat on the single bed in his dirty council flat in Walworth. He was hungry, tired, lonely and broke.

You must have some skills. He's right. I must. What are my skills? What the hell am I good at?

For twenty minutes, Gabe stared at the wall, his mind a blank. Then it came to him:

Women. He was good with women.

Women loved Gabe McGregor. They always had. At school, Gabe regularly charmed his way out of trouble with women teachers, and got the bright girls in his class to do his homework for him. With his broken nose and rugby player's physique, he was not classically handsome. But one look into his playful, spirited gray eyes and grown women had been known to go weak at the knees. Gabe was a natural flirt, a bad boy who needed mothering. It was a lethally attractive combination to the opposite sex.

How the hell do I make money out of that?

Gabe took a shower and changed into his one clean pair of pants and a white linen shirt. Grabbing his last few pounds in change, he walked down to the Elephant and Castle and caught a bus to Knightsbridge.

Thirty minutes later he was standing on Sloane Street. It was six o'clock on a warm July evening, and the stores and bars were still busy. All around him Gabe saw rich, beautifully dressed women. They poured out of Chanel and Ungaro in their Gucci heels and diamonds, flicking their expensively dyed hair as they strode past. Often they were in groups, chatting and laughing as they swung their Harrods shopping bags, sipping flutes of champagne on the sidewalk cafés. Sometimes they were alone. Never, or almost never, were they with a man.

Where are all the husbands? Still at the office in Goldman Sachs, with their A-levels and degrees from sodding Harvard, earning the money to pay for all this designer clobber.

More fool them.

One woman caught Gabe's eye. Brunette, attractive, in her late thirties or early forties, she was standing outside Harvey Nichols, glancing impatiently at her expensive Patek Philippe watch. Whoever was meeting her was evidently late. Irritated, she stuck out her arm to hail a cab, then thought better of it, instead disappearing back into the store.

Gabe ran after her. The driver of a Jaguar E-type beeped at him furiously as he stepped blindly into the traffic.

"Wanker! Have you got a bloody death wish or something?"

But Gabe didn't hear. Plunging through the double doors into Harvey Nichols, he caught up with the woman just as she was stepping into the elevator.

"You're in a hurry." She laughed as the doors whooshed closed. Gabe realized he was panting, he'd been running so fast. "Thirsty?"

"I'm sorry?"

"I said you must be thirsty. This lift goes directly to the fifth-floor bar. Is that what you wanted?"

Gabe grinned. Up close she looked older, perhaps midforties, but she had good legs and the sort of naughty, mischievous smile that boded well for what he had in mind.

"Absolutely."

Her name was Claire, and Gabe lived with her—lived *off* her—for a month, till she finally decided enough was enough.

"You're lovely, darling, you know you are. But I can't spend the rest of my life with a boy young enough to be my son."

"Why not?"

"Because it's exhausting! This morning I fell asleep in the middle of a deposition. I'm a partner in a law firm, Gabe, I'm not Maggie May. Besides, it's time you found yourself something to *do*."

Gabe found himself something to do the next morning. Her name was Angela.

After Angela came Caitlin, Naomi, Fiona and Thérèse. For the first year, life was good. He still had no security. No savings. But he moved from one luxury West End apartment to the next, wore clothes that were not made of polyester and did not scratch, dined at London's finest restaurants, enjoyed regular sex with a string of grateful, well-preserved older women, and had access to more first-class cocaine than he knew what to do with.

At first the coke was under control. Gabe enjoyed the odd line at parties and that was it. But as the boredom and emptiness of his days began to bite (there were only so many times you could go to the gym or go shopping while your girlfriend went to work) the charlie became a lunchtime habit, too. Pretty soon he was getting high at breakfast. That was when the trouble started.

Fiona, a divorced Internet entrepreneur with a stunning Chelsea town house, kicked Gabe out when she came home early from work and caught him snorting drugs off her Conran walnut coffee table with her fourteen-year-old daughter.

Thérèse called it a day after money started going missing from her purse.

"That's funny. I'm sure I had a hundred in my wallet. Didn't I stop at the Lloyds cash point last night?"

"Christ, babe, I don't know. What am I, your mother?"

It was Gabe's anger that raised her suspicions. Convinced she was being paranoid, but scared of being burned again, Thérèse waited till Gabe was away in St. Tropez for the weekend and had surveillance cameras secretly installed in the bedroom.

Two weeks later, Gabe was out on the street.

He wasn't a bad kid at heart. But the drugs took all the decent sides of his personality—the humor, the warmth, the loyalty—and swallowed them whole. He moved on from coke to heroin. Soon all that was left was a husk, a physical shell. Then even that began to crumble. Gabe lost weight. His teeth began to discolor. Without knowing how he got there, he found himself sleeping in doorways and shoplifting to be able to buy food.

He had always had a vivid, active imagination. Now, as his reality became grimmer and grimmer, he retreated ever more into the fantasy world he created for himself. He was a banker, a lawyer, a success. He was rich and respected. His mother was proud.

The house was a grand Victorian mansion. Walthamstow was a rough area, but good transport links to the City meant that the nicer streets had become gentrified. Quite a few young, professional families were moving there, priced out of West London by the Arabs and the Russians. You got more house for your money, but you also got some unsavory neighbors.

Gabe was staying at a homeless shelter a few blocks away. He had next to no memory of that night. A few images, half-remembered dreams. His hand, bleeding. The sound of the sirens. Everything else he'd heard from the police the morning after.

He broke in at around one A.M., high as Mount Kilimanjaro. The police assumed his intention was burglary, although he may simply have been confused and looking for shelter. In any event, he never got the chance to steal anything. The owner of the house, a father of three in his late thirties, heard a noise downstairs and confronted Gabe, swinging at him with a lamp. Gabe picked up the poker from the fireplace and proceeded to "defend himself," hitting the guy repeatedly in the head and upper body. He beat him so appallingly that when the wife came downstairs, she thought her husband was dead.

The police arrested Gabe at the scene. He made no attempt to flee, largely because he didn't know where he was, or what he was supposed to have done.

"Will the defendant please rise."

Gabe was staring into space, lost in thought. He was in a Plexiglas box in the corner of the courtroom. Michael Wilmott, his lawyer, had told him it was bulletproof. Only defendants who were considered a danger to the magistrates or court officials were placed behind the Plexiglas walls.

They think I'm dangerous. A dangerous criminal.

"Stand *up*, please, Mr. McGregor."

Gabe stood up.

"Due to the serious nature of this offense, to which you have wisely pleaded guilty, I am obliged to refer your case to the crown court for sentencing."

Refer? Gabe looked at his lawyer hopefully. *Does that mean they're letting me out?* He hadn't had a hit in three days and was beginning to feel desperate. The Plexiglas was making him claustrophobic.

"Your request for bail is denied. You will be remanded in custody until the date of your next hearing, provisionally set for October fourth. Presentence reports . . ."

Gabe wasn't listening.

You will be remanded in custody.

His gray eyes pleaded with the magistrate. She was a woman after all. But she looked at him impassively, turned and left the room. His lawyer's hand was on his arm.

"Keep your head down," Michael Wilmott muttered. "I'll be in touch."

Then he, too, was gone. Two armed police escorted Gabe toward the cells. Later, he would be transferred to prison.

Prison! No! I can't! I have to get out of here!

No one heard the voices. They were all in his head.

TWELVE

"BUT WHY DO WE HAVE TO GO?" MAX WEBSTER SWUNG HIS legs impatiently, kicking the back of the chauffeur's seat. "We hate the Templetons."

"Nonsense, Max," Keith Webster said firmly. "We don't hate anyone. Especially not family."

Max was traveling across town with his parents to visit his cousin, Lexi in the hospital. Three weeks after her dramatic rescue, she was finally allowed visitors. Keith Webster had insisted to Eve that they should be the first.

By now the whole of America knew about Lexi's kidnap ordeal. Miraculously, Agent Edwards had persuaded the media to hold fire on the story while Lexi was missing. Any press coverage might have put her life in jeopardy, and neither Rupert Murdoch nor Ted Turner wanted Blackwell blood on their hands. But after the debacle at the New Jersey mill, it was open season on the juiciest story to hit the headlines in a generation:

EIGHT-YEAR-OLD HEIRESS KIDNAPPED, DEAFENED IN BUNGLED
   RESCUE
KRUGER-BRENT CHILD MUTE AFTER TRAUMA
FBI HERO FIGHTS FOR LIFE
BLACKWELL KIDNAPPERS STILL AT LARGE

Rumors that Lexi had been abused, or even raped, reverberated around Manhattan high society, adding a delicious frisson of excitement to the summer's party circuit.

Peter heard none of the whispers and read none of the headlines. He had not left the hospital since Lexi was admitted. At night, he kept a constant vigil at her bedside. During the days, he held her hand through the battery of tests, treatments and therapy sessions that had become the new normality for both of them. His hopes had soared when the doctors told him that cochlear implants might restore Lexi's hearing. But after a severe allergic reaction to the first device, Peter refused to put her through any more operations. "She's already been through so much." He did not ask the doctors when they thought Lexi would be able to come home. The prospect terrified him. He dreaded the day when the comforting routine of Mount Sinai would be snatched away and he would be left to care for Lexi alone.

What if he couldn't do it? What if he failed her again?

The thought brought tears to his eyes.

In New Orleans, Robbie watched the news reports of his sister's progress on television. He was staying at the apartment of a man he'd met in a piano bar the night he arrived in the city: Tony. Tony was in his midthirties, a writer, and though he was neither particularly attractive nor wildly dynamic, he was kind and reliable. Tony's apartment was a run-down two-bedroom perched above a restaurant that sold nothing but Cajun chicken. The smell of grease, salt and chicken fat had seeped into everything, from the curtains to the carpets, couch and sheets.

Dom Dellal had chickened out at the last moment and decided to stay in New York, but Robbie wasn't sorry. He needed a fresh start. Tony had given him one.

"What are you watching?"

Tony's voice drifted in from the kitchen, but Robbie didn't reply. His eyes were glued to the screen and the Asian reporter standing outside Mount Sinai Medical Center.

"Eight-year-old Alexandra Templeton was admitted here in the early hours of this morning, along with an adult male said to be in critical condition."

They cut to footage of firefighters battling thirty-foot walls of flame in what looked like an old factory.

"The story just breaking is one of the most dramatic, if not the most dramatic, to involve the celebrated Blackwell family. It appears that the child,

Alexandra, known as Lexi, was abducted from her home more than two weeks ago by persons unknown, and that a ransom of ten million dollars was demanded. Last night, a top secret rescue operation was launched involving both the FBI and the Marine Corps. All we know right now is that the little girl, Alexandra Templeton, is alive. A number of other individuals involved in last night's operation are reported to have died in the fire. More on this incredible story as we get it . . ."

"Rob? What's the matter? You look like you've seen a ghost."

Tony Terrell sat down on the couch beside the radiant blond boy who had miraculously walked into his life two weeks ago. He knew nothing about the kid except that he was beautiful. So beautiful, it was astonishing he'd even spoken to Tony, never mind come home with him and proceeded to make love with sobbing, passionate desperation for five straight hours. Of course, it couldn't last. Beautiful boys like Rob didn't settle down with gentle, neurotic, prematurely balding poets like Tony. But Tony would savor the two weeks they spent together for the rest of his life.

"It's my sister." Robbie was still staring at the TV.

Tony laughed. "Yeah, right. In your dreams, buddy. That little girl's a Blackwell." Then he noticed Robbie's ashen face. "Oh my God. You're serious. She really *is* your sister."

"I have to go home."

Eve stared out of the tinted glass window of the limousine. It was more than a year since she'd set foot outside the apartment. The streets of New York were so intensely alive, they made her eyes hurt. Ice-cream and hot-dog vendors on every corner, two old men fighting loudly over a cab, Wall Street businessmen in smart suits eyeing pretty girl joggers as they passed.

I miss life. I miss the world. This is what Keith stole from me.

She glanced at her son, gazing sullenly out the other window. Max didn't want to be here any more than she did. Eve had taught him to hate his Templeton cousins, fed him on an intravenous drip of loathing since before he could crawl.

We don't hate anyone, Max. Especially not family.

Beneath her veil, a smile danced across Eve's lips.

Lexi was giggling. Sitting cross-legged on the floor with Peter and Rachel, her interpreter, she was playing a game of pick-up sticks.

She signed to Rachel. "I'm winning."

The interpreter, a pretty redhead not more than twenty or twenty-one, grinned and signed back: "I know."

Lexi's progress had been astonishing. Within a week, she had picked up the rudiments of sign language and her lip-reading was quick and accurate. When her body rejected the cochlear implant, Peter had broken down in tears. But Lexi herself was as confident and unfazed as only an eight-year-old could be, taking her deafness in stride. Apart from the lone screaming episode on the first day, she'd displayed no signs of trauma or distress whatsoever.

"It's not uncommon for children to have a delayed reaction to these things," the chief psychotherapist explained to Peter. Using dolls and pictures, Lexi had shown the police and the doctors exactly what had happened to her—the sexual and physical abuse—but she had done so with a cheerfulness that was almost disturbing. "What you're seeing now is a self-defense strategy. But she won't be able to block this stuff out forever."

As part of Lexi's rehabilitation, she was taken to the burn unit to visit Agent Edwards, the man who'd risked his life to save her. Against all the odds, he had survived, but the burns to his torso and face had left him permanently disfigured.

"She may well break down," the psychologists warned Peter. But Lexi did not break down. She walked calmly to Agent Edwards's bedside, took his hand, and smiled.

Afterward, Agent Edwards said to Peter: "That's quite a kid you've got there."

"I know. And she's only alive thanks to you."

That afternoon, Peter deposited $3 million into Agent Edwards's bank account. He couldn't give the poor man back his face. But he could ensure that he lived the rest of his life in luxury. It was the least he could do.

A nurse knocked on the door.

"You have a visitor."

Keith Webster had let Peter know that he, Eve and Max were on their way. The call was a surprise. The two families had never been close. Peter didn't trust Eve as far as he could throw her, and Keith had always struck him as a little odd. But Max seemed like a sweet kid. It would be nice if he and Lexi became friends.

"Show them in."

The door opened. Lexi's eyes lit up like candles on a birthday cake.

"Hey, kiddo. I missed you."

Robbie swept his little sister up into his arms. The two of them clung to each other like limpets.

Peter stood rooted to the spot. It was awful to admit it, but in the last three weeks he had not thought about Robbie once. Lexi's kidnapping had driven every other thought out of his mind. Robbie and his problems felt like part of another lifetime. But now here he was. It was only three weeks since their last meeting, but his son looked different.

"I've stopped drinking, Dad. And the drugs. For good."

Lexi was superglued to her brother's neck as he spoke.

"I made a deal with God. If He saved Lexi, if He let her be okay, I'd get my shit together. I'm gonna make something of my life, Dad. I promise you."

"I hope so, Robert."

Peter put an arm awkwardly around his son's shoulders. He remembered what a beautiful, gentle little boy Robbie used to be. Was that person still inside somewhere? If he was, would he ever be able to forgive his father for what he'd done?

I could have shot him. I could have killed my own son.

Still holding on to Robbie, Lexi put one arm around Peter's neck, pulling father and son closer together. Reluctantly, Peter met Robbie's eyes. The old anger was gone. But there was still a sadness there. Perhaps there always would be.

What a lovely family, thought the interpreter, Rachel. *They've been through so much. No wonder they're so close, poor things.*

"I hope we're not interrupting. We can come back later, if you prefer."

Keith Webster was smiling in the doorway. Behind him stood Eve and Max, hand in hand.

"No, no." Peter pulled away from his children, glad of an excuse to break the tension. "It's good of you to come. You remember Robert?"

"Of course." Keith smiled. "My goodness, you've grown. Last time we saw you, you were knee-high to a grasshopper, wasn't he, Eve?"

"Mmmm." Eve nodded.

Shut up, you obsequious cretin! What the hell is Robert doing here? He's supposed to be shooting up in a doorway somewhere. Lionel Neuman told me he'd signed away his inheritance. Has he come to try to claw back his shares in Kruger-Brent?

Since Alex's death, Eve and Keith had seen Peter and his kids a handful of times at family functions, but the two families were not close.

Years ago, Peter had warned Alex about her twin sister's psychotic personality, a slight that Eve had neither forgotten nor forgiven.

"Max. Go say hello to your cousin." Keith pushed the boy forward. "Why don't you give Lexi her present?"

Reluctantly, Max thrust a brightly wrapped box at Lexi.

The two children eyed each other warily.

Max thought: *I hate you. You and your brother. You want to steal Kruger-Brent from me.*

Lexi thought: *He hates me. I wonder why?*

She opened the present. It was the latest limited-edition Barbie doll. The one with roller skates that she'd been hankering after all summer. Before *it* happened. Before the terror. Before the pig.

The psychiatrists thought Lexi was blocking out what had happened to her. She could read their lips: *Repressed memory syndrome. Classic posttraumatic stress responses.* But they were wrong. They were all wrong.

Lexi remembered everything. Every hair on his forearm, every mark on his skin, every cadence in his voice, every grunt, the fetid smell of his breath.

She may have nightmares. Deep-rooted fear of the bad men returning.

Lexi wasn't afraid. She was determined. She knew her kidnappers had escaped justice and she knew why. Because it was *her* destiny to find them, to pay them back for what they'd done. She had told the police nothing. Pretended that she remembered no details. But she remembered it all.

One day, pig, I will find you.

One day . . .

"Lexi" Rachel was signing at her. "Aren't you going to say thank you?"

Lexi looked down at the doll. She touched her lips with the front fingers of her right hand, then moved her hand away from her face with her palm upward, smiling.

"That's the sign for 'thanks,'" Rachel explained.

Max said, "You're welcome."

His mouth returned his cousin's smile. But his glinting black eyes were as cold as the grave.

THIRTEEN
∞

SOUTH AFRICA WAS BEAUTIFUL.

No question about it. Here was beauty on a grand scale. Epic beauty. Awesome beauty. The sort of beauty that man, over the centuries, had tried to imitate with his cathedrals and temples and pyramids, his feeble attempts at grandeur. Keith Webster was well traveled. He had been to Carnac in Egypt, to the Great Wall of China, to Notre Dame cathedral in Paris. He had stood on top of the Empire State Building, marveled at the Colosseum in Rome, and gazed in wonder at the Taj Mahal in India. Now, standing on Table Mountain with the wind in his hair and the city of Cape Town sprawled out below him, he thought of all those places and laughed. Just as God must have laughed:

You call that beauty? You call that greatness? Is that really the best you can do?

Keith Webster had been in the country for three weeks. He was flying back to America tomorrow, and though he longed to see Eve—it was the longest they had been apart since they married—he realized he would be sorry to leave Cape Town. Not just because it was beautiful. Cape Town was magical in a way that Keith had never experienced before. But because it was here, in South Africa, that he had finally managed to bond with his son. For Keith Webster, Cape Town would always be the city that brought Max back to him. The city of hope, of joy, of rebirth.

It was Eve's idea.

"You and Max should go away somewhere together, on your own. A boys' camping holiday. Just think what fun you'll have!"

Keith thought what fun they'd have: Max ignoring him, pouring scorn on all his suggestions for activities, glaring stony-faced at his jokes. Laughing while he failed to erect the tent. Pleading to be allowed to return to his mother.

"I'm not sure that's such a good idea. I've never really seen Max as the camping type."

It had been two years since Lexi Templeton's kidnapping and rescue; two years since Max had sat in the back of the family's limousine and admitted to his father that he hated his cousins.

Nonsense, Max. We don't hate anyone.

That's what Keith Webster had told his son. But even as he said the words, the thought hit him: *He hates me, too. He always has.* Up until that day, Keith had never admitted this ugly truth, not even to himself. It was easier to make excuses for Max's behavior.

He's overprotective of his mother because she's so vulnerable.

Because he's an only child.

Because . . .

Because . . .

What had Max's teacher said? Yes, that was it. *Your son is extraordinarily gifted, Dr. Webster.* Gifted children often struggled to form attachments. It was nothing to worry about. The boy would grow out of it.

But deep down, Keith Webster knew the truth.

Max hated him.

The only thing he didn't know was why.

Now, though, Max no longer talked about hating Lexi Templeton. Indeed, in the years since he first visited her in the hospital, the boy seemed to have developed some sort of rapport with his poor, deaf cousin. Friendship would be overstating it. But there was something between the two children, some understanding, a flashing of the eyes whenever they met, that had given Keith Webster hope.

If he can learn to love Lexi, maybe one day he can learn to love me?

Keith hadn't wanted to go on this camping trip, but thank God he had. God bless Eve! The vacation had changed everything.

At ten years old, almost eleven, Max was still small for his age. He could easily pass for eight or nine, although grown-ups who knew him well—his teachers, his baseball coach, even his uncle Peter—all noted something jarringly adult beneath the boyish exterior. *An old soul—* that's what people called him. Around Keith, Max was usually sullen and silent. But with others, he was highly articulate.

Keith waited for his son to pooh-pooh the idea of the "boys' holiday," certain that Max would treat it with the same withering scorn he poured on all Keith's efforts to bridge the emotional gap between them. But incredibly, Max was eager to go.

"Can we, Dad? I've never been to South Africa. Lexi and Robert go all the time; it's supposed to be amazing. *Pleeease?*"

"You realize Mommy won't be going." Keith tried to conceal his surprise. "It would just be you and me."

"I know, but Mommy's already been there, loads of times, so I don't think she minds. *Please?*"

Keith felt close to tears. Max wanted to go. With him.

He'd even called him Dad.

Was this it? After ten long years, could this really be the turning point?

"Come on, Dad, come over here. Look how high up we are!"

Keith turned to see Max, right at the canyon's edge, hopping from boulder to boulder like a mountain goat. *He's fearless. Not like me.* Clouds snaked around him like cigarette smoke. Occasionally a larger cloud would descend from the heavens and engulf the boy completely. Whenever that happened, Keith felt his heart stop.

"Buddy, I've told you, get back from the edge. Quit fooling around like that, it's not safe."

Cape Town was the last stop on their great South African adventure, and the only place where they were staying in a hotel rather than camping. Up until now they'd traveled from reserve to reserve and from camp to camp across the Karoo with their guide, Katele, a permanently smiling six-foot Bantu native with the sort of six-pack abs Keith had only ever seen on television commercials for torturous-looking exercise equipment. He looked like an extra from one of the early *Tarzan* movies. Keith felt weak and inadequate in his presence, but he tried not to show it.

Katele told a wide-eyed Max: "The Great Karoo is the largest natural ecosystem in South Africa—and one of the world's great scientific wonders. Its rocks contain fossil remains spanning three hundred and ten million years. You can do everything here. Hot-air balloon flights, horseback riding, stargazing. We have some of the best rock climbing in the country."

"What about the animals?"

Katele grinned. "You won't be disappointed. We have animals you haven't even heard of, my friend. Kudu, gemsbok, aardwolf, klipspringer. And plenty that you have: black eagles, baboons, rhinos, mountain zebras."

"Can you hunt them?"

Keith was shocked. "We're here to observe beauty, Max, not kill it. I'm sorry, Katele."

But the guide was on Max's side.

"It's quite all right, sir. Of course the boy can hunt if he wishes. I'll take you to Lemoenfontein. The big-game hunting there is exceptional."

"Can we, Dad? *Pleease?*"

"We'll see," said Keith.

He did not approve of ten-year-old boys handling guns. In fact, he'd argued with Eve on this very point only days before they left, when she finally admitted to giving Max her grandfather's pistol.

"He's never *used* it, darling," she assured him. "It's never even been out of the safe. Besides, it's so old, I'm sure it doesn't work anymore."

"I wouldn't bet on it." Keith turned the pristine Glock over in his hands. In its own way, it was a thing of beauty.

"I gave it to him as a token," said Eve. "Something from his family heritage to make him feel grown up. Don't be a spoilsport about it."

Max begged to be allowed to bring the gun to Africa.

"Mommy got me the papers specially. I'm allowed to take it because it's a family air balloon."

"Heirloom, darling." Eve smiled indulgently, rolling her eyes at Keith as if to say, *See how innocent he is?*

"I'm not sure, Max. A gun is not a toy."

But in the end, Keith was so overjoyed to be in Max's good graces for once, he'd let his happiness cloud his judgment. The gun was packed, but on the strict condition that it would not, under any circumstances, be used.

"I tell you what." Keith put his hand on the boy's shoulder. "Why don't we forget about hunting for now and start with a hot-air balloon ride? That sounds like fun, doesn't it?"

"Sure, Dad. Whatever you say."

Max was anxious.

He wanted to use his gun. A hunting accident, that was the plan. His mother had told him to stick to the plan. Max had never strayed from Eve's instructions before.

But a hot-air balloon ride? It was a gift.

He played out the scene in his imagination.

I couldn't stop him! I told him to get down, but he was trying to get a better picture. He slipped and . . . oh, Katele, it was awful. I saw him fall, I watched him get smaller and smaller, and then he was gone, I was up there all alone . . .

Damn. That was a problem.

If Keith had an accident hundreds of feet above the Gariep Dam and plunged to his death, Max would be stuck in the balloon by himself. How would he get down?

I'd better figure out how hot-air balloons work.

Katele spoke to Keith: "That's a bright boy you have there, sir. Incredibly curious."

"Thank you. Africa seems to have brought him out of himself."

The guide shrugged. "Naturally. It's in his blood. You know he spent the whole afternoon with our balloon team, learning the ropes."

"Good." Keith forced a smile. "He can help me when I'm up there panicking and forgetting everything they taught me."

"If you prefer to take our pilot . . ."

Keith shook his head. "No, no. I have flown before, many times. Just not recently. I'm sure it'll come flooding back to me."

Keith had decided the balloon ride would be a perfect father-son bonding opportunity. He wanted Max to see him doing something he was good at. Other than surgery, Keith Webster had few talents, and he could hardly have his son sit in on a rhinoplasty. He'd learned how to balloon in college, in a rare moment of daredeviltry, and enjoyed it for a year or so, before the novelty wore off.

Perhaps this would help Max to see him in a new, more heroic light? It wasn't easy to look heroic standing next to Katele.

"You'll be in radio contact all the time." Katele smiled reassuringly. "If you run into trouble, just let us know."

"Don't worry," said Keith. "We'll be fine."

They took off at sunset. It was a perfect evening to fly.

"Little bit of low cloud cover to the east, but the winds are in your favor." Kurt, the technician, checked the propane tanks and the pyrometer, which measured the heat at the top of the balloon, one final time. A gnarled Afrikaner in his early sixties with the sort of grisly gray beard usually associated with fairy-tale villains, Kurt Bleeker was in fact a kind, gentle man. "Winds have been averaging five miles an hour, so you shouldn't go farther than a few miles. As it's your first solo flight in a while, try to stick to forty minutes, but don't panic if you go over. You've got fuel for twice that. Any problems"—Kurt tapped his walkie-talkie—"get on the blower, yah?"

Keith Webster smiled. "Will do."

Now that it was actually happening, his nervousness had completely evaporated.

It'll be a blast. Drifting over the Karoo with my son, like sultans of our own private kingdom. If only Eve was here to see how well we're getting along.

Soon they were airborne, sailing serenely over the koppies, small rocky outcrops that rose up from the arid open plain like boils on an old man's skin. Looking out of the left side of the gondola, the balloon's basket, everything seemed barren and dead. But a glance to the right revealed a magical water world, shimmering like a mirage in the early-evening heat. The Orange and Caledon rivers had carved a winding path through the dusty earth, creating myriad little bays, islands and peninsulas. Far below, Keith Webster could see people sailing and windsurfing close to the jagged shoreline. Close by, a herd of wildebeest had gathered to drink, making the most of the cooler, wetter winter weather. But the views below paled next to the beauty of the sky around them. It was as if an LSD-crazed God had grabbed a paintbrush and daubed a psychedelic canvas of orange and pink across the twilight.

"What do you think, Max? Incredible, isn't it?"

"Hmm."

Max was clasping the aluminum frame of the gondola. He barely seemed to notice the stunning scenery below them. His eyes were glued to the instrument panel. Every time the altimeter or variometer needle flickered, he visibly tensed.

Nervous, thought Keith. *That's normal for your first balloon flight. He'll relax once he gets used to it.*

Max *was* nervous. This was going to be more complicated than he'd thought. He had to wait until they'd floated far enough that they could no longer be seen from the base camp. But if he waited too long, Keith would be busy with the descent and not interested in taking photographs.

"Look down there, Dad."

Max pointed to a small herd of zebra galloping across the plain. Dust plumed behind them like the exhaust fumes from a racecar.

"I want to take a picture."

Keith turned around and screamed. His son had somehow climbed onto the ropes above them. He was perched precariously on the edge of the wicker basket, gripping the ropes one-handed while he leaned out of the gondola with a camera in his other hand.

"Christ, Max. Get down! Are you trying to get yourself killed?"

Still holding the camera, Max jumped back down. He gave Keith a disdainful look. "What? I was only taking a photograph."

"You must *never* climb up like that, buddy. It's incredibly dangerous."

"No, it's not." Max pouted. Under his breath he added, "Katele does it all the time. *He's* not afraid."

Keith stiffened. *Great. Just great. I go to all this trouble to have Max look up to me, and he's still harping about Katele.*

"If you really want a picture, buddy, ask me. Once we're cruising, I'll take it for you."

"Really?" Max's eyes lit up. "Okay, Dad, thanks! That would be terrific."

Twenty minutes later, they'd finally drifted far enough for Max to make his move. They were almost seven hundred feet up now, hovering over the Gariep Dam. The vast concrete structure looked comically small beneath them, like a piece from Max's LEGO set.

"That waterfall's awesome. Can we take a picture of that?"

"Sure."

There was no need to climb up onto the edge of the gondola. You could get a great shot of the dam from inside the basket. But Max had thrown down the gauntlet with his Katele comment.

He wants courage? I'll show him courage.

Looping Max's camera around his neck, Keith got a tentative foothold on the aluminum framing.

"Now remember, son, you must never try this yourself. It's dangerous, and it's only for adults. Okay?"

"Sure, Dad."

Another step. Keith reached for the rope above his head, but it was hard to get a grip. His palm was slick and clammy with sweat. *Jesus Christ, we're high up.* The wind blew through his thin hair and he felt the bile beginning to rise in his throat. He pulled himself up till he was perched on the edge, the way that Max had been, except that Keith had both feet on the gondola and both hands wrapped for dear life around the ropes. Physical terror coursed through his body. He felt dizzy and began to sway. *I must be out of my mind.*

"That's perfect, Dad! Now get the picture!"

To take the photograph, Keith would have to let go of one of the ropes. He began to uncurl his fingers, and immediately felt his balance slipping. *Oh God.*

"Come on, Dad! What are you waiting for?"

"I . . . just give me a second, buddy, okay?"

Max's mind was racing. He estimated that Keith weighed about a hundred and sixty pounds. Roughly a hundred pounds more than he, Max, weighed. If he didn't let go of one of those ropes, would Max have the strength to push him over the edge? What if he tried and failed?

"We're moving faster, Dad. Soon we'll be past it. You're gonna miss your chance."

Keith tried to remember when he'd last felt so frightened. The day that Eve had threatened to leave him, to run off with that actor she'd been seeing. Rory. Back then he'd screwed his courage to the sticking point. He'd done what had to be done.

Just do it! Take the damn picture and you can get down.

Keith let go of the second rope. Suddenly the wind seemed to be blowing violently, pushing them along at a frightening speed. He fumbled for the camera, but his hand was shaking so much he could barely locate the viewfinder.

Silently, Max started climbing up behind him.

Keith leaned forward. He thought the dam was in the frame but he couldn't be sure. Everything was beginning to blur.

"Ground control to Webster balloon. Dr. Webster, do you copy?"

The crackle of the radio startled Keith so much he dropped the camera. He watched in horror as it spiraled silently into the abyss.

"Dr. Webster." There was an urgency to Kurt's voice. "Do you copy? Over. The wind speed is picking up. We need to get you boys down."

Thank God, thought Keith.

Max barely managed to scramble back down into the gondola before his father turned around.

"Answer them. Tell them we copy, I'll bring her down now."

That night, in their tent, Keith tried to cheer Max up.

"Don't look so crestfallen. I'll buy you another camera."

I don't want another camera, you son of a bitch. I want your head on a plate to bring home to my mother.

Katele said: "Your son is an excellent shot, Dr. Webster. Are you sure he's had no training?"

"Quite sure."

Eve promised Keith that Max had never used his treasured gun. Keith had no reason to disbelieve her. But he had to agree with Katele. His son's accuracy on their first hunting trip was quite extraordinary.

"Here, Dad. You try."

Max handed Keith the pistol. They were lying in the long grass with Katele, stalking a young gazelle.

Keith demurred.

"Me? Oh, well, I . . . I'm not much of a shot."

"Go on. It's easy." Max's small boy's fingers encased his father's adult surgeon's hands. "Hold it steady. That's right. Now line up that groove at the top with the white marking between the eyes. See?"

Keith nodded nervously.

"Good. Now squeeze."

Keith pulled the trigger. There was a loud bang. The young gazelle kicked up its hind legs and darted for the safety of some nearby trees.

"Bad luck," said Katele. "It's harder than it looks, isn't it?"

"Apparently so."

Max gave his father a withering look.

"Next time, try keeping your eyes open."

———

They hunted almost every day. But Katele insisted on going with them.

"Can't we go on our own?" Max pleaded with Keith. "It's so much more fun when it's just the two of us."

Keith was overjoyed. He'd been starting to feel a little jealous of Katele. Max seemed to idolize him, and it wasn't hard to see why. To a young boy's eyes, the native must have appeared like a god. The fact that Keith Webster was a world-renowned surgeon and highly regarded, self-made man, and that Katele was one step above a savage, living hand to mouth on an African nature reserve, meant nothing to a ten-year-old. Katele could shoot arrows, fly planes, skin rabbits and make fire with pieces of flint. He was a hero.

"I'm glad you feel that way, sport. I do, too. But this is Africa, Max. It's not safe to go into the bush alone, without a guide."

Keith watched his son's face fall.

"Don't worry." He laughed. "When we get to Cape Town, it'll be just the two of us."

But Max was worried.

There would be no hunting in Cape Town. No chance to carry out his mother's plan.

I have to do it. I promised Mommy. I have to find a way.

The hotel was pleasant. A simple, whitewashed farmhouse on the edge of Camps Bay, it was not the kind of five-star accommodation that Max was used to. But after eighteen days of camping, sleeping in a bed felt like the last word in luxury. The hot showers, in particular, were bliss.

At breakfast, Keith asked: "What would you like to do today?"

I hate you. I detest you. Why are you still alive?

"We could drive up the coast, along the wine route? Or take a picnic to the beach? Or, you know what, we could go shopping. Get you a new camera? Whaddaya think?"

Max didn't miss a beat. "I'd like to go up Table Mountain. There's a hiking route, the landlady told me. It's supposed to be the best view in all South Africa."

Keith beamed. "Sold. Table Mountain it is."

"I mean it, Max. Get away from there."

The wind whipped away Keith's words, turning his shout into a whisper. Max was dancing on one of the small boulders close to the edge of the cliff. Long tendrils of jet-black hair blew against his face, and his slender olive limbs waved rhythmically to some inner music. He was a beautiful child. Almost as beautiful as his mother.

There's nothing of me in there. Nothing except my love.

"Max!"

Reluctantly, Keith Webster began walking toward his son. Below them was a drop of well over three thousand feet. His little stunt in the hot-air balloon had frightened Keith more than he'd realized. Every night since the incident, he'd woken with nightmares. He imagined himself falling, like the camera, spinning around and around in the emptiness, waking just seconds before his body would have slammed into the earth. He could imagine the pain, his bones shattering inside his body like broken glass, his skull caving in like a rotten grapefruit, brains oozing out into the dust.

If anything should happen to Max . . .

Christ. Where is he?

Max was gone. But he couldn't be gone. He'd been right there, pirouetting on the rock, and then . . . Keith felt his stomach lurch and his knees start to give way.

"MAX!" It was half scream, half sob. "MAX!"

Keith was running, sprinting toward the cliff edge, propelled by something bigger than himself, some irresistible force. *Love.* Scrambling up onto the stone, all fear for himself gone, he leaned out, straining his entire body into the emptiness.

"Max! Can you hear me? MAX!"

Below him the clouds lay as thick as butter icing, obscuring everything. A child's picture of heaven.

"I can hear you, Keith."

Keith looked down. On the underside of the rock was a tiny tuft of grass, stuck like a limpet to the side of the mountain. It was so small it could never have borne an adult's weight. But Max, crouched like a leprechaun, could support himself comfortably. Reaching up, he wrapped a hand around Keith's ankle.

"Max, thank God! I thought I'd lost you."

"Lost me?" Max laughed: an awful, maniacal strangled sound that made Keith's blood run cold. "You never had me in the first place. Loser."

Keith felt a tug at his feet. Instinctively, he reached out his arms, grasping for support, but there was nothing. Another tug, harder this time.

Keith looked down. Max was staring up at him, a twisted smile dancing across his face.

He smiles like Eve.

Keith looked into his son's eyes and saw the deep well of hatred there. The last emotion Keith Webster felt was not fear or even sadness. It was surprise.

I don't understand it. We were getting along so well . . .

The clouds rushed up to embrace him, soft, white, welcoming.

Then nothing.

It was the night after Keith Webster's funeral. Max lay in his mother's bed in their New York apartment with Eve's arms wrapped around him. The bedroom window was open a crack, allowing the familiar noises of Manhattan to float in from outside: honking traffic, music, shouts, laughter.

Africa had been beautiful. But this was home.

"You were wonderful, darling," Eve whispered in Max's ear. "No one suspected a thing. I'm so proud of you, my big, grown-up boy."

Eve had been going out of her mind with worry, waiting at home for news of an "accident." She'd rehearsed everything with Max so thoroughly, so endlessly. She really believed he was ready. But as the days turned into weeks and still nothing happened, she began to fear that the boy had lost his nerve. Or what if it was worse than that? What if Max had tried and failed? What if Keith now knew everything and was on his way home to exact his revenge?

But Max had not lost his nerve. He had pulled it off in the eleventh hour, staging a fall so natural that there hadn't even been an inquest. Tourists fell from Table Mountain almost every year, idiots fooling around too near the edge. Keith was just another statistic. A number. A nobody.

"You realize that *you're* the man of the house now?" Eve cooed. "You'll never have to share me again."

Max closed his eyes. He felt the warm silk of Eve's negligee caress his bare back. "Can I sleep in your bed tonight, Mommy?"

Eve sighed sleepily. "All right, darling. Just this once."

Tomorrow morning it would be back to work, for both of them. With Keith gone, it was time to begin the second part of Eve's plan: winning back control of Kruger-Brent. Max would be the linchpin of that strategy, too. But for tonight at least, he'd earned his reward.

Max waited till his mother was deeply asleep. Then he lay awake, smiling, remembering the look of surprise on his father's face as he fell.

You're the man of the house now.

You'll never have to share me again.

FOURTEEN

⚭

PAOLO COZMICI BARKED IRRITABLY AT HIS BOYFRIEND: "SO? Are you going to tell me what it says?"

The world-famous conductor was having breakfast at his usual table at Le Vaudeville on Rue Vivienne in Paris. An Art Deco hangout popular with locals and tourists alike, Le Vaudeville was Paolo Cozmici's home away from home, a place he came to relax. Henri, the maître d', knew where Paolo Cozmici liked to sit. He knew that Paolo liked the milk for his café au lait warm, not hot, that Paolo's *pain chocolat* should always be light on the *pain*, heavy on the *chocolat;* and that Paolo did not expect to have to move to a table near the window in order to chain-smoke his beloved Gauloise cigarettes.

Everybody who knew Paolo Cozmici knew that his Sunday-morning ritual was sacrosanct and unchanging. His boyfriend knew it best of all. And yet the unfathomable boy had arrived for breakfast late, distracted, still dressed in his jogging pants (Paolo *deplored* jogging pants), and bleating on about some ridiculous letter he'd received from his kid sister back home.

I suppose it serves me right for falling in love with an American, thought Paolo philosophically. *Barbarians, all of them, from sea to stinking sea.*

"She wants me to come to her sixteenth birthday party next month. Apparently my father's throwing her a big bash at Cedar Hill House."

Paolo blew a disdainful smoke ring in his lover's direction. *"Où?"*

"It's kind of like a family compound. It's in Maine on a little island called Dark Harbor. You won't have heard of it, but it's a magical place. I haven't been there since my mom was alive."

"You're not seriously thinking of going?" Paolo Cozmici sounded incredulous. "Robert, my sweet, you 'ave concerts booked every week-end in July. Paris, Munich, London. You can't just pull out."

"Come with me?"

Paolo almost choked on his croissant.

"Come *with* you? Absolutely not. Now I 'ave irrefutable evidence, *mon amour.* You have lost your mind."

"Maybe." Robbie Templeton smiled, and Paolo Cozmici felt his resolve melting like a bar of chocolate in the sunshine. "But you knew I was crazy when you fell for me. Didn't you?"

Raising Paolo's hand to his lips, Robbie kissed it softly.

"Hmm," Paolo grumbled. *"Oui, je suppose."*

The love affair between Robbie Templeton, the American piano prodigy and classical music's hottest male pinup, and Paolo Cozmici, the fat, bald, famously irascible Italian conductor, was a mystery to all who knew them, as well as to millions who did not.

It began six years ago. Robbie, then almost twenty, had just arrived in Paris and was living hand to mouth as a freelance piano player, moving from bar to bar and jazz club to jazz club, wherever the work took him.

"You're being stubborn, Robert. I've told you, you can have an allowance."

Peter Templeton had mixed feelings about his son's Great European Adventure. He and Robbie had been reconciled for less than a year. Now Peter was sitting across the table from him at the Harvard Club, being told that he was about to lose him all over again.

"I don't want your money, Dad. I need to do this by myself."

"You've no idea what the real world is like, Robert."

You'd be surprised how much I know about the real world, Dad.

"You don't even speak French."

"I'll learn."

"At least let me set up a bank account for you at Société Générale. You can look on it as emergency money. A safety net, should you need it."

Robbie looked at his father and felt a stab of pity for him. Lexi's kidnapping had aged him permanently. The reality of caring for a deaf child, even one as determined and independent as Lexi, had also taken its toll. Every hour Peter spent away from his daughter was an anxious, guilt-ridden purgatory: he hadn't been there when Lexi needed him most. The least he could do was to be there now, protecting her, loving her, helping her cope with her disability.

The irony was that Lexi was coping just fine. It was Peter who was lost.

Robbie's fixed mental image of his father was of a strong, handsome, youthful man, a sportsman and a scholar. But the truth was that that man had died years ago. The face Robbie saw across the table from him now was broken and defeated, crisscrossed with lines and dark shadows under the eyes. It was a road map of suffering, a lifetime of loss. And it had all started because he married a Blackwell.

Kruger-Brent did that to him. The curse of the Blackwell family. Don't you see, Dad? I can't stay. I can't let myself be broken, like you were.

"Honestly, Dad, I appreciate the offer. But I don't want the money. I've only been clean for eleven months, remember? A big fat French bank account might be more temptation than I could handle."

It was this last argument that had finally won Peter over. He knew that if Robert ever went back to drugs or drinking, he would die. It was that simple.

"Fine. Have it your way. But promise me, when the romance of the whole starving-musician-in-a-garret thing wears off, you won't be too proud to come home. I . . . I love you, Robert. I hope you know that."

Robbie's eyes filled with tears.

I know, Dad. I love you, too. But I have to go.

The first few months were a living hell.

Dad was right. What in God's name have I gotten myself into?

Unable to afford even a shoe box in the city center, Robbie had finally rented a room in Ogrement, a run-down part of the suburb of Épinay-sur-Seine. It was the most depressing place he had ever seen. Ugly sixties tenement buildings with broken windows, the stairwells covered in graffiti and stinking of piss, were home to a plethora of gangs and petty criminals. The gangs seemed to split along racial and religious lines. Ogrement was not a great place to be a Jew, that was for sure. But neither was it overly welcoming of preppy, blond Americans whose six words of French included *foie gras* and *clavier* (piano keyboard), but not *percer* (to stab) or *filou* (pickpocket).

The one language Robbie did understand was drugs. Ogrement was fueled by heroin the same way that China was fueled by rice. It was everywhere, calling to him, tempting him like the siren call of the sea.

It's like renting a room over a kindergarten class to a newly released pedophile. God help me.

Robbie was determined to stay clean. He knew his life depended on it. But it was tough. The loneliness was grinding, soul destroying, and ever present. Not being able to communicate was the worst part.

Why did I have to "find myself" in France? Why couldn't I have gone to London, or Sydney, or some other place where they speak English?

Of course, Robbie knew the answer to that. Paris was the musicians' mecca. The Paris Conservatoire, where Bizet and Debussy had once studied, was a place of mythical significance to Robbie. The newly opened Cité de la Musique, architect Christian de Portzamparc's celebrated ampitheater, concert hall, museum of music, and workshops in La Villette, the old slaughterhouse district, had a new generation of musicians and composers flocking to the city.

The best musical talent in the world came to Paris. It was the center, the hub, the beginning and the end of everything for a would-be concert pianist like Robbie.

Unfortunately, *would be* turned out to be the operative words. Since he had no formal training or qualifications, the conservatoire refused even to see him, never mind hear him play. Simply finding bar work proved far harder than Robbie had imagined. The problem with moving to the most exciting city in the world for classical music was that everyone else had done the same thing. Paris was crawling with hotshit piano players, and most of them had years of experience. Robbie was an unknown Yank whom no one could understand, who'd once had a job playing blues piano in a gay bar in New Orleans for all of three weeks.

Robbie did, however, have three things going for him. Talent, determination and looks. And the greatest of these was looks.

"Pay is fifty francs an hour, plus tips. Take it or leave it."

Madame Aubrieau ("Please, call me Martine") was a fifty-two-year-old ex-hooker who wore a blond wig to cover her bald patches, weighed approximately the same as a young hippo and whose breath smelled of a combination of garlic, menthol cigarettes and Benedictine that made

Robbie want to gag. She wore a low-cut, cheap red top that exposed a quivering expanse of larva-white cleavage, and when she spoke to Robbie, she stared unashamedly at his crotch.

In addition to these attributes, Madame Aubrieau owned Le Club Canard, a dive bar in the twelfth arondissement whose piano player had quit the previous week in a dispute over unpaid wages. Madame Aubrieau liked the look of the shy young American. If he took the job, she would eat him for breakfast. Afterward, she would have him eat her. It was good to be the boss.

Robbie looked at Madame Aubrieau's Jabba the Hut body and felt sick. Fifty francs an hour was not a living wage. On the other hand, his current earnings of zero francs an hour were beginning to irritate Marcel, his Ogrement landlord. Marcel was not a man Robbie wished to irritate.

"I'll take it. When do I start?"

Madame Aubrieau clamped a fat, dirty-fingernailed hand on Robbie's thigh and flashed him a toothless smile.

"Immédiatement, mon chou. Suivez moi."

Robbie first laid eyes on Paolo Cozmici at the Salle Pleyel concert hall on the Rue Faubourg Saint-Honoré. Cozmici was conducting the resident Orchestre de Paris. And he was magnificent.

Like every other musician in Paris, Robbie knew of Paolo Cozmici by reputation. The youngest son of a dirt-poor family from Naples, Cozmici was completely self-taught as a composer, a pianist and, most recently, a conductor. Nicknamed Le Bouledogue—"the bulldog"—by the French musical establishment, Paolo Cozmici had famously won his place as conductor of the Paris Philharmonic by storming unannounced into rehearsals for Tchaikovsky's Symphony No. 5 in E Minor, seizing the baton from a bewildered Claude Dechamel and displaying the sort of instinctive virtuosity that had since made him one of the most sought-after conductors in the world.

In the front row of the glorious Art Deco concert hall, Robbie Templeton sat mesmerized. Later, he would be unable to recall the specific piece that Paolo had been conducting. All he remembered was the beauty and grace of his movements, at one with the music, swept up in the same passion that Robbie himself felt whenever he sat at a piano stool. Robbie could see nothing of Paolo but his back—an ill-fitting tuxedo jacket stretched across broad, workman's shoulders—but it didn't matter. Just watching Cozmici at work gave him a sexual charge so violent it was all Robbie could do not to jump out of his chair and storm the stage.

Afterward he waited at the stage door for hours. When Cozmici finally emerged, tired, grumpy and more than a little drunk, Robbie found to his horror that he was completely tongue-tied. Staring mutely, like an idiot, he watched as his idol began to walk away.

"*Arrêtez! Monsieur Cozmici. Je vous en prie . . .*"

"I don't do autographs," Cozmici barked. "Please, leave me alone."

"But I . . ."

"Yes? What?"

"I love you."

Paolo Cozmici looked at the boy properly for the first time. Even through his drunken haze, he could see that Robbie was extraordinarily attractive. On the downside, he was clearly a lunatic. A sexy lunatic was not what Paolo Cozmici needed in his life right now.

"Get away from me. Understand? Leave me alone, or I shall be forced to call the police."

The next morning, Paolo found a handwritten note in his mailbox.

"I'll be playing piano at Le Club Canard tonight. My set starts at eight P.M. I'll understand if you can't make it, but I hope you can." It was signed: "*Le garcon de la nuit passée. RT.*"

Paolo Cozmici smiled. He had to admire the boy for his tenacity. It was what he was famed for himself.

But no, he wouldn't go. The whole thing was crazy.

Sexy lunatic would have to find someone else to harass.

Robbie peered into the gloomy half light of the club, searching for Paolo Cozmici's face.

He's not coming. I scared him off. Man, of course I scared him off. What kind of fruit loop yells "I love you" in the street to a man he's never met before? The loneliness must be getting to me.

Madame Aubrieau was becoming impatient. It was time for Robbie's set to start. Launching into Bill Evans's soulful "Waltz for Debby" followed by a passionate rendition of "My Foolish Heart," he was embarrassed to find himself fighting back tears. Jazz was not Robbie's preferred genre, but no one could deny that Bill Evans was a genius. The fact that he'd been a heroin junkie, like Robbie, dogged by addiction and self-doubt for most of his life, made the emotional connection even stronger. Robbie closed his eyes and gave himself up to the music. He thought about Lexi and his mother. He thought about home. He wondered how long he could bear to continue in this half-life in Paris, with no friends, no family, no hope.

He heard the applause dimly at first, as if waking up from a dream. He had no idea how long he'd been playing. As so often with Robbie, the music had transported him into a trance-like state where time and space dissolved. But as the cheers and clapping grew louder, he realized that the usually somnolent Canard crowd was on its feet, roaring approval, begging him for more. Robbie smiled, nodding in shy acknowledgment. As soon as he stood up, he found his hand being shaken and his back slapped by a sea of strangers, men and women alike. Some of them pressed notes into his hand.

"*Incroyable.*"

"*Absolument superbe!*"

"Twenty percent of those tips go to the house," Madame Aubrieau reminded him tersely. She considered Robbie her property and disliked seeing him mobbed by other, more attractive women.

"Good evening."

Paolo Cozmici looked even shorter and squatter than he had last night, scurrying away from the stage door at the Salle Pleyel. In a crumpled suit and tie, an incipient paunch spilling over the waistband of his pants, he could easily have been a decade older than his thirty years. But none of that mattered to Robbie. He was so awestruck he could barely force the words out of his mouth.

"I didn't think you'd come."

"Nor did I. You play beautifully."

"I . . . thank you."

"You realize you are wasting your talent in this dump?"

Paolo glared at him aggressively, as if accusing him of some sort of crime. Robbie could see why they called him Le Bouledogue.

"I need the money. I'd love to play classical, but I have no formal training. At least, nothing that's recognized in France."

"*Ça ne fait rien.*" Paolo waved his hand in the air dismissively. "You will play for me. You will play with my *orchestre*. Where do you live?"

"Ogrement."

Paolo looked at him blankly.

"Épinay. It's a suburb . . ."

For the second time in as many minutes Paolo narrowed his eyes, his face alight with disapproval.

"People with your gift do not live in the suburbs. *Non.* You live with me."

Paolo turned and headed for the coat check.

"Qu'est ce qu'il y a? Tu viens, ou quoi?"

"Oui." Robbie laughed aloud. Was this really happening? "Yes. Yes, I'm coming."

The next morning, Paolo introduced Robbie to the Orchestre de Paris.

"This is Robert Templeton. He is the finest pianist in Paris. He will be playing with us tomorrow night."

A sea of bewildered faces looked quizzically at Robbie.

"But, Maestro," Pierre Fremeaux, the regular piano soloist, interjected meekly. "I am supposed to be playing tomorrow."

Paolo shook his head. *"Non."*

"But . . . but . . ."

"It is nothing personal, Pierre. Listen to Robert play. Then you tell me which of you should be onstage tomorrow night. *D'accord?*"

Fifteen minutes later, Pierre Fremeaux was packing his bags.

He was good. But Robert Templeton was out of this world.

"I told you, Paolo, I don't have time for this. I'm not gonna meet some unknown friggin' jazz pianist you met in a bar just because you've got the hots for him."

Chuck Bamber was an A&R man for Sony Records. He was responsible for the label's European classical list, and it was his job to discover and sign new talent. A fat, loud Texan with a passion for T-bone steaks and drag racing, he was as out of place among the Parisian musical elite as a hooker in a nunnery. Everybody in the classical world knew that Chuck Bamber had no soul. They also knew that his commercial ear and instincts were second to none. Chuck Bamber could make or break a pianist's career with a tip of his ten-gallon hat.

Paolo Cozmici was determined to have him meet Robbie.

"You will meet with Robert, or I will walk out of my contract."

Chuck Bamber laughed. "Right, Paolo. Whatever you say."

———

Two days later, Don Williams, head of the legal department at Sony's classical division, phoned Chuck Bamber in a panic.

"Paolo Cozmici's agent just sent me a fax. He's quitting the label."

"Relax, Don. He's bluffing. We've already paid the guy a three-hundred-thousand-dollar advance. He can't leave without paying all that money back. It's breach of contract."

Don Williams said: "I know. They wired the funds last night."

"Cozmici? What the hell is going on?"

"I told you, Chuck. I want you to listen to Robert play. If you refuse . . ."

"Yeah, yeah, I know, you'll quit. You're a fucking prima donna, you know that, Paolo?"

"So you'll see Robert?"

"I'll see him. But I'm telling you, Paolo, he'd better be good. A tight fanny and a set of six-pack abs are not gonna impress me the way they impress you. If this kid ain't piano's answer to Nigel friggin' Kennedy . . ."

"He is, Chuck. He is."

Robert signed a two-album deal with Sony.

The combination of his talent, film-star good looks, and famous family name was every marketing department's wet dream. The only question was in which direction to take him.

"I'd like you to consider a jazz piano album," Chuck Bamber told him over champagne in his palatial office overlooking Notre Dame. "It's sexier than straight-up classical. With your face we could easily brand you as the new Harry Connick Jr."

"*Non.*" Paolo Cozmici shook his head. "We will not do *jazz.*" He practically spat out the word, like rotten meat.

"Jeez, Paolo. Can't you let Robert speak for himself?"

"That's okay," said Robbie. "I appreciate your offer, Mr. Bamber, really I do. But I trust Paolo's judgment. I'd rather stick to classical, if it's all the same to you."

"Eighty percent of Robert's time will be devoted to live performances."

"*Paolo!*" Chuck Bamber lost his temper. "Give me a small break here, okay? I need him in the studio for at least six months. He should come back to America."

"Out of the question."

"Goddammit, Cozmici. What are you, his manager?"

"No," said Paolo simply. "I am his life."

It was true.

For the next five years, as Robbie's career blossomed and he became a bona fide star, his bond with Paolo grew ever closer. They synchronized their various concert schedules to make sure they traveled together whenever possible. When apart, they were resolutely faithful, calling each other on the phone six or seven times a day. Paolo was the best friend Robbie had never had, the strong, constant father he had lost. Robbie was the breath of life in Paolo's cynical, battle-worn, middle-aged body. His elixir of youth. They adored each other.

"You're really serious? You want to go to Maine for a teenager's birthday party?"

Paolo took a sip of his coffee and instantly spat it out again. *Froid. Dégueulasse.*

"She's not 'a teenager.' She's my sister. I love her. And you know, it's been years."

"I know, my darling. And I also know why. You know how your father feels about your lifestyle. About *me.*"

Peter Templeton was proud of his son's success. But he had never fully come to terms with Robbie's sexuality. Now that Robbie was famous and gave interviews in which he spoke openly about his love for Paolo, Peter's disapproval had intensified.

"It's your life," he would tell Robbie grudgingly, during their increasingly rare phone calls. "I don't see why you have to be so flagrant about it, that's all."

"I love him, Dad. The same way you loved Mom. You were *flagrant* enough about that, weren't you?"

Peter was incensed.

"Your involvement with that man bears no comparison to my love for your mother. The fact that you think it does shows just how far off course your moral compass has drifted. I knew it was a mistake, letting you go to Paris."

Paolo had never tried to come between Robert and his family. He didn't have to. Peter's attitude, combined with Robbie's own hectic life in Europe, made the growing distance between them inevitable.

"I wouldn't be going for Dad. I'm doing this for Lexi."

"But Lexi stays with us every summer. Can't you throw her a second birthday party in Paris, after the tour?"

Robbie shook his head. He didn't expect Paolo to understand about Dark Harbor and Cedar Hill House. About what those places meant to him and to his sister. How could he? But the time was right. He had to go back. Lexi's sixteenth was as good an excuse as any.

"You're sure you won't come with me?"

Paolo shuddered. "Quite sure. *Je t'aime, Robert, tu sais ca.* But a Blackwell family get-together on some godforsaken American island, making small talk with your homophobic father? *Non merci.* You're on your own."

FIFTEEN
∽

GABE MCGREGOR STEPPED OUT OF THE GATES OF WORM-
wood Scrubs Prison onto the street. It was six-thirty on a cold November
morning. It was still dark. A light drizzle of icy rain was beginning to
soak through his thin gray woolen jacket.

It was, without question, the happiest moment of his life.

"Got somewhere to go?"

The guard at the gate smiled. Wormwood Scrubs was a shitty place
to work. The screws hated it almost as much as the inmates. But watching men like Gabe McGregor savor their first taste of freedom in eight
long years, reformed young men with their lives still ahead of them, that
was a joy that never got old.

Gabe smiled back.

"Oh yes. I've got somewhere to go all right."

Thanks to Marshall Gresham. I owe that man my life.

On his first night in prison, Gabriel McGregor tried to kill himself.

Michael Wilmott, his lawyer, had told him not to panic. That the
sixteen-year term handed down by the crown-court judge would likely
be reduced on appeal.

"If it goes down to twelve, chances are you'll be out in seven or
eight."

Seven or eight? Years?

The longest Gabe had been without heroin was seven *days*. The worst seven days of his life. It was his first week on remand, and he had not yet learned how to buy drugs inside. Once you knew the system, heroin was easy enough to come by. The big dealers all had guys working inside on a commissioned-sales basis. Heroin and crack were both priced at a 30 percent markup. As long as you had money and a friend on the outside who could make regular payments to the gangs, you were okay. But those first seven days! Gabe would never forget the misery. Nights spent screaming, convulsed by cramps so violent he felt like he were being hanged, drawn and quartered. The sweats, the vomiting, the hallucinations.

A figure on a white horse was coming to get him. Jamie McGregor! In his hand was an ax. As he rode, he swung it to the left and right, slicing off the limbs of the screaming women who surrounded him. Gabe knew the women. There was Fiona. Angela. There was Caitlin, pleading for her life as the man on the horse laughed maniacally, severing her head with a single stroke. All the girls Gabe had used to feed his habit suffered the same fate. Then he saw his mother's face, contorted with terror. She was crying out to him: "Gabriel! Save me! It's Jamie McGregor! He's killing me, he's killing us all!"

Gabe woke up. His sheets were drenched in sweat. He wanted to scream, but his throat was so dry and sore he felt like he'd swallowed a pack of razor blades.

The next day one of his fellow prisoners had given him a hit. On the outside, however desperate he got, Gabe never shared needles. Here, he practically wrenched the syringe from the guy's hand.

The night before he went back to court for sentencing, he heard two of the remand prisoners talking.

"If they send me to the Scrubs, I'm finished. Mike says it's like a bloody desert in there."

"I heard the same thing. The new warden used to work for the drug czar. That place is cleaner that a nun's arsehole."

Gabe thought: *That's it. If they send me somewhere where I can't get drugs, I'll kill myself.*

Like all British prisons, Wormwood Scrubs was overcrowded. The twelve-by-eight-foot cells had been built by the Victorians to house a single inmate. Now the same cramped space was home to three or even four men, each sharing a single lidless toilet.

Gabe's two cell mates did not look up when he entered. Both were black, in their midtwenties and of the same heavyset build as Gabe himself.

At least they don't look gay, Gabe thought. Then he remembered that it didn't matter anyway.

By this time tomorrow he'd be dead.

Climbing silently onto his bunk, he lay back and stared at the ceiling. His original plan had been to hang himself with torn up sheets, but he realized now that that wasn't going to work.

These guys might not be what you'd call sociable, but they aren't gonna sit by and do nothing while I choke myself to death.

Gabe scanned the room. It was bare. No pictures, no hooks, no curtains, no lamps, no nothing. He started to panic.

What the hell can I use?

Then he saw it.

Perfect. It'll hurt, but at least I can do it quickly, while they're asleep.

Gabe was scared. He did not want to die. But anything was better than cold turkey.

Mike says it's like a bloody desert in there.

I'll do it tonight.

Nelson Bradley, the bigger of Gabe's two cell mates, awoke to the sound of groans.

"Keep it down, jock. Some of us is trying to kip."

A few seconds later, Gabe projectile-vomited onto the floor. He started to shake, then convulse.

Nelson Bradley sat up.

"Duane. Wake up, man. Something's wrong."

Duane Wright turned on his handheld reading lamp, pointing it first at Gabe, then at the pool of vomit. Except it wasn't vomit. It was blood. On the floor beside Gabe's bunk was an empty bottle of bleach. The screws must have gotten lazy and left it by the loo after sluicing out.

"Oh, shit. He's only gone and necked the bloody Dettol!" Duane Wright hammered on the cell door. "Get someone in here. Now!"

When Gabe woke up in the prison infirmary, the first thing he thought was: *Christ alive, my stomach is on fire.* The second thing he thought was: *I'm still alive. I failed.* Depression washed over him.

"You're a very lucky man," the doctor told him. "A few more minutes before we pumped your stomach and you wouldn't have made it."

Oh yeah, that's me. Lucky.

The psychologists asked him why he'd done it and Gabe told them the truth. There didn't seem any point in lying.

"You bloody prat." The chief psychiatrist wrote Gabe a prescription for methadone. "You think you're the first addict to walk through these doors? We can help you. There are programs . . ."

But Gabe didn't want programs, and he didn't want methadone. He wanted enough H to put him out of his misery.

When he was well enough, he was transferred to another wing of the prison. This time he had only one cell mate, an ex-junkie lifer named Billy McGuire. Billy was Irish, a former jockey whose life had careened spectacularly off the rails after he got mixed up with drugs. What began as a few "innocent" thrown races and betting scams ended up as internecine gang warfare on the streets of Belfast. An innocent father was killed and Billy was sent down for a minimum twenty-year sentence.

"The IRA aren't what they used to be," Billy told Gabe.

"I'm confused. What did they use to be? Weren't they always a bunch of murdering terrorists?"

"Ah, well, sure they were. But right or wrong, they had a cause. Now it's all about the money. Money and drugs." Billy shook his head in disgust. "That's what heroin does to you, lad. Makes you forget who you are."

Gabe couldn't argue with that. The only trouble was that he *wanted* to forget who he was: a loser with no qualifications, no skills, and now, with a serious criminal record, no future.

I thought my dad was pathetic, wasting his life in the docks.

He was twice the man I am.

SIXTEEN
∽

LEXI LAY SPRAWLED OUT ON THE BLUE-AND-WHITE-striped Ralph Lauren couch at Cedar Hill House, poring over the guest list for her party.

At sixteen, Lexi Templeton had fully emerged from her awkward early teen years. Gone were the hated braces on her teeth and the mornings spent staring longingly in the mirror trying to make her breasts grow through sheer force of will. Draped over the couch like Cleopatra in a pair of cutoff denim hot pants, her lithe, tanned legs stretching out for miles, Lexi was at last a full-fledged sex kitten. Her brown stomach was as smooth and flat as a Kansas prairie, despite the three bowls of Cocoa Krispies she'd wolfed down for breakfast that morning. A simple white bikini top covered breasts as full, round and perfect as small honeydew melons.

To be strictly accurate, the guest list she was studying was not for *her* party. Much to Lexi's chagrin, next week's celebration at Cedar Hill House was officially a joint sixteenth for her and Max.

Why should I have to share my birthday with him? Can't I have any life of my own?

Whatever Lexi did these days, her cousin seemed to show up like a bad penny.

Lexi's father felt sorry for him: "I think he's lonely, honey. Stuck in that apartment with his mother all vacation long. He probably doesn't have many friends."

I'm not surprised. He's so arrogant and stuck-up.

Peter had always put Max's moody silences down to shyness. Over the course of their childhoods, Lexi had formed a different view. Max wasn't shy. He was aloof. She called it his superiority complex, and it irritated the hell out of her.

On the plus side, at least Max's lack of social skills meant that a solid 80 percent of the birthday guests would be Lexi's friends from Exeter, and not a bunch of stuffed shirts from Choate, Max's prestigious Connecticut boarding school.

Lexi examined her list again:

Donna Mastroni, Lisa Babbington, Jamie Summerfield . . . oh, crap. Lisa can't sit next to Jamie. He screwed her over spring break when he was still dating Anna Massey. Where the hell can I put Lisa?

The answer was obvious: Lisa Babbington should sit at Max's table. God knew there were enough spaces. Lexi hesitated. Somehow the idea of seating one of her most attractive girlfriends next to her cousin did not appeal.

The truth was, though she would have died before admitting it, Lexi Templeton had mixed feelings about Max Webster. Three-quarters of the time, she hated him. He followed her around like a bad smell. He was rude, weird and more arrogant than any boy she'd ever met. During their joint internship at Kruger-Brent last Christmas *(I can't even get a job on my own)* Max had made it perfectly plain that he saw himself as Lexi's superior, intellectually and in every other way. Even at fifteen, the staff had begun to defer to him the way they used to defer to Robbie. Because of Lexi's deafness, people just assumed that Max would inherit the company one day. This assumption, fueled by Max's own sense of entitlement, drove Lexi crazy. At Kruger-Brent, Max made a point of playing up Lexi's disability, treating her with kid gloves as if she were some fragile flower. *He never treats me like that when we're alone.*

Lexi might be deaf but she wasn't blind. She saw what Max was up to and it incensed her. She also saw, much as it pained her to admit it, that her cousin had grown into an incredibly good-looking young man. Black-haired and even blacker-eyed, Max had an irresistible air of danger and wildness about him, like Heathcliff or a young Lord Byron. Most boys Lexi's age were gauche and immature. Even the jocks at Exeter seemed to have a built-in geekiness that surfaced in the presence of attractive girls like Lexi. But not Max Webster.

Max looked through Lexi as if she didn't exist.

So why does he hang around me all the time? If I'm so goddamn invisible, so beneath his royal notice, why doesn't he get a life of his own?

Lexi began scratching out names with a pen, rearranging the seating chart.

Lisa Babbington could sit next to Grady Jones.

If Max didn't have enough friends to fill his table, it wasn't her problem.

"Do you like it? I know it's not your official birthday yet, but Rachel thought you might want to wear it for the party."

Lexi's interpreter, Rachel, was her more or less constant companion. Peter Templeton had relied heavily on Rachel's advice when it came to choosing Lexi's birthday present. Watching Lexi's face light up now, he was glad he had.

"Daddy, I *love* it. Oh my goodness."

"Really?" He beamed with pleasure.

"Really."

Lexi ran her fingertips in wonder over the gossamer beaded silk dress. It was Chanel, from the new season's collection. The delicate fabric was the exact same shade of champagne blond as Lexi's hair. The cut was exquisite, plunging and clinging in all the right places, but too much of a work of art to look slutty. It was, without question, the most beautiful item of clothing in existence.

"A beautiful dress for my beautiful girl. You'll look like a princess, my angel."

Lexi smiled."Thank you, Daddy." *He still thinks I'm six years old.* "It's an amazing present."

And it's gonna help me get the birthday present I really *want: Christian Harle.*

Lexi learned early that her deafness was a double-edged sword when it came to dating.

Going to school with an interpreter who rarely left her side was a definite minus. Lexi's lip-reading was excellent and her speech by no means poor, but she was self-conscious about her imagined slurring and preferred to sign whenever possible and have Rachel speak for her.

She was lucky to have had the same interpreter for almost eight years now, since her early days in the hospital. Peter knew that consistency of caregivers would be crucial to his daughter's recovery. Consequently he had thrown money and perks at the then twenty-year-old Rachel, upping the ante every year to make sure she wasn't tempted to leave. Now twenty-eight, Rachel was considerably chubbier than she had been back then, but just as hardworking and sunny-natured. Lexi herself had long since passed the point where she actively noticed her interpreter's presence. To her, Rachel was like her shadow: always there, yet somehow almost invisible.

Unfortunately, boys didn't see it that way.

"Can't you lose Chubby Checker for half an hour after school?"

Pete Harris, a rebel with floppy blond hair, skater tattoos on his chest, and a reputation as the biggest player in tenth grade, leaned over in math class and whispered in Lexi's ear.

His warm breath on her earlobe felt nice. Lexi could pretty much get the gist of his intentions from pheremones alone. But of course, without being able to see his lips, the words themselves meant nothing.

She signed to Rachel. "Ask him to say it again. Tell him to look at me when he speaks."

Rachel duly did as she was asked. Suddenly the whole class had turned around to stare at Pete Harris. He didn't feel so cool anymore.

"Harris, you moron! Don't you know she needs to see your lips to read them?"

"Yeah, c'mon, Pete. Share with the class, man. What'd you say?"

"You guys should definitely date. Deaf and Dumb, what a couple!"

"I . . . I'm sorry," Pete Harris blurted, blushing to the roots of his blond hair. "You're cute, but I . . . I can't do this."

Lexi was philosophical about Pete Harris. He was hot, but he *was* kind of a moron. Besides, she had her sights set on a much bigger fish: Christian Harle.

Lexi had begun Operation Christian in the eighth grade. At fourteen, she was still far too lowly a minnow in the Exeter High School pond for a guy like Christian Harle to notice. Two years her senior, with the body of an Olympic athlete and a face that could make Brad Pitt cry, Christian Harle dated only cheerleaders or models. The fact that he was astronomically out of Lexi's league didn't faze her in the least. On the contrary, it made this the perfect time for her to lay the groundwork of her operation.

Her plan was simple. She would find out what Christian looked for in a woman. (Big tits, pretty face, ditzy manner, IQ of dung beetle.) She would then transform herself into his ideal mate.

Lexi checked off the points on Christian's wish list one by one.

My tits are nonexistent, but they'll grow.

My face is already pretty, or it will be once the braces come off.

I'm smart enough to pretend to be stupid. So what's left?

Ah yes. Ditzy and helpless.

If having Rachel around was a dating minus, Lexi's deafness also provided some unique dating pluses. Because of her disability, boys tended to think of her as sweet and vulnerable—the poor little deaf heiress who needed their protection. Lexi quickly learned how to turn this misconception to her advantage. By ninth grade, she had her phony damsel-in-distress shtick down to a fine art.

"Rachel? Would you ask Johnny to help me with my books? I'm *so* tired this morning, I really couldn't walk another step."

"I'm sorry, Mr. Thomas, but I'm afraid I couldn't finish my assignment this week. I've been having terrible nightmares. Flashbacks about my ordeal."

Lexi's big gray eyes welled with tears. Rachel thought: *She's a fine little actress, this one. She's got them all fooled.*

Christian liked ditzy? Lexi would give him ditzy.

Right along with this stupid-ass virginity burning a hole in my panties.

Lexi was convinced she must be the oldest virgin at Exeter, if not in the whole of America. It was conceivable she was the oldest virgin in the world. Apart from nuns, obviously. And really ugly people like her aunt Eve.

Deep down she was afraid that what happened to her as a child might have spoiled her for sex. She still had nightmares about the pig. *Is that the real reason I've been saving myself for Christian? Did I pick someone I knew was unobtainable because I was too scared to "do it"?*

Whatever her true motivations, the wait was now officially over. Tonight was the night.

As the party drew nearer, Lexi's nerves started to get the better of her.

What if he only likes girls with experience? I guess I'll have to fake that, too.

Sometimes Lexi worried that she pretended so much she'd forgotten who she really was inside.

Maybe I want to forget?

———

"Oh, Max. Max! Don't stop! Please don't stop! I'm coming!"

Max Webster looked down at the girl writhing beneath him and felt ineffably bored. Her name was Sasha Harvey-Newton. Her father owned shipyards. Her mother's father owned oil fields. She was eighteen years old, stunningly beautiful and sickeningly rich. She was widely considered to be one of New York's most eligible young heiresses.

She was also a nymphomaniac.

"Harder, baby! Harder!"

Sasha Harvey-Newton arched her eligible, $20-million back for Max's benefit and let out a whoop of ecstasy.

"Shut up." Max put his hand over her mouth. She started sucking his fingers, and he fought back a powerful urge to ram them down her stupid, vacuous throat. Instead he forced her head down onto the pillow, muting her moans.

"Hey. What'd you do that for?"

Sasha looked up at him, her face flushed an unattractive strawberry red.

"You were making too much noise. What if your mom heard us?"

"What if she did? You know how many times I've had to listen to her and the tennis coach going at it? My mom's a whore."

Max watched Sasha get dressed, pulling on a pair of skintight jeans with no panties, and without bothering to wash first.

Like mother, like daughter.

Sasha smiled. "So. Does this mean I'm your date for your birthday party next weekend? I've always wanted to see Cedar Hill House."

Max wrinkled his nose in distaste.

"No."

"What do you mean, no?" The smile was gone.

"I mean *no.* I realize it's probably not a word you hear very often. But we're already at maximum capacity for the party, I'm afraid. Our security people have insisted, no more guests."

"Your security people?" Sasha snarled. "Who do you think you are? The president? It's a sixteenth birthday party, not a U.N. Security Council meeting. Uninvite someone if you have to."

"Ah, but I don't have to," said Max. "You got what you wanted, Sasha. I'll see myself out."

—

Walking back to Park Avenue, Max reflected on his afternoon's activities. He had not enjoyed the sex with Sasha Harvey-Newton, and he wondered why he'd agreed to go to bed with her in the first place. So he could boast about it? She was considered a good catch, after all. But to whom would he boast? It wasn't as if he had a bunch of male buddies whom he tried to impress. Max Webster needed approval from one person and one person only. His mother wouldn't give a damn that he'd wasted half a day balling some half-witted rich bitch who didn't even turn him on.

That's the problem. None of them turn me on. None of them can hold a candle to Eve.

Max loathed parties. He had only agreed to the joint birthday with Lexi because his mother asked him.

"Keep your friends close and your enemies closer, my darling." That was Eve's motto, at least where Lexi was concerned. She was always pushing the two of them together. "There will be a lot of important people at Cedar Hill House that weekend. Kruger-Brent board members, all the major shareholders and business heads. You can't afford to let Lexi look like the star of the show."

There wasn't much danger of that. No one at Kruger-Brent took Lexi seriously. Not anymore. But, technically speaking, under the terms of Kate Blackwell's will, she still stood a chance of being appointed chairman when she turned twenty-five. Until he, Max, was safely sitting in the chairman's seat, he couldn't afford to get complacent.

Max's old familiar hatred of his cousin had taken a disturbing twist recently. Overnight, it seemed, Lexi had transformed into a sensuous, desirable woman. What made it worse, and more confusing, was that she was starting to look more and more like a young version of Eve. Lexi's mother, Alexandra, had been Eve's identical twin, after all, so perhaps it was inevitable that the likeness would be striking. Still, Max found this genetic irony upsetting. In fact, he found everything about his cousin Lexi upsetting.

The paparazzi had always loved her: the brave, beautiful Blackwell baby, the plucky kidnapping survivor. Eve had once contemptuously described her niece as "America's favorite cripple" and she wasn't far wrong. Now, thanks to Lexi's butterflylike emergence as a society belle, media interest in her life seemed to have quintupled. She was no longer the Blackwell Baby, but the Blackwell Bombshell. Everyone wanted a piece of her.

She loves every second of it, too, Max thought bitterly. Last Christmas, when they'd briefly worked together at Kruger-Brent, he had sensed Lexi silently watching him. As if she were trying to catch him lusting after her, the way that everybody else seemed to.

Forget it. Not me.

Why can't you just disappear? Go to deaf school, marry some other special-ed retard and get the hell out of my life?

Sasha Harvey-Newton didn't know how lucky she was to be missing Max's birthday party. He heartily wished he could have missed it himself.

"Quite a spread, isn't it?"

Tristram Harwood, head of Kruger-Brent's oil and gas division, was talking to Logan Marshall, who ran the mining businesses.

"I wouldn't expect anything less."

Neither of them had been to the Blackwells' Dark Harbor compound since Kate Blackwell's funeral almost seventeen years ago. It was wonderful to see the old house bursting with life and vitality again. Everywhere you turned, America's impossibly beautiful, privileged youth were laughing and talking and dancing with one another while their parents looked on, the mothers dripping diamonds while they gossiped, the fathers grumbling about the latest plunge in the Dow Jones and the new fortunes to be made on the Internet.

Cedar Hill House itself had barely changed since Kate's day. The same Vlaminck floral canvas hung over the fireplace in the living room. Even the rose-and-green-chintz sofas remained, providing a lingering touch of femininity to what was now a man's home. Peter Templeton had inherited the estate upon Alexandra's death, but for years he had found the house too full of painful memories and rarely visited it. After Lexi's ordeal, however, he'd brought her to Maine to recuperate. Slowly, summer by summer, Cedar Hill House had been allowed to live again.

"Ah, there he is. The birthday boy. I suppose we should go and tug our forelocks, get it over and done with?"

Logan Marshall followed Tristram Harwood's gaze. Max was on the veranda, surrounded by a gaggle of admiring teenage girls. In a Ralph Lauren suit and Choate tie, on the surface he looked the epitome of a preppy young gentleman. But neither the clothes nor the old-money, East Coast setting could completely conceal Max's feral nature. He reminded Tristram Harwood of a jungle savage whom some misguided anthropologist had "rescued" and dragged, kicking and screaming, into the civilized world. As if he might at any moment start tearing off his Brooks Brothers shirt with his teeth.

"Happy birthday, young man. I trust you're enjoying the party?"

Max turned around. He wiped the bored expression off his face and greeted the two Kruger-Brent board members warmly. He knew that his mother would be watching.

"Of course. My uncle's gone to a tremendous effort. And you, are you both well?"

Tristram Harwood nodded. "Very well. Business is booming."

For a sixteen-year-old, the boy sure had an adult way of expressing himself. Such maturity. Such poise. Everyone at the firm knew that Kate Blackwell's will favored Alexandra's offspring over Eve's. But when the time came to vote for a new chairman, all board members would be consulted. If they unanimously voted for Max, it would be difficult for the family to ignore their position. And really, how would a deaf woman ever manage to run one of the biggest multinationals in the world? The very idea was laughable.

Eve watched her son schmoozing with Harwood and Marshall and smiled contentedly. She was seated alone in a corner of the living room, next to the French doors that opened onto the veranda. In a full-length black shift, with an exquisitely hand-painted Venetian mask covering her ravaged face, she sat as still and unnoticed as a black widow spider while the party ebbed and flowed around her.

Good boy. Reel them in.

Tristram Harwood had always been a shameless opportunist. Years ago, he'd tried to seduce Eve on almost the exact same spot where he now stood sucking up to her son. Eve had toyed with him a little, until her grandmother stepped in.

"He's a married man, Eve, and a vital asset to the company. Leave him bloody well alone!"

Stupid old bitch. As if she, Eve Blackwell, would be interested in a lowly, chinless drone like Tristram Harwood!

Just then, Lexi appeared on the veranda. She had run up from the bottom of the lawn, followed by a ravishing boy. Her flawless cheeks were flushed from laughter and exertion. Eve felt her heart tighten and a ball of hatred swell in her chest. It was like looking in a twenty-five-year-old mirror.

She looks exactly like me. She's stolen my beauty. My youth. My power. Everything that was taken from me has been given to that cripple. Alex's spawn.

"Holy moly," Logan Marshall whispered to Tristram Harwood. "Somebody's grown up fast."

Max looked on as both men turned to admire his cousin. Lexi was indeed looking stunning. The dress his uncle Peter had bought her clung to her teenage body like shrink-wrap. Her hair, worn up for once and held loosely in place with a vintage diamond-encrusted comb that had once belonged to Kate Blackwell, was escaping in sexy tendrils around her beautiful face. Max felt the beginnings of an erection.

I hate her.

Just then, a loud crash from the boathouse caught everyone's attention.

"What the hell was that?"

A skinny, blond man with incredibly long legs and a long-lens camera slung around his neck was limping toward the harbor. Judging from the hole in the boathouse roof and the debris scattered across the grass, he must have been hiding behind one of the gables and somehow lost his footing.

"Get security!" A grim-faced Peter Templeton emerged from inside. "Someone go after that guy."

"Don't worry, Daddy," said Lexi as Danny Corretti hurled himself into a waiting motorboat and roared off into the night. "It's only paparazzi. I'm used to them."

"Yes, well. You shouldn't have to be used to them," said Peter. To Tristram Harwood he added: "These lowlifes follow my daughter around like a pack of hyenas. It's a disgrace."

Max's eyes were glued to Lexi.

A disgrace? Bullshit. She's loving every second of it.

A liveried butler emerged from the living room.

"Ladies and gentlemen. Dinner is served."

Robbie sat next to his godfather, Barney Hunt.

Barney asked: "So, are you going to play for us tonight? A live performance from the great Robert Templeton?"

Robbie spooned another meltingly good piece of Black Forest chocolate cake into his mouth and shook his head firmly.

"Uh-uh. No way. I'm off duty. Anyway, Dad hasn't asked me. He's got the entire evening choreographed down to a tee. I wouldn't want to upset him any more than I do already. You know, by existing."

It was said in jest, but Barney Hunt picked up the undertone of sadness.

"Come on. Your father loves you. He just . . ."

". . . wishes I weren't gay. I know."

Lisa Babbington, one of Lexi's most beautiful girlfriends, caught Robbie's eye and winked at him lasciviously from two tables away. Clearly, the boy sitting beside her, Grady Jones, was failing to float her boat.

"Looks like your dad isn't the only one." Barney laughed. "Have you had much time alone with your sister yet?"

Robbie looked frustrated. "No. Every time I get near her, she's being whisked off to dance or for photographs. I have to fly back to Paris in the morning, but I can't seem to pin her down."

Barney glanced over at the top table. Lexi's place was empty.

"Hmm. I see what you mean."

On the floor of the boathouse, Lexi lay beneath Christian Harle trying not to feel disappointed.

Is this it? Is this really what I waited two whole years for?

She'd expected . . . what had she expected, exactly? Pain. That's what all the books said. A sharp pain, followed by something momentous, some life-changing, mind-altering feeling of bliss that she would remember for the rest of her life. This was Christian Harle, after all. *Christian Harle!* The biggest catch in Exeter, the boy who had filled Lexi's days and consumed her nights since she was fourteen years old.

After Lexi's kidnapping, the psychiatrists had told Peter that the trauma of sexual abuse would stay with her forever. "She may marry. She may have children. But it's unrealistic to expect her sexual relationships to develop normally." Once again, however, they had underestimated Lexi's willpower.

She *would* enjoy sex.

She *must*.

She would not give the pig another victory.

So why was sleeping with Christian such a terrible letdown?

Still inside her, Christian propped himself up on his forearms so

Lexi could read his lips. Sweat was dripping from his forehead. His cheeks were flushed beet red. He did not look his best.

"Is that good, baby?"

Dear God. Is he talking to me? What is this, twenty questions? Why isn't the earth moving?

Lexi nodded, pulling him back down on top of her. She wriggled around, the way she'd seem Pamela Anderson do it with Tommy Lee on the Internet, and tried to breathe more heavily. Christian had clearly learned his technique from a different sex tape. He started doing some sort of strange, circular motion inside her, like someone vacuuming the interior of a car and wanting to make sure he got his nozzle into every nook and cranny.

At least he's thorough. Thoroughness is an underrated attribute in a man. One can never be too thorough, that's what my old nanny used to say. I wonder how Mrs. Carter's doing these days?

Above Christian's head was the hole in the roof where the paparazzo had fallen earlier.

Poor man. I hope he's okay.

Lexi stared up at the stars. She felt the muscles in Christian's butt and stomach tighten, then relax. The warm wetness between her legs gave her a brief feeling of triumph. *Good-bye, virginity! I won't miss you.* A few seconds later, the warm glow faded. Lexi started shaking.

"What's the matter?" Christian panted. "Hey, are you okay?"

He was looking at her, talking to her. But Lexi couldn't read his lips or see the concern on his face. All she saw was a pig mask.

One word and I'll slit your throat.

She screamed.

Christian Harle started to panic. Lexi's cries were unearthly and getting louder. She wouldn't stop screaming.

What's wrong with her? One minute she's all over me, squirming around like a fish on a hook. The next she's acting like I raped her.

"Stop it, Lex. Please! Someone'll hear."

Not knowing what else to do, he slapped Lexi hard across the face.

Miraculously, it worked. The screams stopped. Lexi watched, dazed, as the pig mask faded away. She found herself looking deeply into Christian Harle's terrified eyes.

You're just a boy. A kid. You're as lost and scared as I am.

What did I ever see in you?

She got to her feet, silently straightened her dress, and walked back to the house.

Peter looked worried. "Where have you been? Rachel says you went off to the ladies' room and never came back."

Lexi signed angrily: "I went for a walk. I needed some air, that's all. Rachel worries too much."

"Yes, well. The dancing's about to start. I thought it'd be nice if you and Max kicked things off."

Lexi looked at him incredulously. "Me and Max?"

"You are the joint hosts, after all."

"He's a freak."

"Lexi, come on now. He's your cousin."

"No. No way. Why can't I dance with Robbie? He's my brother."

Not for the first time, Peter was glad that so few people understood sign language. Lexi could be incredibly rude when she wanted to be, not to mention stubborn. He tried to make excuses for her. Her deafness must be horribly frustrating. Even so, it embarrassed him at times.

"Robbie's playing piano. Uncle Barney roped him into it. Look, Max is coming over now. I'm warning you, Lexi, don't make a scene."

So many bodies in a confined space had made the house stiflingly hot. Max had removed his tie and jacket and rolled up the sleeves of his shirt. With his tanned skin and jet-black hair, he reminded Lexi of a pirate.

All he needs is the cutlass between his teeth.

"Would you like to dance?" He spoke deliberately slowly, as if Lexi were incapable of comprehending ordinary speech. He knew how much it irritated her, and was delighted to see the flash of anger in her eyes as he led her onto the floor. At a nod from Peter, Robbie began playing, Strauss's "Blue Danube Waltz."

Lexi was aware of hundreds of eyes watching them as Max guided her expertly around the room. She disliked dancing. Letting a man lead went against her nature anyway. Being deaf and unable to hear the music meant she had to place even more trust in her partner than other girls did. Lexi did not trust Max Webster as far as she could spit.

"Just relax. Lean into me."

He overenunciated every word.

Lexi thought: *I loathe you.* Pressed against him, she breathed in the scent of his body. He smelled of sweat and aftershave. She was horrified to find herself feeling aroused. *Why didn't Christian Harle turn me on like this? What's wrong with me?*

The waltz ended. Robbie began playing another, and couples started drifting onto the dance floor. Lexi made as if to leave, but Max pulled her back.

"One more dance."

It was not a request. It was a command. Lexi contemplated storming off, but they were already moving, swept up in the rhythm of the waltz. Max spun her around so she could read his lips.

"I know what you've been up to."

Lexi ignored him

"You reek of sex."

The words were so unexpected, at first she thought she'd misread what he said.

"What?"

"So, who was he? Anyone I know?"

This time there was no mistaking him. The sneer on Max's face spoke a thousand words.

"Why don't I take a guess? Christian Harle. Am I warm? Everyone knows you've had the hots for that Neanderthal since seventh grade."

Lexi blushed furiously. *Did everybody know? How?*

"Maybe I'm jumping to conclusions. I guess it could've been anyone, right? You're probably as much of a slut as your mother was."

How dare he talk about my mother! Lexi felt sick. Violated. She tried to wriggle free but Max's grip was like iron. She could feel the friction burns forming on her wrists.

"Not so high-and-mighty now, are we?" Max taunted her. "What's it worth for me not to tell your doting daddy what his princess has been doing tonight? Or should I say *who* she's been doing? How about we go somewhere quiet, you suck my dick like a good little girl, and I'll forget I know anything?"

Max laughed, spinning Lexi around and around till she felt nauseous. Someone tapped her on the back. It was one of her girlfriends, Donna Mastroni.

Thank God!

"Lexi, some guy's here to see you. He says it's important. Security stopped him at the gate, but he won't leave."

With Donna standing there, Max had no option but to let Lexi go.

With a parting look of purest hatred, Lexi followed Donna into the night.

———

The man was short and sallow-skinned. In his midfifties, he wore a cheap, shiny blue suit. His shoes were worn and scuffed with age. He introduced himself as Tommy King and handed Lexi a ratty-looking business card with visible thumb smudges at the corner.

KING & ASSOCIATES
Investigations
(212) 965-1165

Glancing around to make sure she was alone, Lexi whispered: "We can't talk here. Far too dangerous."

Tommy King followed her to a secluded corner of the grounds, far from the prying eyes of the security guards.

"Can you do the job?"

Tommy King smiled, revealing a crooked row of teeth more gold than enamel.

"I can do the job, princess. But it might take a while. You haven't given me much to go on."

Lexi cut to the chase.

"How much?"

"A hundred bucks a day. We bill monthly. You get a progress report at the end of each month, photographs, any other material we've managed to dig up. Expenses are extra."

Lexi nodded.

"I'll need a deposit to get started. Seven hundred plus five hundred for expenses."

"You can have five hundred today. No more. I'll pay you the rest when I get your first report."

Tommy King scowled. Why was it always the richest clients who were the cheapest? The dress Lexi was wearing looked like it cost more than his apartment. Still, he figured, he shouldn't be greedy. If he played his cards right and strung the thing out, the Blackwell girl could wind up being a gold mine.

"Fine. Five hundred. You have it with you?"

Lexi fumbled down the front of her dress and pulled a tightly rolled wad of notes from her bra. Looking around again, she thrust it into Tommy's eagerly sweating hand.

After he was gone, she thought: *What have I done? What if he runs off with that money and I never see hide nor hair of him again?*

It was a risk worth taking. After years of saving, squirreling away her allowance and birthday and Christmas gifts in a secret account, Lexi now had over $30,000 in her own name. It wasn't a fortune. But it was a start.

The time had come.

Prepare to die, pig.

SEVENTEEN
∞

A CHANCE MEETING IN THE PRISON LIBRARY CHANGED Gabe McGregor's life.

Thanks to Billy, and the zealous attentions of the young prison doctor who ran the Wormwood Scrubs drug program, Gabe was clean for the first time in three years. But temptation was everywhere. The irony was that those guys on remand had been talking out of their arses. Gabe had tried to kill himself, corroding his intestines with bleach, because he thought he wouldn't be able to get a hit here. The truth was there was plenty of heroin available if you knew the right people.

Gabe responded well to the methadone. Billy told him: "You can't go back now, son. It's the road to hell, sure you know that as well as I do."

"I won't go back, Billy."

Gabe heard himself saying the words. He felt himself wishing they were true. But every time he thought of the years of boredom and loneliness stretching ahead, of how he'd let his mam down, of the mountain he would have to climb if he ever *did* get out of here, the hopelessness and despair became unbearable.

It was only a matter of time before he went back to heroin, and he knew it.

The prison doctor liked Gabe. Sensing his patient's weakening resolve, he arranged a job for him cataloging books in the prison library.

"It's one of the better places to work in this dump. Quiet, decent blokes in there, no real hard cases. You'll be earning money and you'll be busy."

Gabe was grateful. The doctor must have pulled quite a few strings to get him such a cushy job. But still he found the work monotonous and soul destroying, arranging books alphabetically by author, title and subject matter.

"That's the trouble with you bleedin' Scots. No imagination."

Gabe turned around. Behind him, seated at one of the Formica work-tables surrounded by fat legal tomes, was a small, middle-aged man. He was completely bald and sported a thick, black Charlie Chaplin mustache that made him look as if he belonged in another century, like a music-hall performer or a magician from a Victorian circus.

"I beg your pardon. Are you talking to me?"

"Yes, jock, I'm talking to you." The man's cockney accent was almost comically strong. "Every day you come in 'ere, and not once 'ave I seen you read so much as a page. It's like watching a kid stack shelves in a candy store and never stick his hand in the pick-and-mix."

"I'm not much of a reader."

The man laughed.

"Take a seat, jock. Go on. Pull up a pew."

Gabe looked around. Both the librarians were engrossed at their computers. He wasn't supposed to stop and chat on the job. In fact, nobody was supposed to talk in the library at all. He'd have to make it quick.

"Marshall Gresham." The bald man proffered his hand as Gabe sat down.

"Gabe McGregor."

"Let me ask you a question, Gabe McGregor. You've seen me in 'ere, right? Most days?"

Gabe nodded.

"Ever wondered what I'm up to? With all these boring-looking books?"

"Not really," Gabe admitted.

Gabe's gray eyes met Marshall Gresham's blue ones. Marshall had amazing eyes. They literally sparkled, like sunshine bouncing off the sea, and they seemed to invite confidences.

"I'll tell you, shall I?" said Marshall. "I'm working on my appeal. You see, Gabe McGregor, I 'ave a low opinion of the legal profession in general, and of my own brief in particular. The thought crossed my mind that while I'm banged up in 'ere, fending off shit-stabbers for the next ten years of my life, my poncey bloody solicitor is going home every night for steak-and-kidney pudding and a shag with his missus. Now, which of the two of us would you say is more motivated to see me walk through those gates to freedom?"

Gabe laughed.

"Ah, but motivation isn't everything, is it, Mr. Gresham? Your lawyer is a professional. He knows how the appeal system works. You don't."

"I *didn't*." Marshall Gresham gestured to the books around him. "But now I bloody do. Tell me, Gabe McGregor. How's *your* lawyer getting on with *your* appeal? Heard much from him, 'ave you?"

Michael Wilmott. Christ. Gabe had almost forgotten the man existed. He'd been so preoccupied with his addiction and the daily struggle to get clean, he'd filed everything else in his life under *P* for "pending." Permanently pending.

Marshall Gresham raised a bushy black eyebrow. "I'll bet his wife makes a mean steak-and-kidney pudding."

The first thing Gabe did was sack Michael Wilmott. The second thing he did was swallow his pride and write to everyone who might be able to help him raise money to pay for a new lawyer. He composed a simple note, countersigned by the prison doctor, telling people he was clean and determined to make a fresh start. Marshall Gresham helped him with the spelling. ("Bollocks to dyslexia. You have to work harder than other people, that's all.") Gabe sent the letters out to everyone he knew who wasn't a user or a criminal, expecting little. He was overwhelmed by the response.

Thérèse, his last "girlfriend," the one who'd kicked Gabe out after he stole from her, sent him a thousand pounds.

You could be anything you want to, Gabriel. Make me proud.

When he got her note, Gabe burst into tears.

More money followed, gifts of hundreds from classy London friends (almost all women), tiny donations of a few quid from old mates back in Scotland that again brought tears to Gabe's eyes. *These people have nothing. They can't afford to help me. But here they are, trying.* His mother, Anne, who had not heard from Gabe in almost two years, sent him fifty pounds stuffed into a card that said, simply: *I love you.* No mention of the fact that he was in prison. Not one word of a reproach.

I love you, too, Mam. One day, I'll repay your faith in me.

Day by day, as the money trickled into his life and the drugs trickled out of it (he was almost off the methadone now), Gabe's natural optimism and faith in human nature revived. Claire, his first London sugar mommy, was a lawyer. "I know a great criminal guy, Angus Frazer. He owes me a favor or twenty. Let me see what kind of deal I can do for you."

Marshall Gresham was impressed.

"I'll tell you what, kid. You either have the biggest knob in Scotland, or you're a charming little bastard. You fleeced every one of these birds, but here they are falling over their knickers to 'elp you out."

Angus Frazer was not quite as brilliant a lawyer as Claire had made him out to be.

He was at least five times better.

A handsome Old Etonian with a hooked nose and regal bearing, Angus Frazer could play judges the way that Gabe McGregor could play women. When Angus Frazer finished his summing-up, the appeals-court judge was starting to think that perhaps Gabe shouldn't be in prison at all. Perhaps the Walthamstow home owner whose skull had been crushed should be the one doing time? After all, it was *he* who had wantonly derailed the life of this bright, promising, determined young man. A young man whose glamorous ladyfriends packed the court's public gallery like hopefuls at a Hollywood casting call.

Gabe's sentence was reduced to ten years, the minimum possible for his offense. Angus Frazer told him: "You've already served four. With good behavior, you'll be out in another three."

Three years! Only three more years! To the new Gabe, it was nothing. Thirty-six months.

"I don't know how to thank you, Mr. Frazer. You do understand, I can only pay half your fees today."

Angus Frazer smiled. He was a wealthy man, not usually given to doing favors for ex-junkies. But in Gabe's case, he was glad Claire McCormack had twisted his arm. There was something about the boy . . . it was hard to put into words. But Gabe McGregor made Angus Frazer feel glad to be alive.

"Don't worry about it, Gabe. You'll pay me back one day, I'm sure."

Yes, sir, I will. On my father's grave, I'll pay you back ten times what I owe you. One day.

———

Marshall Gresham was inside for fraud.

"So, how much money did you steal, then?"

It was the sort of question Marshall would only have tolerated from Gabe McGregor. The two men had become fast friends.

"I didn't steal any money, Gabriel. That's why I'm appealing my conviction. I *rearranged* quite a bit."

"How much?"

Marshall allowed himself a small smile of pride.

"Two hundred and sixty million."

Gabe was silent for a full minute.

"What business are you in, Marshall?"

"Property."

Another minute's silence.

"Marshall?"

"Hmm?"

"I think I'd like to learn the property business. Will you teach me?"

"Why, Gabriel!" Marshall Gresham's twinkly blue eyes sparkled even more brightly than usual. "I'd be delighted."

Suddenly thirty-six months felt like thirty-six minutes.

There was so much to learn, and so little time. Indeces, interest rates, prices per square foot, building costs, planning law. It went on and on and on and for Gabe it was like learning not only a new language, but a whole new way of thinking.

Marshall Gresham told him: "A lot of things have changed in the markets these past few years. All this new Internet money." He shook his head disgustedly. "People have lost their 'eads. Don't listen to anyone who tells you that the fundamental market forces are any different than what they've always been."

Gabe nodded silently, drinking in Marshall's advice. It was his new drug. He couldn't get enough of listening to the older man's voice. Every word from Marshall Gresham's lips sounded like money, like hope. Gabe's future made flesh.

"Location. That's the key. If I were going into this game fresh, from scratch, I'd stay out of London."

Gabe was silent, but his face said *why?*

"Overinflated. Too many bleeding Poles. And Russians. Too many barriers to entry. To be honest, I'd forget the U.K. altogether. And America. You want a market that's still up-and-coming. Get in on the ground floor, like I did."

Get in on the ground floor.

Yeah, sure. But where? And with what?

Marshall Gresham made it sound so easy.

Marshall was right about the Wormwood Scrubs library. Look past its linoleum floors and filthy, chipped Formica tables; past the well-thumbed Dick Francis novels and fashion-model autobiographies—My Life: The Untold Story, *by Misty Holland. Who on earth read that crap?*—and a world of infinite possibilities was there for the taking.

A lot of cons took Marshall Gresham's route and went straight for the law books. Some had even done open-university degrees while inside. Others lost themselves in fiction, an escape of sorts from the grim reality of prison life. For Gabe, whenever he wasn't wading through books on real estate and business, it was history he turned to. Specifically the history of his famous forebear, Jamie McGregor.

It was amazing how much had been written about Gabe's great-great-uncle and the illustrious company he founded. In America, Gabe discovered, there were professors who'd devoted their entire lives to the study of Kruger-Brent, Ltd. As if it were a country or a war, a great king or a pandemic disease.

No wonder my father and grandfather were so obsessed. Apparently they weren't the only ones.

Gabe had always known that Jamie McGregor died a wealthy man and that his direct descendants—the Blackwell family—had become even wealthier. But the sums of money he read about now were so large, simply thinking about them made his head ache. It was like trying to imagine the distance to the moon in inches, or the number of grains of sand there were on a beach.

But it wasn't the money that fired Gabe's interest. Nor was it the company whose interests spanned the globe and now even reached into space, thanks to a 1980s acquisition of a Finnish satellite business. It was the man, Jamie McGregor himself, who fascinated Gabe.

Gabe read about Scotland in the 1860s, the life of crushing poverty from which Jamie had escaped. It made his own childhood seem positively luxurious. He learned about the treacherous sea crossing from London to Cape Town. Thousands had perished on the journey from hunger, exhaustion or disease, chasing their own dreams of striking it rich in the Namib diamond fields. Not one in a million had done it. But Jamie McGregor had been that one, triumphing over inconceivable odds.

Years later, just months before the stroke that incapacitated him for the last years of his life, Jamie McGregor was asked by a South African newspaper reporter what he considered to be the secret of his success.

"Perseverance," he'd answered. "And courage. I went into places that most people considered far too dangerous. Trust no one but yourself."

Gabe thought about this. *I trust Marshall Gresham. And my mother. And Claire. And Angus Frazer. Maybe if I follow rules one and three, I'll be two-thirds as rich as Jamie McGregor was.*

Then out of the blue, another thought struck him.

What had Marshall said? *Find a market that's still up-and-coming. Get in on the ground floor.*

And Jamie McGregor? *I went into places that most people considered far too dangerous.*

Suddenly the answer was obvious.

A little bit of research confirmed Gabe's excitement. The South African rand had all but collapsed against the U.S. dollar since the fall of apartheid. Property in Cape Town was going for a song as white families fled, fearing a new explosion of black violence. Fearing revolution.

If the revolution comes, I'll lose everything. But if it doesn't . . .

At last, Gabe McGregor had a plan. He would go to Africa to seek his fortune.

Just like Jamie McGregor had done before him.

By 7:30 A.M., Gabe was on a subway into central London.

By nine, he was waiting outside the glass doors of the exclusive Coutts Private Banking offices at number 100 The Strand.

"Can I help you, sir?"

The security guard gave Gabe a look that made it perfectly clear that the *last* thing he wanted to do was help him. Gabe didn't blame the guy. He'd shaved and smartened himself up as best he could, but in his thin gray jacket and ancient, rain-soaked jeans, he did not look like a typical Coutts customer.

I've left you a little something at Coutts. Just to get you started.

It was typical of Marshall Gresham's generosity. He'd already done so much, kick-starting Gabe's appeal, teaching him the real-estate business. Billy and the prison doctor might have gotten Gabe clean, but it was Marshall Gresham who'd kept him that way. Marshall had given Gabe hope, something to live for other than heroin. He hadn't so much saved his life as given him a whole new one.

And now he wants to make sure I have money for a bed and a meal tonight.

It was both touching and much needed. Gabe had walked out of Wormwood Scrubs with only five pounds to his name, and that had gone on his subway fare and a bacon sandwich at Kings Cross. This afternoon he'd start looking for construction work. Friends inside had given him a few contacts. But it was nice to know he wouldn't have to sleep rough on day one.

"I'm here to see Robin Hampton-Gore." Gabe spoke softly but with confidence. "I believe Marshall Gresham informed him I'd be coming."

The guard's look now said, *And I believe you're a chancer come to try your luck with a sob story. Well, if you are, good luck to you, mate. You won't get far with Mr. H.-G.*

Out loud he said: "Wait here, please, sir."

Gabe waited there. Five minutes later, as much to his own surprise as the guard's, he found himself being escorted into a corner office by a genial man in a pin-striped Savile Row suit and the shiniest pair of wing-tips Gabe had ever seen.

"Mr. McGregor, I presume?"

The man sat down behind a comfortingly solid mahogany desk. He gestured for Gabe to take the chesterfield chair opposite.

"Robin Hampton-Gore. Marshall told me you'd be coming. Waxed quite lyrical about you, in fact. He assures me you're going to be the next Donald Trump."

Gabe laughed uncomfortably. For a ritzy banker, Robin Hampton-Gore seemed suspiciously friendly toward an ex–heroin addict, just out of prison for burglary and aggravated assault, whose only recommendation came from a convicted fraudster.

"Marshall's an old friend of mine," Robin explained, as if reading Gabe's thoughts. "He made me in this business. He was my first big client and he stuck with me, long after he became so rich he could have insisted on someone far more senior handling his account. I owe him a lot."

"So do I," said Gabe.

Robin Hampton-Gore unlocked the drawer of his desk with an old-fashioned brass key and pulled out a crisp white envelope.

"This is cash," he explained unnecessarily, handing it to Gabe. "Marshall thought you'd need some immediately."

Gabe broke the seal and gasped. Inside was a small fortune. There was a smattering of tens and twenties, then hundred after hundred after hundred, the distinctive red-inked bills fluttering between Gabe's shaking fingers like rare butterflies as he thumbed through them, trying to count.

"There's only ten thousand there. It's a float. The rest is in an account in your name. I have all the details here."

Robin Hampton-Gore passed Gabe a second envelope. This one was already open, with a sheaf of Coutts letterheaded paper sticking out of the top.

Gabe stammered, "I . . . I don't understand. What do you mean 'the rest'? I think there must have been a mistake. I only need a couple of hundred quid."

Robin Hampton-Gore laughed. "Well, you've *got* a couple of hundred thousand." He handed Gabe a third envelope and his business card. "It's a letter from Marshall. I trust it explains everything, but if you've any further questions, don't hesitate to call me."

Gabe's hands were still trembling. As ever with Marshall Gresham, the letter was short and to the point.

Dear Gabriel,

It's not a loan. It's an investment. Fifty-fifty partners.

Love, M.

P.S. Don't forget to write from Cape Town.

Gabe felt a lump in his throat and swallowed hard. Now was not the time to get emotional. He had too much to do. There were so many people he was indebted to. Marshall Gresham, Angus Frazer, Claire, his mother. He couldn't let them down.

I'll pay you all back. Every penny.
I'm going to Africa to make my fortune.
I won't be back till I'm as rich as Jamie McGregor.

EIGHTEEN

∽

AUGUST SANDFORD GRIPPED THE SIDES OF HIS CHAIR AND ground his perfectly straight white teeth with frustration.

The team meeting of Kruger-Brent's new Internet division had run over by almost an hour now. Max Webster, Kate Blackwell's twenty-one-year-old great-grandson and Kruger-Brent's probable future chairman, was on his feet, pontificating.

August thought: *I didn't spend eight years at Goldman Sachs to sit here and listen to some business-school freshman talking out of his ass. Or did I?*

August's girlfriend, Miranda, had warned him about joining Kruger-Brent.

"It's a family company, babe. However huge, however global, at the end of the day the Blackwells will always call the shots. You'll hate it."

August had ignored her warnings for three reasons. The headhunter from Spencer Stuart had promised to triple his salary and bonus; he'd be fast-tracked onto the Kruger-Brent board, and he wasn't in the habit of taking career advice from his girlfriends. August Sandford picked his lovers according to a strict set of criteria involving largeness of breasts and flatness of stomach. He wanted a lioness in the sack, not a life coach.

"Don't worry, sweetie," August told Miranda patronizingly. "I know what I'm doing."

But he didn't know shit. Miranda was right. On days like today, August Sandford yearned for his old job on the Goldman derivatives desk like a shipwrecked man yearns for dry land. No salary was worth this.

"You're being shortsighted." Max Webster's black eyes blazed with passion. "Kruger-Brent should be allocating more money to its Internet businesses, not less."

His speech—*more like a sermon*, thought August bitterly—was directed entirely at his cousin Lexi Templeton. As if the two Blackwell heirs were the only people in the room. Both Max and Lexi were on a six-month leave from Harvard Business School. When they graduated, both would join Kruger-Brent. But only one would ultimately take on the mantle of chairman, a position reserved for family members only.

The general consensus was that that person would be Max. Aside from the obvious drawback of her hearing, Lexi was seen as too much of a party girl to be taken seriously. She showed up for the first day of her internship on the back of a Ducati, her long legs wrapped around its owner, Ricky Hales, and her trademark blond hair flying in the wind. Ricky Hales was the drummer with the latest hot rock band, the Flames. More tattoo than skin, with a heroin habit that made Courtney Love look like Mother Teresa, Ricky was almost as much of a paparazzi favorite as Lexi herself. Lexi gave Ricky a lingering kiss on the steps of the Kruger-Brent building, a shot that made the front cover of every gossip rag in America the next morning.

Lexi Templeton was an enigma. Part vulnerable child, part vixen, she kept the press guessing and the Blackwell-obsessed public intrigued. But August Sandford sensed that Lexi's little show with Ricky Hales was not intended for the media. It was a deliberate attempt to goad her cousin, the brooding Max Webster.

The rivalry between the two Blackwell heirs was intense.

They reminded August of the Williams sisters, announcing at their first Wimbledon tournament that they considered their only competition to be each other, thereby instantly alienating every other women's tennis player on the international circuit. Unlike the Williams sisters, Lexi and Max further fueled the flames of their competitiveness with a sexual tension so strong you could practically smell it in the air. Not that either one of them would admit it, even to themselves.

Miranda's voice rang in August's ears: *It's a family company. The Blackwells will always call the shots.*

August looked around the table. Apart from Max, Lexi and himself, there were three other Kruger-Brent executives at the meeting. Harry

Wilder, a gray-haired former academic with mad-scientist eyebrows, was nominally the most senior. A board member for a decade, Harry Wilder was a golf buddy of Peter Templeton's, Kruger-Brent's current chairman. Other than a decent handicap and an affable clubhouse manner, however, it was hard to see what value he added to the company. Nobody took him seriously, least of all August Sandford. The fact that Harry Wilder was the board member chosen to head up the Internet division did not bode well for any of them.

Next to Wilder sat Jim Bruton. Jim Bruton was an up-and-comer at Kruger-Brent. A dead ringer for a young Frank Sinatra, Jim's most meaningful personal relationship was with his mirror. Second came his busty personal assistant, Anna. In distant third was his loyal wife, Sally, mother of Jim's three legitimate daughters, Corinna, Polly and Tiffany, always referred to pretentiously by Jim as "the heiresses." (His two illegitimate sons, Ronnie and Carlton, lived with their mother in Los Angeles, unbeknownst to Sally and the girls.)

To say that August Sandford despised Jim Bruton would be an understatement. But even August had to admit that Jim was sharp. He'd tripled the profits of the biotech division during his stint as head in the early nineties. Jim made no secret of the fact that he intended to make Kruger-Brent Internet his next money-spinning fiefdom.

Over my dead body, thought August.

Beside Jim Bruton was a young woman named Tabitha Crewe. Recently hired from Stanford Law School, Tabitha was attractive in a neat, regular-featured, hair-pulled-back-in-a-ponytail sort of way. Apparently she'd started and sold a small dot-com while at college and made herself a little nest egg, hence her assignment to the team. August looked at Tabitha's impassive, makeup-free face and found it hard to imagine her having the get-up-and-go to start a washing machine, never mind a business. She seemed so . . . blank. Especially when she sat next to Lexi Templeton.

Now there's a chick with a fire in her crotch. If she weren't so obsessed with her prick of a cousin . . . how much would I like to screw all the haughtiness out of her? Sexy, opinionated, stuck-up . . .

"Mr. Sandford. Are we boring you?"

Jim Bruton was staring at August, a wry smile playing across his lips. *Yes, you're boring me. You're all boring me stiff.*

"I apologize." August returned the smile. "What was the question?"

"Mr. Webster here is proposing we make a formal submission to the board, asking for a bigger budget with which to make acquisitions. Ms.

Templeton disagrees. Harry and I were wondering where you stood on the matter?"

August opened his mouth to reply but was interrupted by Lexi. Her deafness made her speech slower and more deliberate. She also had a habit of moving her hands when she spoke, unconsciously signing her words. August watched her long, slender fingers perform their delicate dance and found himself wondering what they'd feel like wrapped around his cock. He started to get hard, which irritated him even more.

Lexi said: "I'm all in favor of expanding our online reach. What I'm *not* in favor of is throwing money at a random bunch of start-ups before we've done our due diligence. My cousin seems to think that no economic fundamentals apply to Internet companies. I disagree."

"So do I," said August.

Max glared at him. Jim Bruton and Harry Wilder followed suit. Both had clearly decided that the chances of a deaf woman taking over Kruger-Brent were slim to none, whatever Kate Blackwell's will might say, and were pinning their colors firmly to Max's mast.

If I had any sense, I'd do the same, thought August. *I don't even like the girl, so God knows why I'm defending her.* But the fact was, Lexi was right. Max was talking out of his ass, jumping blindly and greedily onto the Internet bandwagon like every other Harvard Business School groupie.

"Any acquisition proposal we make to the board needs to be specific and backed up by hard data." August stood up to leave. "Now, if you'll excuse me, I'm afraid I have an important lunch appointment."

That night in the bath, Lexi Templeton thought about August Sandford.

He's not the ugliest man in the world, she conceded grudgingly, picturing his thick chestnut hair, strong jaw and almond eyes, offset by a butterscotch tan acquired, no doubt, on the beaches of East Hampton this past summer. Lookswise he was the exact opposite of Max. Brad Pitt to Max's Johnny Depp. Or so August probably thought.

He's almost as good-looking as he thinks he is. Not half as smart, though.

Lexi knew scores of August Sandfords at Harvard. Handsome, rich, well-educated, chauvinist pigs. *Take one rampant ego, sauté lightly in wealth and privilege, top with a blue-chip business card, and voilà! August Did-I-Mention-I-Was-at-Goldman? Sandford. Yawn.*

The bright young things at Harvard bored Lexi, but they served a purpose. She slept with all of them. Ever since the night of her six-teenth birthday party, when she'd lost her virginity to Christian Harle, Lexi had been haunted by the thought that her childhood abuse might have ruined her for sex as an adult. Having worked so hard to overcome her deafness, it was terrible to imagine that the pig might have won after all. That he might have turned her into some sort of sexual crip-ple. Determined not to let this happen, Lexi threw herself into college sex with all the single-minded fervor of a sailor on shore leave. Harvard was an education on every level: algorithms by day, orgies by night. Threesomes, bisexuality, sex toys, role-play; Lexi wanted to discover it all. To prove to the world and to herself that she was *not* a victim, that the pig had *not* defeated her. It was an open secret on campus that Lexi Templeton was the best lay at HBS. But an unspoken code of loyalty prevented her classmates from spreading rumors in the newspapers. Harvard was a closed world, a safe place to explore one's wild side. Out-side the college walls, it was a different story.

At Kruger-Brent, I'll have to be more careful.

Lexi brought her thoughts back to August Sandford. At least he'd stuck up for her against Max today, which was more than those other stuffed shirts had done. Lexi was well aware that 99 percent of Kruger-Brent's senior management had written her off. Kate Blackwell's will fa-vored her over Max for the chairmanship, but then Kate Blackwell had never known that Lexi would grow up to be deaf. In any event, a unani-mous board decision could see Max usurp her position. Most people at the company, including Max himself, not to mention Lexi's own father, seemed to view this as a foregone conclusion. It drove Lexi wild with rage.

How dare they write me off? My GPA has always been higher than Max's. I'm smarter than he is, I have more business sense. Okay, so I can't hear. But Max can't listen. That's the real handicap. He loves the sound of his own voice too much.

Lexi rubbed soap under her armpits and breasts with a sponge. Men were all the same. So impressed with themselves, beating their chests like baboons. August Sandford, Jim Bruton, Max . . . they were just grown-up versions of Christian Harle and the other Andover jocks. They patronized Lexi, the way they patronized all women, only in Lexi's case her deafness seemed to make it worse. That and the fact that she was beautiful, rich, famous and smarter than all of them com-bined.

August Sandford might have thought he had his poker face on today. But Lexi could see the envy in his eyes.

He hates me because I'm better than he is. He hates me because he wants to sleep with me and he can't. He hates me because—

A flashing light on her PC screen in the living room caught her attention.

New message.

Grabbing a towel, Lexi leaped out of the bath and ran, dripping, across the polished walnut floor of her apartment. Unlike mommie's-boy Max, who still lived at home with Eve, Lexi had her own place on the Upper East Side and reveled in her independence. A sleek, modern two-bedroom in a classy building on Seventy-seventh Street, between Park and Madison, it was decorated in neutrals and whites with huge floor-to-ceiling windows overlooking the city. A delicate Christopher Wray chandelier in glass and stainless steel hung from the living-room ceiling above a cream pony-skin rug. In the far corner, perched on a Danish Modern desk was Lexi's white Mac—her portal to the hearing world. She'd often wondered how on earth the deaf had managed before the advent of the Internet and thanked God she'd been born in the age of the text.

Scrolling past e-mails from Robbie and her father, her Harvard professor Dr. Fairford, and countless lovers, Lexi said a silent prayer.

Please be from him.

Finally, she reached the new message. Clicking it open, her heart gave a little leap of excitement. The subject heading read:

I've found him.

Tommy King did not like Thailand.

There was only so much Asian pussy that one man could enjoy. Once you'd seen the first hundred girls fire Ping-Pong balls out of their assholes, smoke cigars with their pussies, and exhaust the rest of their repertoire of bizarre sexual party tricks, it actually got kinda tame. And then what were you left with? Fried bugs, stinking hot weather and friggin' dysentery, that's what.

Tommy King wanted a Big Mac, *Monday Night Football,* Fox News and sex with a white woman over thirty who considered her asshole to be an exit not an entrance. After five long years, he wanted this godforsaken assignment to be over. The guy was obviously dead, like his two buddies. Why couldn't the Templeton girl just accept that?

When Tommy King first met Lexi Templeton at her sixteenth birthday party, he thought he was onto a cash cow. Little had he known that the search for the girl's kidnappers would take five long, fruitless years.

Years that had seen the sallow-skinned PI clock up more air miles than Henry Kissinger, and for what? Sure, the job had netted him a tidy little nest egg. But he was sixty-two already and tired as all hell. Besides, what use was money in a dump like Phuket?

Agent Edwards, the FBI hero (schmuck) who pulled Lexi out of the burning mill all those years ago had tried to warn him. Tommy King went to visit Agent Edwards at his place on Long Island, a huge French Country pile paid for by the girl's grateful father. Crunching his way up the graveled drive, Tommy King thought: *Jeez, Blackwell money goes a long way.* Then he saw Agent Edwards's barbecued face and thought: *But not far enough.*

"You'll never find them. Believe me, we've tried."

They'd sat outside in the garden on a joyously warm spring day. A maid brought them fresh lemonade. Tommy King watched Agent Edwards sip it with what used to be his mouth and tried not to wince.

"What makes you so sure?"

"The fire destroyed everything, all the physical evidence. All we had to go on were Lexi's own descriptions. They were fairly detailed in some respects, but it wasn't enough." Agent Edwards shook his head sadly. "We're as sure as we can be that none of the major crime syndicates were involved."

"No Mob?"

"Definitely not. We looked into everyone close to the Blackwell family who had a grievance. Real or imagined. It's a long list."

"I'll bet." Tommy King took a sip of his own lemonade. It was ambrosial.

"Kruger-Brent employees, household staff. We even looked at Dr. Templeton's old patients. He was a psychiatrist, you know, before his marriage. We figured maybe some whack job with a thing for little kids?"

Tommy King shivered.

"Anyway, after two years and a pretty much unlimited budget, we dropped the case. I wish you luck. But you're looking for three needles in a haystack the size of Canada."

Two years later, Tommy King found the first two needles: William Mensch and Federico Borromeo. Billy Mensch was a small-time drug dealer turned contract killer from Philadelphia. Borromeo was a friend Billy had made in juvenile detention in 1970, a con artist and compulsive gambler with no known history of violence.

Both had died in a car crash in Monaco in 1993, the year after Lexi's rescue.

When Tommy King first told her, Lexi, then aged eighteen, refused to believe it. She wrote to Tommy, demanding to see pictures of the bodies. After four months spent painstakingly grooming the lonely, overweight receptionist at the Monaco Medical Examiner's Office, Tommy obliged. Along with the pictures he sent a bill, and a note of his own, asking if Lexi wanted to continue to search for the third man.

In two years, I've discovered no trace of him. As you know, the FBI also drew a total blank. I feel it only right to advise you that, in my opinion, we will not be able to track down this individual and that continuing the case would be a waste of both my time and your money.

One week later, Tommy King received a check for $20,000 from Lexi Templeton, along with a one-word note.

Continue.

Two years later, he got a lead on a man calling himself Dexter Berkeley, a known rapist and petty thief from the San Francisco area. Berkeley regularly visited the Far East as a sex tourist.

Tommy King booked a flight to Bangkok.

In Thailand, Dexter Berkeley had disappeared again like a fish swimming into a sewer. Every few months, Tommy King saw him leap like a salmon out of the river of filth. In Bangkok, he surfaced as Mick Jenner, insurance salesman; in Pattaya, he was Fred Greaves, toy manufacturer; in Phuket, he was Travis Kemp, taxi driver. Only in his latest incarnation had Tommy King been able to get any sort of grip on his slimy, sewage-slick form:

John Barclay, aka prisoner 7843A.

John Barclay had taken a ten-year-old hooker back to his five-star hotel room and been arrested at gunpoint by a Thai vice squad fifteen minutes later with his pants around his ankles.

Ten years. No parole. No prepubescent pussy.

Too bad, Dex. Or whoever the hell you are.

Tommy King sat at the bar, waiting for his BlackBerry to buzz.

One thing you could say for Lexi Templeton. She wasn't one to let the grass grow under her feet. Not with news like this.

Sure enough, within sixty seconds, Tommy's phone jumped to life. He allowed himself a single, gold-toothed smile.

Thank you. Your employment is now terminated. I will wire the rest of the money to your Bahamanian account first thing Monday morning. Good-bye, Mr. King.

Tommy wondered briefly what would happen now. Would Lexi wait ten years for the guy to get out—assuming he lived that long—before taking her revenge? Or would she consider a decade taking it up the ass in a Thai jail punishment enough?

Whatever. It wasn't his problem anymore.

Good-bye, Ms. Templeton.

Good riddance.

Six blocks from Lexi's apartment, Max was having dinner at home with his mother.

"What's the matter, darling? You look tense."

Six feet of gleaming mahogany separated Eve from her son. The table was laid formally, as usual, with full silver service. A Cordon Bleu cook prepared all Eve's meals, taking care to keep her daily calorie intake below eighteen hundred. Keith may have stolen her face decades ago, but even now, at fifty-five, Eve was vain enough to obsessively maintain her trim figure. Unable to go to restaurants for fear of being photographed, she tried to make meals at home as luxurious and pleasurable as possible. She dressed for dinner, and expected Max to do the same. Tonight she was wearing a full-length jade-green evening dress with a high neck and deep V that plunged down her back, almost to the start of her buttocks. It was a young woman's dress, but Eve could carry it off.

"It's nothing." Max forced a smile.

Eve examined her son's handsome face, its predatory, sensual features accentuated by the stark black of his tuxedo.

He's breathtaking. Not an ounce of his father in him. But how could a son of mine be such a terrible liar?

"I don't think it's nothing, Max. Tell me what's wrong."

Max hesitated. "It's Lexi. We had a team meeting today. She kept trying to shoot me down."

Eve's scarred, stretched eyelids narrowed. "Go on."

"She's got August Sandford eating out of her palm. I'm sure Jim Bruton wants to screw her, too." Max shook his head. "At first I thought the board was just humoring her with this internship. But now I'm not so sure. She wants the chairmanship as much as I do. She's smart."

"She's deaf, Max." Eve's voice dripped with disdain. "Are you telling me you can't outwit a girl who slurs her words like a drunk? Like a retard?"

"Of course not, Mother. I—"

"She's a slut! She's a joke!" Rancor poured out of Eve like pus from a boil. "Falling out of nightclubs at five every morning with her skirt pulled up around her hips."

This wasn't exactly true. Lexi might be promiscuous, and she might enjoy a party or twenty, but she was very conscious of her public image. Not that Max was about to argue. He loathed his cousin every bit as much as Eve did. The fact that he wanted her sexually only made his loathing stronger. Lexi was all that stood between him and Kruger-Brent. Between him and his mother's love. Lexi was trying to take Eve away from him. She was ruining everything.

Eve raged on. "You're not a man. You're a queer like your cousin Robbie. Like your father."

"No! I'm nothing like Keith."

"You don't have the *balls* to run that company."

"Mother, I do. I—"

"What exactly was today's meeting about?"

Max told Eve about his proposal to siphon more money into the Internet division, and Lexi's objections. Eve sat silently for a few moments.

"All right," she said at last, pushing aside her plate. "This is what we do."

Harry Wilder was on his third glass of claret at the golf club bar when the steward tapped him on the shoulder.

"Telephone call for you, sir."

"For me?"

He wasn't expecting any business calls. It was Saturday. His wife, Kiki, was shopping with friends and besides, she never rang the club. Perhaps something terrible had happened? One of the grandchildren?

"You can take it in the library."

Harry Wilder hurried into the deserted, oak-paneled room trying not to let his imagination get the better of him. Kiki was always telling him not to be such a worrywart. Professor Panic, that was her pet name for him.

"Hello?"

"I know about Lionel."

The voice was unfamiliar. Harry wasn't even certain if it was male or female.

"I beg your pardon?"

"Lionel Jakes. I know."

Harry Wilder felt his mouth go dry. His tongue began to swell.

"Who is this?"

"Don't tell me you've forgotten, Harry? Lovely Lionel? The way his cock felt in your mouth? The taste of his cum?"

"Jesus." Harry spluttered. "How do you . . . ? We were children, for God's sake. Little boys. It was fifty years ago. I'm a happily married man."

Laughter. "Your wife knows about Lionel, does she? And Mark Gannon?"

Harry Wilder felt a painful tightening in his chest. *Who was this person? How could they possibly know about Mark? He'd been dead for twenty years.*

"What do you want?"

When the voice told him, Harry was incredulous.

"That's it? That's all? You don't want money?"

But the line had already gone dead.

Staring down at his empty bowl, he felt the familiar ache of hunger gnawing in the pit of his stomach.

"Mi piang por." It's not enough.

His four cell mates began rattling their spoons against their bowls in protest. Their normal ration of rice—one full bowl at breakfast and another in the afternoon—had been cut by two-thirds with no explanation for the second day running.

"Gla'p maa!" Get back! the Thai guard barked, and the men cowered back like dogs, their teeth bared but their backs arched in submission.

They were all white, all five of them. Samut Prakan Prison was full of child sex offenders, but the white men received the roughest treatment and had to be segregated from the other prisoners. This was good, because it meant they were five to a cell and not eight or ten like the

Thais, who stank. *Revolting animals.* On the other hand, he suspected the whites were last in the food line. Getting the poorer-quality stew was bearable. Being starved of rice was not.

He closed his eyes and thought about America. Happier days. At other times, when he'd been fed, he allowed his mind to wander back to the Blackwell twins. Sweet Eve and uptight Alexandra. How perfect they'd been as young girls. How smooth, how tiny. He thought about the girl Lexi, Alex's daughter. Thanks to Federico, that wetback pussy, he never got to rape her. Not fully. Of course, there'd been hundreds of little girls since then: Thais, Burmese, Singaporian, all adorable, squealing virgins. But he still felt robbed.

I wanted that girl. She was promised to me. Three million dollars, and little Lexi with her thighs spread wide. And what did I get? Second-degree burns and the FBI up my ass.

Now, though, all he could think about was food. Like the pink elephants in *Fantasia*, the images danced through his brain: cheeseburgers dripping with ketchup and fat, chili, fried onions, marshmallows dipped in chocolate and peanut butter . . .

"Effing nips. They're trying to bloody kill us."

Barry, the most cadaverous of his cell mates, had deep sunken brown eyes and skin like paper hanging from his caved-in cheekbones. Barry was British, and referred to all Asians indiscriminately as "nips."

"I can't take much more of this. GIVE US OUR FUCKING RICE, YOU BASTARDS!"

Barry ran his spoon along the bars of the cell, shrieking and yelling like a madman.

Stupid fool. He's going to earn us all a beating.

The guard returned. He winced and covered his head, waiting for the inevitable blows to rain down. But instead, to his astonishment, a cauldron of broth was wheeled into the cell. The guards withdrew, leaving it there.

For a second, all five men stood frozen, staring at the steaming food as if it were a mirage. Dumplings bobbed on the surface amid a thin smattering of noodles. It smelled faintly of chicken, more strongly of cabbage. Then they moved as one toward the pot.

Someone called, "Don't spill it!" Then ten hands plunged into the boiling liquid. He fought like an animal for his share, cramming noodles and thin wisps of meat past his shriveled lips, reveling in the salty broth that scalded his tongue and fingers. When nothing but liquid was left, he grabbed his bowl and the others followed suit, gulping down every last drop into their distended, rice-deprived bellies.

In less than a minute, it was all gone. He crawled back to his corner, exhausted and, for a short, blissful moment, sated.

At first, he thought it was just cramps. He often got pains after a meal here, especially if rations had been scarce. But then he felt a stab so violent it made him cry out, as if someone were grinding razor blades into his appendix.

He looked across the cell at Barry. He was on his knees, vomiting.

Bam! Another razor blade. *What the . . . ?* His back went into spasms, arching so violently it felt as if his neck would snap. Soon his entire body was jumping, contorting in a grotesque dance of death conducted by an invisible cattle prod that delivered shock after shock after shock.

They've poisoned us! The bastards have poisoned us!

He opened his mouth to call for help and a volcano of blood and vomit poured out of it. He heard shouts. The little Thai guards came running toward the cell, their short legs pounding the concrete in panicked stampede. Then a red mist came down and everything was quiet.

In the prison kitchen, the new pot scrubber waited till all the cooks had gone.

Something terrible's happening in the cells. Do you hear that? Let's go take a look.

Then he slipped out of the back door, as quiet and unnoticed as a cockroach, and climbed into the rear of a delivery truck.

Two minutes later the truck bumped through the prison gates, out onto the bustling streets of Bangkok. At the first intersection, the pot scrubber opened the doors and jumped out, disappearing into the maze of alleys and courtyards that he had known from boyhood.

When he was sure he was alone, he reached into his pocket and pulled out a cell phone.

Lexi stared at August Sandford in disbelief.

"I don't understand it. How did this happen?"

August bit his tongue. *Which part? The Internet division getting its budget tripled overnight? Or me being kicked off the team?*

Out loud he said: "I don't know. Harry Wilder got the budget changes past the board. Then he quit, appointed Jim Bruton to head up the team with Tabitha as VP. Next thing I know, I'm booted into the real-estate division."

"But it doesn't make any sense. You were the best-qualified person in that division."

Tell me about it.

"Doesn't it? I think it makes perfect sense to your cousin. Max is not my number one fan. He's been guaranteed a place in the Internet division when you guys graduate. Did you know that?"

Lexi didn't know. There was only one associate-level job available in the Internet division. *Her* job.

"Apparently you're scheduled to start in real estate. With me."

It took Lexi less than forty-five seconds to reach her father's office. Bursting in, too angry to speak, she began signing at Peter at a hundred miles an hour.

"What the hell are you playing at, cooking up a deal with Max behind my back?"

Peter played dumb. "Slow down, darling. No one's cooked up anything."

"You signed off on the Internet budget increase!"

Peter shrugged. "Harry Wilder made a strong case."

"It wasn't Harry's case, it was Max's. He wants to make a whole bunch of acquisitions, companies that he knows *nothing* about. It's madness. Wilder and the others are only backing him because they think he's going to be chairman."

Peter was silent. He'd made no secret of the fact that he did not want Lexi to take over Kruger-Brent. Had things been different with Robert, maybe he could have assumed the mantle one day. That was what Kate Blackwell had wanted. But Robert had chosen his own path. The idea of Lexi taking his place filled Peter with horror. She'd already been through so much. She had no idea what Kruger-Brent really was: a monster, a curse that swallowed people whole. Kate Blackwell had been consumed by it. Her son, Tony, was driven mad. Peter's own hopes and dreams had been sacrificed to the monster, for Alex's sake. But he wanted something better for Lexi. A normal life, a husband, children.

Lexi, however, had other ideas.

"August Sandford told me you've guaranteed Max a job in Internet. Is that true?"

Peter looked uncomfortable. "It was Jim Bruton's decision."

"You're the *chairman*, Dad. You *knew* that's where I wanted to work. They've dumped me in real estate, a total dead end."

"Listen, darling—"

"No, Dad. *You* listen. Just because *you* don't want me to become chairman, you think you and Max can bury me in real estate. Well, screw you and your little boys' club. It's because I'm a woman, isn't it?" Lexi was furious. "This is such *bullshit*. Kate Blackwell was a woman and she was the best chairman Kruger-Brent ever had."

"She was," Peter murmured. It couldn't be denied. "Master of the game. That's what people used to call her."

"Mistress," Lexi shot back. "*Mistress* of the game. Which is exactly what I'm going to be, whatever you or Max or any of the other sexist pigs around here think."

Peter watched her go, a whirlwind of righteous indignation, slamming his office door behind her.

She's so like Kate, he thought.

His heart was filled with foreboding.

Outside in the corridor, Lexi forced herself to take deep, calming breaths.

Real estate? Why not accounting? Why not the goddamn mail room?

The real-estate division was known to be one of Kruger-Brent's sleepier businesses. If there was a fiery center to the company, real estate was as far removed from it as it was possible to be.

Max thinks he can bury me alive in there with August. Out of sight, out of mind.

We'll see about that.

Lexi's cell vibrated in her pocket. New message, sender unknown. She read the four words on the screen. Suddenly nothing else mattered. Not Max, not Kruger-Brent, not anything.

She bolted into the ladies' room, walking straight into a cubicle and locking the door. Only when she knew she was alone did she read the text again, allowing her eyes to linger on the most beautiful sentence she had ever read:

The pig is dead.

Lexi's knees gave way and she slumped onto the toilet seat, tears streaming down her face. For years she'd allowed herself to believe that she'd shaken off the ghosts of her childhood, and the terrible things that had happened to her. Now she saw this for the fantasy it was. The pain would always be there. Always.

There could be no closure. Not in this lifetime.

Only vengeance.

Lexi savored its sweetness for a few precious moments. Then she dried her tears, erased the text from her phone and walked back to her office as if nothing had happened.

NINETEEN

⁓

CAPE TOWN WAS UTTERLY UNLIKE ANYTHING GABE MC-Gregor had ever seen.

After a twelve-hour economy-class flight on SAA that was a circus in itself—a family of eleven tried to bring a crate of live chickens on board as hand luggage, and several grown men fell asleep in the aisles—Gabe emerged bleary-eyed into the arrival hall at Cape Town International Airport to begin the new millennium not just on a new continent, but in a new world. People of every different race and creed swarmed the marble concourse like multicolored ants. Men in traditional African robes and women balancing brightly woven blankets or earthenware on their heads mingled with Asian businessmen in bespoke suits. Half-naked street children skipped around the luggage carousel alongside towheaded American kids dressed head to toe in Ralph Lauren, visiting Cape Town with their parents for the glitzy millennium New Year's parties. Unpleasant, sour smells of sweat and travel were overlaid by the sweet coconut scent of shea butter, expensive aftershave and the delicious, barbecue tang of boerewors, the traditional Cape Dutch sausages sold by vendors outside. Every one of Gabe's senses was assailed by something new.

I wonder if this is what it felt like for Jamie McGregor all those years ago. Stepping off his boat, the Walmer Castle, *onto a wharf of unfamiliar sights and sounds.*

Like Jamie, Gabe had never been away from home before. Unless you counted three days in St. Tropez, or family holidays on the Isle of Mull in an RV when he was eight (Gabe didn't). Both men had come to South Africa to make their fortunes, determined to love the country, to make it their home.

Soon all these sights and sounds and smells will seem normal to me. I have Africa in my blood, after all.

"I hate sodding Africa. I want to go home."

Gabe was slumped on a bar stool in an Irish pub in Camps Bay. *Did they have Irish pubs on the moon yet? Probably. At least one McGinty's.* He'd been in Cape Town for a week, during which time he'd been mugged at gunpoint, had his wallet and passport stolen, developed a mysterious stomach bug that had him on his knees over the toilet bowl every night, and failed to find a place to live. Oh, and had every square inch of his white Scottish skin bitten to death by mosquitoes the size of small bats.

"Why don't you, then?"

The girl was American. A brunette with merry green eyes and a full, womanly body that Gabe couldn't take his eyes off of. After eight years in prison, he'd learned an even deeper appreciation of the female form, and this girl's form was exquisite.

She introduced herself as Ruby.

"Why don't you go home?"

"I can't." Gabe hoped he wasn't blushing. Christ, she was gorgeous. "I only just got here. I can't go home till I'm rich enough to pay everybody back."

"You're not rich, then?"

"Not yet."

"Why d'you hate Africa?"

"How long have you got?" Gabe locked his gray eyes onto Ruby's green ones and decided he hated Africa a lot less than he did two minutes ago. "Let me buy you a drink and I'll tell you about it."

They chatted for more than hour. Ruby was from Wisconsin. She'd come to Cape Town ten years ago to model.

"Ten *years* ago? How old were you then? Six?"

Ruby smiled. "I was thirteen. I quit the business at seventeen."

"Why?"

"Too old."

Gabe roared with laughter.

"And too short. At seventeen, your growing days are over."

Gabe glanced down at her endless legs.

"You realize there are NBA pros shorter than you? Hell, there are probably apartment buildings shorter than you."

Ruby laughed, a low throaty chuckle that made Gabe want to rip her clothes off there and then. He told her his own story, leaving out the part about living with a string of older women. No need to *completely* shoot himself in the foot. But everything else was the truth: his addiction, prison, Marshall Gresham, his family connections to South Africa.

"You're related to *the* Jamie McGregor? Kruger-Brent? You're not putting me on?"

"I swear on my mother's life. Don't get the wrong idea, though. I'm not from the Blackwell side of the family. My lot got nothing. That's why I'm here—to make my own fortune."

Gabe told Ruby about his ambitions for a career in real estate.

"I might be able to help you there. A friend of mine, a guy named Lister, is a developer out in Franschloek. He's still relatively small-scale, but I know he's on the lookout for a partner."

Gabe's eyes danced with excitement. *At last! A contact. A start.*

Ruby's hand was on his leg. Her eyes were on the bulge in his jeans.

Gabe blushed. "Sorry. It's been a long time."

Ruby grinned. He was even better-looking when he got flustered. "No need to apologize on my account." She downed the last of her drink. "Let's go to bed."

Gabe lived with Ruby for six months, the happiest six months of his life. Ruby introduced him to her friend Damian Lister, a local architect-turned-developer, and the two men hit it off instantly. Damian was tall and rake thin with a prominent nose and Adam's apple. He reminded Gabe of a Dr. Seuss drawing come to life. Luckily for Gabe, Damian was a soccer fan, which helped break the ice. They talked about Celtic's lackluster performance this season, and whether Ashley Cole deserved his place on the Arsenal squad, and suddenly they were old friends. Damian's own brother, Paul, had spent five years inside for embezzlement, so Damian was relaxed about Gabe's criminal record.

"We all make mistakes. The important thing is to learn from them. You've clearly learned from yours."

Damian Lister was developing a new residential estate in Franschloek, a popular wine-route town and tourist destination about an hour outside Cape Town. He'd done well on similar investments in Stellenbosch and Bellville, both local commuter towns.

"My problem is the bloody banks, you know? The rand's on the upswing, but they're still so cautious about lending, even to someone with a track record like mine."

"Why not borrow from a foreign bank?" Gabe asked. "I'm sure the Americans would finance you."

"I could," Damian agreed. "But I prefer to have a partner. Someone who I know and trust. Someone who won't pull the rug out from under me as soon as the blacks start kicking off again, making our economy look unstable."

The one negative thing about Damian was his racist way of talking. Gabe put it down to his culture and upbringing. You couldn't wipe out centuries of prejudice overnight.

Besides, it's a terrific stroke of luck for me that he wants a partner. With his local knowledge and contacts, I'll get a far bigger return on Marshall's money than I would on my own.

Gabe spent his days on-site at Franschloek, overseeing the construction, while Damian stayed in his Cape Town office, managing the finances. Gabe loved watching the development take shape, running his hands lovingly over the bricks and mortar that were going to make his fortune. Marshall had taught him so much, but it had all been book learning. This was the real deal. It filled Gabe with an exhilaration almost as strong as a heroin rush.

At night, Gabe went home to Ruby. She would cook them something simple, steak and salad or oven-baked fish with rosemary roast potatoes, and they would eat on the terrace of her light-filled apartment overlooking the ocean. After a glass or two of Cape wine, usually Stellenbosch, they would talk for hours about their lives, hopes and dreams. Ruby said little about her past. She talked only vaguely of her family, in broad brushstrokes. After a few weeks, Gabe realized that, despite all their talks, he knew almost nothing about the minutiae of Ruby's daily life when he wasn't with her. She was an art dealer and spoke about wanting to open a gallery in Spain one day. But Gabe never saw any paintings or heard her take a business call.

When he pressed her for more details, Ruby laughed and asked him:

"Does it matter? I live in the moment. The now. When I'm with you, you and I are all that matters. It's the key to happiness."

Making love to her on the beach under the stars, Gabe began to believe it. So what if he didn't know what galleries she represented or the name of her first dog? Ruby was the most loving, sensual, incredible woman he had ever met. She had transformed South Africa from a nightmare into a dream. He should be grateful, not pestering her with questions.

The one-hour drive from Cape Town to Franschloek in the morning was the best part of Gabe's day. Rattling through the mountains and vineyards in his ancient Fiat Punto—determined not to waste a penny of Marshall's money, Gabe had bought himself the cheapest car he could find—he never failed to be moved by the breathtaking scenery. Franschloek means "French corner," named after the persecuted French Huguenots who first settled its steep slopes over three hundred years ago. They brought with them a culture and cuisine for which the town was still famous. Being a Scot, Gabe knew little of either culture or cuisine, but he still felt an affinity with the Huguenots. Like him, they were outcasts, come to this strange, distant place to make a fresh start. Most lunchtimes Gabe sat and ate his sandwich by the Huguenot monument at the top of the village. Main Street was packed with enticing coffee shops and restaurants offering some of the best food in the country, but Gabe always packed his own lunch. Until he had paid everyone back—Marshall, Claire, Angus Frazer—he had no right to indulge in luxuries.

This morning, Gabe parked the Punto as usual at the top of main street and walked the six blocks to his and Damian's development. They were building eight "executive homes," comfortable, ranch-style houses with pools and grassy backyards. *The kind of house I wish I'd grown up in.* Gabe knew it was foolish to feel an emotional attachment to a business venture. But now that they were starting to take shape, he was proud of the homes he and Lister were creating. He could picture the families who would live there, protected by the magnificent mountains on either side of them, secure within the strong, solid walls that Gabe had built.

I hope they're happy.

Turning the corner into the construction site, Gabe stopped. For a moment he just stood there, blinking, as if his eyes were deceiving him.

The place was deserted. What should have been a hive of activity—men, drills, cement mixers, trucks full of gravel spinning their wheels in the summer mud—had been transformed into a desolate wasteland. It wasn't simply that no one was working. All the equipment was gone. The piles of sand and bricks. Even the foreman's office had been dismantled. All that was left were eight half-finished shells of buildings, their skeletal beams stretching up hopelessly toward the blue African sky.

Gabe's first thought was: *We've been robbed.*

He pulled out his cell phone, then remembered he hadn't charged it. He had to call Damian. And the police. Sprinting to the nearest house, Gabe knocked on the door, breathless, his heart pounding. A woman answered in a bathrobe.

"I'm sorry to disturb you so early. But could I possibly use your phone? It's an emergency."

The woman was middle-aged with short-cropped, bleached hair and a once-pretty face grown tired with the drudgery of motherhood. She looked at the Adonis-in-distress on her front porch and cursed the fact that she had not yet had time to put on her makeup. Straightening her hair and sucking in her belly, she gestured for Gabe to come in.

"I know you, don't I? I mean I've seen you around. You're the site manager of those Lister Homes."

Gabe nodded distractedly, looking for the phone. "I'm afraid we've been robbed. The site has been stripped bare."

The woman looked at him curiously. "But that was *your* guys," she said. "I thought it was strange, them showing up for work on a Sunday."

"My guys were here yesterday?"

"Yah, crack of dawn, with a load of trucks. My husband went out to complain, about the noise, you know? The foreman told him you and your partner had gone bankrupt and skipped town. They had six weeks of wages owing, so they took what they could carry and left." She pronounced it "lift."

Gabe felt weak at the knees. He sank down into an armchair and tried to think.

Why would they think we'd gone bankrupt? And why didn't Jonas, the foreman, call me?

Then he remembered his dead phone. He'd been unreachable all weekend. Ruby had persuaded him to accompany her on a boat trip and to leave his phone behind. It would just be the two of them, living in the moment. "The now," as Ruby liked to call it in that cute New Age

American way of hers. They swam and fished and made love. It was a magical weekend.

Gabe dialed Damian's office number. There had obviously been some terrible misunderstanding.

After six rings, an automated voice announced dully: "The number you have called has been disconnected."

Panic rising in his chest, Gabe called Damian's cell. A single, long, no-such-number beep rang in his ears. He called the apartment, hoping to catch Ruby, but she wasn't home. He pictured their white cordless phone on the coffee table, ringing forlornly in the empty living room, and suddenly felt ineffably sad. Ruby's cell was switched off, too. Not knowing what else to do, Gabe finally contacted the police.

"And this is Gabriel McGregor I'm speaking to, is it?" The desk sergeant sounded excited, almost disbelieving, as if Gabe were some sort of celebrity.

"Yes, I've told you. I'm calling from a house across the street. My properties have been robbed, my partner seems to have gone missing—"

"Just stay where you are, Mr. McGregor. Someone will be with you very shortly, I promise."

While Gabe was on the phone, the lady of the house put on some lipstick and changed into a pair of frayed denim shorts and a pink Labatt's Beer T-shirt that showed her nipples. Gabe didn't even register the changes. She made him a cup of hot, sweet tea, which he drank, his mind racing. After what seemed like an age, the doorbell rang.

"That'll be the police," said the woman.

"Thank God." Gabe got to his feet. Four uniformed officers walked into the living room. He extended his hand in greeting. "Boy, am I happy to see you."

"The feeling's mutual, mate," said the senior officer.

He slapped a pair of handcuffs onto Gabe's wrists.

Only a series of miracles kept Gabe out of prison for a second time.

Detective Inspector Hunter Richards, the officer in charge of the case, saw something in Gabriel McGregor's sad gray eyes that he trusted. The lad had been a fool. He'd lost millions of rand, played straight into Damian Lister's hands. But DI Richards did not believe he had intended to defraud anyone, even if he was an ex-con. The Franschloek locals spoke glowingly of Gabe's character. As the investigation continued, and more and more victims of con artists Ruby Frayne and

Damian Lister came to light, the case against Gabe gradually began to unravel.

Ruby and Damian had been lovers and partners for over a decade. There was no art dealership, no imprisoned brother, no wholesome, small-town family back in Wisconsin. Every ounce of Gabe's happiness during the last six months had been built on lies. It was his first taste of the betrayal his London girlfriends must have felt when they discovered he was using them for their money. The irony was not lost on Gabe.

Not everyone was convinced of Gabe's innocence. For a terrifying few months, he lived with the threat of prosecution hanging over him. But any court case was going to be lengthy and expensive. In the end, the police decided it would be more cost-effective to focus on Lister and Frayne. At the end of the day, they were the ones with the money. Gabe had nothing.

The day the case against Gabe was formally dropped, he went back to the bar where he'd first met Ruby and drank himself unconscious. Even after everything that had happened, he still missed her. He couldn't help it. When he woke the next morning, he was lying in the street, laid out next to the trash cans like a lump of human refuse. Someone had stolen his shoes. There was nothing else to take.

This is it. Rock bottom. I can go back to the drugs, back to the streets. Or I can pick myself up and fight back.

It wasn't an obvious choice. Gabe was tired of fighting, tired to his bones. He blamed himself entirely for what had happened.

I can't become like my father, blaming other people for my own misfortunes. It's my own stupidity that got me here.

But in the end, Gabe told himself, he didn't have an option. Too many people had believed in him, Marshall Gresham most of all. What right did he have to give up before he had paid his debts? Until then, Gabe reasoned, his life was not his own to throw away.

I'll pay Marshall back. Then *I'll decide if I've anything left to live for.*

The first year was hell. Marshall Gresham generously assured Gabe he was in no rush to get his money back, but Gabe's own pride drove him on. He *had* to start earning money. With his record, no one was going to give him a white-collar job in real estate. His only option was manual labor, working on construction sites till he earned enough money to get back into developing.

I've done it before and I can do it again. I'm not afraid of hard work.

But this wasn't London. It was Africa. Nothing had prepared Gabe for the backbreaking work, hauling bricks and mixing cement in the hundred-degree heat, bitten to death by mosquitoes and sand flies. Often he found he was the only white man on a crew, which was lonely and dispiriting. The blacks all spoke Swahili to one another, laughing and joking as they lifted huge slabs of stone with no more effort than a mother lifting a baby. Gabe had always considered himself strong and physically fit. But at thirty, with a white man's muscle tone, he was no match for the nineteen-year-old local boys. Every night he crawled back to his filthy single-room apartment on Kennedy Road and collapsed on the bed, his body screaming with pain. For the first six months, before his skin hardened, Gabe's hands would blister and bleed so badly he looked like he had stigmata. Worst of all was the loneliness. It followed him everywhere, like a stalker, even into his dreams at night. Sometimes he could go an entire week without talking to anyone other than the foreman who paid him his wages. Gabe had to make a conscious effort not to slide into depression and despair.

I got through heroin. I got through prison. I can get through this.

And slowly, as the months rolled into years, he did get through it. Giving up drinking was the first step, not so much a choice as a physical necessity. Gabe's body was already stretched to the limits of endurance. There was no way he could work with a hangover. With the booze out of his system, he started sleeping better. His mood and energy levels began, imperceptibly, to lift. Once he raised his head and smiled at the black men working beside him, he found that they were not so standoffish after all. The thought struck him that perhaps it was *he* who had kept himself isolated, not them.

He made friends with a man named Dia Ghali. Dia was a joker, sunny-natured, with a deep, booming laugh that erupted frequently and incongruously from his skinny body. Dia was a foot shorter than Gabe, and as black as Gabe was white. Standing side by side, they looked like a comedy act. But Dia was every bit as serious as Gabe about making something of his life.

"I grew up in Pinetown. You know what happened last week, in the street where I lived? A baby girl, four months old, was killed by a rat. *Killed*. By a *rat*."

Gabe looked suitably horrified.

"The city refuses to collect the trash so the bloody rats are everywhere. They say the shack dwellers are 'illegals' and not entitled to services. As if we *choose* to live that way. Well, it's not happening to my child. No way. I'm getting out."

By pooling his money with Dia, Gabe was at last able to afford to move out of his single room. Together the two men rented a minuscule two-bedroom apartment downtown. It was a shoe box, but it felt like the Ritz.

"You know what we should do?" Gabe emerged from his first hot shower in a year and a half to find Dia watching cricket on their second-hand TV. "We should go into business for ourselves, in Pinetown. That's the problem in South Africa. There are shantytowns and mansions, but nothing in between. Low-cost, cooperative housing my friend. It's the future."

Dia nodded absently. "Fine. But you know what we should do first?"

"What?"

"Get laid."

Gabe hadn't had a woman since Ruby. Alcohol had deadened his libido. Since he gave up drinking, he'd begun, slowly, to notice women again. But he was too poor, and too exhausted, to spare much thought for dating. Cruising the bars of the Victoria and Albert Waterfront with Dia, watching the girls in their miniskirts and heels dolled up for a night out, Gabe felt like a tortoise emerging from hibernation. His first few attempts to chat up women were met with blunt rejection.

Gabe couldn't understand it. He'd always found flirting so easy.

"It's because you're with me," Dia told him. "Women don't trust a white guy who hangs out with a native."

"A *native*?" Gabe laughed. "Come on, Dia. Apartheid's been over for years."

Dia raised an eyebrow. "Really? Where have you been the past two years, brother? In a cave?"

He was right. Glancing around, Gabe saw that none of the groups hanging around the Waterfront were of mixed race. Whites and blacks might frequent the same stores and bars, but they each stuck with their own. Gabe thought of his ancestor Jamie McGregor and his lifelong friendship with Banda, a native revolutionary. A hundred and fifty years had passed since those days. *But how much has really changed?*

Happily, Dia was not in the mood for philosophizing. "Check out that honey standing by the fountain." He pointed out a tall, slender black girl in tight jeans and a sequined vest. When she looked up and saw him staring, she smiled.

Dia grinned at Gabe. "You're on your own, my friend. Don't wait up."

The black girl's name was Lefu. Less than a year later, Dia married her.

"Quit complaining," Dia told Gabe as he taped up the last of his boxes. He and Lefu were moving into their own place a few blocks away. "Now your crazy white women can make as much noise as they like through the walls."

Gabe would miss Dia. But it was true, he *could* use the privacy. It hadn't taken him long to rediscover his magic touch when it came to women. Cape Town, he quickly learned, was a mecca for Eastern European models. Girls flocked to join the hot new agencies—Faces, Infinity, Max, Outlaws—taking advantage of South Africa's year-round sunshine and perfect photographic conditions. Gabe McGregor made it his personal mission—more like his Christian duty—to ensure that the poor things didn't get too homesick.

"I'm providing a free service," he told an envious Dia and disapproving Lefu as yet another Amazonian Czech breezed out of the apartment in hot pants. "Someone has to make the poor loves feel welcome."

Now that Gabe had finally been promoted to foreman, he was working shorter hours and earning good money. He'd already repaid Angus Frazer and everyone who'd loaned him money for his appeal. On his thirty-fourth birthday, he put in a call to Marshall Gresham. Marshall had been released from Wormwood Scrubs the previous Christmas and was now living in splendor in a spanking-new mansion outside Basildon.

Marshall said: "I thought you'd done a runner."

It was a joke, but Gabe was horrified.

"I would never do that. It took me a wee bit longer than I expected to raise the money, that's all. But I've got it, every penny. Where should I send the check?"

"Nowhere."

Gabe was confused.

Marshall said: "I told you five years ago, didn't I? That money's an investment. What I want to know is when are you going to get off your lazy Scottish arse and start a new company?"

Gabe tried not to show how touched he was.

"Even after what happened? You'd still trust me?"

" 'Course I trust you, you wanker. Just don't take on any more dodgy partners."

"Ah. About partners."

Gabe told Marshall about Dia and their plans to develop low-income housing close to the impoverished Pinetown and Kennedy Road areas. Marshall was skeptical.

"Your plan sounds fine. But I don't understand why you need this black fella. What does he bring to the party?"

"He grew up in Pinetown. He knows the area far better than I do. Plus, ninety-eight percent of the population in these dumps is black. I need a black face on the team if I'm going to get the locals to trust me."

Gabe didn't add that Dia's friendship meant more to him than any business. That even if it meant returning Marshall's investment, he would never leave Dia in the lurch. Luckily he didn't have to.

"Fine. You know what you're doing. Call me once you've doubled my money."

Gabe laughed. "I will."

He was back in business.

Gabe and Dia called their new company Phoenix, because it had risen from the ashes of their old lives.

At first, everyone thought they were crazy. Fellow developers laughed in Gabe's face when he told him Phoenix's business plan.

"You're out of your mind. None of the shack dwellers can afford a home. And anyone who *can* afford one isn't going to want to live within twenty miles of those areas."

Others went even further.

"You go home at night, the kaffirs'll torch the place. Those shanty-town kids have got nothing better to do. Who d'you think's going to in-sure you in Pinetown?"

As it turned out, insurance *was* a problem. None of the blue-chip firms would give Phoenix the time of day. Just when Gabe was starting to give up hope, Lefu came to the rescue, introducing Dia to a boyfriend of one of her cousins who worked for an all-black building insurance agency in Johannesburg.

"The premiums are high." Dia handed Gabe the quote.

"*High?*" Gabe read the number and felt faint. "This guy must have *been* high when he came up with this rate. Tell him we'll pay half."

"Gabe."

"All right, two-thirds."

"Gabriel."

"What?"

"It's our only option. He's doing this as a favor to Lefu. As a friend."

"With friends like him, who needs enemies?" Gabe grumbled.

They paid the full rate.

By the end of their first year, Phoenix was 700,000 rand in the red. They had built thirty small, simple prefab houses with running water and electricity and sold none. Gabe lost fifteen pounds and took up smoking. Dia, with one baby at home and a second on the way, remained inexplicably upbeat.

'They'll sell. I'm working on it. Give me time."

Gabe had worked out a financial model for shared ownership that he knew a number of the shanty families could afford. The problem was that none of them believed it.

"You have to understand," Dia explained. "These people have been lied to by white men their entire lives. Many of them think it was white doctors who first spread AIDS here."

"But that's ridiculous."

"Not to them. They think you're trying to steal their money. The idea that they could afford a home—never mind a home with water and a roof that doesn't leak—it's totally alien to them. You may as well tell them you've found a way for them to live forever, or that you can turn horse manure into gold."

"So what do we do?"

"*You* do nothing. Go away for a few weeks, take a vacation. Show one of your Polish teenagers something other than your bedroom ceiling for a change."

Gabe shook his head. "No way. I can't leave the business, not now."

"I'm not asking you, I'm telling you," said Dia. "Bugger off. I know what I'm doing."

Gabe spent two weeks at Muizenberg, a local beach resort, with a girl named Lenka. Once the site of a famous battle between the British and the Dutch, Muizenberg was now the go-to resort for affluent Capetonians, an African version of the Hamptons.

"Gorgeous!" Lenka gasped as they strolled past the Victorian mansions on the promenade.

"Gorgeous!" she enthused, taking in the wide sandy beaches and turquoise water of False Bay.

"Gorgeous!" she cooed, when a spaniel puppy bounded up to Gabe on the beach and promptly urinated on his deck shoes.

After two days, Gabe was climbing the walls. One more "gorgeous" and he'd be forced to try to hang himself with the hotel sheets.

I will never, ever go on vacation again with a girl with the IQ of a dog turd. Even if she does look like a movie star.

Muizenberg was dull. Deathly dull. But it could have been one of the Seven Wonders of the World and Gabe would still have hated it. His mind had never left Pinetown.

The morning he got back to Cape Town, he raced to the office. He hadn't felt so nervous since the day he stood in the dock at Walthamstow, waiting to be sentenced.

"So?" he asked Dia breathlessly. "Did you make any progress?"

"A little."

Gabe's heart sank. *A little? They didn't need a little. They needed a bloody miracle. He'd have to give up the apartment. Move back to Kennedy Road. Or perhaps the time had come to go* home *home? To admit defeat and go back to Scotland? There was no work at the docks, but maybe . . .*

"I sold them all."

It took a moment for Dia's words to sink in.

"But . . . I don't . . . how . . . but . . ."

Dia teased him. "You know, after two weeks away, I'd forgotten how articulate you can be."

"You . . . but . . . *all* of them?"

"Every last one."

"How?"

"Faith, my friend. Faith."

Gabe looked at him blankly. Dia explained.

"I went to see the pastor at my old church and asked if he would let me speak there. He wasn't keen at first, but I persuaded him. Church meetings around here are packed."

"What did you say?"

"The same thing you've been saying, but in their voice. I talked about my own childhood. About the kids I knew who died as a direct result of the appalling living conditions, the lack of sanitation. I tried to let them know that I've been where they are, that I'm one of them. People started asking questions. From then on, it was easy. I talked them through your model, explained the financing. The next day I moved to another parish, then another.

"I actually sold the last unit three days ago. But I figured it could keep. I didn't want to ruin your holiday with the lovely Lenka."

Gabe thought about the nightmarish last few days in Muizenberg and didn't know whether to laugh or cry.

"Aren't you going to say something?"

Striding over to Dia, Gabe picked him up in a huge bear hug and danced around the room, whooping for joy.

"Gorgeous!" He laughed. "Dia Ghali, you are bloody gorgeous!"

TWENTY

∞

THE DAWN OF THE NEW MILLENNIUM USHERED IN A PEriod of great change in the business world. Companies that had once been seen as untouchable giants began to disintegrate, outpaced by minuscule dot-com start-ups. Greed was still the name of the game. But the *rules* of the game had changed.

On April 8, 1999, former housewares salesman Craig Winn became a billionaire . . . for a day or two. When his three-year-old Internet startup, Value America, went public, the stock price veered wildly from $23 a share to almost $75 a share, before settling at $55. The forty-five-year-old Winn went to bed that night with a paper fortune of $2.4 billion. Not bad for a company that had never made a profit—and never would.

Within a year, the share price had fallen to two dollars. Over half of Value America's employees had been fired and investors had lost millions. In August 2000, the company filed for bankruptcy.

In boardrooms across America, CEOs of what were now termed "old-economy" companies—giants like Kruger-Brent—watched these developments with dismay. Everything was changing. While the dot-com boom burned itself out in a spectacular fireball of ignorance and greed, the sands of world power were also shifting. China and India were on the up. The dollar began to falter. In investment banking and pharmaceuticals, two of Kruger-Brent's key profit sectors, companies were merging and acquiring one another faster than the analysts could keep up. In banking, many of the great names of the 1980s—Salomon Brothers, Bankers Trust, Smith Barney—disappeared literally overnight, swallowed up by bigger, often foreign, rivals. In pharmaceuticals, the likes of Glaxo and Ciba faded as new brands like Aventis and Novartis emerged. In car manufacturing, Ford went on an acquisition spree, buying Volvo and Mazda and Aston Martin, then turned on a dime and began selling, first Jaguar then Land Rover. Meanwhile, the prices of oil and land—real estate—continued to rise like floodwater. Every year, every month, economists predicted a correction, but it never seemed to come. Banks fell over themselves to offer cheap credit, pouring gas onto the flames of an already overheated market.

They were exciting times. And dangerous times. For Peter Templeton, it was all too much. In 2006, he retired quietly to Dark Harbor, alone at last with the memories of his beloved Alexandra. His departure caused barely a ripple in the market. Everybody knew that Peter had never been more than a puppet chairman of Kruger-Brent. Tristram Harwood quietly took the helm and corporate life continued much as before.

As head of Kruger-Brent's oil-and-gas division, Tristram Harwood had spent the past decade playing solitaire on his computer while his group's assets quadrupled in value. He applied the same sit-back-and-do-nothing philosophy to his chairmanship. After all, it was only going to last for three years.

In three years' time, the two Blackwell heirs, Max Webster and Lexi Templeton, turned twenty-five. According to the terms of Kate Blackwell's will, twenty-five was the age when one of them would take control of Kruger-Brent.

The general assumption was that that person would be Max.

But in the new economic world order, assumptions were made to be broken.

Within a week of starting work in the Internet division, Max knew he had made a mistake. During the summer of his and Lexi's last internships, it had looked like the Internet sector was about to enter into a second period of rapid growth. Real estate, by contrast, was long overdue a correction. This combined with the fact that it had always been one of Kruger-Brent's least dynamic businesses was what had prompted him to railroad Lexi into it.

Unfortunately, by the time the cousins graduated from business school and joined Kruger-Brent full-time, the market had performed another of its disconcerting backflips. Jim Bruton had done his best to stem the tide of losses. But when Max showed up for his first day at work, Kruger-Brent's Internet division was hemorrhaging money so fast, he was plunged into twenty-four-hour damage control.

Meanwhile, Lexi and August Sandford had galvanized the sleepy real-estate division and were making money hand over fist. Under August's guidance, Kruger-Brent extended its reach into Europe and Asia. While Max was locked away with auditors in a windowless office in Manhattan, Lexi was flying all over the world, to Tokyo, Paris, Hong Kong and Madrid, clinching deal after deal in property. She made sure the press knew about every one of her successes.

Lexi knew that media interest in her could be a double-edged sword. On the one hand, of course, it was flattering. When she was a teenager, paparazzi followed her everywhere. She was America's sweetheart: brave, beautiful and blessed. Her face was on the cover of countless magazines. All across the country, large numbers of baby girls were being christened Alexandra. Lexi could not remember a time when she hadn't been famous. She could not imagine what that might feel like, although she tried: to be anonymous, just another face in the crowd. Sometimes it seemed an appealing prospect.

Lexi was well aware that her fame had almost cost her her inheritance. Max had successfully used it against her, painting her to the Kruger-Brent board members as vacuous and a lightweight. *It girl. Party girl.* They had seemed like innocuous nicknames at first. But when Max outmaneuvered her for the Internet job, Lexi woke up with a jolt to just how damaging they could be.

I already have two strikes against me. I'm deaf. And I'm a woman. Three strikes and I'll be out.

From that day onward, Lexi worked hard to redefine her relationship with the media. Like all American heroines—all the ones who lasted, anyway—she was a mistress at the art of reinvention. Just as Madonna had gone from crucifix-wearing nymphomaniac to patron saint of Kabbalah in a heartbeat, so Party Girl Lexi was erased from America's memory and replaced by a new creation: Businesswoman Lexi. Her face was still on the covers of magazines. But instead of *InStyle* and *Us Weekly*, Lexi now gazed down from newsstands from the cover of *Time* and *Forbes.*

Max tried vainly to raise his own profile, but it was no good. He hadn't been kidnapped as a child. He hadn't fought back bravely after losing his hearing in an explosion. In America's eyes, he was just another rich, handsome trust-fund kid. Lexi was the star of the family, and her star was rising. Suddenly all the goodwill that Max had built up at Kruger-Brent in his teens seemed to count for nothing. Lexi had turned the tables, apparently without even trying. Unless something drastic changed soon, she was on course to become the firm's next chairman.

Antonio Valaperti handed Lexi a solid silver Montblanc pen and watched her sign the contract. A gratified smile spread across his face.

Such a beautiful girl. It's almost a shame to watch her signing away a fortune.

Almost . . .

Antonio Valaperti was the biggest property developer in Rome. Bigger even than the Mob. In his midsixties, with a vulpine face and small, watchful hazel eyes that missed nothing, he liked to boast at dinner parties that the last Roman to own as much of the city as he did was Julius Caesar. Antonio Valaperti had torn down slums and bulldozed churches. He had burrowed deep into the city's ancient earth to build parking garages, and redefined her skyline with his apartment and office buildings. Half of Rome admired him as an innovator and visionary. The other half loathed him as a vandal. Antonio Valaperti was arrogant, brilliant and ruthless. He was tight with money, but enjoyed the good things in life: fine food, fast cars, beautiful women. He did not like Americans. But in the case of Lexi Templeton, he was prepared to make an exception.

"Now that our business is concluded, *bella*, perhaps we can turn our minds to pleasure?"

His eyes crawled over Lexi's body like lice. She was wearing a form-fitting Marchesa suit that did full justice to her voluptuous figure. Her cream silk blouse revealed the merest hint of lace detailing on her bra. Antonio Valaperti thought: *She wants me. I've seen it a thousand times. She's young, but she's turned on by power. Perhaps that's why she's been so foolish with this deal? She's too concerned about getting her pussy licked.*

Lexi watched the old man across the table and suppressed the urge to laugh out loud.

There's no fool like an old fool. He actually thinks I'm attracted to him!

After all the hype about Antonio Valaperti—the way August Sandford talked about him, you'd have thought the man had magical powers—

Lexi was almost disappointed by how easy it had been to outsmart Rome's answer to The Donald. She had just sold Valaperti what *he* believed to be highly valuable land just south of Villa Borghese Park, in one of the city's most upscale residential areas. In fact, the forty-acre parcel was about to become all but worthless. With a few well-placed bribes, and the help of her trusty low-cut blouse—*they should really put my cream silk Stella McCartney on the front page of* Forbes, she thought. *It's saved Kruger-Brent a lot more money on this trip than I have*—Lexi had discovered that all development permits within a kilometer radius of the Spanish Steps were about to be rescinded.

Of course, it never occurred to Antonio Valaperti that an outsider, an *American*, might have greater access to Italy's corridors of power than he had. Especially not this pretty little slip of a girl young enough to be his daughter. Deaf, too, God bless her. Americans really did have some very strange ideas about how to run a business.

"Would that I could, Antonio. Would that I could." Every head in the restaurant of the Hotel Hassler swiveled to watch Lexi as she stood up to leave. "But I'm afraid I have pressing business in Florence tomorrow morning. I must get an early night. Good night."

Antonio Valaperti watched her leave, biting back his irritation.

Little tease. She thinks she's played me. He signaled to the waiter to bring him the check. *When you find out how much that land is really worth, sweetheart, you'll see who's played whom.*

Then you'll know what it feels like to get fucked in the ass by Antonio Valaperti.

At ten o'clock the next morning, Lexi checked in to the Villa San Michele, an idyllic former monastery turned luxury hotel perched high in the Florentine hills.

I love Italy, she thought as she stepped out of her traveling clothes and into the marble-tiled shower. She'd chosen the San Michele because its high walls made it impossible for the paparazzi to disturb her there. For once in her life, Lexi felt in need of a break from all the attention and this was the perfect place to get it. Robbie had told her that Italy was astonishingly beautiful. But not even his elaborate praise had done it justice. Rome was so spectacular Lexi found she was catching her breath at every turn in the road. It was like stepping back in time. But if the Villa San Michele was anything to go by, she had a suspicion she was going to enjoy Tuscany even more.

Her triumph over Valaperti was all the sweeter because August Sandford had been so sure she would fail. Lexi herself had had her doubts. She found lip-reading much harder with foreigners, who formed English words differently, and had even considered traveling to Italy with an interpreter.

*Thank God I didn't. All those cozy dinners-*à-deux *with Valaperti were what clinched us the deal.*

Over the past year, Lexi's relationship with August had thawed, somewhat. She still thought he was arrogant and sexist. He still resented her for being Kate Blackwell's great-granddaughter. But each of them had developed a grudging respect for the other's business skills. August was flying in to Florence that night, and for once Lexi was looking forward to having dinner with him.

Maybe now he'll admit I might actually make a good chairman. That I'm as capable of running Kruger-Brent as he is.

The restaurant at the Villa San Michele spilled out onto a medieval terrace covered with thick vines. From her table, Lexi could see the formal monastery gardens with their box hedges and gravel paths. Beyond the gardens lay the distinctive terra-cotta rooftops of Florence, spread out like a blanket in the warm, rosemary-scented evening air.

It's so romantic! How much nicer it would be to be having dinner with a lover here, instead of my boss.

Lexi felt a tap on her shoulder and spun around. The smile of contentment dissolved on her face.

"What are you doing here? Where's August?"

"In Taiwan, I believe. Something came up. Have you ordered yet? I'm famished."

Max sat down and snapped his fingers imperiously for the waiter. Without looking at the menu, he rattled off his order in flawless Italian. He was speaking too fast for Lexi to make out much of what he said. But she did notice he'd asked for a two-hundred-dollar bottle of Antinori red wine, and that he'd taken it upon himself to choose food for her, too.

Her eyes narrowed. "What are you doing here, Max?"

"We're thinking of buying an online recruitment company." His tone was casual. "Starfish. It's like a European version of Monster.com. They're based out of Florence, believe it or not."

Lexi didn't believe it. *He's up to something.*

Although they lived in the same city and even worked in the same building, it had actually been months since Lexi had seen Max. She traveled constantly. On the rare occasions when she was at Kruger-Brent, she didn't exactly seek out his company. Tonight he was wearing a blue open-necked shirt and black Armani suit pants. He smelled very faintly of an old-fashioned, lemon-ish cologne, and his naturally olive skin was more deeply tanned than usual. She'd forgotten how attractive he was and found herself irritated by it.

"How did it go in Rome? I gather Valaperti is a tough *cantuccini.*"

Part of Lexi would have liked to ignore him. But the urge to boast was too strong.

"It went great. Valaperti was putty in my hands."

"Really?"

"Uh-huh. I sold him that land for over a hundred million dollars."

Leaning in closer, Max signed: "Did he try to sleep with you?"

Lexi looked amazed.

"When did you learn to sign?"

Max shrugged. "I only know a few phrases, but I'm working on it. I figured, you know, we're going to be working together for a while, so I should probably make the effort."

He seems genuine. But why is he being so nice and reasonable all of a sudden?

"So did he?"

"What?"

"Try to sleep with you?"

"No! Well, kind of. Maybe a little bit." Lexi found she was smiling despite herself. "Our friend Antonio evidently thinks of himself as quite the catch."

"How old is he?"

"Sixty-five? Seventy maybe?"

"Dirty old goat."

Lexi was surprised to find she was enjoying herself. Sitting in this divine, romantic spot with her lifelong enemy, the evening seemed to be flying by.

The wine arrived, along with two Tuscan bread salads. Before long, Lexi was happily tipsy. Max kept her amused with stories of doom and gloom in the Internet division.

"The only person who's gonna get a bonus this year is whoever wins the Jim Bruton Divorce Case Sweepstakes. His wife's finally leaving him, and the whole division's put money on how much she'll get."

"That's terrible! Poor man." Lexi giggled.

"Poor man, my ass. He had two kids with another woman and never paid a cent for either of them. When you're chairman, you should fire him."

Lexi sobered up immediately. Had she read his lips correctly?

"What did you say?"

"I said when you're chairman, you should can Jim Bruton. Come on." Max stood up, gallantly offering her his hand. "Let's go inside and talk. It's getting cold out here."

The hotel lounge and bar were both full, so they went back to Lexi's junior suite. Opening onto the gardens, it had its own private terrace as well as a study and separate living room, complete with antique Italian furniture and roaring log fire. Max fixed them both a whiskey from the minibar and sat down on the couch next to Lexi.

"Look. Starfish wasn't the real reason I came here. At least, it wasn't the only reason."

Watching his lips move, Lexi felt a powerful urge to lean forward and kiss them.

I must be drunker than I thought. She put down her whiskey.

"Go on."

"I want to call a truce."

For almost a minute, Lexi was silent. The entire evening had been surreal. August's no-show, Max turning up out of thin air, his uncharacteristic charm offensive. Now he was talking about truces? Finally, she said: "Why?"

Max smiled. "I'm not going to lie to you, Lexi. I want the chairmanship as badly as you do. I always have. But I recognize that's now unlikely to happen." When Lexi didn't respond, he went on. "Kate Blackwell hated my mother. I don't know why, but she did. And I hated her for that, even though she died before I was born."

"Max."

"Let me finish. Because Kate's will tried to lock me out of Kruger-Brent, I felt I had something to prove. I didn't see why I should roll over and let them hand the company to you on a plate."

"Kate's intention was to hand it to Robbie on a plate," Lexi reminded him. "I've had to fight for a seat at the table, too, you know."

"I know. That's why I'm here." Max took her hand in his. His palm was warm and dry. Lexi felt a pulse begin to throb between her legs. It was making it hard to concentrate. She swallowed hard.

Max said: "We're not kids anymore, Lexi. It's time we both stopped acting like kids. Kruger-Brent means everything to me. Everything."

There were tears in his eyes. "If . . . *when* you take control at the company, you're going to have some tough challenges ahead. You're going to need people around you that you can trust."

Trust and *Max* were two words that, until this moment, Lexi had never had cause to put together in a sentence. Was it possible that he really *had* grown up? She wanted to believe it. And yet . . .

"I don't know what to say. That's—that's very generous of you."

"You know our market cap dropped almost twenty percent last year." There was a flash of something that looked like anger in Max's black eyes. "Tristram Harwood's a dinosaur. He has no idea what he's doing, no vision, no game plan."

Lexi nodded quietly. "I know."

"So what do you think? Do you want to try playing on the same team for a change?"

Max's leg was touching hers. Lexi could see the outline of his thigh muscle beneath the thin cotton of his pants, lean and strong.

I think I want to see you naked.

I think I want you in my bed tonight.

I think I definitely had too much wine at dinner.

"Sure." She smiled back at him. "Why not?"

That night in bed, Lexi lay awake, staring at the ceiling. Was Max for real? If anyone had asked her that question twenty-four hours ago, she'd probably have laughed in his face. Her and Max Webster, a team? And yet he did seem sincere. She cast her mind back over the last few months at Kruger-Brent. Max had supported her in that crucial board vote over the new share issue. And he hadn't said a word about her new, larger office space. Was it possible she'd misjudged him? Or was sexual frustration clouding her judgment now?

She'd thought that the roar of her libido would fade once the effects of the alcohol wore off. But now, hours later, her leg still burned from where Max's thigh had brushed against it, and the lemon scent of his cologne lingered deliciously on her skin. *Goddamn him. Why did he have to come here?*

Lexi had had scores of lovers in her life. Perhaps even hundreds. But she realized tonight that none of them meant anything to her. *I never wanted any of them. Not really. Deep down, it's always been Max.*

Closing her eyes, she slowly moved her hands down her warm, naked body. She cupped her breasts, then let her fingertips graze the soft, flat expanse of her belly. Finally, tentatively, she began to stroke the hot, silky wetness between her legs.

She pictured Max's lips moving:

Kruger-Brent means everything to me . . . I want the chairmanship . . . but it's not going to happen.

Her fingers worked faster, more rhythmically.

I've beaten him.

I've won.

She imagined Max on top of her, inside her. She imagined them as one.

Kruger-Brent is mine.

She gasped, her body racked by a series of shudders as the orgasm ripped through her.

Oh God, Max. I want you.

From a pay phone at Taoyuan International Airport in Taiwan, August Sandford bellowed at his secretary.

"It's not good enough, Karen! I flew halfway across the world for this damn meeting, only to have Mr. Li tell me that the stupid hotel is no longer for sale."

"I'm sorry, Mr. Sandford. I don't understand how the wires could have gotten crossed. His secretary confirmed the meeting to me only yesterday. She said they had another bidder and it was vital that you fly out right away."

August slammed down the receiver, too angry to speak. Thanks to this wild-goose chase, he'd had to cancel two important client meetings in Europe, not to mention his rendezvous with Lexi.

Then a strange thought struck him.

His secretary confirmed the meeting . . . she said they had another bidder.

August met with Mr. Li's secretary less than an hour ago.

Mr. Li's secretary was a man.

Eve called Max while he was driving.

"Did you see her?"

"Yes, Mother. I saw her."

"You played it the way we discussed?"

"Yes."

"And? Do you think she trusts you?"

Max thought about this for a moment. He remembered the way that Lexi's pupils had dilated when he took her hand; the heat when their legs had touched. There was something new between them, all right. But he wouldn't necessarily call it trust.

"I think she's starting to."

Eve sensed the hesitation in his voice. She asked him sharply: "You didn't sleep with her, did you?"

"No, Mother. Of course not."

"Good." Eve sounded mollified. "You'll have to eventually, of course. But not yet. It's too soon."

Max hung up feeling uneasy. He pictured his mother pacing their New York apartment in her silk robe, a caged tigress waiting for him to return from the hunt. Things had gone better than he'd expected with Lexi this evening. But still. His discussion with Eve last week was vividly branded in his memory. The tension in her voice, the pent-up rage coiled inside her body, ready to burst through the skin.

It's your last chance, Max. Our last chance! That bitch is going to take Kruger-Brent from us. You have to do *something!*

I will, Mother. Don't worry. I will.

But would he? *Could* he?

What if he failed?

Swerving to the side of the road, he stopped the car and fumbled in the glove box. Pulling out a clear plastic pillbox and a bottle of Jack Daniel's, he swallowed four Xanax, washing them down with the raw, scorching liquor.

I won't fail you, Mother.

I promise.

TWENTY-ONE

IT SEEMED TO LEXI THAT THE NEXT YEAR WENT BY IN A
blink.

She had a natural flair for real estate. Kate Blackwell always believed
that an instinctive feel for a market was worth a hundred MBAs. Lexi
agreed. It wasn't Harvard that had given her a nose for business. Business was in her blood. She lived for the high of clinching deals, thriving
on stress and tension the way that other people thrived on eight hours'
sleep and regular meals. Kruger-Brent's real-estate holdings were enormous and growing all the time. It was such an exciting sector, it was easy
to forget that it was just one of hundreds of industries that the company
was involved in.

As Max's and Lexi's twenty-fifth birthdays moved ever closer,
Kruger-Brent's ten-man board of directors decided that they should both
spend some time learning the ropes of *all* of the company's myriad business areas.

"It's important that you feel intimately familiar with every aspect of
the firm." Tristram Harwood addressed his remarks to the two of them,
but by this point, both Lexi and Max knew that "you" meant Lexi.

"I daresay you feel you've grown up here and that you know the
business inside out. But you might be surprised by just how vast your
empire really is."

"Patronizing old fossil," said Max as they left the office.

"He's pathetic," agreed Lexi. "Our *empire* indeed."

But Tristram Harwood was right. Kruger-Brent *was* an empire. And Lexi *was* surprised. Flying back and forth across the globe like a deranged bat, visiting the company offices in India and Russia, Prague and Hong Kong, Dublin and Dubai, it dawned on her that to run Kruger-Brent she must be more than just a brilliant businesswoman. Much more. She must be a stateswoman. A diplomat. A general. She must lead, of course, but she must also delegate. Kruger-Brent was infinitely too huge to be managed by one human being. For the first time, she saw for herself just how important it would be to have a team of people around her whom she trusted implicitly.

August Sandford. He's a pain in the ass, but I trust August.

And Max, of course.

Since Lexi's return from Italy, there had been a sea change in Max. At work, he was helpful, respectful and relaxed. Where once Lexi would have gone to August Sandford with her problems, she now used Max as a sounding board. When she visited a microchip-manufacturing subsidiary in India and found that the managers there could not understand her when she spoke, despite their fluent English, she was mortified.

They looked at me like I had just landed from Mars. Lexi poured her heart out in a late-night e-mail to Max. *I felt like such a fool. All these years people have been telling me my speaking voice is fine. But it's bullshit. I obviously sounded like a deaf, slurring freak to these guys.*

Max responded calmly. Indian English and American English were not the same thing. They'd probably have looked at him the same way. Lexi should travel with a signing interpreter as well as a regular language interpreter, just in case. No big deal.

It was exactly what Lexi needed to hear.

The sexual tension between them grew daily. Max infuriated Lexi by blowing hot and cold. It was the one element of his character that continued to perplex her. One minute she felt sure he was about to make a move. The next he switched, and started acting all brotherly toward her. Used to men dropping at her feet like flies, Lexi had no idea how to handle Max's hard-to-get routine. She dated other guys—discreetly; now was not the time to reignite the party-girl rumors—but found the sex to be utterly unsatisfying. The thought crossed her mind that she might be in love with her cousin, but she quickly pushed it aside.

I don't have time for love. There's too much to do at Kruger-Brent.

Lexi's world tour opened her eyes to the grievous problems the company was facing. Unquestionably, the biggest issue was size. Kruger-Brent was too big. Under Kate Blackwell's leadership, the firm had swallowed every competitor it came across like Pac-Man, regardless of its fit with the rest of the group's businesses. In the two years before Kate Blackwell's death, Kruger-Brent became the proud owner of a diamond mine in Zaire, a children's book publisher in Scotland, a biotech research firm in Connecticut and a swath of Brazilian rain forest approximately the size of Pennsylvania, to name only four of Kate's scores of acquisitions.

Lexi's great-grandmother had been master of the game of business. But the game had changed.

When I'm chairman, I'll be playing by new rules. We need to be leaner. Fitter. Faster. Or we won't survive.

Lexi knew she wanted to grow the real-estate business. Oil and gas would also be crucial. Her most recent trip to Africa had strengthened her growing belief that the continent, with its wealth of land and natural resources, might well hold the key to Kruger-Brent's future. Just as it had once held the key to its past.

There were fortunes to be made in African land and property. Prices were tripling every year, but most big American firms were losing out, too nervous about the volatile politics and economy to invest in the region. Meanwhile, local conglomerates like the Olam Group and Africa Israel Investments were making out like bandits. In South Africa, what should have been Kruger-Brent's heartland, new companies like Endeavour and Gabriel McGregor's Phoenix were outpacing them, leveraging themselves up to the hilt and audaciously grabbing market share from right under their noses.

Lexi admired Phoenix's brilliantly simple business model. She made a mental note to copy it, then squeeze Gabriel McGregor out of business at the earliest opportunity.

Jamie McGregor built this firm in Africa. He wasn't afraid to take a risk. Nor am I.

The week before Christmas, August Sandford asked Lexi to have lunch with him.

"I never see you these days. Real estate is horribly quiet without you."

Lexi smiled. It was the closest he'd ever come to paying her a compliment. She agreed to lunch the following day.

The concierge at the Harvard Club looked disapprovingly at the group of photographers mobbing Lexi as she emerged from her town car. In a cream cashmere coat from Donna Karan, her famous gray Blackwell eyes covered with oversize Oliver Peoples, she looked every inch the budding tycoon.

"Sorry, John." Lexi smiled. The concierge melted faster than the snowflakes on the sidewalk. "I've been out of town for a few weeks." She nodded toward the paparazzi. "I'm afraid they're worse than usual. Has Mr. Sandford arrived yet?"

"Yes, Ms. Templeton. His usual table."

August watched Lexi as she weaved her way through the other diners toward him. She wore a crisply tailored pantsuit she'd had custom-made in Hong Kong, and looked professional and poised. August thought: *She's grown up.* Though he'd die rather than let her know it, he'd become genuinely fond of Lexi these past two years. His initial, envy-fueled attraction had been replaced by something worryingly close to friendship. August Sandford had never been friends with a woman before. Perhaps that was why this whole thing felt so awkward?

August was not looking forward to today's lunch. He had things to tell Lexi that he knew she wouldn't want to hear. Things that might make him look foolish in her eyes. Or paranoid. Or jealous. Or all three.

Lexi sat down.

"So what's been going on? What've I missed? Did you close the Hammersman deal yet?"

August grinned. He loved the way she cut straight to the chase.

"We did. Yesterday. How was Africa?"

"Interesting. Hot. The food sucked."

"You missed New York?"

"I missed the office. But don't tell anyone."

They ordered food. Lexi could tell August had something on his mind.

"Was there something you wanted to talk to me about?" She took a bite of her turkey club sandwich. After two weeks of boerewors and Mrs. Ball's chutney washed down with rancid rooibos tea, it tasted like manna from heaven.

August bit his lip. "Have you seen Max since you got back?"

"Not yet. Why?"

"It may be nothing." He paused. "It's just . . . some of the things he's been doing recently. Are you sure he's given up all hope of the chairmanship?"

Lexi put down her sandwich.

"Of course I'm sure. What's this about, August?"

"I overheard Max in the men's room a few weeks ago. He was talking to Tristram Harwood, claiming credit for selling one of the online gambling businesses."

"Jester. I know. He sold it to KKR."

"Except he didn't." August took a sip of his iced water. "That was never Max's deal. It was Jim Bruton's."

"Was it?"

"Uh-huh. Jim challenged Max about stealing his thunder. Four days later, he was packing up his desk."

Lexi shrugged. "So? Bruton got canned. What do you care? I thought you hated him."

"I do. That's not the point." August tried a different tack. "Max was supposed to be in Switzerland last month, touring pharmaceuticals. As soon as he heard you'd been sent to Africa, he canceled the trip. He's been in New York the whole time you were gone, playing golf with Harwood and Logan Marshall. He even invited me to dinner at the Lowell, then on to Cindy's. I'm telling you, he's been schmoozing big-time."

Lexi felt her chest tighten, but not for the reason August Sandford intended. Cindy's was a strip joint, known for having the most beautiful pole dancers in the city. The thought of Max fondling some seminaked goddess while she was in Africa made her sick with jealousy.

"Did you go? To Cindy's?"

August ran his hand through his hair in frustration. "No. Lexi, I don't think you're hearing me. I think Max is plotting against you behind your back. I think he's up to something."

"You're wrong."

"Am I? What happened in Italy, Lexi? That time that I was supposed to meet you in Florence."

"Nothing happened." Lexi sounded defensive. "You disappeared to Taiwan without bothering to call me. Max was in Italy for some deal or other. We had dinner. Who cares? It was a year ago, for God's sake."

"Taiwan was a setup. There was no meeting. Someone called Karen, my assistant, posing as Mr. Li's secretary. I flew halfway around the world for nothing."

Lexi laughed.

"And you think it was Max? Come on! It's a bit *Mission: Impossible,* isn't it?"

August was silent for a few moments.

"Lexi," he said at last. "Are you and Max an item?"

The red flush on Lexi's cheeks was as much from anger as embarrassment.

"Excuse me?"

"It's a simple question. Are you sleeping with him?"

Lexi stood up. "In what alternate universe would that possibly be your business?"

Furious, she turned and stormed out of the restaurant.

Who the hell does August Sandford think he is? My father?

August was about to call after her, then remembered that she wouldn't be able to hear him. He got up and followed her into the street.

It was still snowing. Grabbing Lexi by the shoulder, August spun her around to face him. Only then did he realize that they were surrounded by snapping photographers. By this time tomorrow, the gossip columns would no doubt be touting him as Lexi Templeton's new love interest.

"I think you're in love with Max." Having come this far, he might as well get it off his chest. "And I think it's clouding your judgment. He's using you, Lexi."

Click click click.

Angrily, Lexi shrugged off his hand.

"If anyone's judgment is clouded, it's yours. You're jealous. You're jealous because Max and I . . ."

"What? Max and you what?"

At that moment John, the Harvard Club concierge, scurried out of the club like a groundhog. He forced his way through the knot of paparazzi, carrying Lexi's coat over his arm. Stepping in front of August, he bundled Lexi into it.

"For heaven's sake, Ms. Templeton. Leaving without your coat? You'll freeze."

"Thank you, John."

Grimly, Lexi buttoned the cream wool up to the neck. With a last, furious look at August, she climbed into the back of her town car. The driver sped away, spraying the photographers with filthy, traffic-blackened snow.

Lexi stared through the smoked-glass windows, trying to collect her thoughts.

"Back to the office, miss?"

"Not yet, Wilfred. If you wouldn't mind just driving around for a little bit."

Damn August and his stupid suspicions! What does he know? She ran through everything he'd told her again. *Max and Jim Bruton had fallen out over a deal.* So what? It happened all the time. *Max canceled a trip to Europe.* That could have been for any number of reasons. *Max was playing golf with board members.* Hardly a hanging offense. Admittedly the Taiwan thing was weird. But Lexi was sure there must be a perfectly rational explanation.

What she wasn't sure about was why she couldn't shake the feeling of unease lurking in the pit of her stomach.

She still felt sick that evening when she got home to her apartment. Normally cooking and watching close-captioned reruns of *Friends* helped her to destress, but tonight nothing was working.

Changing into her pajamas and settling down on the couch with a family-size tub of Phish Food ice cream, Lexi decided to call her brother. Robbie always helped her put things into perspective, and for once he was actually in her time zone, playing a bunch of concerts in Pittsburgh. Thanks to Lexi's new Geemarc screen phone, a brilliant invention that enabled her to speak normally into the telephone then have the other person's speech translated into text in front of her, she was gradually starting to escape the tyranny of e-mail. (Kruger-Brent had made a bid for Geemarc last year but lost out to a German rival. The next morning Lexi had her broker buy as much of the acquirer's stock as he could get hold of. Today those shares were worth three times what she paid and were still rising.)

There was no answer in Robbie's hotel room. He must have left for the Mellon concert hall already.

Maybe I should call Max directly? Talk to him about this stuff. But there was no way she could do that without landing August in the shit. As angry as she was with August, the last thing Lexi wanted was to have him and Max getting into some sort of office feud. *They're the two people at Kruger-Brent I trust the most. I'll need them both on my side when I become chairman.*

A red light flashed on the wall above the TV. Someone was downstairs. Flicking on the video screen by the front door, Lexi saw a male figure, shoulders hunched against the wind. When she saw who it was, she smiled.

He never comes to the apartment. I wonder what he wants at this time of night?

Buzzing him up, she dashed into the bathroom and brushed some bronzer onto her cheeks. Africa had been roasting, but Lexi's schedule had left her precious little time to tan. Traveling always made her look drained and washed out. In her hurry, she managed to spill bronzing powder all over the bathroom floor. She was still on her hands and knees cleaning up when Max walked in.

"Jesus, what happened in here? A sandstorm?"

Lexi stood up and kissed him on the cheek.

"I wasn't expecting you."

"I know. I was on my way home from dinner and I thought I'd stop in. But look, if you're too tired . . ."

"No, no. It's fine." In a thick cable-knit sweater and jeans, he looked even more handsome than usual. August's words floated back to Lexi. *I think you're in love with him.*

"Drink?"

"I'll have a Scotch, thanks."

She went into the kitchen to fix it for him. A few moments later, she jumped out of her skin. Creeping up behind her, Max slipped two cold hands around her waist. Then, so gently Lexi could barely feel it, he dropped a kiss on the bare skin on the back of her neck.

Okay. Now, that's a move. Surely that counts as a move?

Or does the neck thing make it brotherly?

Crap.

She turned. Max was looking at her, his predatory eyes wandering over her features, as if seeing them for the first time.

"You had lunch with August Sandford today."

How did he know that?

"Yes."

"Did he make a move on you?"

Lexi was so surprised, she burst out laughing.

"Is that a yes?" Max asked angrily.

"No, it's not a yes! It's a no. Of course he didn't make a move. August doesn't think of me like that."

"Sure he thinks of you like that. Every man on earth thinks of you like that."

Max took Lexi's face in his hands and drew her toward him. Suddenly his lips were pressing hard against her own and his tongue was in her mouth, eager, hungry. Then, just as suddenly, he pulled away. He looked angry.

"I don't want you having lunch with him again."

Lexi bridled. "Now wait just a minute. I don't know where you think you get off telling me who I may or may not have lunch with. But if—"

Another kiss. This time Max's icy hands slipped under Lexi's shirt, grabbing hungrily at her breasts. All Lexi's feminist instincts told her to push him away. But her groin seemed to have missed the Germaine Greer lecture. Instead of showing him curtly to the door, Lexi found herself pulling Max's sweater over his head and fumbling for the belt buckle on his jeans.

Oh God. What was it August said about clouded judgment?

"I thought you weren't attracted to me," she murmured.

"You thought wrong."

Yanking off Lexi's pajama bottoms, Max carried her into the bedroom. Clothes from her Africa trip littered the bed, but Max didn't bother to move them. Throwing her down on top of the mess, he spread her legs, bent his head low, and began to lick her, his tongue darting like an eel into the slippery wetness between her thighs. Lexi moaned. She felt her muscles tense and her back start to arch. Wriggling helplessly, she tried to move his head away. *I mustn't come too quickly. I mustn't let him know how long I've wanted him.* But it was no use. Lexi seemed to have no control over her body whatsoever. She bucked wildly as waves of pleasure coursed through her.

The instant her orgasm was over, Max pulled off his pants and crawled up the bed so that his face was over hers. Lexi looked into his eyes. She expected to see excitement, arousal, joy. Instead she found herself gazing into two bottomless black pools of . . . nothing. She felt a momentary stab of fear.

You aren't Max. You're a stranger. Who are you?

It was a fear tinged with excitement. Even in the days when she'd convinced herself she hated him, Lexi recognized something wild and animalistic in Max. Something dangerous. It was the part of him she had always secretly wanted to possess, to unleash. Now she was about to unleash it. She could barely breathe.

Max felt her trying to read him, trying to gauge who he really was. He flipped her onto her stomach so she couldn't see his face. Then he entered her from behind, his huge penis filling her completely, satisfying her at last.

Lexi gasped with pleasure,

This is it. This is what sex is supposed to feel like.

Soon she was aware of nothing but the incredible sensations ripping through her body.

Max, too, was lost in the moment. He tried to hold himself back, but it was impossible. Lexi's breasts felt like his mother's breasts. Her hair, her skin, reeked of Eve. He was doing this for his mother. It was all for Eve. And yet Max felt unfaithful, dirty, pounding away like an animal on his cousin's bare back.

It shouldn't feel so good. Not with Lexi. Max hated Lexi.

I hate you.

Max came, screaming his mother's name.

Unable to see his face, Lexi couldn't hear him.

Lexi's affair with Max was like a child's secret treasure: too precious to be shown to others. When Lexi was a little girl, she'd had a beautiful antique box that she used to fill with special "nature things"—a bird's egg that had fallen from a nest and landed, unbroken, on the lawn at Dark Harbor; a rabbit's skull with bones worn so white that they glowed in the dark. If she could, she would have hidden Max's love in that box. Taken it out at night when she was alone, like the rabbit's skull, and gazed at it in wonder. The fact that no one at work knew they were together only added to the thrill of the relationship.

Max said: "We're cousins. And colleagues. People wouldn't understand."

Lexi agreed. One day soon, she would be Max's boss. Everyone's boss. Discretion at Kruger-Brent was vital.

"People" would have understood even less had they been flies on the wall observing Max and Lexi's love life. Since losing her virginity at sixteen, Lexi had been on a sexual mission, determined not to let her childhood abuse blunt her adult libido. She'd been so busy *proving* her sexuality, so busy showing lover after lover how much she enjoyed sex and how in control she was, she'd never stopped to figure out what it was that she actually wanted.

Max was the answer to all the questions Lexi had never asked. Not only did his sex drive match her own, but he made love with a violent desperation that left her breathless and begging for more. She never imagined she could enjoy being dominated in bed. In life, in the boardroom, *she* was Mistress of the Game. But Max opened the door to another side of her psyche. The games were gentle at first: he held her hands down on the bed or lightly tapped her butt during sex. But as Lexi's responses intensified, Max pushed further and further into full-blown S&M—sodomy, bondage, humiliation—nothing was off-limits.

Lexi felt liberated. At home, in bed with Max, she could throw off the armor that she wore all day at Kruger-Brent, the same armor she'd worn at business school and with the media, the same armor she'd been wearing all her life. The armor that said: *Yes, I'm deaf and I'm a woman. But don't think you can fuck with me.* With Max, she could finally be herself. Real, vulnerable, unguarded.

It was the best feeling in the world.

The only downside to the relationship was that they didn't spend enough time together. Lexi, especially, still had an insane travel schedule. And Max was up to his neck in Kruger-Brent politics at home.

Max told her, "It'll be better when you're chairman. You'll be in New York more. We'll have control over our own schedules."

Lexi could hardly wait.

Eve asked Max: "Have you found anything yet? There must be something you can use against her."

"Not yet, Mother. I'm working on it."

"Well, work faster. You're wasting too much time screwing her, aren't you?"

"No."

"Yes, you are. You're too busy enjoying yourself to remember who Lexi is. She's your enemy, Max. She's trying to *steal* from us. Time is running out."

"I know." Max hated disappointing his mother. He was also afraid Eve might be right. Sometimes, when Lexi screamed and writhed and moaned beneath him, he could almost believe that he *did* love her. That he'd forgotten why he had seduced her in the first place. Forgotten that this was all a game. A game in which the winner got to keep the greatest prize of all: Kruger-Brent.

Eve reminded him in no uncertain terms.

"You know what to do, Max. Fuck her. Fool her. Finish her."

Max nodded grimly.

He knew what to do.

Lexi lay back and tried to slow her breathing.

Dr. Cheung said: "Don't be nervous. Think of it as a flu shot."

Right. A flu shot that might give me back my hearing.

Lexi never imagined that hope could be so painful. Ever since Max told her about Dr. Cheung and the pioneering work he was doing with gene therapy, she'd been unable to sleep. It was like meeting a psychic who claimed to be able to contact your lost loved ones from beyond the grave. You want to believe it. But to do so means ripping open old wounds. Lexi had long since accepted the fact that she would never hear again.

Then Max casually passed her the *New Scientist* over breakfast one morning and blew her world apart.

"Look at this. Some guy in China's found a gene that makes deaf guinea pigs get their hearing back."

Lexi read the piece. The gene was called Math1. Dr. Cheung had developed a genetically engineered adenovirus containing the gene and injected it into the cochlea of deaf guinea pigs. Incredibly, the hair cells of the animal's inner ear had begun to regrow. Eighty percent of the sample recovered full hearing in a matter of weeks.

She passed the magazine back to Max. "He's never tried it on humans. Scientists are always coming up with these so-called breakthroughs. It won't work."

"Says here he started human trials last month. Aren't you even curious to meet him?"

"No."

"He comes to New York regularly."

"I said no, Max, okay? I don't have time to meet with some Chinese whack job."

Lexi pressed a Band-Aid onto her arm. "How long does it take? To feel the effects?"

"It depends. I've had patients start hair regrowth almost immediately. For others, it can be weeks, or even months. You may need a second shot. Can you check back with me in two weeks?"

Dr. Cheung was almost as nervous as Lexi. If the therapy was successful with such a high-profile patient, he would be set for life. If it failed, he could wave good-bye to his funding, not to mention his medical reputation.

"It's important to rest as much as you can, especially during the first week. This is an immense change for your body."

"I'm afraid that's impossible." Lexi gathered up her purse. "I'm due to assume the chairmanship in a month. There's so much to do at Kruger-Brent."

Dr. Cheung tried not to sound panicked. "Ms. Templeton. You *must* rest. This is your hearing we're talking about. Even if you were to look at it purely from a business perspective, I think you'll agree it's an investment worth making."

Max said the same thing.

"Go to Dark Harbor. See your dad. It might be the last chance you get to take a vacation. Once you're chairman, you'll never get away."

Reluctantly, Lexi agreed. But on one condition. "Promise me you won't tell anyone about the treatment? I don't want to raise expectations. Not until the outcome is certain."

Max took her in his arms and kissed her.

"I promise. Now, for heaven's sake, get out of here. Go get some rest while you still can."

"So did you hear? Santa Claus just landed his sleigh at Grindle Point Lighthouse."

Robbie Templeton sat in a coffee shop in Dark Harbor, across the table from his sister.

"Grindle Point? Wow."

Lexi read Robbie's lips, but her thoughts were miles away. Dr. Cheung had said it could take weeks for her hearing to begin to return. *He also said that twenty percent of the study had no reaction to Math1.*

Robbie continued. "The fat man's planning to take over the galaxy using the lighthouse as his base."

"Right."

"Rudolph's in charge of the first attack wave. After that, the whole show's wide open. It could be Donner. Blitzen. Any one of those guys."

"I see. Brilliant."

Robbie reached across the table and pinched Lexi's arm, hard.

"Ow! What'd you do that for?"

"I've been trying to get your attention for the last fifteen minutes. You haven't taken in a single word I've said. I might as well go back to Paris and be done with it."

"Sorry."

This trip to visit their father was the first time brother and sister had spent real time together in over five years. Robbie was a huge star now, filling concert halls and stadiums all around the world. Finding a window in his schedule was like winning the lottery. But as much as Lexi delighted in his company, it was hard to keep her mind off her hearing.

Or rather the lack of it. She was also itching to get back to Kruger-Brent.

How am I supposed to rest when my mind is racing?

"You think Dad would be super upset if I flew back to New York early?"

Robbie frowned. "I don't know. *I* would be. What's the rush?"

He was worried about Lexi. She'd lost a ton of weight since he'd last seen her, presumably from stress. Nothing could dim her luminous beauty, but to his brotherly eyes, she looked gaunt and more tired than he'd ever seen her.

Lexi looked at him and wondered when it was, exactly, that they'd grown so far apart. She still loved Robbie dearly. But whereas once he'd understood her, almost like a second self, now he asked her questions that made no sense to her at all.

What's the rush?

How could she answer that? What did it even mean? *Business is the rush. It's the life in my veins. I may never hear again. But I'll always have Kruger-Brent.*

Max would have understood.

Tristram Harwood looked at the screen in front of him. With each new image, his rheumy seventy-year-old eyes widened. The speakerphone was still on.

"You see the scale of the problem, Tris?"

Kruger-Brent's CEO said grimly: "I do. Is there any way . . . can this be contained?"

The voice on the speakerphone laughed.

"Contained? It's all over the Internet! In a few hours, those pictures'll be on Fox News and our stock'll fall through the floor. You need to make a statement."

Tristram Harwood hung up.

He'd spent three years "minding the store" at Kruger-Brent. Three peaceful, scandal-free years. And now, in his very last week . . .

"Stupid girl," he muttered under his breath. "Stupid, stupid girl."

Cedar Hill House had been Kate Blackwell's dream home, an oasis of tranquillity in her turbulent life. The views were spectacular, the decor comfortable, welcoming and peaceful. The house had once held too many painful memories for Peter Templeton. But as he grew older, and his children became adults, he found himself increasingly drawn to the place. Kate had come here to escape the world. When he retired, he decided, he would do the same.

He made a few crucial changes. There was no longer a television in the house, or a phone. If one was going to escape the world, one might as well do it properly. A single, ancient desktop computer squatted on Peter's desk, but it remained unplugged.

Robbie enjoyed the feeling of being cut off. It helped him relax. Lexi loathed it.

Thanks to Peter's communications phobia, Lexi didn't receive August Sandford's e-mail till almost eight o'clock at night. She was strolling down by the water with Robbie when her BlackBerry suddenly and unexpectedly buzzed into life. It kept on buzzing.

Seventy-seven new messages.

The one from August had so many red exclamation points attached to it she opened it first.

Robbie saw the blood drain from her face.

"What? What is it?"

"I have to get back to the city. Right now. I need a plane." Lexi was texting as she spoke, her thumbs working at lightning speed.

"It's eight o'clock at night, sweetie. It's too late to—"

"GET ME A PLANE!"

"All right. All right," said Robbie. "I'll see what I can do."

Kennedy airport was swarming with reporters.

Vultures, come to eat me alive.

"Lexi, have you seen the pictures?"

"When were they taken?"

"Will you step down from Kruger-Brent?"

"Do you have any idea who posted the images on the Net?"

Yes, I have an idea. I know who. I know why. I know when.

But none of that is going to help me.

The Kruger-Brent boardroom was built in the round. Perched like a squat, circular turret on top of the Park Avenue building, it afforded phenomenal views of Manhattan, Central Park and the East River. In its center was a round mahogany table, large enough to seat thirty people.

Today, twenty chairs had been positioned around it: fifteen for the board, including Tristram Harwood. Three for Kruger-Brent's most senior attorneys. And one each for Lexi and Max.

Nineteen of the chairs were filled. It was five o'clock in the morning.

"Where is she? After everything she's put this company through, the least she can do is show up on time."

Logan Marshall, the oldest serving board member, made no attempt to mask his irritation. Glancing around the table, it was clear that his colleagues echoed his sour mood. When the markets opened later this morning, they could each expect to see as much as a third of their net worth go up in smoke. There was only one person to blame.

"I'm here, I'm here. We can start."

In a pale peach pencil skirt and cream Marc Jacobs jacket, teamed with heels so high they looked more like launching gear than footwear, Lexi had dressed to kill. August Sandford thought: *She's not giving up without a fight. But she can't win. Not this time.* He flashed her an encouraging smile, but Lexi was too psyched up to return it. She launched into her pre-prepared speech:

"First of all, I would like to apologize to all of you for putting you— putting us—in this position."

Silence.

"Obviously our key concern this morning is our stock price. My view is that before we make any other decisions, we need to act now to limit the damage and reassure our shareholders."

Silence.

Lexi plowed on.

"My first thought on seeing these pictures was to resign immediately." August heard the mutterings of "hear, hear." Mercifully, Lexi didn't. "But we all know that sudden and unexpected management change is the *last* thing likely to restore investor confidence. Our stock has risen steadily for the last six months on the expectation that I would take over as chairman next month. I don't believe that me throwing myself on my sword is going to help us."

Logan Marshall whispered to August: "Pity she didn't think of that before she threw herself on all those college boys' swords at Harvard. And on film, too. What was she thinking?"

"I disagree."

Max got to his feet. He looked confident, poised and rested. Lexi thought: *How the hell does he manage to look so beautiful at five o'clock in the morning?*

"Let's look at what we're dealing with, shall we?" Max pulled a remote control from his pocket. A second later, a screen descended from the ceiling. On it was an image of Lexi, naked and on her knees, giving oral sex to a faceless man while two other men looked on.

August Sandford objected: "Is this really necessary? We've all seen the pictures."

"Yes, and we've had a whole weekend to digest them," said Max. "Think about our shareholders, waking up this morning and looking at that for the first time."

He jabbed at the button on his remote. Another picture: Lexi snorting cocaine. And another. And another. They'd all been taken at the same party, during freshman week at Harvard. The "friend" who took them had been persuaded years before (with the help of a fat check) to hand the chip from his digital camera over to Lexi. She should have destroyed it at the time. But some crazy impulse made her keep it, locked away in the safe at her apartment. A reminder of the "Party Girl Lexi" she had left behind, the old, promiscuous self she had shed like a snake's skin since falling in love with Max.

Falling in love.

Only one another person knew the code to that safe.

Max was still talking. He made eye contact with each board member in turn. When he came to Lexi, he looked through her as if she were a ghost.

No wonder you were so anxious to ship me off to Dark Harbor. How long have you been planning this, you bastard?

"It's not only our shareholders. We have to think about the damage this can do to Kruger-Brent internally. I've already had e-mails from the heads of the Dubai, Kuwait and Delhi offices, all threatening to quit if Lexi becomes chairman. Tristram, have you gotten any calls?"

Tristram Harwood nodded grimly. America might be prepared to forgive its favorite daughter her youthful indiscretions. But Kruger-Brent operated all over the world, in Muslim and Hindu countries. Having a woman chairman, a *deaf* woman chairman, was bad enough. But this sort of stigma? It would cripple them.

Lexi sat and watched in silence while the men around her debated her future. Only it wasn't a debate. It was a show trial. The verdict, guilty, had been decided before she ever walked into the room.

Of course it was Max who had betrayed her. He'd played her, just like August said he would. Images of their lovemaking, the wild, pagan passion of the last six months, swept unbidden through Lexi's mind.

Was it all just a game to him? Part of his battle plan? It must have been. And yet his desire, his love for her, felt so real.

She weighed her options:

I could tell them. I could tell the board it was Max who stole those pictures and made them public. Max who precipitated this crisis. Max who got us all into this mess.

But even as she thought it, Lexi knew she would never do that. The market had already lost its faith in her. Kruger-Brent's share price would plunge this morning as a result. If Max's name was tarnished, too, investors would have nothing to cling to. The company would fall out of Blackwell-family hands. It might even collapse altogether.

Kruger-Brent was the one great love of Lexi's life. She could not allow it to go under.

She looked at Max. *That's what you were counting on, wasn't it? You knew I wouldn't turn you in. You knew I love this company too much.*

She hated him for what he'd done to her. But she hated him even more for what he'd done to Kruger-Brent. To secure the chairmanship for himself, he'd put the entire firm in jeopardy.

Lexi got to her feet.

"Enough."

She held up a hand for silence. The muttering ceased.

"It's clear that you all feel the same way. Therefore, for the good of the company, I will withdraw my name from the chairmanship ballot. I will formally resign from Kruger-Brent this afternoon."

The attorneys' shoulders slumped visibly with relief.

Max opened his mouth to speak. But when he looked into Lexi's eyes, the words died on his lips. The things he wanted to say meant nothing now: *I'm sorry. I still love you.* He'd had to destroy her in order to win Kruger-Brent for Eve. It was his destiny, his life's purpose. He'd had no choice. One day, he hoped, Lexi would see that. She would understand.

With a quiet dignity that made August Sandford want to cry, Lexi gathered up her briefcase, turned and left the room.

"Good luck, Max."

Lexi waited for the elevator doors to close before unclenching her fists. Blood dripped from her palms from where she had dug her own fingernails into the flesh.

Good luck, Max.

Good luck, Judas, you treacherous son of a bitch.

Her Bible studies came back to her.

"And Jesus said, 'I tell you solemnly, one of you will betray me. But woe to that man, the betrayer! It would be better for that man if he had never been born.'"

Lexi was going to make Max wish that he had never been born.

Her cousin had won the battle.

But the war had only just begun.

BOOK TWO

TWENTY-TWO

⚭

LOS ANGELES. FIVE YEARS LATER

PAOLO COZMICI LOOKED AT THE EXQUISITELY DECORATED
Bel Air drawing room and scowled.

"Too many flowers. It looks like somebody died."

Robbie Templeton kissed him indulgently on the top of his bald
head. "The flowers are perfect. Everything's perfect. Relax, babe. Have
a drink."

Tonight was Robbie's fortieth birthday party. With typical altruism,
he had decided to mark the milestone with a charity event that he
hoped would raise a million dollars for the Templeton/Cozmici AIDS
Foundation. Stars from the worlds of classical and pop music, as well as
a smattering of Hollywood movie actors, would soon be pulling up to
Robbie and Paolo's wrought-iron gates, where a huddle of eager paparazzi was already gathered. The sprawling Bel Air estate had been
home to classical music's happiest couple for the past three years. The
real-estate agent described it as "a French Country manor," a turn of
phrase that had reduced poor Paolo to paroxysms of laughter.

"'Ave you ever been to France?"

It was in fact a vast, vulgar, wedding cake of a house, smothered in
enough climbing roses to make Martha Stewart wince. The gardens

came complete with a fake stream powered by a hidden electric pump and a faux-medieval bridge. It was the epitome of tackiness: brash, American, suburban. *Disney.* But it was also incredibly comfortable, boasted heart-stopping views from almost every room, and—crucially—afforded total privacy. Robbie and Paolo had been blissfully happy there.

"Ah, Lex, there you are. Would you please tell Monsieur le Grinch here that the house looks awesome?"

"The house looks awesome."

It was hard to believe that Lexi Templeton was thirty years old. Skipping down the stairs in a vintage gray Hardy Amies ball gown, with diamonds gleaming at her ears, neck and wrists, her skin still shone like a teenager's. She wore her hair long and loose, another girlish touch that belied the steely businesswoman within.

After Lexi left Kruger-Brent five years ago in a storm of scandal, most business pundits wrote her off. Overnight, her picture stopped appearing on the front covers of magazines. Lexi made no statements, responded to no rumors, approved no messages through "friends" or "insiders." She stopped attending celebrity parties, charity auctions, gallery openings. Word was that she'd left America, but no one knew for sure. As the months went by, people ceased to care.

But those who assumed Lexi had crawled under a rock to lick her wounds had profoundly underestimated the strength of her ambition, not to mention the resilience of her spirit.

Ten days after Max's coup, Lexi awoke to the sound of horns blaring outside her new, rented apartment. The media had driven her out of her old place. The noise was muffled at first, as if everything had been covered with a fresh fall of snow. But during the next few days, the snow slowly started melting. Sounds became sharper, crisper. Lexi delighted in each one like a newborn child. Water gushing from the faucet in her bathroom made her laugh out loud. Vendors cursing on the street below brought a lump to her throat. Strangest of all was her own voice. It didn't seem to belong to her at all.

Dr. Cheung was elated. "Congratulations, my dear. I'm only sorry that so much of what you're hearing at the moment is so unpleasant."

Like everyone else in America, Dr. Cheung had seen the pictures and read the reports. They were hanging the poor girl out to dry.

Lexi, however, seemed unfazed: "Don't worry about me, Doctor. I can hear again. That's all that matters."

And it was. Suddenly Lexi felt invincible. Raising capital against her

MISTRESS OF THE GAME | 219

Kruger-Brent stock—despite the drop in value, Lexi's stake was still worth over $100 million—she quietly started her own real-estate company, Templeton Estates. She began buying up cheap tracts of land in Africa, following the same business plan she'd intended to adopt as chairman of Kruger-Brent. Within two years, the company was outperforming almost all of its African competitors. *This* year Lexi had finally had the immense satisfaction of watching Templeton's market share in Africa overtake Kruger-Brent's.

Only one company, Gabriel McGregor and Dia Ghali's Cape Town–based Phoenix Group, consistently outperformed them. But then Phoenix had had a five-year head start on Templeton. No one could deny that for a five-year-old business, Templeton Estates had made one hell of a mark.

As her company flourished, so Lexi's own self-esteem started to revive. When Max betrayed her, releasing those awful, degrading pictures, part of her wanted to crawl away and die. Now, with both her hearing and her fortune restored, she found herself taking her first baby steps back into public life. On the spur of the moment, she showed up one night at the opening of a friend's restaurant in her native New York. Wearing a vintage Bill Blass dress, Lexi utterly stole the show, cutting as dazzlingly glamorous and enigmatic a figure as she had in the old days. Soon afterward the floodgates opened. Once again, men flocked to her. And not just any men. Lexi dated musicians, businessmen, movie stars, always moving on within a few weeks, keeping the tabloids guessing. With the dollar at an all-time low and the economy in the doldrums, America craved glamour and excitement like a crack whore craving a fix. What better way to revive the national spirit than to welcome this conquering, beautiful Blackwell daughter back into the collective American fold?

So she had a wild and crazy youth. So what? Who didn't?

She can hear again and she's back on her feet.

Lexi was a star, a fighter, a winner. She had reinvented herself once again. Once again, America was glued to the edge of its seat.

Paolo Cozmici needn't have worried. The party was a terrific success, with just the right amount of scandal to satisfy Hollywood's gossip fiends:

A famous music producer got locked in the bathroom with a beautiful singer who was not his wife.

The singer's name was David.

A movie actress was so wasted climbing into the hot tub that she forgot about the hairpiece she wore to hide her bald spot. When her twenty-year-old boy glanced down and saw what he thought was a dead rat floating between his legs, he passed out. The poor kid nearly drowned.

Michael Schett, this year's "Hollywood's Hottest Hunk" according to *People* magazine, arrived with *Playboy*'s Miss September, but dumped her like a campaign promise when he laid eyes on Lexi. Unfortunately for Michael Schett, Lexi wasn't interested.

Michael cornered Robbie Templeton by the bar. "You gotta help me. I'm crashing and burning here. You're her brother. Tell me how to impress her."

With his Cary Grant looks, legendary prowess in the sack, and a string of hit movies to his name, Michael Schett was not used to rejection. He hadn't had a girl dismiss him like this since seventh grade.

Robbie grinned. "Lexi likes a challenge. You could always start making out with me. Maybe she'll try to 'turn' you?"

Michael Schett roared with laughter. He'd known Robbie and Paolo for years.

"Nice try, Liberace. She's cute, but no girl is *that* cute."

"Hey, you know what they say, Michael. You're not a man till you had a man and didn't like it."

In the wee small hours of the morning, once all the guests had gone, Paolo went to bed, leaving Robbie alone with Lexi.

"You know, Michael Schett is really into you."

Lexi rolled her eyes.

"What? He's a nice guy. Most women would bite his hand off. Christ, *I'd* sleep with him."

"You would *not*. You and Paolo are fused at the hip and you know it."

"Actually, we're fused at the heart. But I know what you mean."

Robbie was worried about Lexi. On the surface, she seemed to have pulled her life back from the brink. But her continued obsession with Kruger-Brent and their cousin wasn't normal. As for her working hours, Lexi regularly clocked in days that would put most self-respecting Taiwanese sweatshop workers to shame.

"Work isn't everything, you know, Lex. Don't you ever think of settling down?"

Lexi laughed. "With Michael Schett? His movies last longer than his relationships!"

"Okay, fine, forget Michael. But everyone needs love in their life."

"I have love in my life. I have you."

"That's not what I mean. Don't you want to have children one day? A family of your own?"

"No. I don't."

Lexi sighed. How could she explain to Robbie that after Max, she would never love again? He had no idea about her affair with Max—no one did—still less that it was Max who had distributed the pictures that very nearly ruined her. But Lexi knew. She knew love was for fools. Love had blinded her. Because of love, she had lost Kruger-Brent. The only thing that mattered now was destroying Max and taking back her beloved company. As for children, Kruger-Brent was Lexi's child. She had trusted in Max, and he had torn her child from her arms, ripped it from her breast and carried it off into the wilderness.

She had rebuilt her life and her reputation against the odds. Templeton Estates was a huge success. But inside, the longing for Kruger-Brent corroded Lexi's life like acid leaking from a battery. It turned every triumph to ashes.

Seeing she was upset, Robbie changed the subject.

"You're in Cape Town a lot these days. Have you come across a guy called Gabriel McGregor?"

Now he had her attention.

"I have. I've never met him. He co-owns a company called Phoenix. They're competitors of ours."

"Any good?"

"Very good, unfortunately," Lexi admitted. "He's a shrewd businessman."

"But?"

She paused. "I don't know. Like I say, we've never met. But there's something about him I don't entirely trust. You know he claims to be related to us? Says he's a descendant of Jamie McGregor."

"Isn't he?"

"I have no idea. I suppose he could be. How do *you* know him?"

Walking over to his desk, Robbie pulled out a handwritten letter. He passed it to Lexi.

"He and his wife are heavily involved in AIDS relief over there. He wrote asking me if Paolo and I would be interested in working with his charity. I'm flying out to meet with him next week."

Lexi read the letter, twice. It *seemed* genuine. But she couldn't quite shake the feeling of foreboding. Who was Gabe McGregor, really? A lot of people wanted to claim a connection to her family. This man was too rich in his own right to be a fortune hunter. But even so . . .

She found herself saying: "I'm going out there on business next week, as it happens. I can go and meet him with you if you like?"

Robbie's face lit up. He'd been trying for years to get Lexi interested in his charity work.

"That'd be great! I can book us on the same flight. It'll be just like old times. Hey, you remember going to Africa with Dad when we were kids? Those boring old Kruger-Brent tours? Man, Dad never shut up: 'Jamie McGregor had a diamond mine here, Kate Blackwell went to school here,' blah blah blah blah blah." He laughed.

"Of course I remember."

Those tours with her father felt like yesterday.

Lexi had loved every second of them.

"Jamie! Take Thomas the Tank Engine out of your sister's cereal right now or you're going on the naughty step."

Gabe McGregor fixed his four-year-old son with what he hoped was a stern stare.

Jamie said seriously: "I'm sorry, Daddy. I certainly can't do that. Thomas has crashed and bust his buffers. Now he must wait for the breakdown train to rescue him."

"Cheer—ohs! *Cheeeeer ooooooohs*!" Collette, Jamie's two-year-old sister, burst into ear-splitting wails. "Don't *wanna* train! *My* Cheer-ohs!"

"Stop crying, Collette," said Jamie angrily. "You're giving Thomas a head-gate."

"Jamie!" Gabe shouted.

Marching silently over to the breakfast table, Tara McGregor removed the offending train from Collette's cereal bowl, dried it with a paper towel and handed it to her protesting son. "Any more moaning, Jamie and Thomas is in the trash. Finish your toast and you can have a chocolate milk."

To Gabe's astonishment, Jamie promptly forgot about his train and focused on stuffing peanut-butter toast into his mouth. Pretty soon his cheeks bulged like a hamster's. "Finished."

"Are you sure he won't choke?" Gabe glanced worriedly at Tara. "He looks like a snake trying to swallow a rabbit."

Tara didn't look up. "He'll be fine."

As usual, Tara McGregor's morning routine was a ridiculous juggling act: cooking breakfast, feeding and dressing the kids, refereeing World War III and helping Gabe remember where he'd put his socks/laptop/phone/sanity.

Gabe watched his wife frying bacon for his sandwich with one hand while checking e-mails on her BlackBerry with the other. With her glossy red hair, slender waist and long, gazellelike legs, there was an old-fashioned sexiness about Tara that motherhood seemed only to have enhanced. From behind, she looked like Cyd Charisse. From the front, the impression was more innocent and wholesome. Rosie the Riveter meets Irish farmer's daughter. Pale skin. Freckles. Large, womanly breasts. A smile so broad it had knocked Gabe off his feet the first time he saw it, and still made him want to take her upstairs and ravish her now, six years later.

By nine o'clock this morning, Tara would be at the clinic, up to her elbows in dying babies.

She's an angel. One in a million. How the hell did a girl that smart and beautiful ever fall for a guy like me?

Tara Dineen loathed Gabe McGregor on sight.

"That guy? You mean the cheese ball?"

Tara and her girlfriend, Angela, were in a trendy new bar at the Waterfront. Angela had singled out Gabe as a "hot guy." Tara begged to differ.

"What's wrong with him?" asked Angela. "He's got Tom Brady's body and Daniel Craig's face. He's edible."

"And he knows it," said Tara archly. "Look at him, flashing his cash in front of all those toothpicks."

As usual, Gabe was surrounded by a gaggle of models, whom he was ostentatiously plying with Cristal.

"Let's go over there," said Angela.

"No thanks. You're on your own."

Angela made a beeline for Gabe. They chatted for a while, but Gabe's eye kept wandering back to the redhead giving him death stares from across the bar.

"Doesn't your friend want to join us?"

"No," said Angela, annoyed. Why did Tara always get all the male attention? "If you must know, she thinks you're a cheese ball."

"Does she, now?"

Gabe put down his drink. Marching over to Tara, he demanded: "Do you always judge a man before you've spoken to him?"

On closer inspection, Gabe could see that the girl wasn't classically beautiful. She had an upturned nose. Her eyes were set slightly too wide. She was tall and strong. The word *strapping* sprang to mind. And yet there was something compelling about her, something that set her apart from the *Vogue* beauties he usually dated.

"Not always, no. But in your case . . . well."

"Well what?"

"It's obvious."

"What is?"

"You!" Tara laughed. "Come on. The overpriced champagne? The Rolex watch? Your little harem over there? What do you drive? Don't tell me." She closed her eyes in mock concentration. "A Ferrari, right? Or . . . no. An Aston Martin! I'll bet you fancy yourself as a regular little James Bond."

"As a matter of fact, I drive a perfectly ordinary Range Rover," said Gabe, making a mental note to put his Vanquish up for sale tomorrow morning. "Give me your number and I'll take you out for dinner in it."

"No thanks."

"Why not? I'm a nice guy."

"You're not my type."

"What's your type? I can change."

"For heaven's sake, I'm not *your* type." Tara gestured to the nineteen-year-old Heidi Klum clones blowing Gabe kisses while they took turns warming his bar stool. "Take some friendly advice and quit while you're ahead."

But Gabe didn't quit. He found out where Tara worked—she was a doctor at a Red Cross AIDS clinic in one of the shantytowns—and had dozens of roses delivered to her every day. He asked her out on countless dates, sent her theater tickets, books, even jewelry. Everything was firmly but politely returned.

After three months, Gabe was on the point of giving up hope when he received an unexpected e-mail from Tara, sent to his work address. When her boss discovered one of his doctors was being pursued by one of the owners of Phoenix, he'd practically frog-marched Tara to the clinic's computer.

"Do you have any idea how much that company is worth? One donation from this McGregor guy and we could buy enough antivirals to see us through the next five years."

"But I'm not interested in him."

"Bugger 'not interested'! People are dying out there, Tara, I don't need to tell *you*. Now you flutter your eyelashes, and you get Gabriel McGregor back in here with his checkbook, pronto."

"Or what?" Tara laughed. She loved her boss, especially when he tried to lay down the law, bless him.

"Or I'll send you to your room without any supper, you cheeky cow. TYPE!"

Gabe's visit to the Red Cross AIDS clinic at Joe Slovo Shantytown changed his life forever.

Gabe had lived in camps himself. With Dia, he had seen firsthand the hopeless, crushing poverty of the slums. But nothing had prepared him for the depths of human misery at Joe Slovo.

Baby girls as young as two were brought in daily by female relatives after their uncles or fathers had raped them. Apparently the widely held belief that HIV could be "cured" by having sex with a virgin had mutated into a the-younger-the-better theory. Most of the children died from their internal injuries long before they could develop AIDS, their tiny, fragile bodies shattered from the force of penetration.

"Twenty rand buys ten of these child-rape kits," Tara told a clearly shaken Gabe. She handed him a plastic bag with a picture of Winnie the Pooh on the front. Inside was a sanitary napkin, a pair of child's panties, some sterile wipes and a sugar lollipop.

"That's it? A little kid gets raped and that's what you give her?"

Tara shrugged. "They get drugs if we have them. Children are first in line for antivirals. There's nothing else we can do."

After an hour touring the wards—dying girls in their twenties pleading with nurses to save their babies, young men shrunk to skeletons staring listlessly at the ceiling—Gabe excused himself. Tara found him sitting outside, tears streaming down his face. For the first time, she wondered if perhaps she'd been too hard on him. He was so bloody handsome it was hard not to distrust him. But his distress around the kids was obviously genuine.

"I'm sorry. I shocked you."

"It's okay." Gabe's hands were shaking. "I needed to be shocked. What can I do? What do you need?"

"Everything. We need everything. You name it, we need it. Drugs, beds, toys, food, syringes, condoms. We need a miracle."

Gabe reached into his pocket and pulled out a checkbook. Without thinking, he scribbled down a number, signed it, and handed it to Tara.

"I can't do miracles, I'm afraid. But maybe this will help. Just till I can work out something more long-term."

Tara looked at the number and burst into tears.

Their first date was a disaster. Hoping to impress her as a serious-minded citizen, not just another rich playboy, Gabe got them tickets to the premiere of a political documentary that had gotten rave reviews. Tara loved the movie. It was the additional sound track of Gabe's snores she objected to.

"I'm sorry! But you have to admit it was dull."

"*Dull?* You know it won the Palme d'Or at Cannes."

"Palm Bore more like it," muttered Gabe.

"How could you find that boring? The West's treatment of refugees is one of the most fascinating, complex issues facing modern society."

Not as fascinating as your breasts in that T-shirt.

When they sat down to dinner—Gabe had deliberately chosen a low-key steak house in a quiet neighborhood, nothing too flashy—things got worse. Tara leaned forward, her gorgeous wide-set eyes dancing in the candlelight. For one glorious moment Gabe thought she was about to kiss him.

Instead she asked earnestly: "So what *are* your politics, Gabe? How would you define yourself?"

"I wouldn't."

"Come on. I'm interested."

Gabe sighed. "All right. I'm a capitalist."

Later that night, alone in bed, Gabe wondered if he'd somehow misspoken and said "I'm a Nazi child-killer" or "I'm a horse fetishist. You?" The very word *capitalist* sent Tara into such an apoplexy of rage, she stormed out of the restaurant before they'd even finished their entrées.

He'd had to beg for a second date. This time he decided to keep it simple. Uncontroversial. He took her ice skating.

"I've never done this before." Wobbling uncertainly on the ice in jeans and a pair of pink leg warmers, Tara looked about thirteen. Gabe had never wanted a woman more.

"It's a cinch." He smiled, reaching for her hand. Pulling her toward him, he skated around behind her, wrapping his arms around her waist. "Just step . . . and glide. Step . . . and glide. Let me lead you." He began to skate forward.

"No, no, no, it's okay. Don't push me. I can do it."

"It's all right. Just relax. I won't let you fall." He started to build up some speed, gliding the two of them across the ice.

"No, Gabe. I don't want you to . . . I prefer—watch out!"

The guy who plowed into them must have weighed at least two hundred pounds, a human Mack truck with no brakes. Gabe needed six stitches in his forehead. Tara fractured a rib and broke her arm in two places.

"You look good in white," Gabe joked in the emergency room, when they finished setting her arm in a cast.

"Thanks."

She wasn't smiling. *Oh God, I've blown it. She'll never go out with me again. Not after this.*

"I'm not very good at dates, am I?"

"No."

"That was probably the worst date you ever had."

"Unquestionably."

"Apart from the one before."

"Apart from that one, yes."

"The thing is . . ."

"Yes, Gabe?"

"You're laughing at me."

And she was. Tears of laughter streamed down Tara's face. Instinctively she moved her arm to wipe them away, only to whack herself in the face with her cast. For some reason, this made her laugh even harder.

"I'm sorry. But you look so adorable with your face all bashed up. And you are the most useless date in the universe. I mean you're bad on a superhuman scale."

"I know." Seizing the moment, he leaned down and kissed her, a full, passionate kiss that took both of them by surprise. It was a nice surprise, though. So they did it again. And again.

"I love you," said Gabe.

Tara grinned. "Disappointingly, I'm afraid I love you, too."

"I know I'm a crap date. But I'd be a good husband."

"Oh, really? So is that a proposal?"

"I don't know. Is that an acceptance?"

"Come back with a ring and I'll think about it."

Three months later, they were married.

Phoenix's offices were on Adderley Street, the main artery of Cape Town's thriving central business district. Robbie and Lexi were shown up to the twelfth floor.

"Wait here, please. Mr. McGregor will be with you shortly."

The waiting area was comfortably furnished with deep, squashy sofas and tables piled high with magazines. Floor-to-ceiling windows offered spectacular views of Table Mountain. The overall impression was one of wealth and ease.

Robbie asked: "Didn't Kruger-Brent used to have a satellite office on this street?"

"They still do."

"McGregor must be doing well to afford headquarters here."

Lexi, who'd been thinking the same thing, nodded glumly. It was her suggestion that they meet at Phoenix's offices. "It'll give us a chance to get to know one another before we drive out to the clinic." In fact, her real intention was to size up her competition. Now she wished she hadn't bothered. *These Antoni couches alone must have set him back twenty grand. I wonder how much Phoenix made last year?*

"Sorry to keep you waiting. I'm Gabe. Would you like to come through?"

They followed Gabe into his office. For a moment Lexi was lost for words. She'd pictured Gabriel McGregor as an ordinary, balding, middle-aged executive.

Why didn't Robbie warn me he was so attractive?

"Lexi Templeton." She shook his hand coolly.

"A pleasure to meet you, Lexi. Tara and I were really excited when we heard back from your brother. Robbie and Paolo have done so much for the AIDS cause."

Lexi thought: *Quit sucking up. What do you really want?*

"I had no idea you were involved in the charity, too."

"I'm not. I'm in Cape Town on business."

"Ah, that's right. Templeton Estates. That's your company, isn't it?"

You know it is. Don't play dumb with me, pretty boy.

"Amazing that three people with the same great-great-great-grandfather should find themselves in the same city, involved in the same charitable cause *and* the same business. Don't you agree?"

Lexi gave a peremptory nod.

Gabe thought: *I wonder what's eating her? She's about as warm and cuddly as a piranha that just got slapped with a parking ticket.*

He'd seen countless pictures of Lexi Templeton over the years, including the infamous sex shots. He knew she would be beautiful. But none of the photographs had managed to convey Lexi's *presence* in the flesh; the way she seemed to fill a room simply by walking into it. She was already dominating this meeting, stealing her brother's thunder.

The silence was getting awkward.

"I'm sorry Paolo couldn't be here," said Robbie. "His health is not what it was, I'm afraid. He finds all the travel terribly tiring."

"That's quite all right. Perhaps next time? I know my wife will be pleased to see you, Lexi. She gets fed up with all the guy-talk."

Lexi's frown deepened. *So he thinks I'm the "little woman," does he? Here to spend the next two days shoe shopping with his trophy wife while he fleeces Robbie's foundation? Well, he can forget it. I'm here to protect my brother's interests.*

Out loud she said. "I look forward to meeting her. Shall we get going?"

Without waiting for an answer, Lexi started for the door.

After you, Your Majesty, thought Gabe.

It was going to be an interesting day.

Later that night, in bed at their sprawling, Cape Dutch farmhouse in the hills above Camps Bay, Gabe asked Tara what she'd thought of the Templetons.

"He's a sweetheart. She's a card-carrying bitch."

Gabe laughed. "You're so tactful, darling. Why don't you tell me what you really think?"

"Oh, come on. You can't have liked her." Tara turned off the bedside lamp. "And she certainly didn't like *you*. All those barbed comments?"

It was true. After a long and grueling day touring three new AIDS clinics that Phoenix had funded, Lexi's negativity had begun to grate on everyone's nerves.

"Anyone would have thought you wanted her brother's money for yourself. Here you are, trying to help these poor, suffering people, and this woman talks to you like you've just given her herpes."

"Another lovely image. Thanks for that, darling."

Tara teased: "You're *sure* you never slept with her?"

"Quite sure."

"It would explain a lot. There were so many, Gabe. She might have slipped your memory."

"Ha ha. Believe me, if I'd slept with her, she wouldn't look so damned miserable."

"Arrogant bastard!" Tara hit him over the head with her book. Thankfully, it was a paperback. "Seriously, though. Why do you think she has it in for you?"

Gabe had been pondering the same question all day. He noticed the sour look that came over Lexi's face whenever he alluded to their family connection. Perhaps that had something to do with it? Phoenix had out-bid Templeton on a couple of deals recently, but he couldn't believe that a serious businesswoman like Lexi would take something like that personally.

"She's probably just protective of her brother. Doesn't want to see him being taken advantage of."

"Bollocks," Tara said roundly. "Robbie Templeton's forty years old and richer than Croesus. He can take care of himself. Besides, this is what his foundation *does*. They help people with AIDS. I couldn't believe how cold that woman was. Everyone cries when they see clinics like ours for the first time, but not that one. Oh no. Couldn't have cared less, could she?"

Gabe wasn't so sure. Lexi was certainly withdrawn. Aloof, even. She had declined to hold the babies when offered the chance, and seemed uncomfortable amid so much suffering and sickness. But people reacted to tragedy in different ways. Reaching out, Gabe ran a hand over his wife's belly. Since Collette was born, Tara's body had lost some of its firmness. Tara felt self-conscious about it, but Gabe adored her new soft contours. She had given him his children, brought a joy and purpose to his life that no words could ever fully express, nor any action of his could ever hope to repay. He loved her more than life.

He whispered in her ear: "I love you."

Tara sighed. "I love you, too, Gabe. But I'm absolutely bloody knackered. Be a sweetheart and piss off to your own side of the bed, would you?"

Ah! The sweet delights of matrimony.

For once in her life, Tara McGregor was dead wrong. The truth was that Lexi had been deeply moved by what she saw at the clinic. Those tiny, doll-like babies with their stick arms and bulging joints. When the nurse offered her a little girl to hold, Lexi was gripped with an irrational terror that she might break her. Her skin was paper thin . . . what if she gripped her too tight? The thought of causing that child one more ounce of pain was unbearable. The pleading look in the little girl's eyes would haunt Lexi forever. She'd been determined not to betray any emotion or weakness in front of Gabe McGregor. But as soon as they got back to Cape Town, she broke down in Robbie's arms.

"How can this still be happening? Those kids are just being left to die. What about the international aid programs?"

"They're overwhelmed," Robbie explained patiently. "They need private-sector money desperately. That's why I'm so eager to develop this relationship with Gabe McGregor. Can't you cut him a little slack?"

Lexi dried her tears. "I'll write you a check right now for those babies. But I don't trust McGregor. I'm sorry, but I don't."

Over the next two years, Lexi Templeton and Gabe McGregor crossed paths more frequently, at charity events and business conferences, as well as occasionally in the boardroom when they found themselves on opposite sides of a deal. Templeton Estates was investing in emerging real-estate markets all across the globe, from Georgia to Iran to Tibet. But something kept drawing Lexi back to South Africa. The returns were high. But it went beyond that. South Africa was the birthplace of Kruger-Brent. Lexi felt a powerful urge to succeed there.

Phoenix, whose investments were limited to South Africa, remained the market leader. Dia Ghali had cashed out of the business last year, leaving Gabe McGregor as the man to beat in real estate. Lexi Templeton fully intended to be the woman to beat him. But Templeton was not the only target in her sights.

Her thoughts were never far from Kruger-Brent. Templeton did no business in New York, but Lexi insisted on keeping an outrageously expensive office there purely because she had a good view of the Kruger-Brent building from her window. She had admitted it to no one. But deep down, Lexi had always seen Templeton as a stepping-stone. A stopgap measure until she could figure out a way to win back Kruger-Brent, destroying Max Webster in the process.

On the face of it, she knew her goal must sound insane. Kruger-Brent was a giant, a hundred times Templeton's size. It was a behemoth. Untouchable.

Lexi saw things differently.

Size is their weakness. They have too many vulnerable points, too many exposed businesses ripe for the picking. And I have the inside scoop on all of them. Kruger-Brent's a twelve-headed monster, and none of the heads talks to another. By the time Max realizes he's under attack, it'll be too late.

Business was a game. Toppling Kruger-Brent would be like playing a multibillion-dollar game of Jenga. Yes, Max's tower was infinitely taller than Lexi's. But remove a few strategic blocks from the bottom, and the whole edifice would come crashing down. The hard part was going to be controlling the explosion when it came. Lexi needed the company to weaken before she could strike, but not to collapse so totally that there was nothing left of her birthright.

So far, Max was doing most of the hard work for her. He was a brilliant diplomat and a natural schemer, but his performance as chairman had been distinctly lackluster. Lexi remembered her Harvard Business School professor's damning remark about one of his students, a young man who fancied himself as the next Warren Buffett.

"Jon Dean? Please. That guy couldn't sell a dollar for ninety cents."

Max Webster, it appeared, couldn't sell a dollar period. He had inherited Kate Blackwell's penchant for indiscriminate growth, a brilliantly successful strategy in the 1960s and '70s, but a disastrous one in today's wildly fluctuating markets.

Max could wait. So could Kruger-Brent.

For now Lexi had to focus on the job at hand: annihilating Gabe McGregor.

The safari was Gabe's idea. He cornered Lexi at a real-estate convention in Sun City, after Sol Kerzner's closing address.

"I've got reservations for a week at the Shishangeni Lodge next week. Tara and the kids were supposed to be coming, but Jamie's got some awful stomach bug. I wondered if you might be interested?"

Dressed formally in a dark gray suit that highlighted his tan and brought out the pale gray in his eyes—Lexi's eyes—Gabe looked even more handsome than he had the last time Lexi saw him. *Is that part of the reason I don't like him? Because he's so attractive?* It was possible. Max had burned her badly. The very thought of desiring someone again filled her with dread.

"That's kind of you, but I'm afraid I can't. I'm traveling for the rest of the month."

"What a shame." Gabe shook his head. "It's supposed to be the best safari experience in the country."

"I'm sure you'll have a wonderful time." Lexi looked pointedly at her watch.

"It would have been the perfect opportunity for us to talk about the Elizabeth Center, too. But if your schedule's too full . . ."

Damn him. He's got me on a string and he knows it.

The Elizabeth Center was going to be the biggest shopping mall in the country, built on two hundred prime commercial acres in a wealthy suburb of Johannesburg. Every real-estate firm worth its salt was bidding for a piece of the action, including Templeton. Somehow, Gabe had managed to wrangle a private deal for Phoenix and now owned a 10 percent stake in the venture, making him the second-largest single shareholder. A word from Gabe could open the door for Templeton. Or close it.

"Next week, you say?"

Gabe grinned. *Gotcha.*

"I'll have my assistant send the details to your office."

Lexi nodded tightly. "Thanks."

"You know, you might even enjoy it. Stranger things have happened."

Lexi was by no means sure that they had.

The Shishangeni Private Lodge is the jewel of Kruger National Park's crown. Made up of twenty-two thatched chalets, it boasts a swimming pool, library, conference facilities and a better wine cellar than most Michelin-starred restaurants. Every chalet has a private game-viewing deck as well as a bar, fireplace and outdoor shower—for those wishing to feel at one with nature without forgoing such necessities as deviled quail's eggs for breakfast and parfait of foie gras for dinner.

"How's your room?"

Gabe joined Lexi for dinner by the pool. It was their first night at Shishangeni. Above them, a livid African sun bled the last of its rays into the land, oozing burnt orange over the tapestry of rich greens. On the drive from Kruger Mpumalanga Airport, all Lexi's resolutions not to be impressed had flown out the window. She'd been visiting South Africa since childhood, but the extraordinary beauty of this corner of the national park took her breath away.

"It's fine, thank you."

Lexi's chalet had views of the Crocodile River in the south. To the east, she could almost see to the Mozambique border—mile upon mile of some of the most stunning country on earth.

"The water's a little slow to heat up."

Gabe frowned. "That's unusual. I'll have a word with the management."

In fact, Lexi's shower had been perfect, piping hot, powerful, its jets easing away every ounce of tension from her tired back and shoulders. She just didn't want Gabe to think she was enjoying herself.

This isn't a vacation. It's a fact-finding mission. I'm here for the Elizabeth Center, not the frigging zebras.

"Are you looking forward to the safari tomorrow?"

"Sure. I guess."

"Apparently we've a good chance of seeing all the big five: rhino, elephant, buffalo, lion and leopard."

"Great."

Gabe gritted his teeth. *One more monosyllable and I'm going to strangle her.*

Bringing Lexi to Shishangeni had been Tara's suggestion. Gabe could hear his wife's voice now:

"It's been two years, and you still have no idea why this woman hates you. Personally, I don't know why you give a shit. But seeing as you so obviously *do,* for God's sake take her away somewhere and find out what her beef is."

It seemed like a good plan at the time. Now, sitting opposite Lexi's beautiful, truculent face as the waves of hostility washed over him, Gabe also wondered why he gave a shit.

Because they shared a common, distant ancestor?

Because Lexi was a business rival?

Because she was Robbie's sister?

Or were his motives more selfish than that? Was the *real* reason he was sitting there that he couldn't stand the idea of any sexy, intelligent woman dismissing him the way that Lexi did? The last woman who'd been immune to his charms was Tara, and he'd wound up married to her.

Am I being a fool? I love Tara. Whatever this thing is with Lexi, I mustn't let it threaten that.

Lexi broke the silence: "So, the Elizabeth Center. I understand there are a number of interested parties?"

Gabe waved down the waiter.

"Let's order, shall we? I'm a little too tired to discuss business to-night."

"Sure." Lexi forced a smile. "There's plenty of time."

She tried not to notice the way Gabe's broad chest stretched the blue fabric of his shirt. Or how his big, rugby player's hands tore the warm bread rolls in half as easily as if they'd been a piece of tissue paper.

I should never have come. I'll leave in the morning. Tell him something came up in New York.

She didn't leave in the morning. By six A.M., she was half asleep in the back of a jeep, bouncing off into the wilderness.

"We'll be sleeping under canvas tonight." Gabe looked rested and happy in an ancient pair of cargo pants and a khaki shirt. Indiana Jones without the bullwhip. Lexi, by contrast, looked like what she was: a sleep-deprived New Yorker longing to crawl back into bed, or at least into the nearest Starbucks for a triple-shot vanilla latte. "Are you excited?"

"Thrilled."

The roar of the jeep's engine as they clattered over the deeply rutted track made conversation difficult. For half an hour, silence reigned.

Then Gabe yelled out: "Look! Over there!"

A lioness emerged from the Delagoa thornbushes, yawning and stretching her long, gold limbs in the early-morning sun. Gabe took pictures.

"Did you see her? Incredible! This is going to be an amazing day."

Lexi thought: *He's like a schoolboy. I wonder if business excites him this much?*

They stopped at noon to eat lunch under the shade of a baobab tree. Lexi jumped out of her skin when two natives approached them. Both were barefoot, armed with spears and wore feathered loincloths around their waists.

"It's all right," said Gabe. "They're San. Trackers. San have roamed these lands since the early Stone Age."

"What do they want?"

"Food, probably." Gabe held out his hand, offering the men some bread. They declined, pointing at Lexi and smiling. One of them pulled a pouch of dried leaves from beneath his feathers and offered it to Gabe.

"Ah. My mistake." Gabe grinned. "It looks like you're the big draw." He shook his head at the San tribesmen. "Sorry. She's not for sale."

"They wanted you to trade me for a bunch of leaves?" said Lexi indignantly, once the men had gone. "Shouldn't they at least offer, like, an ox or something?"

"The San don't keep animals. But they're expert botanists. They know every poison, medicine and narcotic to be found out here. To them, those leaves may have been priceless."

"You should have made the trade," Lexi quipped.

Gabe looked at her for a long time.

"How could I? You're not mine to sell."

Lexi felt the blood rushing to her face.

"Why did you ask me here?"

"Why do you hate me so much?"

The driver shouted from inside the jeep: "Time to pack up, guys. If we want to reach Crocodile River by sunset, we'd better get a move on."

Lexi spent the rest of the afternoon in silence, feigning interest in the wildlife. Inside, her mind was racing.

He wants me. That's why he brought me here. Do I want him, too?

She tried to look at things dispassionately. Gabe was married. Very happily married, if Robbie was to be believed, and Lexi had no reason to doubt him.

Maybe that's part of his attraction? He's a strong, solid family man. A good husband, a good father. He's built the kind of life that I can never have.

She thought of her past lovers, from Christian Harle through all the rock musicians and bad-boy actors. She thought about the wild sex she used to have in college. About Max and the destructive, animal passion they'd shared. *In some ways, we still share it. We always will.* Men like Gabriel McGregor, good men, honest men, never fell for Lexi. *They watch me and admire me from afar, like safari tourists ogling a tigress. They know it's dangerous to get close.*

As they approached the clearing where they'd be spending the night, the jeep stalled in a deep pothole and Gabe's body was thrown against Lexi's. The contact lasted no more than a couple of seconds. But it was enough.

They talked by the campfire till late into the night. Gabe spoke about his childhood. How he'd watched his father's obsession with the Blackwells and Kruger-Brent eat away at him like cancer. "I knew I never wanted to be like that. Embittered, clinging on to the past. I had to make my own way."

"So you don't care about Kruger-Brent? You don't want it?"

From her tone, it was clear that Lexi found this hard to believe.

"No, I don't want it. Why should I? It's just a name to me. Besides, from what I can see, it's brought as much suffering to your family as it has riches."

He's right. But he doesn't understand. Kruger-Brent is a drug. Once you have it in your system, it takes over. Nothing else matters.

The more Gabe spoke, the more Lexi understood the connection he felt to her family. It went beyond the gray McGregor eyes and a single common forefather. Gabe shared Lexi's wanderlust, her magnetic yearning for Africa. Like Robbie, he'd been an addict and crawled back from the abyss. Beneath his gentle-giant exterior, Lexi sensed a powerful ambition.

Like me and Max. Like Kate Blackwell.

Gabe had grown up in a family at war, a family pulled to pieces by bitterness and envy. When he spoke about his father, Lexi immediately thought of her aunt Eve, trapped in the past, enslaved by it.

Max and I are enslaved by it, too. But not Gabe. He's broken free.

He's like us, but he's not one of us.

All of a sudden, like switching on a light, she realized why she'd hated Gabe for so long. It was so obvious, she laughed out loud.

"What's so funny?"

"Nothing."

I envy you. That's what's funny. I envy you your freedom, your goodness, your happy marriage. I envy your ability to care for others. Those kids with AIDS. The slum families you and Dia housed. You can feel. Your heart is still open.

My heart closed when I was eight years old.

That night, Lexi lay wide-awake in her tent, thinking. There was something there between her and Gabe. She hadn't imagined it. It was real.

Part of her ached to get up, crawl into Gabe's tent, and make love to him. Just to know what that would feel like, to be held and wanted and made love to by someone good, someone whole. But a bigger part of her knew that she could never do it. Gabe belonged to another woman. He also belonged to another world.

By the time Gabe awoke the next morning, Lexi had left the camp. Eighteen hours later, she was back in New York.

The next week Templeton Estates were offered a 5 percent stake in the Elizabeth Center development, at highly advantageous terms.

They turned down the offer.

Twenty-Three

MAX WEBSTER WAS ON HIS HONEYMOON.

He and Annabel, his young English bride, were walking on Table Mountain. Annabel raced ahead, her long honey-streaked hair dancing in the wind. Her feet were lost in a carpet of flowers. Above her head, the sun shone a dazzling azure blue.

Max shouted: "Be careful! Don't get too close to the edge!" But the wind whipped away his words. Annabel danced on. She was singing an old folk tune Max's mother used to sing to him in the bath when he was a little boy. *Uncanny. How does she know that song?* Max tried to hum along, then realized he had forgotten the melody.

The other walkers had gone now. They were alone, and the distance between them was growing. Annabel was right by the edge of the cliff.

Max was screaming. "Come back! It's not safe!"

"What did you say?"

Thank God. She heard me. Annabel stopped and turned around so Max could see her face. Except it wasn't her face. It was Lexi's, swaying back and forth over the abyss like a reckless child.

Max rushed toward her. "Lexi, come back. I love you. I'm sorry." He reached out his hand to pull her to safety, but he was too late. Her fingers slid through his and she staggered backward. She was falling.

Max leaped after her. They were in each other's arms in midair, the ground rushing up to meet them. Lexi's features began to morph grotesquely, like melting plastic. She was turning into Eve.

"You killed Keith. You murdered your father. You didn't really believe you'd get away with it, did you?"

But, Mother, I did it for you. Everything has been for you. Mother!

"Max." Annabel Webster shook her husband awake. "Max! You're dreaming. Wake up, darling. It's all right. It's only a nightmare. It isn't real."

She held him in her arms till he calmed down, like a baby. This was the third time this week. Whatever pills Dr. Barrington was prescribing, they evidently weren't working. When he stopped shaking, she said: "Honey, you need to talk to someone. This isn't normal."

Max mopped his brow with the bedclothes and slumped back against the pillow. "I'm all right. I'm a little stressed at work, that's all. It'll pass. Go back to sleep."

The marriage had been Eve's idea. Everything was always Eve's idea.

She was berating Max over one of their weekly lunches. "You need an heir. Someone to take over the business and undo all of your mistakes. Someone who can make Kruger-Brent great again."

"I'm trying, Mother," Max said weakly.

"You're failing. Get married."

Max knew he was a poor chairman. He knew that Kruger-Brent's once bright light was fading, spluttering out slowly like a dying star. It didn't help having his mother second-guessing his every decision, bullying him into taking one direction then blaming him when the hoped-for profits failed to materialize.

It was Eve who had insisted that they sell their holdings in the Ukraine: "If there was oil in those fields, they'd have found it by now. Alternative energy, that's the future. Are you *completely* stupid?"

Max dutifully sold Kruger-Brent's five thousand acres to Exxon, investing the money from the sale in a wind farm in Israel. Six months later, Exxon struck oil. A year after that, the wind farm filed for bankruptcy. Eve blamed Max.

"You never drilled that land properly. What do you expect if you do a half-assed job? This is business Max, not some childish game. God help me, you're your father's son."

Eve brought up Keith's name more and more often these days. It was almost as if she'd transferred the hatred and rage she once felt for her husband onto her son. Max had destroyed Keith Webster, but the monster Keith had created lived on in Eve. Max had done everything his mother wanted. Killed Keith. Betrayed Lexi. Won back Kruger-Brent. But every trophy he brought her was like gasoline poured on the flames of Eve's hatred. He could feed the fire. But he could never put it out.

Meanwhile, Lexi's star continued its inexorable rise. No one remembered the sex scandal that had driven her out of Kruger-Brent. When people saw Lexi Templeton today, they thought of glamour, of resilience, of success. No one at Kruger-Brent said it to Max's face. But the whispers behind his back were deafening:

We made a mistake. We should never have gotten rid of her. Lexi's the winner in the family, not Max. We backed the wrong horse.

By the time he met Annabel, Max was drinking heavily. He was thirty-five but looked ten years older. His looks were fading. *Like everything else about me.* Annabel Savary was fifteen years Max's junior, beautiful and everything he was not: sensible, happy, healthy and uncomplicated. The product of a blissfully happy marriage—her father was an English lord, her mother an American socialite—Annabel was in New York doing an internship at Christie's when Max met her at an auction. He was outbid on the Constable he was after. But he left the auction room that day with a far more valuable prize.

Annabel Savary loved Max Webster in the same way that she had once loved her pony, Trigger. Everybody told Annabel that Trigger was too old and bad-tempered to be broken in. But the nine-year-old refused to give up. Trigger was a beautiful pony, intelligent, strong, fast as a bullet. With patience, and after suffering numerous bites, kicks and other signs of Trigger's displeasure, Annabel transformed him into a sweet-natured, loving animal. By the time he died, when Annabel was eighteen, Trigger had won a boatload of "first" rosettes and was famed across Derbyshire for his devotion to his young mistress.

Annabel was as certain that Max could change as Max was certain that he could not. He knew he should let her go. *She has no idea how fucked up I am.* But Eve wouldn't hear of it. She thoroughly approved of Annabel, believing her to be too young and naive to pose any threat to her influence.

"Marry her quickly, before she changes her mind. Get her pregnant."

Max did as he was told. The wedding was a blur. When he looked at the photographs later, he could barely remember having been there. All he could think about on the way to the church was whether Lexi would show up—she didn't—and whether his mother's pleasure with him would last this time.

Max knew how badly Eve wanted a grandchild. For different reasons, Annabel was also eager to give him a son. Max found the performance pressure unbearable. With Lexi, he'd allowed his sexuality free rein. Somehow, in his mind, Lexi and Eve had merged into one being, the mother-lover, the fulfillment of all his deepest, darkest fantasies. Lexi had allowed him to pour his rage and frustration into her body. She knew the wildness in him, the twisted savage inside, and she wanted it. Sodomy, violence, bondage, nothing had been forbidden. With Lexi, Max had gorged his inner beast. But Annabel must never know that monster. She was pure and lovely. Max must not defile her, the one piece of goodness in his life.

Only Annabel's stubborn, superhuman patience saved the marriage. After six miserable, sexless months, she took matters into her own hands, literally. Ignoring Max's protests, she reached over in bed one night and began stroking his limp penis. Nothing happened.

"I'm your wife, Max. I'm a woman. Put it inside me."

"Stop it!" Max loathed hearing her talk this way.

"No, I won't stop it. Enough is enough."

"Christ, Annabel. I can't get it up on command, okay?"

She took him in her mouth. In spite of himself, Max started to get hard. Images, hateful, degrading images of his mother and Lexi, poured into his mind like sewage. "Please stop." But Annabel didn't stop. Straddling him, she inserted his penis between her legs, bucking and squeezing until at last, with a sob, Max came. Afterward he cried in her arms for hours.

That was the night Annabel realized he was sick. It was also the night she conceived their twin sons.

Max waited till Annabel's breathing settled into a deep, regular rhythm before getting out of bed. Taking a handful of prescription pills from the bathroom cabinet, he swallowed, splashing his face with cold water. His reflection in the mirror looked ghostly.

I have to get it together before tomorrow's board meeting. August Sandford's out to get me. One sign of weakness and he'll move in for the kill.

It was Sandford who'd demanded tomorrow's emergency session.

From the start, he had been a vocal opponent of Max's strategy to abandon foreign real estate and focus exclusively on the U.S. market. August wanted Kruger-Brent to follow Templeton's lead. Eve wouldn't hear of it.

"You're not Lexi's puppy, Max. Kruger-Brent leads, it doesn't follow."

Hundreds of millions had been wiped off the firm's balance sheet as a result. Now the board wanted answers.

Tiptoeing into the nursery, Max gazed in wonder at his sleeping boys. George and Edward were almost three now. They were so perfect, sometimes Max felt scared to touch them. Tiny, male replicas of Annabel, blond and sturdy and sweet.

"Darling. It's four in the morning." Annabel stood in the doorway, yawning. "For heaven's sake, come back to bed."

"Coming. Sorry."

Max followed her into the bedroom.

I wonder if my father ever looked at me while I slept?

I wonder if he loved me, like I love those boys?

The dreams began again.

Tara McGregor giggled to herself as she put the children's cake mixture into the oven. *Ridiculous! I'm behaving like a sixteen-year-old.* But her happiness refused to be contained.

Gabe was coming home early this afternoon. It was his birthday. The kids had baked him a cake and made homemade presents from toilet paper, glitter and glue. Jamie opted for a magnificent rocket, while Collette had surprised no one with her *Little Mermaid*–themed effort. Gabe would be thrilled. But Tara was saving the best present for last. She couldn't wait to see the look on Gabe's face when she told him.

She was pregnant again. A complete accident. *At forty-one!* Ever since she saw the pink line on the pee stick yesterday morning, she'd been unable to stop laughing. She looked at the kitchen clock: three-thirty. Gabe should be home by four.

The doorbell rang. *He's early! Two miracles in one day.* Tara skipped to answer it before Mala, the maid, beat her to it.

"Happy birthd—oh. Can I help you?"

A huge black man loomed in front of her. In his late twenties, with an acne-scarred face and a blank, cold expression in his eyes, he made Tara feel instantly uneasy.

"Your husband home?"

It was half question, half sneer. Tara's unease turned to fear. Adrenaline surged through her body.

"Yes. He's upstairs," she lied. "I'm afraid he's busy at the moment. Come back another time." She started to close the door. Smiling, the man forced his way in. The next thing Tara knew, he was holding a screwdriver to her throat.

"Quiet, and I don't kill you, bitch." His breath smelled of marijuana. "Where's the safe?"

Mala appeared on the stairs. When she saw what was happening, she screamed.

"The children!" yelled Tara. "Get them out!"

The maid turned and ran. Tara felt a sharp pain. The man had slashed the screwdriver across her cheek, narrowly missing her left eye. Blood poured from the wound.

"I say QUIET!" he roared. Suddenly the entryway was filled with men—six, maybe seven of them. All were black and all were high. Tara scanned their faces, looking for one that she recognized. They were bound to come from one of the nearby townships. If she knew someone's family, if she could appeal to them as a person . . .

Upstairs, Collette was screaming. Tara felt her blood run cold.

"Don't hurt her! Please. Take what you want. But don't hurt my children."

Two of the men came downstairs, carrying Collette and Jamie under their arms. Collette was hysterical. Seven-year-old Jamie saw his mother's bloodied face and wriggled free. Hurling himself at Tara's captor, he bit him savagely on the leg.

"Leave her alone! You get away from my mummy."

The man yelped with pain. Pulling back his foot, he kicked the boy's head as if it were a football. Tara heard Jamie's skull crunch as he collapsed at the knees. Her son lay on the floor, motionless.

"Open the fucking safe, bitch. Open it NOW or we kill you all."

Gabe leaned on his horn. *Sodding traffic.* It wasn't even rush hour, but every road into Camps Bay was jammed solid.

On the passenger seat of his Bentley lay the card Jamie had given him that morning. It was a picture of the two of them fishing, two grinning stick figures beside a blue felt-tip-pen river. "I love you, Daddy" was written across the top in bright red glitter.

"I love you, too, buddy," Gabe murmured to himself.

If only the stupid roads would clear, he'd be home in ten minutes.

Tara was on her knees. She felt the cold metal of the screwdriver pressing against her temple, but tried not to think about it, or about her darling Jamie lying unconscious in the hallway.

She pressed the numbers on the keypad of the safe: Four . . . six . . . one . . .

"Type in some security code and I'll slit your kids' throats. The first siren we hear, they're dead. Got it?"

Tara hesitated, her finger hovering in midair. One set of numbers would open the safe. Another combination opened the safe while simultaneously alerting the police.

God help us.

She pressed the final number.

At last the roads were clearing. Cruising along the shore, Gabe swung left onto the winding road that led up to the house. He thought about Tara. She'd been in an unusually good mood this morning, bouncing out of bed like Tigger. Before he left for work, she gave him a long, lingering kiss in the driveway with the promise of a "birthday treat" this evening. Gabe grinned. So much for women losing their libido at forty. Tara was sexier in his eyes now than she had ever been.

When he thought about how close he'd come to losing her two years before on that insane safari with Lexi Templeton, Gabe felt sick. He regretted the way things had ended with Lexi. They hadn't spoken since that day, even though Gabe now considered Robbie Templeton a good friend. But it couldn't be helped. Whatever his feelings for Lexi, Tara was his life. Thinking about her now, he felt a familiar stirring of longing.

He put his foot down harder on the gas.

The man was stuffing a diamond necklace into his Nike backpack. Tara looked past him into the entryway. Jamie wasn't there. Where was he? Upstairs with the other men? The whole house had gone eerily silent. A dark puddle of blood stained the white oak floorboards from where that bastard had kicked Jamie's head. *What sort of animal could do that to a little boy?*

"Nice." The man's eyes gleamed with greed as he caressed the priceless stones. The necklace was an anniversary present from Gabe. Its centerpiece was a flawless six-carat stone from Klipdrift, the diamond-rush town where Jamie McGregor made his first fortune. It was stunning, but Tara had never worn it. There wasn't much call for six-carat diamond necklaces at the AIDS clinic.

Is that what my children might die for? A stupid necklace?

"Take it. Take everything." She wept. "Just please let me go to my son. I'm a doctor. He needs medical attention."

"Later." The man zipped up the bag. He looked at Tara as if seeing her for the first time. It was a look she'd seen thousands of times from young men at the clinic. Distrust. Hatred. Envy. Barely repressed rage. The curse of this beautiful country.

She knew what was going to happen.

"You people, you take everything from us." The man's hands were at her throat. "Our land. Our food. Our diamonds. White devils."

"I work with your people, every day." Tara tried not to show her terror, but she knew he could see it in her eyes. "I work at the AIDS clinic in Pinetown."

"AIDS? YOU gave us AIDS! You white doctors. You kill our children."

"Bullshit." Anger was Tara's last defense. "You kill your own children with your ignorance. We try to help you. My husband has given millions—"

One big black hand covered her mouth, forcing her to the floor. The other tore at her shirt, grabbing hungrily at her breasts. Tara knew better than to fight. The bastard would probably enjoy it. Instead she retreated from her body, barricading herself in her mind.

It's only my body. It isn't "me." He can't touch me.

She felt him on top of her, inside her, the stench and weight of him, the rage with which he forced his huge, grotesquely swollen cock inside her body.

Think about the children. If he gets what he wants from me, maybe he won't hurt them.

He wasn't fucking her. He was stabbing her, frenziedly pounding himself into her flesh, his entire body a weapon.

The police will come, or Gabe. Oh God, Gabe! She stifled a sob. The clock on the wall said ten after four. *Where are you?*

—

Gabe crouched by the side of the road, his hands black with oil.

Stupid Bentley. He'd had new tires put on only last month and already one of them had a flat. He was annoyed about being late again. Tara was always berating him about it, and for once he'd made a real effort to leave the office in good time. As he heaved the spare out of the trunk, it occurred to him that he hadn't changed a tire since he was a teenager back in Scotland. *Bloody hell, I'm getting old.*

Two police cars roared past him, sirens wailing.

Must be another break-in.

He got to work.

Tara heard the sirens. Hope welled up within her.

The man stopped raping her and pulled up his pants. Fear flickered in his eyes. He shouted to his companions: *"Masihambe! Amaphoyisa!"*

Tara understood the Zulu. "Let's go. Police." She started to shake with relief.

Thank God. Oh, thank God. It's over.

For the first time, she wondered if the rape would mean she'd lost her baby. There was blood on her thighs.

Five men charged down the stairs and leaped out of the ground-floor windows like gazelles. *Weren't there six of them before? Had she miscounted?* She tried to get a closer look at their faces, but it was impossible, they moved so fast.

Grabbing his backpack, the ringleader started after them. Then he stopped and turned around.

"Fucking bitch. You typed in the alarm code, didn't you?"

He moved toward the stairs. Tara's blood turned to ice. *The children.*

"No!" She lunged at him, but her legs collapsed beneath her like Jell-O.

He started to climb.

The electric gates were closed.

"No sign of forced entry. You sure this is the place, man?"

"Yah." The police sergeant nodded. "McGregor. It's the Phoenix guy. Maybe they got in around the back."

"You know how to open these things?"

The senior officer looked wearily at the Fort Knox–like gates. He was called out to break-ins almost every day. Nine times out of ten it was a false alarm. Kids playing around with the safe, or some dumb Bantu maid getting spooked and hitting the panic button.

"You can't. Not without the code. We'll have to climb over, boss."

The senior officer sighed. He was getting too old for this.

"Come on, then. Dax, Willoughby, you drive around the back. Wits about you lads, eh? You never know. This could be the real thing."

"Sure, boss." They all laughed.

Five o'clock. Forty minutes to change a stupid tire. *You're pathetic, Gabe McGregor. Pathetic.*

Turning the corner, Gabe saw two squad cars parked outside his gates.

"Sorry, sir. You can't go up there."

"What do you mean I can't go up there? This is my house. What's happened? Where's my wife?"

Blood drained from the young cop's face. "Just stay here, sir. I'll fetch DI Hamilton." He set off at a run up the drive.

Bugger this, thought Gabe. Grinding the Bentley's gears into first, he slammed his foot down on the gas pedal, sending his wheels spinning and throwing up a plume of dust like a sandstorm.

"Sir! Stop!" But it was too late. Gabe's car shot up the hill like a bat out of hell. Seconds later, he sprinted into the house. Cops swarmed the entryway like sand flies.

"Tara!" Gabe shouted into the rafters. He could hear the panic in his own voice. "Tara? Darling?"

A policeman approached him.

"Gabriel McGregor?"

Gabe nodded mutely. "Where's my wife? Where are the children?"

"If you'd just sit down a minute, sir . . ."

"I don't want to sit down. Where have you taken my children?"

A man appeared at the top of the stairs. In his arms was a gray canvas body bag.

It was only four feet long.

TWENTY-FOUR

THE BRUTAL SLAYING OF GABRIEL MCGREGOR'S WIFE AND children was a story that gripped not just South Africa but the world. It was a Greek tragedy: the white philanthropist and his doctor wife, attacked by the very people they had spent their lives trying to save.

A few weeks after the killings, the gruesome drama took another, unexpected twist. Gabe McGregor walked out of Phoenix's office one lunchtime as usual. He hadn't been seen or heard from since.

Conspiracy theories abounded on the Internet: *Was Gabe involved in the murders? Maybe Tara was planning to divorce him, and he had her killed to protect his fortune? He discovered the kids were not his and murdered them in a jealous rage? Had he killed himself out of remorse? Had he assumed a new identity and fled justice?*

Of course, there wasn't a shred of evidence to support such lurid speculation. But that didn't stop tabloids around the world from dredging up every buried secret from Gabe's past, his drug addiction, his record for assault and battery, his investigation for fraud, dissecting each of them in salacious detail and salivating over their imagined "implications." Many people spoke up in Gabe's defense, among them the police investigating the McGregor killings, Robbie Templeton, the world-famous pianist and AIDS campaigner, and Dia Ghali, Gabe's former partner at Phoenix and a hero to many black South Africans. But their voices were drowned out by the baying of the mob.

Race relations had come so far in the new South Africa. No one wanted to believe that this beautiful white doctor and her photogenic children had been slaughtered by a gang of angry black men whom the cops had no chance of catching. Not when there were so many other, more interesting possibilities.

For those who knew Gabe and Tara, however, this was no soap opera. It was sobering, unimaginable reality.

Lexi was in her office in New York when she got word of the murders.

"But they can't *all* have been killed. Not the children, too. There must be some mistake."

There was no mistake. Lexi's first feeling was pure compassion. *Poor Gabe. All of them, his whole family, gone!* She wanted to call or write to him, but quickly realized how inappropriate that would be. She and Gabe hadn't spoken in more than two years. And for a very good reason. As she was fond of telling Robbie and anyone else who would listen, Lexi Templeton hated Gabe McGregor.

Lexi saw the world in black and white. She did not operate in grays. Ever since she was a little girl, playing with her dolls, she'd divided the people around her into two camps: friends or enemies.

Robbie was her friend. Her love for him, and her loyalty, were bottomless and would remain so all her life.

The men who kidnapped her were her enemies. Max was her enemy. Now, since her revelation on safari, Gabe was her enemy. Enemies must be destroyed.

Hovering above this black-and-white worldview loomed a single, even greater imperative: Kruger-Brent. Kruger-Brent was the beginning and end of everything. It was Lexi's religion. Her god. Max had stolen Kruger-Brent from her. That made him the greatest of all her enemies. But Gabe McGregor ran a close second. Not only had he outperformed Lexi in business, but he had also succeeded in keeping his soul intact. For this crime alone, he must be damned, eternally undeserving of her compassion.

And yet Lexi did feel compassion. How could she not? When she heard about Gabe's disappearance, she felt something even deeper. She imagined him alone in the bush somewhere, tortured, crawling away to end his life in unutterable grief and despair. And all at once the world became grayer. For the first time in her life, Lexi Templeton took a day off from work. She spent it in her apartment sobbing, unable to get out of bed.

David Tennant came to see her. A senior member of the Templeton board, David was a lawyer by training. He looked like a character from a Dickens novel. He wore full Victorian sideburns, carried a pocket watch, and had a long bulbous nose that always made Lexi think of Mr. Punch. But beneath his comic appearance, David Tennant was sharp as a tack. He was one of Lexi's most trusted advisers.

"What's Cedar International?"

Lexi assumed a look of studied blankness. "What?"

David Tennant wasn't buying the innocent routine.

"Cedar International. What is it? Or how about DH Holdings? Does that ring any bells?"

Lexi tried to brazen it out. "Of course. They're both offshore investment vehicles. Why do you ask?"

"Oh, I don't know." David Tennant smiled wryly. "I suppose I was just curious as to why you've been siphoning off Templeton assets into them like a South American dictator about to go on the lam."

Lexi smiled. Perhaps charm would work where brazenness had failed?

"Relax, David. I'm not going anywhere. I set those companies up to make investments outside of Templeton's core portfolio."

"I'll say they're outside of our portfolio! We're a real-estate company, Lexi. Cedar International owns two paper mills, a failing diamond mine in the Congo, and a chain of European waste-disposal companies. DH Holdings owns an Internet bank and"—he consulted his notes—"a coffee-processing plant in Brazil. Have you gone quite mad?"

How typical of David to be so observant. And how irritating.

Forget charm. I'll try the angry-boss card.

"Templeton Estates is my company, David. I don't need you to remind me of our business plan."

"Don't you? Then would you mind telling me what all these acquisitions are *for*? And why the dodgy shell companies?"

Damn. She'd forgotten it was impossible to bully David Tennant. That must be why he was her closest adviser and why she'd allowed him to buy a 10 percent stake in her company.

He's entitled to an explanation. I just have to think of one that will appease him without revealing the truth.

"Look, perhaps I should have told you. But not all of these trades worked out as well as I'd hoped. I didn't want to appear, well, foolish."

Silence.

"I knew they were risky deals, so I stripped them out of our balance sheet."

More silence. Lexi plowed on.

"If it looks as if there's no rhyme or reason to the portfolio, that's because there isn't. I set up Cedar years and years ago to buy up any wacky, failing business I thought looked interesting. It's been around almost as long as Templeton."

"I know. You registered it in the Caymans in 2010."

"Right." *How the hell did he know that?*

Lexi ensured she left a trail so complex and convoluted, no one should have been able to trace the company to her, still less link it with Templeton Estates.

I must have gotten careless. That can't happen again.

"I also noticed that two of the companies, the mine and the coffee plant, belonged to Kruger-Brent."

Actually, they all belonged to Kruger-Brent . . . once. With the others, I bought shares in the acquirers, then sold them on to my shell companies after a suitably discreet interval. I guess you didn't get that far, Sherlock Holmes.

Lexi kept her voice casual. "Yes. Purely coincidence."

David Tennant looked skeptical. Lexi had been becoming more and more secretive and reclusive recently. She'd been furious when a recent *Vanity Fair* article drew comparisons between her and Eve Blackwell, her agoraphobic aunt. Maybe the truth hurt?

"I should have told you, David. I'm sorry."

He softened slightly.

"As you say, Lexi, this is your company. Just don't bleed us completely dry, eh? Too many transfers of the size you've been making recently and our cash flow . . . well, I don't need to tell you of the risks."

After he'd gone, Lexi sat at her desk for a long time, thinking.

Her Jenga strategy wasn't working. She'd thought she could chip away at Kruger-Brent discreetly, making strategic acquisitions here and there without anyone connecting them to her. But David Tennant had already made the connection. More important, Kruger-Brent was showing no signs of imminent collapse.

I need a new strategy. Something bigger, bolder. I need to think.

It was time to face facts. Gabe's disappearance had shaken her deeply. She wasn't sleeping. She often found herself crying for no reason. Worse still, it was starting to affect her judgment at work. She had appeased David Tennant, for now. But she knew David. The man was a rottweiler. He never let go. Next time . . .

No. There mustn't be a next time.

She wrote an e-mail to her brother:

I've changed my mind. If it's still open, I'd like to take you up on your offer. I've been working too hard recently. I need a break.

Three weeks at Robbie and Paolo's farmhouse in the South African wine country might be just what the doctor ordered.

The week Lexi arrived in South Africa, Gabe McGregor was officially pronounced dead.

"It's a legal formality," Robbie told her. "No one knows for sure what happened. But given his state of mind and the length of time he's been missing . . . he hasn't touched his bank accounts. He left his passport in the office."

Lexi nodded. She had accepted weeks ago that Gabe was gone. Even so, having his death confirmed in the newspapers felt strange and sad.

I never got to say sorry. I wish he'd known how much he meant to me.

Robbie Templeton opened the lawyer's letter at breakfast.

"Oh dear, oh dear," Paolo teased. "Been harassing the busty sopranos again, have you? Bad boy."

"It's from Gabe McGregor's law firm. I've been asked to come to the reading of his will. According to this, I'm a beneficiary."

Lexi asked to see the letter.

"I didn't know you and Gabe were that close." She felt unaccountably jealous.

"We were friends. But I never would have expected anything like this. To be blunt, it's not as if I need the money. Gabe knew that."

"One always needs the money, Robert," said Paolo firmly. "I intend to become shamefully extravagant in my old age. Don't force me to leave you for someone younger and richer, *chéri*."

Robbie laughed. Lexi couldn't.

I've been asked to come to the reading of his will.

His will.

He really is dead.

———

Robbie hated lawyers' offices. They reminded him of sitting opposite Lionel Neuman as a teenager, the old man's rabbit face twitching as Robbie renounced his inheritance. What dark days those had been. And how happy he was now. Walking away from Kruger-Brent was the best decision he'd ever made. Even so, attorneys still scared him, and Frederick Jansen was no exception. One look at Jansen's severe, dark suit and craggy face crisscrossed with lines, like a clay bust left too long in the sun, and Robbie felt like a naughty kid again. It didn't help that the five other men in the room had all worn suits. Robbie, in jeans and an L.A. Philharmonic T-shirt, felt like a fool.

"The bulk of Mr. McGregor's assets were held in a family trust." Jansen droned on. The legalese washed over Robbie: "*intestate . . . tax efficient structures . . . trustees making provision . . . distinguishing between bequests and wishes . . .*" A few words took root in his brain, among them *charitable endowments.* When Gabe wrote his will, he'd expected to be survived by his children. In the event that he was not, his wealth was to be divided among a select group of charities, including the Templeton/Cozmici AIDS Foundation.

"Sorry. If I could just interrupt you for a moment."

The lawyer looked at Robbie as if he were asking permission to deflower his daughter.

"How much, er . . . how much exactly would our foundation be in line for?"

Frederick Jansen's nose wrinkled in distaste. *Was this man a fool? Had he not* read *paragraph six, point d, subsection viii?*

"The percentage of Mr. McGregor's tax-deductible bequest—"

"Sorry again." Robbie held up his hand, his heart hammering. "I'm not very good with percentages. If you could give me an overall number. You know. Ballpark."

"*Ballpark?*" Frederick Jansen's jowls quivered with distaste. He couldn't imagine what had possessed his client to leave so much money to this vulgar, American queer. "Mr. Templeton, as is explicit in the document before you, your foundation stands to receive a lump sum in the region, the *ballpark*, if you will, of twenty-five million U.S. dollars. Now, if we *could* be allowed to move on with the reading?"

The lawyer repositioned his reading glasses and resumed his monologue, but Robbie was no longer listening. *Twenty-five million!* It was an astonishingly generous bequest from a man with his own charity to support. If there was a heaven, Gabe McGregor must undoubtedly be in it.

"Excuse me, Mr. Jansen." A nervous, plain-looking mouse of a woman appeared in the doorway. Robbie thought: *Poor thing. I wouldn't be this fella's secretary for all the tea in China.* "There's a gentleman here to see you."

Frederick Jansen's sour expression soured still further.

"Sarah. I made it perfectly clear I was not to be interrupted under any circumstances."

"Yes, sir. But—"

"*Any* circumstances! Are you deaf?"

"No, sir. But the thing is, sir . . ."

She got no further. A man appeared in the doorway. Frederick Jansen's mouth fell open. The papers slipped from his hands and fluttered slowly to the floor, like feathers.

"Hello, Fred." Gabe smiled. "You look like you've seen a ghost."

Frederick Jansen knew Gabriel McGregor as a client. The other suits in the room had all dealt with him through their businesses or charities. Only Robbie knew Gabe as a friend. Jumping to his feet, he threw his arms around him.

"You sure know how to make an entrance! I suppose this means I won't get my twenty-five mil?"

Robbie joked in order to break the tension and to hide his own shock. Gabe looked terrible. He'd always been so big, a great, friendly bear of a man. The man standing in front of Robbie now had visibly shrunk. He must have lost fifty pounds. His face looked sunken and aged. But the biggest shock of all was his hair. The thick blond mop of old was gone. Gabe's hair had turned completely white.

"Let's just say you won't get it yet. Listen, Robbie, can you do me a favor?"

"Of course. Anything."

"I'm pretty sure some people in the lobby recognized me when I came in."

Robbie thought, *I wouldn't bank on it.*

"The press'll be here in a minute. I can't go home. Any chance I could hide out with you and Paolo for a while?"

"Of course. As long as . . ." Robbie hesitated, not sure how to put it. "You're sure it wouldn't bring back too many painful memories?"

Gabe and Tara had stayed at Robbie's compound last summer with their children. It had been a magical vacation for all of them.

Gabe was touched by Robbie's concern. "It's okay. The memories aren't painful. They're all I have."

"Fine, then. In that case, let's get out of here."

Robbie had a hundred and one questions he wanted to ask Gabe. *Me and the rest of the world*. But they could wait. The main thing was to get him home and fed, away from the prying eyes of the media.

He's family now. He's one of us. Paolo and I will protect him.

When Robbie walked through the door of the farmhouse arm in arm with Gabe, Lexi fainted. When she came to, tucked up in bed in one of the guest rooms, she had a lump on her head the size of a duck egg.

"Sorry." Her voice was hoarse. "I think I must be more exhausted than I realized. I thought I saw Gabe. It was so real! As if he were standing right next to you. Do you think I need a psychiatrist?"

"Unquestionably." Robbie grinned. "But not because you're seeing things. It turns out our friend Gabriel isn't *quite* as dead as we all thought he was."

"Hi, Lex."

An old-man version of Gabe appeared at Lexi's bedside.

She promptly passed out again.

It was a full twenty-four hours before it sank in that Gabe was not only alive, but here, at Robbie's house, with her. While Lexi came to terms with reality, Gabe washed, ate and slept for the first time in weeks. By nightfall, the story had leaked into the media that Gabriel McGregor was back from the dead. It took the press about a minute and a half to discover his whereabouts. Luckily, Robbie and Paolo's estate was completely hidden from prying lenses, set back behind a long driveway and surrounded by an impenetrable wall of trees. Paolo persuaded the local police to place a ban on low-flying helicopters. Once they realized there was no picture to be had, the paparazzi reluctantly slunk back to Cape Town, pitching camp instead outside Phoenix's offices. Gabe couldn't hide out with Robbie Templeton forever. Eventually he'd have to surface, and when he did, they'd be waiting.

For the first week, Gabe slept eighteen hours of every twenty-four. At mealtimes he ate well but in silence, exchanging occasional grateful smiles with Robbie and Paolo. He barely looked at Lexi.

A doctor was called. He gave Gabe a clean bill of health. Not wanting to risk any more press leaks, Robbie contacted his godfather in New York, Barney Hunt, and asked him to fly out and examine Gabe.

"I'd say he's in good shape mentally," said Barney, "considering the magnitude of the trauma he's just been through. He's allowing himself to recover."

"But he barely speaks," Robbie protested. "He won't say where he's been all this time. He hasn't mentioned Tara or his children once. If I get one 'pass the pepper, please,' that's a good day."

"He'll talk when he's ready. How about Lexi? How's she doing?"

It seemed like an odd non sequitur. "Lexi? She's okay, I guess. Mad as a box of frogs, obsessing about Kruger-Brent as always, but what's new. She came out here to relax, which I took as a good sign."

"And is she? Relaxing?"

"Gabe showing up kind of threw her. I don't know. She's been out of the house a lot. Riding. Do you think I should be worried?"

"No, no." Barney Hunt smiled reassuringly. "I'm fond of your sister, that's all. I care about you both. As does your father."

Robbie stiffened. It had been years since he'd seen Peter. Their estrangement now was as wide and deep as it had ever been.

"I've got enough on my plate right now with Gabe and Lexi," he said defensively.

"I understand," said Barney. "Just remember, your father is not going to live forever. Gabe has years to work through what he's feeling. So does Lexi. But you and Peter . . ."

"Thanks, Barney. I'm okay. We're okay."

The conversation was closed.

Lexi lay in bed, unable to sleep. In two days' time, she would head back to New York. Back to reality. The vacation with Robbie was supposed to have cleared her head. But she felt more confused than ever.

Gabe was alive. That was a good thing. Obviously. So why did his presence in the house make her feel so . . . *so what?* There was no word for it. Lexi and Gabe moved past each other like ghost ships on a hopeless sea. Sometimes Lexi felt him watching her. Almost as if he were waiting for her to say something. But say what?

Sorry I don't know how to talk to you? Sorry your wife and kids got their throats cut? I'm glad you're alive, but I wish you'd get the hell out of my brother's house?

At other times, she sensed hostility in his gaze. *He felt something for me on that safari years ago, and we both know it. Does he blame me for that? Do I make him feel guilty?*

Lexi didn't understand Gabe's passivity. If she were in his shoes, she would be filled with bloodlust. She would think of nothing but wreaking terrible, righteous revenge on those who had slain her family. But Gabe showed no anger. No hatred. Lexi couldn't understand it.

She looked at her bedside clock. Four A.M. Her mind was racing. There was no hope of sleep. Hauling herself wearily out of bed, she pulled a bathrobe over the old pair of Robbie's pajamas she was wearing and tiptoed downstairs. Maybe a cup of warm milk would help.

"What are you doing here?"

Lexi jumped a mile.

"Jesus, Gabe. You scared me."

Gabe was lurking in the half shadow, his face eerily illuminated by the first pale rays of dawn sunlight.

"I couldn't sleep."

"Welcome to my world. You know, when Collette was born, we got no sleep for a year. Tara and I would fantasize about how great it would be to wake up late on Sunday mornings. Now I can wake up as late as I like. But I never make it past dawn. Never."

"I'm sorry."

God, it was so inadequate. What a small, useless little word. Like firing a water pistol into a volcano.

"I was going to do it, you know. I was going to kill myself."

"Gabe, really. You don't have to tell me this."

"But then I thought, Why should *I* be allowed to rest in peace, after what I did? I should have to wake up every day, *every day*, and see their faces. Hear their screams."

Gabe started to cry. Lexi stood rooted to the spot, unsure what to do. Then instinct took over. She wrapped her arms around him.

"It wasn't your fault."

"It was!" he sobbed. "It was my fault. I should have been there. If I hadn't been late. If I hadn't stopped to change that stupid tire! Oh God, Lexi. I loved them so much!"

He clutched at her like a drowning man clinging to a buoy. Then suddenly he was kissing her, they were kissing each other. Lexi could taste the hot salt of his tears in her mouth, his face pressed against her cheek, her neck, her breasts. There was a terrible desperation to the way he ripped her clothes off, pulling her down onto the cold flagstone floor.

As if by making love to her he could somehow bring himself back to life.

He entered her with an anguished cry, like an animal in its death throes. Lexi gripped him tightly to her. Closing her eyes, she could feel the pain flowing from his body to hers. *It's all right, Gabe. It's all right, my love.*

In the beginning, Max used to make love to her the same way. Desperately. As if Lexi could save him. But that was another lifetime. Gabe was not Max. Gabe was good and decent and kind. Gabe was suffering because he had loved. Max suffered because he could not love. Because he was broken.

Like me.

Maybe Gabe and I can save each other?

When Robbie came downstairs later that morning, he found his friend and his sister fast asleep on the couch, entwined in each other's arms. He smiled.

Paolo put on some coffee. "I wouldn't look so happy if I were you." He nodded at the sleeping lovers. "That's trouble."

"Why? You said yourself that Gabe should find somebody. That he needs love to live again."

"Yes, but Lexi?"

Robbie bridled. "Why not Lexi? God knows she could use someone normal in her life. Someone to break her of this obsession with Kruger-Brent."

"I love your sister, Robbie. You know that. But lovers can't 'fix' each other."

Robbie thought: *You're wrong. What about us? We fixed each other.*

"Give it a chance. She loves him, you know. I'm convinced of it. When he went missing, she pined like a lost puppy. Lexi acts tough on the outside, but she feels things deeply."

Paolo said nothing.

He hoped he was wrong, for all their sakes.

TWENTY-FIVE

GABE, LEXI AND ROBBIE WERE IN LEXI'S NEW YORK APART-
ment, playing cards.

Gabe was explaining the rules. "The game's called hearts. The aim
is to dump as many hearts as you can on your opponent, without winning any yourself. Every heart counts against you, so the ten of hearts is
minus ten points, the ace is minus twenty-five and so on. The most
dangerous card in the pack is the queen of spades—the black Mariah. If
you win her, that's minus fifty points. With me so far?"

Robbie said: "I think so. Losing is good, winning is bad, right?"

"Sounds like a stupid game to me," grumbled Lexi.

She was not in a good mood. Normally she loved having Robbie stay
over. They saw him too rarely. He was a good, calming influence on Lexi
and Gabe's fiery relationship; a reminder that their love ran deeper than
the silly arguments and competitiveness of daily life. But today, not even
Robbie could lift her spirits.

Lexi had spent the morning watching helplessly as Kruger-Brent's
share price rallied, up almost twenty points. For years she'd been
quietly pursuing her Jenga strategy: buying up strategic parts of the
Kruger-Brent empire piece by piece, through anonymous shell companies. The idea was that if she could only remove the right piece at the
right time, the whole edifice would collapse in on itself. Max would be

fired. She, Lexi, would return in a blaze of glory to lead the company back to greatness.

But it hadn't happened. Kruger-Brent was like a giant spider. Every time you cut off one of its legs, it grew back. Max was winning the game. The bastard was beating her.

Her temper was not improved when she comprehensively lost the first two rounds of the card game. "This is ridiculous. Whoever heard of a game where you're not supposed to win?"

Robbie laughed. He adored the furious look on Lexi's face. It was the same look she'd had at age six when she lost at Chutes and Ladders, and demanded that either he or the nanny agree to a rematch.

"You *are* supposed to win. But you have to win by losing."

"Actually, there's another rule," said Gabe. "I didn't tell you about it before because it basically never happens. But if you somehow manage to win *all* the hearts *and* the black Mariah—if you get every conceivable penalty card against you, in other words—then you have an option either to halve your own minus points or double your opponents'."

Lexi was quiet. A few minutes later, her bad mood miraculously evaporated. Scooting across the couch, she wrapped her arms around Gabe and kissed him.

"Come on, then, let's play. Whose turn is it to deal?"

Robbie watched Gabe's face light up.

"What was that for?"

"Nothing. I love you, that's all."

Later that night, Gabe and Lexi made love for the first time in weeks. Lexi had been so preoccupied with work recently, she'd been neglecting Gabe. But tonight she made up for it, teasing and caressing him till he begged to get inside her, whispering her undying love in his ear. Afterward, Gabe fell into a deep, contented sleep.

Lexi lay awake, her mind racing, too excited to close her eyes.

At last, at long, long last, she'd figured it out. It was Gabe who'd given her the idea.

I know how I'm going to win back Kruger-Brent.

I've been playing the wrong game all along.

Lisa Jenner, Eve Blackwell's maid, brushed her mistress's long gray hair and let her mind wander. The old woman was rambling again.

"Rory loved me. He was going to marry me, you know. But then that man tricked me. He waited till I was helpless, unconscious, and he did *this*." Eve ran her wizened, veiny hands across her face, probing the scars with her fingers.

"Which man, madam?" Lisa had only been working for Ms. Blackwell for a month, but was already used to her insane outbursts.

"My husband, of course!" Eve snapped. "Max."

"Your husband is dead, madam. He was killed in an accident a long time ago. Max is your son. Remember?"

Eve frowned. *Max is my son. My son?*

"My son is a fool. He's destroying Kruger-Brent. He's weak, like his father."

Lisa Jenner twisted Eve's hair into a high, tight bun and secured it with an ivory pin. Then she replaced her mistress's veil.

"There we are. All done," she said brightly. "Max is waiting for you in the drawing room with Dr. Marshall. Would you like me to take you through?"

"No!" Eve's voice was shrill with panic. "My face! Don't let him touch my face! He's not a doctor. He's a maniac!"

"It's all right, Lisa. I'll handle this."

Annabel had insisted on coming with Max today. The last time he visited his mother on his own, he came home a wreck, his frail nerves stretched to the breaking point. She wasn't about to let it happen again.

"Come along now, Eve. Dr. Marshall isn't here to hurt you."

"Who are you?"

"It's Annabel, Eve. Max's wife. Max and I are here to have a chat with the doctor. We brought you some of that smoked cheese you like."

"She's a good breeder, Max's wife." Eve got unsteadily to her feet. "He should hurry up and marry her. Kruger-Brent must have an heir."

Kruger-Brent. How Annabel had come to loathe those two words. The pressure of running Kruger-Brent had brought poor Max to the brink of a nervous breakdown. His mother seemed to expect him to wave a magic wand and recoup all their losses overnight. She had no idea of the reality of the market. Then again, how could she?

The old battle-ax barely knows her own name.

"Hello, Mother. You look well."

Eve shuffled into the drawing room. Age had not crept up on Eve Blackwell. It had ambushed her suddenly. In a matter of months, her ramrod-straight spine had become bowed and stooped. Faint veins on the backs of her hands stood out like tree roots. Liver spots burst like a plague over her once flawless skin. But none of these changes mattered to Max. In his eyes, his mother was eternally beautiful.

He moved forward to kiss her. Eve brushed him aside.

"I know what you did," she hissed. "I'm going to tell everybody. *Then* you'll be sorry."

Annabel watched Max shrink. *Why does he let her crush him? What power does she hold over him?*

"That's enough, Eve," she said. "You're confused."

While the doctor took Eve's blood pressure, Max took Lisa Jenner aside.

"Has she been like this the whole time? Or is it worse, you know, when I'm here?"

"You mustn't blame yourself, sir," the maid said kindly. "She has her lucid moments. But this is pretty much par for the course. She's been writing a lot. That seems to calm her."

"Writing? Writing what?"

"I don't know. Just rambling, I think. She won't let me see it. She keeps all her papers locked in the desk drawer."

Later, Max repeated to Annabel what Lisa had told him. "Do you think I should open the drawer? Take a look?"

"No," Annabel said firmly. "She may be old and mad as a hatter, but she's entitled to her privacy."

In fact, Annabel Webster couldn't have cared less about her mother-in-law's privacy. Her only concern was for Max. *God knows what venomous drivel is in those papers. As soon as she drops dead, I'll open the drawer myself and burn them.*

Lexi was late home. Again.

Gabe couldn't hide his disappointment. "I made dinner. Two hours ago. Where the hell have you been?"

"At work." As always when she was in the wrong, Lexi's tone was aggressive. "Just because you've lost your ambition, it doesn't mean I have to."

Gabe's face crumpled with hurt. The irony was that he'd taken a backseat at Phoenix in order to spend more time with Lexi. He hoped eventually to persuade her to marry him and start a family. But whenever he brought up either subject, she either ducked the question or put her "bitch" hat on.

"You're lying. I called the office. You left hours ago."

"Oh, what, so you're spying on me now?"

"Not spying. You were late. I was worried."

"I'm a big girl, Gabe. If you must know, I was at a business meeting."

"With whom?"

"None of your damn business!"

Lexi stormed into the bedroom, slamming the door behind her. Pulling off her clothes, she tried to get her head together.

Why am I doing this? Why am I pushing him away?

Lexi loved Gabe as much as she ever had. More. But her stress levels were through the roof. She was preparing for the greatest battle of her life—the battle for control of Kruger-Brent—and she couldn't tell Gabe, or anyone, what she was doing. The stakes could not be higher. If she failed, she would lose everything. Her fortune, her company, perhaps even her freedom.

Actually, there's another rule. I didn't tell you about it because it never happens . . .

You are supposed to win. You have to win by losing.

What if she won back Kruger-Brent, but lost Gabe?

She pushed the thought from her mind. She would win the game. She had to. Once she had Kruger-Brent, and her revenge on Max was complete, then she would make it up to Gabe. He wasn't going anywhere.

Kruger-Brent failed to make payments on a loan in Singapore. The bank foreclosed on one of its properties. The amount involved was so small, Max never even knew about it. A Singaporian middle manager was fired. Kruger-Brent refinanced. End of story.

A few weeks later, a similar oversight in Germany led to another loan being called in. Again the amount was small.

Lexi made a note of the dates.

Karen Lomax, a financial journalist at the *Wall Street Journal*, received a phone call. After she hung up, she turned to her colleague Daniel Breen.

"Hey, Dan. You heard anything about credit problems at Kruger-Brent?"

Daniel Breen shook his head. "Have you?"

"Some lady just called. Said I should look into bad loans in Asia. Think there's a story in it?"

Daniel Breen shrugged. "Only one way to find out, I guess."

The cards were being dealt.

Gabe opened the file in front of him, skimming through the pictures.

"So she's *not* having an affair?"

The private investigator shook his head. "From the evidence I've seen, sir, no, she's not." Gabe's shoulders sagged visibly with relief. "However . . ."

Gabe looked up.

"There are some . . . anomalies."

"What sort of anomalies?"

"Financial. If you turn to page twelve of the written document, it's all in there."

Gabe turned. Slowly, methodically, he started to read.

The first few weeks of Gabe's love affair with Lexi had been like a dream.

Gabe had not believed it possible that he could love again after what had happened to Tara and his children. Certainly not while his grief was so raw. But in those first miraculous weeks at Robbie's African hideaway, Lexi had breathed life into his deadened heart. When Gabe woke in the small hours, sweating and screaming Tara's name, Lexi would wrap her arms around him and hold him till the nightmare passed. Gabe spoke about his children often, returning again and again to the terrible events of his birthday like a dog crawling back to its vomit. Lexi listened. He poured his guilt into her hands, and she took it from him, as gently and graciously as if he'd been giving her a bunch of flowers.

But eventually, inevitably, real life intruded upon their lovers' idyll. Gabe handed over the day-to-day running of Phoenix to others, content to focus on Lexi and his charity work. If Tara's murder had taught him one thing, it was that love and life were too precious to be wasted pushing paper around an office.

Lexi didn't see things that way. She could no more stop working than stop breathing. Templeton was based in New York. Gabe moved to the city to be with her. He enjoyed New York, the energy and the excitement, but he never stopped feeling like a guest in Lexi's apartment.

As a first step toward building a new, joint life together, Gabe bought an exquisite period house in Bridgehampton. Somewhere for them to get away, to make time for each other.

"What do you think?" He led Lexi around the wood-paneled rooms, each simply but beautifully furnished with chesterfield couches and Irish linens from the White Company. "I tried to make it peaceful. An escape from the city."

"It's . . . it's cute." Lexi tried to sound enthusiastic. But inside she thought: *I don't want to escape from the city.*

Gabe's face fell. "You don't like it."

"I do! It's not that. It's just . . . when are we going to use it?"

"On weekends."

"I work weekends, baby."

Lexi didn't just work weekends. She worked early mornings and late nights. She worked Thanksgiving and Labor Day. Gabe hadn't realized that her fateful trip to visit her brother in South Africa was the first vacation she'd taken in over five years.

It wasn't only the long hours. It was the secrecy. Lexi often talked in her sleep, rambling about Kruger-Brent and Max and revenge. She seemed to be anxious that time was running out. But when Gabe asked her, "Time for what?" Lexi pretended not to know what he was talking about. Not long ago, Gabe had been shocked when David Tennant, Lexi's right-hand man at Templeton, mentioned in passing that the company was in trouble.

"Lexi's been liquidating assets faster than any of us can keep up. The money disappears into these obscure holding companies, then *poof,* it's gone."

When Gabe challenged Lexi about this, she was dismissive.

"David's a worrywart. I've moved some cash around, that's all."

"He says you're stripping Templeton bare."

"He's exaggerating."

Conversation closed.

Recently it had reached the point where Gabe felt he had to make an appointment to speak to Lexi at all. When he did, all the subjects *he* wanted to discuss—marriage, children, their future—were off the agenda.

"I can't have children, Gabe. I've told you."

"Can't or won't?"

This made Lexi angry.

"Fine. Won't. What's the difference?"

"There's a lot of difference! Why won't you? What are you so afraid of?"

"I'm not afraid of anything. Stop harassing me! You want me to spend more time with you, but when I do, you give me the third degree."

Hiring the private investigator was a low point. But Gabe couldn't take any more. He had to know what it was that Lexi was keeping from him. He loved her, but he was tired of sitting home, alone while Lexi flew God knows where on a never-ending business trip. He wasn't her lover. He was her layover. That's when it hit him.

Maybe she's found someone else?

"I'm afraid I don't fully understand this." Gabe handed the file back to the PI, a fat man with the ruddy cheeks of a heavy drinker and a paunch so swollen it spilled over the edge of the couch, hanging almost to his knees.

"Ms. Templeton is a trustee of your charity?"

"She is, yes."

"She's authorized to make financial transactions on its behalf?"

"Yes. But that's just a formality. Lexi's celebrity is a useful tool for us. It helps to raise money. She's not involved in the day-to-day business of the foundation."

"Which makes it all the more curious that she's made a number of sizable withdrawals from the charity's accounts."

The PI pulled a red pen out of his jacket pocket. He handed the relevant sheet of paper back to Gabe with the amounts and dates circled. Gabe stared at it for a long time.

"You're sure it was Lexi who authorized these withdrawals."

"Yes, sir."

She's stealing from me? From the charity? It makes no sense.

"Do you know why?"

"No, sir. Not yet. I'm afraid your fiancée is a regular David Blaine when it comes to money. As soon as she get her hands on it, it vanishes. The paper trail around her is so complex, it's damn near impenetrable."

Gabe pulled out his checkbook. Scribbling down a number, he ripped off the check and handed it to the investigator. The fat man's eyes bulged.

"Penetrate it."

"Yes, sir. We will, sir. Thank you, sir."

———

Waddling down the driveway of Gabe's Bridgehampton beach house, clutching his check like a talisman, the PI marveled at the stupid things men did for love.

The PI had seen hundreds of pictures of Lexi Templeton. Blow-job lips on an angel's face. Tits and ass to die for, but classy with it. A woman like that could screw any man she wanted. But she'd picked this old, white-haired shell of a guy who just *happened* to have bucket loads of money and a trusting nature?

Maybe McGregor thought he was safe because the lady was rich herself. If so, he was an even bigger fool.

Didn't he know that rich women were the greediest of all?

It was Friday morning. Max sat in his corner office at Kruger-Brent staring at the photographs on his desk. His little boys, George and Edward, were five years old now. Max's office had countless silver-framed pictures of them, hand in hand, grinning at the camera. There were photographs of Annabel, too, and of Eve as a young woman at the height of her beauty. But it was Max's sons who mesmerized him, their innocence flooding the room like sunlight.

That's what childhood ought to look like. Happy. Pure.

August Sandford stormed in.

"Have you seen our share price? What the hell's happening?"

August Sandford had not aged well. His once thick chestnut hair had thinned, exposing too much middle-aged scalp. The muscled physique of his twenties had long since turned to fat. Kruger-Brent had made him a rich man, on paper. But this morning, August had seen the value of that paper drop by almost 15 percent. With a wife, three kids and a demanding mistress to support, August's stress levels were permanently set on high. This morning, the sweat patches under his arms had grown so big they were about to start dripping.

Max pulled up Bloomberg on his PC screen. *Jesus.*

August was shouting, "Some bastard's shorting us."

It was true. Somebody out there was borrowing massive amounts of Kruger-Brent stock and selling it at a discount. Effectively they were taking a bet on the share price going down. The problem was that by shorting on this scale, the seller was turning his prediction into a self-fulfilling prophecy.

"That piece in the *Wall Street Journal*, that's what started this. That bitch journalist, making out like we're some kind of major credit risk! Two lousy loans and the whole market's turning on us. How the fuck did she know about Singapore? That's what I'd like to know."

"I don't know."

"Well, you *should* know. You're running this company, Max. We're leaking bad news like a ripped condom and you're sitting in your ivory tower with your finger up your ass!"

Max's head began to throb. He closed his eyes. When he opened them again, August was gone. *Thank God.* Standing in his place was an elderly man. He was leaning heavily on a wooden cane, clutching the handle with delicate, liver-spotted hands.

"Can I help you?"

The old man shook his head. "No. I'm afraid no one can help me anymore. It's too late."

Something about his voice sounded familiar. His sadness tugged at Max's heartstrings. "Too late for what, sir?" he asked kindly. "Perhaps I can help."

"Too late for everything. I'm dead, you see. My boy killed me."

Foul green slime began to ooze from the old man's nostrils.

"Why did you do it, Max? I loved you so much."

Keith?

A terrible, unearthly stench filled Max's office. He started to choke, clutching his desk for support.

"Get out! You're dead! Get out and leave me alone!"

"Max?"

"I said GET OUT!"

August Sandford was shaking Max by the shoulders.

"Max! Can you hear me? Are you all right? Max?"

"Oh God. I killed him!"

"Killed who?"

That was all they needed in a crisis. A chairman who was losing his marbles.

Slowly, Max emerged from the nightmare. The terror began to fade. *It's okay. I'm in my office. August's here. It was a dream, that's all. Just a dream.*

"I'm sorry." He smiled weakly at August Sandford. "The stress gets to me sometimes. I'm fine."

Like hell you are.

Max forced himself to look at the screen in front of him. This was the real nightmare. And he hadn't the first clue what to do about it. Sensing his indecision, August took charge.

"You need to call a board meeting. Right now. We need to find out who's short-selling our stock and why. If it's the credit rumors, we can address that. But we have to act fast."

August Sandford hurried out of the room. Max stared at the open door, half expecting his father's ghost to reappear. *Annabel's right. I need help.*

He pressed a buzzer on his desk.

"Tell the board I'm convening an emergency meeting."

His computer screen was flashing.

Fifteen percent down.

Sixteen . . .

"I want everyone around that table in fifteen minutes."

Lexi was clearing her desk at Templeton when David Tennant knocked on her open office door.

"Come in." She smiled at him warmly. David Tennant did not return the smile, or the warmth.

"I came to give you this." He handed her a sealed white envelope.

Lexi joked. "I take it from your expression that it's not an early Christmas card?"

"No. It's my resignation."

Lexi looked taken aback. "Are you serious?"

"Dead serious. I thought we were partners, Lexi. But partners don't lie to each other."

"David! I haven't lied."

David Tennant shook his head in disbelief. "Haven't lied? You've done *nothing* but lie for months. Lexi, you've plundered the company balance sheet without mercy, despite solemnly promising me you would stop. Our cash reserves are so low we can barely afford a hot dog. You refuse to tell me, to tell any of us, what you've been buying."

"I haven't been buying anything," said Lexi truthfully. "It's true that at one time I was acquiring businesses."

"From Kruger-Brent."

"Yes," Lexi admitted. "But I stopped that years ago."

"Really. So where *is* the money, Lexi?"

Lexi picked up a brass paperweight on her desk and studied it intensely. When she spoke, she did not meet David Tennant's eye.

"I'm afraid I can't tell you."

David Tennant turned to go.

"Wait! Please, David. Trust me. All the money I've borrowed from Templeton will be repaid. With interest. This deal that I'm working on could make us a fortune."

"And if it doesn't?"

"It will. But if worse comes to worst, I can refinance Templeton."

"How?"

Lexi looked at him brazenly. "By borrowing against my Kruger-Brent stock."

"Lexi, have you looked at the markets this morning? Kruger-Brent's stock is in free fall."

"What do you mean 'free fall.' They're down?" She switched on her computer, trying to hide her excitement. *It's started.*

"Not down. Crashing. Something's going on over there. People are dumping KB shares as if they were live hand grenades. Unless Max Webster can turn the tide, they could be bankrupt by Monday morning."

The stock price popped up on Lexi's screen. Her hands started to tremble.

In other circumstances, David Tennant might have felt sorry for her. If Kruger-Brent did go under, Lexi stood to lose a fortune. But having watched her strip the value out of his 10 percent stake in Templeton without a shred of remorse—seven years of work up in smoke!—he wasn't feeling at his most charitable.

He walked out of the office without looking back.

After he'd gone, Lexi sat at her desk for a long time.

They could be bankrupt by Monday morning.

If this doesn't work, I've destroyed the thing I love most in the world.

An hour later, Lexi left the office and drove out to the Hamptons. This weekend with Gabe had been on the schedule for months. She couldn't cancel. She had to behave normally. *Act like nothing has happened.*

Gabe saw Lexi's Aston Martin DB7 pull into the graveled driveway. He watched from their bedroom window as she stepped out of the car.

"Our" bedroom. That's a joke. Lexi can't have spent more than six nights here all year.

As always, her beauty took his breath away. She wore a plain gray wool business suit and cream silk blouse, her blond hair pulled back in a simple ponytail. But she still shone brighter than the polestar. *She always will to me.* He couldn't bear the thought of losing her. Maybe, somehow, she'd have an explanation for taking the money? For all the secrecy, all the lies? Clinging to faint hope, he went downstairs.

Lexi dropped her weekend bag in the entryway and hugged him fiercely. Gabe saw instantly that she'd been crying. *Tears of remorse? Guilt?*

"What's the matter?"

Lexi followed him into the sitting room. She sank down onto the white couch that only a few short hours ago had borne the weight of the fat PI.

"Is there something on your mind? Something you want to tell me?"

Not until that moment did Lexi realize how much pressure she'd been under. The greatest gamble of her life was under way. She longed to unburden herself to Gabe. But she knew she couldn't.

"I'm not sure where to begin."

Gabe felt the love well up inside him like freshly struck oil. She looked so forlorn and vulnerable.

She really is sorry. She's going to confess everything. I'll forgive her. Everything will be all right.

"Templeton's going under."

Gabe hid his surprise. It wasn't what he'd expected to hear. Was *that* why she'd stolen from his charity? To prop up her business? Hardly the most noble of reasons, but perhaps in desperation . . .

"David Tennant resigned today. I'm going to have to let the others go, too."

"I'm sorry, darling. I know how much that business means to you."

Lexi looked up at him with genuine surprise.

"Templeton? It doesn't mean that much to me."

Now Gabe was confused. "But . . . you've been crying."

"Not about Templeton." Lexi sniffed.

This is it. This is where she's going to come clean about the money. Ask to make a fresh start.

"Kruger-Brent's share price got decimated today. Wiped out. They could . . . it might mean the end of the company."

Gabe recoiled as if he'd been stung.

Kruger-Brent? She's crying over Kruger bloody Brent?

It was the last straw. Gabe hadn't hit another human being since almost killing that poor man in London thirty years ago. But he could feel his fists twitching. Did Lexi have no shame at all? She'd stolen money, not just from him, the man she was supposed to love, but from the thousands of AIDS victims who desperately needed it. But that didn't bother her. Oh no. All she cared about, all she'd *ever* cared about, was that godforsaken company. Gabe remembered his father, how he'd died broken and embittered, destroyed by his obsession with Kruger-Brent. *I traveled halfway across the world to avoid the same fate. And here I am, in love with a woman every bit as poisoned and corrupted by Kruger-Brent as my dad was.*

Oblivious to his anger, Lexi went on.

"There have been some credit problems. I didn't realize it was that serious, but obviously it must be. The market can sense Max's weakness like a shark smelling blood."

"I don't care." Gabe's voice was barely a whisper.

"What?"

"I said I'm NOT INTERESTED!"

Suddenly he was shouting. Screaming. Lexi had never seen him so angry.

"Kruger-Brent can go to hell, for all I care, and the same goes for Max Webster. You stole from my foundation."

Lexi said nothing. Gabe could see the wheels turning in her brain as she calculated her options. Deny? Explain? Apologize?

Everything's a game to her. It's all about winning and to hell with the truth.

Eventually she said: "I didn't steal. I borrowed."

"Why?"

Another pause. "I can't tell you." She hung her head. "But it was for something very important."

"More important than getting retrovirals to terminally sick children?"

"Yes," Lexi answered without thinking, from the heart.

Gabe looked at her with a mixture of horror and disgust. Was she really so far gone that she thought a business deal was more important than saving lives? Apparently so.

His disappointment was more than Lexi could bear. Tears welled up in her eyes.

"You'll get the money back, Gabe. You'll get twice what I took. I promise."

"It's not about the money." Gabe put his head in his hands.

Lexi thought: *He looks so tired. So defeated. Have I done that to him?*

"It's over, Lexi. I love you. But I can't go on."

Lexi felt the walls caving in. She wanted to cry, to scream: *No! I love you. Please don't leave me. Don't go!*

And yet she knew she couldn't keep him. Gabe was good and honest and true. He deserved a normal, happy life. She had done what she had to do. Gabe would never understand it, even if she told him. Which, of course, she never would.

It took every ounce of her self-control for Lexi to stand up, pick up her bag and walk to the door.

"I love you, too, Gabe. I'm sorry. You'll get your money."

Gabe stood in the doorway, watching her car drive away.

Good-bye, Lexi.

On Monday morning, when the markets opened, Kruger-Brent stock was down by almost 90 percent.

On Wall Street, rumors were rife. *Someone* had inside information about Kruger-Brent, and it was bad:

The default on the Singapore bank loan was the tip of a bad-debt iceberg.

A massive accounting fraud was about to be uncovered.

One of the "wonder drugs" of the firm's pharmaceutical division was going to be exposed as a lethal killer.

Not since the banking crisis of 2009 had the markets seen such a huge company brought to its knees overnight. A couple of traders emerged from the woodwork, admitting that they'd taken huge bets on the company's demise. Carl Kolepp, owner of the legendarily aggressive hedge fund CKI, was one. The *Wall Street Journal* estimated that over the weekend, Kolepp had personally made $620 million out of Kruger-Brent's misery.

Lexi Templeton, like the rest of her famous family, had lost everything.

Max Webster made a statement on CNBC, appealing for shareholders to stay calm, echoing Roosevelt's famous line that there was "nothing to fear but fear itself." Like millions of others, Lexi watched Max's broadcast live. She was shocked by how ill he looked, how frail and gaunt. The world was on fire, and Max was burning.

Think of it as preparation for the flames of hell. Bastard.

Max's statement calmed no one. By Tuesday, it was all over. Hundreds of thousands of Kruger-Brent employees all around the world woke up to find themselves out of a job. Tens of thousands of shareholders saw their money go up in smoke. Across America, the headlines screamed:

KRUGER-BRENT BANKRUPT!
U.S. GIANT COLLAPSES!

In the midst of all the commotion, few people noticed the short press release from Templeton Estates, announcing that the firm had ceased trading.

By Thursday, the press stopped hounding Lexi for interviews. She had given a statement, expressing her profound sorrow at Kruger-Brent's passing and making it clear that she had nothing more to say.

The entire extended Blackwell family was door-stepped by photographers, gleefully cataloging their spectacular fall from grace. Talk about the mighty fallen! The media gorged itself on schadenfreude like a blood-drunk mosquito. Footage of Peter Templeton looking old and frail outside Cedar Hill House was aired on all the major news channels, who were running back-to-back retrospectives of Kruger-Brent's illustrious history. Interviews with Kate Blackwell from the 1960s were dusted off and replayed, pulling in enormous ratings for the TV networks. America had grown up with the Blackwells and Kruger-Brent. It was, as Robbie Templeton told reporters outside the Royal Albert Hall in London, the end of an era.

Eve Blackwell, as ever, remained barricaded in her self-imposed prison on Park Avenue.

Max Webster's whereabouts were unknown.

Two weeks later, the furor began to die down. Lexi Templeton slipped quietly out of her apartment one night at about six o'clock. Taking a series of taxis, making sure she wasn't followed, she arrived at a nondescript Italian diner in Queens around seven.

He was at the table, waiting for her.

Lexi sat down. "Have all the transfers been made?"

"As agreed. Seventy percent for you, thirty for me. A bit harsh really, considering I did all the work," he joked.

Lexi laughed. "Yeah, and I took all the risk. I staked every penny I have on borrowing the additional stock we needed. I broke my own company—begged, borrowed and stole." She pushed the thought of Gabe from her mind. "If the market hadn't panicked, I'd have been wiped out."

"But they did, though, didn't they?" Carl Kolepp grinned. "How do you feel?"

Lexi grinned back. "Rich."

"Good. The spaghetti's on you."

They ate and celebrated. What they'd done was completely illegal. Short selling was one thing. But manipulating a company's stock price through an orchestrated campaign of misinformation? That was something else. Lexi had used her inside knowledge to defraud shareholders. If she and Carl were caught, they were both looking at a long stretch of prison time.

But we won't be caught.

This time Lexi had covered her tracks completely. All threads linking her to Carl Kolepp had been meticulously destroyed. Unless one or the other of them confessed, they were home free.

Carl asked Lexi: "So what'll you do now? Buy yourself an island somewhere peaceful? Fill your swimming pool with Cristal?"

The suggestion seemed to amuse her.

"Of course not. This is where the real work begins."

"What do you mean?"

"I'm going to rebuild the company, of course. Buy back all the decent businesses. Get rid of all the dross Max acquired in the last ten years. I've halved my own score. Now I'm going to double my opponents'."

"Excuse me?"

Lexi laughed. "Forget about it. Private joke."

"Let me get this straight." Carl Kolepp looked puzzled. "You bankrupted your own company just so you could rebuild it?"

"Uh-huh. I lost so I could win."

"Has anyone ever told you you're a little bit nuts?"

Lexi smiled. "A few people. Apparently it runs in my family."

TWENTY-SIX

∽

FELICITY TENNANT WAS DEPRESSED. SHUFFLING OUT TO the mailbox in her pajamas, she did not return her neighbors' cheery waves on this glorious, sunny September morning. Behind Felicity stood the idyllic white clapboard house where she and her husband, David, had lived happily and harmoniously throughout twenty years of marriage. Until last month.

First rule of a happy marriage: Get Your Husband Out of the House.

Ever since David quit his job at Templeton, he'd been moping around at home like a bear with a sore head, getting under Felicity's feet. For reasons Felicity did not understand, they had apparently lost a lot of money. David was even talking about selling the house and moving somewhere more modest. Perhaps even leaving Westchester County.

Over my dead body.

The morning mail did not lift Felicity's spirits. Bills, bills and more bills. There was only one white envelope among the brown and red. *(Red bills! The shame of it!)* Felicity would have liked to open it, but David got terribly prickly when she opened his mail. Then again, David got terribly prickly about everything at the moment.

"Here." Back in the kitchen, she handed him the letter, along with the bills. "For you."

David Tennant opened the envelope without interest. Since Templeton folded, it was as if a black cloud had descended over his life. Nothing seemed to matter anymore. Inside the envelope was a note and a check. David Tennant read both. Twice. Felicity noticed that his hands had started to shake.

"What? What is it?"

He handed her the note.

Dear David, I am sorry this has taken so long. And I'm sorry I was not able to be more open with you. I hope this check will go some way toward restoring your faith in me. Your friend, Lexi

"Humph." Felicity Tennant was unimpressed. "Guilty conscience got the better of her, has it? It's about time. *Your friend*, indeed! After the way Her Ladyship has treated us."

Silently, David Tennant passed his wife the check.

"Jesus, Mary and Joseph!" Felicity Tennant clutched the kitchen table for support.

The check was for $15 million.

It was going to be a good day after all.

Yasmin Ross smiled at her boss when he walked into the office.

"Morning Mr. M. The mail's on your desk, next to the latte and skinny blueberry muffin. I moved the morning meeting to a quarter after so you'd have time to eat something."

Gabe smiled back gratefully

"Yaz, you're an angel."

Poor man. Yasmin watched him go into his office, shoulders slumped, head down. Gabe's smiles didn't fool her, or anybody else at the charity offices. Ever since he'd broken things off with Lexi Templeton, the joy seemed to have drained out of him like air from a punctured tire. *Lexi must be crazy, letting him slip through her fingers. I wouldn't kick Gabe McGregor out of my bed, not for any money.*

Sitting at his desk, Gabe picked at his muffin. He knew his assistant was worried about him, and her concern touched him. He hadn't been eating well lately. Or sleeping, for that matter. Sighing, he turned his attention to the mail. Every day Gabe received scores of begging letters, asking for gifts from his foundation. Saying no was the part of his work he liked least, but it had to be done. If they spread themselves too thin, they'd achieve nothing. There was still so much work to be done.

Recently Gabe had been saying no even more than usual, thanks to the hole in the charity's funds made by Lexi. Legally, Gabe was obliged to report the theft to the police. But he hadn't been able to bring himself to do it. Not yet, anyway.

When he saw the handwriting on the plain white envelope, he choked on his coffee, spraying brown liquid right across the desk. Gabe hadn't heard a word from Lexi since that awful day in the Hamptons.

What could she want? A reconciliation?

Is that what I want, too?

He opened the letter. Except there was no letter. Only a check.

It was for exactly three times the amount Lexi had stolen.

August Sandford was suspicious.

"I don't know, Jim. Who else is going?"

Jim Barnet was the head—ex-head—of Kruger-Brent's manufacturing division. Along with a select group of other divisional heads, Jim had been summoned to a meeting by the firm's receivers. Apparently, a potential cash buyer had come forward, interested in bidding for some of Kruger-Brent's more profitable businesses.

"Me, Mickey. Alan Dawes, I think. Tabitha Crewe."

"Tabitha? They want mining?"

"Apparently. And real estate."

"And nobody has any idea who this mystery benefactor is?"

"Nope. But come on, man. It's not like we're exactly inundated with offers. Most of the market still seems to think we're toxic."

August hung up the phone.

"Who was that, darling?" Leticia, his mistress, rolled over in bed, pressing her soft breasts against his chest. Since Kruger-Brent went bust, August's performance as a lover had dropped off a cliff. It was like there was an invisible thread connecting his dick to his net worth. When one shriveled, so did the other.

"Jim Barnet. Some cash-rich buyer wants to talk to us apparently."

"That's good, right?"

Reaching beneath the Frette sheets, Leticia gently ran her fingers over August's balls. He used to love that in the old days.

"Maybe." August felt the first stirrings of an erection. *A good sign?*

"I hope so."

———

Mandrake & Connors was one of the largest, most respected accounting firms on Wall Street. In Kruger-Brent's glory days, it'd made a fortune acting for the firm. Now, in an ironic twist of fate, it found itself handling its bankruptcy. Unraveling the accounts of such a vastly complex network of businesses was expected to take months, if not years.

August Sandford sat with five of his former colleagues in one of Mandrake & Connors's conference rooms. A month before, the six Kruger-Brent board members would have called the shots at such a meeting. Today, Whit Barclay, the accountant, was in charge. He was loving every minute of it.

"You all know why you're here."

Whit Barclay was a small man with a weak chin, receding hairline and permanently wet lips. A drone who had made it to the top of his anthill full of drones by the simple expedient of staying in the same job for thirty-two years.

"It goes without saying that everything that is discussed within these four walls today remains strictly confidential."

The Kruger-Brenters murmured their assent.

"A company known as Cedar International has approached us, expressing an interest in a number of Kruger-Brent's more profitable business areas."

"And mining," muttered August Sandford. Tabitha Crewe shot him a venomous look. Everybody knew that Tabitha's division, which had been responsible for Kruger-Brent's gold and diamond mines, was a lame duck.

"Indeed," Whit Barclay averred. "In any event, Cedar International—"

August Sandford interrupted again. "Who are these guys? I'm sorry to piss on everybody's picnic. But has anyone heard of this company?"

"Really, Mr. Sandford. There's no need for coarse language."

"I haven't," said Jim Barnet.

"Me neither." Mickey Robertson and Alan Dawes agreed.

"How do we know they're for real?"

Whit Barclay flushed with anger. *He* was supposed to be chairing this meeting.

"I can assure you, Cedar International is a legitimate, *highly* capitalized firm with—"

"Yeah, but who are they? What do they do? They're not active in any of our business areas or we would have heard of them."

The door to the conference room opened. Everybody turned around.

Whit Barclay said stiffly: "Allow me to introduce the CEO of Cedar International."

August Sandford's jaw almost hit the table.

"Hello, August. Everybody." Lexi smiled sweetly. "It's been a while."

Lexi had done her homework. She knew exactly which of Kruger-Brent's businesses were viable and which had become dangerous drains on the firm's resources. She could afford to pick and choose, buying up the cream of the crop at bargain-basement prices. The only area where she'd let her heart rule her head was in mining. Jamie McGregor had built Kruger-Brent on diamonds. Kruger-Brent without a mining division would be like Microsoft without Windows. Besides, she was convinced she could turn the business around, once she'd fired Tabitha Crewe and the rest of the lazy yes-men whom Max had allowed to bleed the company dry.

Once word got out that Lexi Templeton had bought the Kruger-Brent name and was rebuilding the firm, the press went wild for the story.

BLACKWELL BEAUTY BUYS BACK BUSINESS
KRUGER-BRENT RISES FROM ASHES
LEXI CLINCHES LAST-MINUTE DEAL

The American public didn't think to question where Lexi had found the money for her epic business-buying spree. She was a Blackwell. Of course she was rich. Those closer to her were more suspicious.

"What'd you do? Rob a bank?" asked Robbie.

Lexi was coy. "Ask me no questions and I'll tell you no lies."

August, who had some idea how much money Lexi ought to have lost when her Kruger-Brent stock got wiped out, was even more perplexed. But he didn't dare bring up the subject. Lexi had thrown him a lifeline. He was in no hurry to start cutting the rope.

One night in October, August and Lexi were working late, going through their European property portfolio. The smaller, leaner

Kruger-Brent now operated out of Templeton's old offices. They were a lot less grand, but half the price, a proposition that worked for August. Sitting on the floor of Lexi's office amid a sea of paperwork—the new furniture had yet to arrive—they were both starting to get tired.

"All right. Italy." August yawned, rubbing his eyes. "I say we keep the commercial stuff and ditch the residential."

"Agreed." Lexi put her hand over her mouth. "Oh God."

"What?"

She staggered to her feet. "I think I'm gonna throw up."

She came back from the bathroom a few minutes later looking white as a sheet.

"You okay?"

"I'm fine. I think I'm a little exhausted. Stress. Whatever."

August remembered his conversation with Max Webster the day their shares started crashing. *I'm fine. These Blackwells wouldn't know "fine" if it bit them in the ass.* No one had seen Max since the firm went under. Rumors were rife that he'd had a complete mental breakdown. August Sandford could well believe it.

"You should see a doctor," he told Lexi.

"I'm fine." She picked up the next bulging file. "Romania. Are we in or out?"

"Out. You should see a doctor."

Lexi rolled her eyes. "If I still feel bad on Monday, I'll go, okay?"

Lexi had no intention of seeing a doctor. For one thing, she didn't have time. For another, medical science had yet to come up with a cure for heartbreak.

Running Kruger-Brent was all Lexi had ever wanted. She'd risked everything to beat Max, and she'd done it. She'd won. But without Gabe to share it, her victory felt joyless and empty: a beautifully wrapped birthday present with nothing inside.

Sleep, that's what I need. And a vacation.

It was the stress. Stress made people sick all the time, right? If anyone found out that she and Carl had deliberately manipulated Kruger-Brent's share price, they could both be looking at a decade in jail.

That's what's making me nauseous. Not Gabriel stupid McGregor.

George and Edward Webster found their mother in the garden.

"Mommy," said George. "Daddy's got a tummy ache."

"I think he needs some pink medicine," added Edward.

Annabel put down her gardening shears. Gardening was her therapy, her escape. Since Kruger-Brent's collapse, she'd retreated to her rose beds more and more frequently, unable to bear watching Max tear himself apart with guilt. It was Eve's disappointment that haunted him most. Tortured by the idea that he'd let his mother down, Max longed for her forgiveness. But of course, the crazy old bitch hadn't called or returned a single one of Max's calls.

"What were you doing in Daddy's room? I told you not to go in there. Your father needs to rest."

George said indignantly: "We didn't go in."

"He was lying on the floor in the hallway," Edward explained. "We had to step over him to get our boots. Didn't we, George?"

Annabel wasn't listening. Running across the yard to the house, her face and hands smeared with soil, she found Max curled up in a fetal position on the floor, groaning.

"Darling! Max. What did you do? Have you taken something? MAX!"

She shook him hard. Max mumbled incoherently in response. Annabel could only catch a few words. "Eve . . . Keith . . . she made me do it . . ." Frantically, Annabel searched Max's pockets for pills.

"Please, honey. Tell me what you've taken." But it was no good. Leaving him clutching his stomach and moaning into the carpet, she dialed 911.

"The good news is there's nothing physically wrong with him, Mrs. Webster."

Annabel tried to focus on the psychiatrist's words. She was sitting in an office on the ground floor of a private sanatorium. It was a calming room, painted a restful sky-blue, with a large window overlooking the gardens. The psychiatrist, Dr. Granville, was about Annabel's age, blond-haired and handsome in a preppy, unthreatening sort of way. He seemed kind. At the general hospital, the staff had been too busy to reassure her. All their focus had been on Max. Understandably. By the time Annabel got him to the ER, he'd started having seizures, frothing at the mouth like a rabid dog. He had to be sedated before the doctors could examine him. It was awful.

"There was no overdose. No attempt at self-harm. That's good, too."

Right. It's all good. It's all completely fabulous.

"So what *is* wrong with him?" Annabel wrung her hands despairingly.

"Try to think of his body as an electrical circuit, with the brain as its center. Your husband's circuit simply overheated. All the fuses blew at once."

"A nervous breakdown?"

Dr. Granville grimaced. "I don't like that term. I wouldn't describe your husband's symptoms as a nervous condition. He is deeply depressed. I believe he may have lived with untreated schizophrenia for many years. There appear to be repressed memories—"

Annabel interrupted. "What can you *do*?"

Schizophrenia . . . depression . . . these were just useless labels. She wanted to know that Max was going to get better.

Dr. Granville was sympathetic. "I know it's very difficult. You want answers, and I don't have them for you. Eventually we will put him on drug treatment and into therapy. With the right combination of medication, symptoms can often be effectively managed."

"But not cured?"

Dr. Granville looked at the beautiful, exhausted woman in front of him and wished with all his heart he had the magic wand she needed.

"No one can be cured of being who they are, Mrs. Webster."

For the next two weeks, there was no change in Max's condition.

Annabel begged Eve to come and visit him.

"He asks for you constantly. For God's sake, Eve, he's your son! Whatever he's done, or not done, whatever happened at Kruger-Brent, can't you forgive him?"

But the old woman's brain was as addled as her son's. Max was her husband, Keith. Max was her sister's husband, George Mellis. Max had raped her, disfigured her, stolen Kruger-Brent from her.

"Don't speak his name to me!" Eve screeched at Annabel on the phone. "He's dead, dead and gone, and I hope he burns in hell!"

Stripping off his pajamas, Max felt peaceful. He was going to see his mother at last. Everything would be all right.

He made rips in the sleeves and pant legs with a loose bedspring and began to tear. He should never have slept with Lexi. That was when the poison got into his system. He'd been unfaithful to his mother. That's why Kruger-Brent had been taken from him. He was no longer clean.

Calmly, methodically, he tied the strips of fabric together using a true lover's knot, a camping knot that his father had taught him in South Africa when he was a little boy.

Come here, Max. Let me show you.

He had to remember to teach the knot to Edward and George. They'd go camping next summer. It'd be a blast. Now that he wasn't working, he'd have more time for the family. *My darling boys.*

Standing on the bed on tiptoes, naked, Max threw the knotted fabric over the ceiling beam. The noose felt wonderful against his neck, caressing his skin like a lover's fingers. He closed his eyes and let his mind drift back. His eighth birthday. The gun.

What is it?

Open it and find out.

Eve's voice was low and sensual.

You're too old for toys. Keith doesn't understand that, but I do.

Max smelled her perfume. Chanel.

Do you like it?

His head was pressed against her soft breasts, breathing her in, adoring her.

I love it, Mommy. I love you.

Smiling beatifically, Max leaped into his mother's arms.

Twenty-Seven

∞

LEXI SAT ALONE IN THE DOCTOR'S WAITING ROOM, GLANC-ing impatiently at her BlackBerry. How much longer were they going to keep her waiting? Didn't they realize she had a business to run?

It was late October, ten days after Max Webster's shocking suicide, and New York had suddenly plunged headlong into winter. In other years, Lexi's spirits always lifted with the first frost. She loved the cold bite of the air on the city streets, the smell of the chestnut vendors outside her building, the blinding glare of winter sunlight in the crisp ice-blue sky. It roused some childish excitement in her: the promise of Christmas, Santa Claus, brightly wrapped boxes and ribbons, wood smoke, cinnamon. This year, however, the New York cold seemed to have seeped into her bones. She felt drained. Listless. Max's death had neither elated nor shattered her. She was numbed with a cold that froze from the inside out, from her heart to the tips of her Gucci-gloved fingers.

"Ms. Templeton?"

The receptionist was a plump black woman dressed from head to toe in orange. Even her cheap plastic earrings were Halloween-hued. She tapped Lexi on the shoulder.

"We've been calling you, ma'am. Dr. Neale will see you now."

Dr. Perregrine Neale had known Lexi Templeton since she was a child. A keen tennis player in his midsixties, he prided himself on his still-trim figure. With his distinguished gray hair, deep voice and strong, masculine features, Perry Neale was particularly popular with middle-aged women patients; a category to which Lexi now technically belonged, although looking at her clear skin and blond hair without so much as a hint of gray, it was hard to believe she was forty years old.

"Come in, Lexi. Have a seat."

"I won't, if you don't mind, Perry. I'm in kind of a rush. If you could just let me have my test results and a prescription, I'll be out of your hair."

Perregrine Neale gestured to the Ralph Lauren armchair in the corner. "Please. This won't take long. You look tired."

Lexi sat down.

"I am tired. That's why I'm here. I'm sick and tired of being tired."

Perregrine Neale laughed.

"That's to be expected. The first trimester is often the most exhausting."

"I'm sorry?"

"I said it's normal to feel excessively tired in the early stages of a pregnancy. You're pregnant, Lexi."

Now it was Lexi's turn to laugh. "I don't think so, Perry. You must have mixed my blood sample with someone else's. Not to put too fine a point on it, I haven't had sex in months. Not to mention the fact that I'm forty years old and I've been on the pill since dinosaurs roamed the earth!"

"Be that as it may, you're pregnant. I would estimate you're about three months gone. We'll have to do a scan to be sure."

Perregrine Neale's face was deadly serious. Lexi was suddenly glad she was sitting down. Cold beads of sweat began to roll down her spine. She gripped the sides of the chair, fighting back a rising tide of nausea.

"I can't be pregnant."

Painfully, she cast her mind back to the last time she and Gabe had slept together. It was two weeks before she made her move on Kruger-Brent. How long ago was that? She'd come home late, wound up like a clockwork toy after a tense, secret meeting with Carl Kolepp. When Gabe tried to touch her, Lexi pushed him away. But for once, he'd forced the issue, stroking and exciting her as only he could, bringing her to orgasm twice before finally pushing himself inside her, obliterating the tension from her mind and body.

Perregrine Neale was still talking.

"... twelve weeks ... nuchal scan ... baby's neck measurements ..." His voice washed over Lexi like an echo, distant and unreal. "... older first-time mothers ... elevated risk ..."

"No."

Lexi spoke so softly that at first the doctor didn't hear her.

"What did you say?"

"I said NO!" This time the panic in her voice was unmistakable. "I can't be pregnant."

"Lexi. You *are* pregnant."

"I mean I can't ... I can't have a baby. I can't go through with it."

Perregrine Neale paused. "You want to terminate?"

Lexi nodded.

"I can arrange that, of course. But don't make any rushed decisions. Clearly, the pregnancy was unexpected. Perhaps if you gave yourself a chance to get used to the idea—"

"No." Lexi shook her head fervently. Her mind was filled with images of Gabe, his face, his body. Forcibly, she pushed them out, screwing her eyes closed. "I can't do it, Perry. There's work. Kruger-Brent. We're only just starting to rebuild. The timing couldn't be worse."

"Lexi, please don't take this the wrong way. But you're forty years old. You may not get another chance at pregnancy, at least not naturally. There's always IVF, of course, but statistically the odds are not great."

"I don't want another chance." Lexi stood up. She was shaking, but her voice was firm. "I don't want children, Perry. Please set up a termination as soon as possible."

She walked out of the office, slamming the door behind her.

Gabe McGregor sat on the veranda of his new Cape Town apartment, lost in thought. Maybe he should have waited? Shopped around a bit before signing the lease? It was the first place the real-estate agent had shown him that met his requirements: private, not too big, excellent security, ocean views. Gabe had signed on the dotted line within a minute of walking through the door.

But now he thought: *What am I doing here? This isn't home.*

What had he expected? He'd moved back to South Africa because, after Lexi, he had to leave New York. And because he had nowhere else to go. Scotland wasn't home anymore. London was cold and gray, not a city to move to when trying to escape depression. South Africa had been his home once. Maybe it could be again?

Or maybe not. Cape Town was so charged with memories of Tara and the children, of Dia and Phoenix, of happiness found and lost, that when Gabe walked the streets, even the air smelled of grief. He'd hoped his new bachelor apartment might jolt him out of his sadness. Something modern and fresh, with no womanly touches, nothing to remind him of Lexi or his marriage. But it was no good. A fresh start wasn't about geography or chrome kitchen fixtures or black marble bathrooms. It was about moving in his heart. Sipping his Beck's beer, gazing at the bleeding blood-orange sunset, it came to him with searing clarity.

I don't want to move on in my heart.

I want Lexi back.

He'd thought about contacting her after she sent the check. He'd even picked up the phone a couple times and gotten halfway through her number before hanging up, cursing himself for being a fool. *It wasn't the money that broke us up. It was the distance, the secrets, the lies. I never really "had" Lexi. Kruger-Brent did, and it still does.*

Gabe followed the news about Kruger-Brent's revival with a sort of agonized compulsion. Every article, every TV news story, was a connection to Lexi that both thrilled and tortured him. In interviews, she looked poised and confident, a brilliant businesswoman on her way back to the top. There was no trace of pain, let alone heartbreak, beneath the flawless studio makeup. When Max's suicide hit the news, Gabe expected—hoped?—to see some cracks in Lexi's invulnerable facade. But even her response to that had been cool and on message.

"My heart goes out to his wife and family, of course. But at Kruger-Brent it's business as usual."

No one watching her would have guessed that she had once loved Max with all her heart. That they'd grown up together, as Lexi herself used to say, like two sides of the same person.

It was getting cool. Gabe finished his beer and walked inside his pristine, state-of-the-art apartment.

He'd never felt more lonely in his life.

Lexi woke at five A.M., sweating.

The dreams were getting worse.

She was six years old, walking along the street in Dark Harbor with her father, pushing a doll carriage. Max, adult and naked, ran up to the carriage and snatched the doll. Except it wasn't a doll, it was a baby. Their baby. He wrapped his hands around its tiny, fragile neck and started to choke it.

Lexi was going into labor. Gabe was pushing her through the hospital corridors in a wheelchair. He spun the chair around and said: "I know you're lying to me. Tell me the truth about Kruger-Brent and I can save you."

"Save me from what?"

Blood started gushing from between Lexi's legs, torrents and torrents of blood, till the hospital floor was no longer a floor but a thick, viscous red swimming pool. She was drowning, screaming for Gabe to help her, but he couldn't. *"I love you. But I can't go on."*

Weakly Lexi crawled out of bed and into the shower. Her appointment wasn't till this afternoon. *How am I going to make it through the next ten hours?* She rubbed shower gel all over her wet skin, washing not because she was dirty but because it was something to do. Cupping her breasts in her hands, she marveled at the weight of them. The baby—it—was about the size of a pinhead, but already her boobs were preparing to feed the five thousand. She wondered how long it would take them to go back to normal afterward. Days? Weeks? Her usually washboard-flat stomach now had a slight but pronounced curve to it, but it looked more like middle-aged spread than pregnancy. This wasn't her body. It was the body of a stranger. Soft. Maternal. All the things that Lexi was not. Could never be.

She thought about Gabe. Maddeningly, the tears started to well up. She tried not to think of "it" as a baby, still less as Gabe's baby. Even so, the knowledge that she was about to destroy the last piece of what they'd had together . . .

Lexi put her head in her hands and sobbed.

Goddamn these stupid hormones.

All Lexi wanted was for the nightmare to be over.

"I see this is your second scheduled appointment with us?"

Lexi glared at the abortion-clinic receptionist. *Are you asking me or telling me?*

"You canceled a previous procedure on . . ." She scrolled down her computer screen. "On the tenth. Is that right?"

"Yes."

"And what was the reason for the cancellation?"

Gee, well, let me think. I'm throwing away my last chance at natural motherhood? I'm killing the child of the man I love, the best thing that ever happened to me, not to mention my own baby? I'm scared of hemorrhaging to death on the operating table like some kind of sacrificial lamb, being punished for all the sins that no one knows I've committed?

"I had a business meeting."

The receptionist raised an eyebrow.

"An important business meeting. It couldn't be rescheduled."

"Right. So you're quite sure about this afternoon's procedure?"

"Quite sure." Lexi signed the consent forms. "When can I go to my room?"

"As soon as you're ready, Ms. Templeton. One of our nurses will show you through to the patient suites."

The girl sighed as she watched Lexi disappear through the double doors. It didn't matter if it was a panicked teenager or a world-weary CEO, and it didn't matter how tough a front they put on. Abortion was always sad. Part of Lexi Templeton's heart would break today, never to recover.

Next week, the receptionist decided, she would look for another job.

The captain's voice rang out through the cabin speakers.

"I appreciate your patience, folks. We've been asked to circle around for just a few more minutes. Should have you on the ground shortly."

A collective groan from the passengers jolted Gabe awake. Through his tiny plastic window he could see New York sprawled out below. He wondered for the hundredth time what the hell he was doing coming back here.

You know why you came.

Because you had to.

Your heart never left.

"We're running a little behind today." The nurse smiled sympathetically as she bustled about Lexi's room, drawing back the curtains and refilling the pitcher of water. "You'll probably go down to the operating room at around four. Can I bring you some magazines? I'm afraid we can't offer you anything to eat."

Lexi smiled wryly. *As if I could eat!* Maybe something to read would help distract her.

"Do you have today's *Wall Street Journal*?"

"Er . . . no. I'm afraid not." The nurse looked apologetic. "We have *Vogue* and *InStyle*. I think we may have the new *Us Weekly*. Would you like to see that?"

"No thanks."

Mindlessly, Lexi grabbed the remote and turned on CNN. *Four o'clock. Three whole hours.* She'd have written a check for a million dollars to jump the line and get it over with now. What use was it, having money, if it couldn't get you what you wanted?

Gabe jumped into the cab. It was filthy and smelled of stale tacos.

"Park Avenue, please. The Kruger-Brent building."

"They ain't there no more." The cabdriver turned around. A blubbery whale of a Mexican, he had sweat patches under his arms the size of dinner plates. When he spoke, he blasted Gabe with taco breath. "They went bust, remember? You don't watcha news?"

"Right, right. I forgot."

Of course. Lexi must have moved to new premises. But where? Gabe looked at his watch. It was three o'clock already and he was dog tired. Maybe he should forget going to Lexi's office? He could go to his hotel, get some sleep and see her this evening at the apartment.

"You know what? I changed my mind. Just take me to the Plaza."

"You got it, boss. Plaza hotel it is."

Lexi felt the medication course through her veins.

The nurse said: "You should start to feel a little woozy. Just relax. I'll be back to get you in half an hour."

Lexi slumped back against the pillow. When the nurse was gone, she started to cry.

I'm sorry, baby.

Outside, the nurses were talking.

"Even without makeup she's *really* pretty."

"I know. You'd never think she was forty. You think she's had Botox?"

"No way. You can always tell."

"Yeah, but with her money she could get, like, the best. Invisible."

"How rich is she, exactly?"

"She bought Kruger-Brent for cash, so I'm guessing Bill Gates–rich. You know, if *I* had tons of money and looked like she does, I'd figure I had something to smile about. She looks so sad."

"C'mon, Pearl, give her a break. She's here for an abortion. She's hardly gonna be doing cartwheels down the hall."

"I guess. I wonder who the daddy is?"

They ran through the list of Lexi's past lovers like they were discussing a character on a TV soap until the doctor arrived and put an end to the gossip.

It didn't matter who the father was anyway. In a couple of hours, there would be no father.

The doctor was a woman. Lexi wondered if she'd ever been through an abortion herself. *How do doctors get into this line of work anyway?*

"Once the anesthetic is in, I want you to count backward from twenty. Okay?"

"Okay."

A sharp prick. "Start counting."

"Twenty, nineteen . . ."

Lexi thought about her mother giving birth to her. Had she known she was going to die? That she would sacrifice her own life for the new life inside her?

". . . fifteen, fourteen . . ."

Max's face. He was making love to her, violently, passionately. She was coming, screaming his name.

". . . twelve, eleven . . ."

The light was fading. She could feel herself sinking, sliding deeper and deeper into the darkness.

Gabe was here. He was talking to her. She could see his face, his lips moving, but she couldn't hear him. He was waving his arms around wildly, shouting. Something was wrong.

"I'm sorry," she murmured. "I'm sorry, Gabe."

Then he was gone.

At first she thought she was dreaming. Only when Gabe took her hand did she realize he was real.

She was in bed in her room, the same room she'd been in before the operation. Gabe was sitting by the bedside.

"What happened? Is it over?"

He kissed her on the forehead. "You mean the operation? No. I wouldn't let them go through with it. I convinced the doctor that you were still unsure."

Tears streamed down Lexi's face.

"Was I wrong? Do you want to get rid of our baby that badly?" He looked anguished. "It is *our* baby, isn't it?"

Lexi nodded miserably.

"How did you know I was here?"

Gabe told her how he'd jumped on a plane in Cape Town, desperate to see her. "I was going to my hotel, but I changed my mind at the last minute and swung by the old Templeton office."

"Kruger-Brent," Lexi said weakly.

"I know. I hoped you might have moved there, but I wasn't sure. Then I ran into August Sandford in the elevator. As soon as he saw me, his face changed. I knew there was something terribly wrong."

"August *told* you?"

"Don't be mad. I forced it out of him. I got here as fast as I could, but they told me you were already in the operating room. My God." Gabe shook his head. "If I'd been thirty seconds later . . . Why didn't you tell me you were pregnant?"

Lexi reached out and touched his face.

"I didn't want to hurt you. I'd already hurt you enough. I knew I couldn't keep it."

Gabe's voice trembled. "Why not? What are you so afraid of, Lexi?"

At last, it all poured out. Her terror of giving birth. Her certainty that, even if she lived, she would make a terrible mother.

"I'm not like you," she sobbed. "I'm different. Max and I, we were both different. We were born with this . . . *thing*. Obsession, I suppose you'd call it. Max wanted Kruger-Brent as much as I did. I killed him, Gabe." She put her head in her hands. "When I took the company away from him, I signed his death warrant."

All the grief she'd been suppressing burst out of her like an exorcised demon. Lexi had hated Max for so long, she'd convinced herself that all the love was gone. But it wasn't. Max's death was like a part of herself dying. She knew that now.

Gabe let her finish.

Once she'd cried herself out, he said gently: "You didn't kill Max Webster. The man was ill. He killed himself."

"But, Gabe, you don't know. You don't know *me*. I've done some terrible things. Unforgivable things."

"Nothing is unforgivable." Gabe stroked her hair. "That's why I got on the plane. Whatever you've done, Lexi, I don't care. I love you. I love you as you are."

"But, Gabe, you don't know. You don't know what I've done."

"No, and I don't care. I thought I wanted the truth, but I don't. The past is the past and it can't be changed. It's the future I'm interested in." He reached down and stroked her belly. "*Our* future. Have the baby, Lex. Marry me. I know Kruger-Brent will always come first. But I'll take second if that's what it takes to be with you."

He opened his arms. Lexi fell into them, clinging to him for dear life. She loved him so much, it terrified her. As for the baby . . .

"I'm frightened, Gabe," she said at last, pulling away. "My mother died giving birth to me. My grandmother died giving birth to *her*. It's not even death I'm afraid of. It's dying before I've had a chance to make Kruger-Brent great again."

Gabe looked at her with a mixture of wonder and pity.

The tragedy is, she means it.

"You're not going to die, Lexi. Marry me."

I can't. It will never work. There's so much you don't know about me. So much you must never know.

"Yes."

Gabe's face lit up. "Seriously? You will?"

"Yes!" Lexi was crying and laughing, touching and kissing him everywhere, unable to let him go. "Yes, I'll marry you. I love you so much, Gabe."

She knew she didn't deserve a happy ending. But she wanted one so badly.

Kruger-Brent. Gabe. A baby.

At last, Lexi Templeton was going to have it all.

Eve knew the end was coming. She could feel death all around her, a smothering blanket she could not shake off. Panic surged up in her throat like vomit.

No! Not yet! It's not my time. Please! I haven't finished.

She was young and beautiful, far more beautiful than Alex. Men fought one another for the privilege of going to bed with her. She was a goddess, rich, blessed, untouchable. Then the ghosts came in and spoiled it all.

Kate Blackwell, her grandmother. *You're a wicked child, Eve. Alexandra shall inherit Kruger-Brent. You will get nothing.*

Keith Webster. *It's just a minor operation, to get rid of those fine lines around your eyes. You mustn't worry, darling. I'll take care of you.*

Max, her gypsy boy, her savior. *We're going under, Mother! Someone's short-selling our stock. There's nothing I can do.*

Fools, all of them. Thieves, liars and fools!

Kate Blackwell was pressing the blanket down over Eve's face. She couldn't breathe. Overwhelmed with terror, Eve felt her bowels opening. She caught the rancid smell of her own filth, felt the sticky wetness on her legs and back.

No! Not now! Not like this!

With her last ounce of strength, Eve pushed her grandmother off. She reached into the bedside drawer, her gnarled fingers scrabbling desperately for pen and paper. She started to write, a frenzied, barely legible scrawl. Folding the paper over, she wrote a name on the back.

Almost there . . .

Keith Webster snatched the pen from her hand. George Mellis held her down. The last thing Eve saw was Kate Blackwell walking toward her with the blanket of death in her hands.

The old bitch was smiling.

Twenty-Eight

LEXI TEMPLETON'S WEDDING TO GABRIEL MCGREGOR WAS the society event of the decade. Held at Cedar Hill House in Dark Harbor, it was attended by prime ministers and kings, billionaire tycoons and movie stars. But the most important guest was none of those illustrious figures. It was a newborn baby girl—Maxine Alexandra Templeton McGregor. As the sole heiress to Kruger-Brent, Lexi's daughter was already the richest child in America. Her photograph, however grainy, would be worth a fortune to the lucky paparazzo who snapped it first.

But no one was going to get her picture at the wedding. Security was so tight, not even a housefly got into the estate grounds without a permit. For today, at least, little Maxine could sleep peacefully, untroubled by the prying eyes of the world.

"Isn't she beautiful?"

Lexi bent low over her daughter's crib. The terror of Maxine's birth already felt like a distant memory. Nothing had gone wrong. Lexi had been worrying over nothing.

"*You're* beautiful." Robbie Templeton kissed his sister on the cheek. As Gabe's best man, he was supposed to be having a pre-ceremony drink with the groom. But he couldn't resist snatching these few final moments with Lexi and his niece. Little Max already had her famous uncle wrapped around her finger.

"You're biased. I'm still fat." Lexi patted her nonexistent belly through the white lace of her wedding dress. "Do you think it's ridiculous to wear white at my age?"

"Not at all," said Robbie. "It's the color of new beginnings."

New beginnings. Yes. A fresh start.

Lexi still found it hard to come to terms with her new happiness. Under her direction, Kruger-Brent was once again thriving. They were smaller than they had been in Kate Blackwell's heyday. But they were on their way back to the top, and the climb was exhilarating. With every passing month, Lexi worried less and less about being exposed for what she and Carl had done. The SEC hadn't so much as sniffed at either of them. They were in the clear.

Better yet, she had Gabe to share her happiness. Gabe and the miracle that was their daughter. It was hard to tell who Maxine looked like. Being so tiny, her eyes were still baby blue, and her hair was a shock of chimpanzee black. Gabe said she looked like Lexi, but that was only because she clenched her fists and pouted a lot, and screamed blue murder when she didn't get her way.

Paolo put his wrinkled, old man's face around the door.

"Robbie, Gabe needs you. It's five minutes to showtime."

Robbie looked at Lexi.

"Next time I talk to you, you'll be Mrs. Gabe McGregor."

"I know." Her smile could have lit up the whole state of Maine. "I just hope I don't wake up before I get to that part."

The entire garden of Cedar Hill House, a vast sloping lawn that led from the house right down to the water, was covered with a white canvas tent. Inside, a hundred-foot "aisle" lined with thousands of white roses led to a dais-style altar.

Peter Templeton's eyes filled with tears as he walked his daughter toward her husband. Frail and elderly, a shadow of the burly quarterback of his youth, at times Peter appeared so weak that he had to lean on Lexi for support. But there could be no mistaking his joy. After so much suffering, God had at last granted a happy ending to his beloved child.

"Do you take this woman . . . ?"

"I do."

"Do you take this man . . . in sickness and in health, till death do you part?"

"I do! I do."

Lexi felt her shoulders lighten and her chest release. She gazed with love into Gabe's eyes and saw her love reflected back. *I will never be alone again.*

At the gates to Cedar Hill House, a man produced his ID card.

"Special delivery for Ms. Templeton."

"Okay. You can leave it here."

"No can do. My employer gave me strict instructions to deliver it to Ms. Templeton personally. It contains a very important document."

The security guard laughed.

"I don't care if it's the original stone tablet of the Ten Command-ments. You ain't going up there."

The man hesitated.

"If I leave it with you, will you be sure Ms. Templeton gets it? To-day?"

"Sure, buddy. Like I said. Leave it with me."

He waited till the man had gone, then looked at the package. It was a plain, stiff brown envelope from a lawyer's office. Boring. Who wanted to look at that shit on their wedding day?

Behind the guard lay a huge mound of unopened wedding presents and cards, junk mostly, left by well-wishers and members of the public. Without thinking, he tossed the envelope onto the pile.

Gabe felt like he was being sucked into a cyclone. All around him people were clamoring to shake his hand and pat him on the back.

"Beautiful ceremony."

"Lexi looked gorgeous."

"Congratulations, man. Where's the honeymoon?"

The vice president of the United States, unquestionably one of the most boring men on the planet, cornered Gabe for ten solid minutes af-ter the speeches. Even after most of the guests began drifting home, Gabe found himself pressing the flesh with one dignitary after another, shaking hands till his wrist ached. Spotting Robbie in the crowd, he grabbed his arm as if it were a branch in a tsunami.

"Oh my God. This is insane. I haven't drawn a breath in the last three hours."

Robbie smiled. "It's your wedding day. You're popular."

"Is this what it's like for you, after a concert? Getting mobbed by fans?"

"Ha! I wish. Have you seen Lexi?"

Gabe sighed. "I was about to ask you the same question. We've only been married half a day and already she's disappeared on me."

"Try the study," said Robbie. "She's probably on the PC, checking Kruger-Brent's stock price."

It was a joke. But Gabe said: "You know what? That's not such a bad idea."

Lieutenant John Carey of the Maine State Police shook his head in disbelief.

"It's April first and no one told me. Right?"

Detectives Michael Shaw and Antonio Sanchez shook their heads.

"You're serious about this?"

Antonio Sanchez said, "Yes, sir. I mean, we only got the information last night. But it seems to check out."

"*Seems to?*" Lieutenant Carey's blood pressure was rising. "Do you know how powerful this woman is? And you come to me with *seems to?*"

The detectives were silent. Both of them were glad it wasn't their call. Eventually the lieutenant spoke.

"Bring in the other guy. Kolepp. Let's talk to him first."

Detectives Shaw and Sanchez looked at each other nervously.

Lieutenant Carey groaned. "What?"

"We tried, sir. Last night. He's gone."

"What do you mean, 'gone'?"

"To South America, sir. We think. He emptied all his accounts."

"Shit." John Carey had been a cop for over thirty years. This sort of thing—billion-dollar frauds, tip-offs from beyond the grave—didn't happen much in Maine. The contents of Eve Blackwell's deathbed letter to the police were explosive. *Explosive enough to blow up my career if I screw this up.*

"Should we bring Ms. Templeton in, sir?"

Lieutenant Carey thought for a moment. "No, don't do anything yet. Not till we're certain. Let's not forget, Eve Blackwell was as crazy as a June bug. This whole thing could be a hoax."

He needed time to think. Perhaps this drama was a blessing in disguise? Perhaps, after three thankless decades on the force, the gods were offering him, John Carey, a final shot at fortune and glory?

If it was a hoax and he arrested Lexi Templeton on her wedding day, he'd be a laughingstock.

If it wasn't, and he didn't . . .

At least there was a silver lining in all of this. Carl Kolepp might be able to disappear. But Lexi Templeton had one of the most recognizable faces on the planet.

She's not going anywhere.

Lexi sat in an upstairs bedroom at Cedar Hill House, thinking. All the noise and clamor downstairs was too much. She had to escape.

I did it! I married Gabe. I have everything I've ever wanted.

She remembered childhood summers spent in this house. How her father's grief for her mother had coated everything with a cloying patina of sadness, freezing the Dark Harbor estate in a sepia haze of loss. Except for Peter, who still lived there, rattling around the empty halls like a ghost, all the old generation were gone now: *my mom, Uncle Keith, Aunt Eve. Even Max. Poor Max.*

When Father dies, I'm going to strip this place bare and start again. Make it a happy home for Maxine. She's going to have the childhood I never had.

"Sorry to disturb you, ma'am. I didn't know anybody was in here." Conchita, one of the housemaids, staggered in with a preposterously large pile of wedding presents and cards. "The gatehouse hasn't room for any more." She dumped the pile unceremoniously on the bed.

"These were all left at the gate?"

"Yes, ma'am. It seems a lot of people want to wish you well."

Lexi sat down and began to unwrap the gifts. Before she knew it, hours had passed. The party downstairs was almost at an end. Some of the presents were expensive: Lalique vases, Tiffany lamps, first editions of Hemingway and Mark Twain. Others were simple, but given from the heart. Lexi was particularly touched by a pottery mug one of the local grade-school kids had made for her, engraved with her wedding date and her and Gabe's initials intertwined. *Sweet.* By the time she came to the stiff brown envelope, she was starting to get tired. *This'll be the last one. I'll open the rest later.*

Pulling out the single sheet of paper she recognized her aunt Eve's handwriting immediately. Thirty seconds later, Lexi knew she would never open her other wedding presents. Her world had changed forever.

Think. You don't have much time.
What would Kate Blackwell have done?

"Sir, take a look at this."

Detective Michael Shaw was pointing to numbers on his computer screen. Big numbers.

"These are transfers made from Cedar International to Carl Kolepp's business account forty-eight hours before Kruger-Brent went under."

"So?"

"So Kolepp used this money"—Detective Shaw pulled up another screen—"to borrow Kruger-Brent stock from a whole bunch of banks. Which he then sold short, pushing the share price down. But it wasn't enough. So on the Monday he borrowed a bunch *more* stock. From these guys. DH Holdings."

"Who the hell is DH Holdings?" Lieutenant Carey frowned.

"It's no one. It's a shell. The chairman is one Jennifer Wilson. Who also happens to be the founder, owner and sole shareholder of . . ." Another screen.

"Don't tell me. Cedar International?"

The detective nodded. "Jennifer Wilson *is* Lexi Templeton, boss. She's traded under that name on and off for nearly fourteen years. She even registered it with the SEC."

So crazy old Eve Blackwell was right. How the hell had she known?

"Shall we bring her in now, sir?"

Lieutenant Carey made a decision.

"Yes. But we need this done discreetly. It's her wedding day. Half of Congress are up at that house this afternoon. I do *not* want a circus. Is that clear?"

"Yes, sir. Clear as day."

TWENTY-NINE
⚬

LEXI WATCHED THE TWO PLAINCLOTHES POLICEMEN WALK up the path toward the house.

Her plan was audacious. She calculated its chances of success at around 20 percent. *Better odds than Jamie McGregor had when he survived those land mines in the Namib desert.*

Forcing herself to stay calm, Lexi folded Eve's letter and slipped it into her bra. Then, making a deliberate effort to slow her breathing, she walked downstairs. By some miracle, the entryway was deserted. She could hear Gabe and Robbie's voices in her father's study. She would have to act quickly.

"Come in. I've been expecting you."

She opened the front door to the house with a smile. Two cops stood on the porch. One was young, not more than thirty, good-looking and Hispanic. The other was older, about Lexi's own age, pale-skinned and balding. *I wonder which one is the boss?*

Both men looked awkward. To be greeted by Lexi Templeton herself, still in her wedding dress, seemed to throw them off stride. *Didn't people like her have butlers to answer the door? And how in the hell was she expecting them?*

Lexi said, "Follow me. I'll take you somewhere we can talk in private."

Detective Shaw looked at Detective Sanchez. Normally, *they* took the lead when making an arrest. But Lieutenant Carey had made it very clear he wanted this thing handled "softly softly." They decided to let it slide.

"Sure thing, ma'am. After you."

Lexi took them to the library. On the second floor of the house, it had once been Kate Blackwell's pride and joy. A sumptuous, welcoming room with wine-red brocade chairs and cozy, wood-paneled walls, it oozed understated wealth and breeding. *Class.* Lexi gestured for the policemen to sit down. She locked the door behind them. "So we won't be disturbed."

Detective Shaw began. "We're sorry to have to do this on your wedding day, ma'am."

Lexi shook her head. "Please, don't apologize. You're doing your job. I'm assuming you received a copy of a letter from my aunt, Eve Blackwell?"

The detectives exchanged glances again.

"That *is* why you're here, isn't it?"

Detective Sanchez said: "I'm afraid we're not at liberty to discuss that, ma'am."

"You do know she was insane? Toward the end, she barely knew her own name, poor thing."

"I think it would be better if we had this conversation at the station."

Lexi's face fell. "I see." She looked so beautiful, so vulnerable, in her wedding dress, Detective Sanchez felt horrible. He wanted to make love to her, not arrest her.

"Am I under arrest?"

"Well . . . we'd rather not make it formal till we get to the station," he said kindly. "You have the right to have a lawyer present. I think the less said right now the better."

Lexi nodded calmly. "I quite understand. Can you give me a few minutes to change and talk to my husband?"

Detective Shaw looked uncomfortable. "I don't know about that, ma'am."

"Please. I'd like to explain to him about this misunderstanding before we leave."

Detective Shaw thought: *Misunderstanding, my ass.*

Detective Sanchez said: "Of course. Take your time."

Once Lexi had gone, Detective Shaw let his partner have it. "What the hell was that about? We're supposed to be bringing her in for fraud, not asking her on a date."

"Come on, man. It's her wedding day. Have a heart, would you?"

"She's a crook, Antonio."

Detective Sanchez shrugged. "It's still her wedding day."

Gabe ran into Lexi at the top of the stairs.

"There you are. Where on earth have you been? I've been looking for you for hours."

"I'm sorry, darling." She kissed him, savoring the feel of his lips on hers. *I can't lose him. I can't.*

"Do you know the police are here? Security just spoke to Robbie. They said they had to speak with you urgently."

"I know. I let them in. They're here to arrest me."

Gabe's eyes widened. "*Arrest* you? Arrest you for what?"

Lexi took his hand and led him back into the bedroom, locking the door behind them. There was no way around it. She would have to tell him the truth. Without Gabe's help, and Robbie's, her plan would fail.

"You remember when you proposed to me? At the abortion clinic?"

Gabe shuddered. Memories of that day—how close they'd come to losing little Max—still gave him nightmares.

"Of course I do."

"Do you remember what you said to me?"

"Something along the lines of 'Will you marry me,' I suspect. Why?"

"No." Lexi looked at him urgently. "Your exact words. Do you re-member?"

"Not exactly, no. But why is it so—"

"You said: '*Nothing is unforgivable.*'" Lexi clasped his hand. "You said: '*Whatever you've done, Lexi, I don't care. I love you as you are.*'"

Gabe remembered. He remembered his desperation that day. He'd have done anything to get her back.

"Did you mean it?"

He thought for a moment.

"Yes. I meant it. Whatever trouble you're in, Lex, you can tell me. We'll face it together."

Reaching down her dress, Lexi pulled out Eve's letter.

"Read this."

THIRTY

GABE READ THE LETTER IN SILENCE. THEN HE READ IT
again. By the time he looked up, Lexi had changed out of her wedding
dress into a jeans and a sweater and was hastily packing an overnight bag.

Gabe had a million questions: How, why, when? But there was no
time for any of them. Lexi, as ever, was in control.

"Two detectives are waiting in the library. When I get to the station,
they're going to arrest me. We don't have much time."

"Time for what?" Poor Gabe couldn't keep up. A few short hours
ago he'd been the happiest man in the world. Now he was sleepwalking
through a nightmare.

Stuffing her passport into the overnight bag, Lexi zipped it up and
thrust it into his hands. "Time to escape, of course. Now listen carefully.
This is the plan."

All the other wedding guests had left, but August Sandford was still in
the kitchen. Deep in debate with Paolo Cozmici over a bottle of Ychem
that was too good to be hurried, he'd lost track of time.

"Christ." He looked at his watch. "I gotta go. My wife'll think I've
been fooling around with one of the bridesmaids." Swaying happily, he
staggered out onto the front lawn. Lexi, flanked by two cops, was

climbing into the back of a squad car. A few feet away, Gabe McGregor stood watching, ashen-faced.

August rubbed his eyes. He must be drunker than he thought.

"Gabe? What the hell's happening?"

"They're arresting her." Gabe's voice was a monotone. He was clearly still in shock. "Eve Blackwell's lawyers are accusing Lexi of fraud. Something to do with short-selling Kruger-Brent stock. It's all bullshit."

"Of course it is." August put a comforting arm around Gabe's shoulders. "Jesus. What a screwup. Is there anything I can do?"

"No. Just keep it to yourself. Lexi's attorney should have things straightened out in an hour or so." Gabe looked dazed. "We're supposed to be on our honeymoon."

"You will be," said August. "Seriously, don't worry. This is obviously just a crazy mistake."

Alone in his car two minutes later, sober as a judge, August put in an urgent call to his broker.

"Bill? I think you'd better sell my Kruger-Brent stock. Uh-huh, yes. All of it. As soon as the markets open on Monday, I want you to dump the lot."

August Sandford had no idea what sort of trouble Lexi had gotten herself into this time. And he didn't want to know. She had brought Kruger-Brent back from the dead once. He'd always be grateful to her for that. But one more scandal and they were finished.

Not even Lazarus rose twice.

THIRTY-ONE
⁓

GRETA, MAXINE MCGREGOR'S NANNY, HAD MISSED THE drama of her boss's arrest. A thirty-year-old Swede with flaxen hair and strong, childbearing hips, Greta Sorensen had been a professional nanny for nine years. Long enough to know that jobs like this one, working for rich and famous clients like Lexi Templeton, might *sound* glamorous, but in reality, they were damned hard work. With so many people in the house today, it had taken Greta ages to settle little Max down to sleep. Now, with her charge at last dozing in her crib, the nanny was slumped on the nursery sofa in front of *Who Wants to Be a Millionaire?*, snoring loudly.

Gabe walked in and shook her by the shoulder.

"Sorry, sir." Greta jumped. "I was just resting my eyes. Max is fast asleep next door. I'd have woken up if she stirred."

"It's all right, Greta."

"I thought you and Mrs. McGregor had left for your honeymoon. Did you want to say good-bye to the baby?"

"Actually, there's been a change of plan. Mrs. McGregor's been . . . er . . . detained. She'll be flying out to join us in a day or two."

The nanny looked puzzled. "To join *us*?"

"Yes. We've decided to take Maxine on the honeymoon with us after all. Lexi couldn't bear to leave her in the end, so you'll fly out with me tonight. How soon can you pack?"

Greta gritted her teeth and turned off the television. "I'll need an hour to get all the baby's things together, sir." *Why did rich people always change their minds at the last minute, and expect everybody else to pick up the pieces? Traveling with an infant was like a major military operation. You couldn't just get up and go.*

"You've got twenty minutes," said Gabe. "Ask one of the maids for help if you need it. There's a boat waiting at the jetty to take us to the mainland. It's a short ride to the airport from there."

"May I ask where we're going, sir?"

"Turks and Caicos."

"Oh."

"Don't look so worried," said Gabe. "You'll love it."

Lieutenant John Carey felt the sweat beading on the back of his neck. He had taken a big risk, arresting Lexi Templeton right here in Dark Harbor and bringing her in to the local police station for questioning. This case was so huge, the biggest fraud since Bernie Madoff. Once word got out, everyone would want a piece of it: the FBI, the fraud squad, Interpol. But John Carey had decided to make them all wait.

Why should I let some FBI hotshot waltz in and steal all the glory from right under my nose? We made a nice, clean arrest. All I need now is a nice, clean confession.

"So, Ms. Templeton. Let's get to the point, shall we? Was bankrupting Kruger-Brent, Limited, your idea? Or Mr. Kolepp's?"

Mark Hambly, Lexi's bull terrier of an attorney, whispered in her ear.

"You don't have to answer that."

Lexi had known Mark for years. A squat, broad-shouldered man with a wide neck and short, muscled arms, he looked more like a bare-knuckle prizefighter than a lawyer. Appropriately, since plenty of prosecutors had left courtrooms where Mark Hambly was defending feeling like they'd gone ten rounds with Godzilla. Other defense attorneys relied on subtlety, coaxing juries, pointing out nuances and shades of gray in the evidence. Not Mark Hambly. He ran over juries like a dump truck. It was one of the many things Lexi loved about him.

Thank God I invited him to the wedding, thought Lexi. *If Mark had been in New York and I'd had to get some local lawyer . . .* She shuddered at the thought.

Lieutenant Carey pressed on. "Were you aware that Mr. Kolepp was intending to flee to South America?"

Mark Hambly shook his head at Lexi. *Don't answer.*

"When was the last time you spoke to Mr. Kolepp?"

Another head shake.

Lieutenant Carey lost his temper. Who did this fancy New York attorney think he was dealing with?

"Listen, you arrogant prick. I'm asking the lady, not you. She's not doing herself any favors by being so obstructive, you know. You think these tapes are gonna sound good in court? Do you?"

Lexi spoke up. "It's all right, Mark. I'm happy to answer the Lieutenant's questions. I've got nothing to hide. You can go home now."

Mark Hambly's jaw practically hit the Formica table. Lexi Templeton was a smart cookie. She couldn't be serious about talking to this schmuck without a lawyer present. Could she?

"Lexi, trust me, that's not a good idea. You're not thinking clearly."

"Really, Mark. It's fine."

A grin of triumph spread over Lieutenant Carey's face.

"You heard her, *Mark.* Go home."

"Perhaps there's a more comfortable room we could use, Lieutenant?" Lexi gave John Carey her most winning smile, the same one that had melted the heart of Detective Sanchez earlier. "My sense is this is going to take a while. These chairs are awfully hard."

Mark Hambly pleaded: "Lexi, come on, this is crazy. Don't talk to this idiot alone."

"This idiot?" It was all John Carey could do not to grab the lawyer by the throat and throttle him. "Are you deaf, buddy? She asked you to leave."

Mark Hambly looked helplessly at his client, but it was no use. He picked up his briefcase and left without another word.

Lieutenant Carey turned his attention back to Lexi.

I'm starting to like this woman.

"We'll move into room three, Ms. Templeton. There's a couch in there. I'll have my guys bring you something to eat if you like."

"I'd appreciate that. Thank you."

My pleasure. You talk to me, sweetheart, and you can have anything you want.

Greta Sorensen looked worried. She was in the back of a limousine with Gabe, speeding toward the airport.

"I'm not sure, Mr. McGregor. I could get into trouble."

"Not if you stick to the story. The airline is fully informed."

Greta frowned.

"I'm still not sure."

Gabe pulled out his checkbook. "Would fifty thousand dollars help to ease your mind at all?"

Greta looked at the check. Then she looked at Gabe. Finally, she looked at baby Maxine, dreaming away in her car seat, blissfully unaware of the high-stakes game in which she was about to become an unwitting pawn. Greta held out her hand.

"You know what, Mr. McGregor? I believe it *would* ease my mind."

Gabe grinned and passed her the check.

He'd always liked Swedish girls.

The new interview room was painted a bright, cheery yellow, with a striped rug, paintings on the wall, and a pair of matching faux-suede couches. Someone brought Lexi a sandwich and a cup of coffee. Lexi thought: *This must be the "good cop" room. Perfect.* The clock on the wall said a quarter after eight.

She had thirty minutes.

"Talk to me about Carl Kolepp."

Lexi talked, slowly. It was important that she sound relaxed on the tape. But at the same time, she had to measure every word. *I can't afford to incriminate myself. I have to tread carefully.* She told Carey about her first meeting with Carl. Her respect for him as a trader. She talked about Kruger-Brent. "It's important you understand a little bit about the company history, Lieutenant. What happened to our stock price was not simple cause and effect. It was not one single event but a complex web of events."

John Carey nodded. "Go on."

Twenty minutes . . . Keep him talking . . .

Twelve minutes.

John Carey didn't understand half of what Lexi was saying. Indices and margin calls and hedges, it was all Greek to him. But it didn't matter. The point was she was *talking*. And it was all on tape.

Hawaii. That'd be a good place to retire. Maybe a time-share on Kaanapali Beach?

Lexi checked the clock. Seven minutes. Frowning, she rested a hand on her belly.

"Everything okay?"

"Yes. I . . ." Lexi clutched her stomach again. "Would you mind stopping the tape for a moment, Lieutenant?"

Carey got up and switched off the recorder. It was irritating having to stop when they were on a roll, but he didn't want to alienate Lexi, not when she was being so helpful.

"Are you sure you're all right, Ms. Templeton?"

"I'm fine. Thank you." Lexi smiled bravely. "I didn't want this to go on record. But I actually just found out I'm pregnant again. The sickness . . . you know."

"Oh. Sure." Carey looked embarrassed. He wasn't good with women's problems. "Sorry. I didn't know. Can I . . . is there anything I can do?"

"I'll be fine. I could maybe use some fresh air."

"Of course. You want to use the ladies' room first?"

Lexi nodded gratefully. "Thanks."

"Follow me."

Carey led her down the hall to the restrooms. Normally suspects would be escorted to the toilets by a female officer, but he didn't see the need in this case. *This is Lexi Templeton. She's hardly likely to try to shimmy out of the window like a common criminal.*

Sure enough, five minutes later, Lexi emerged into the corridor. She looked deathly pale.

"I know you want to get back to the interview, Lieutenant. But do you think I could step outside for a few minutes? I don't feel at all well."

"Of course. Take your time."

He led her out into a small paved area at the back of the station. There was a metal table and a couple of chairs, both littered with cigarette butts. A lone ceramic planter stood forlornly in the corner, containing something very, very dead.

Lieutenant Carey was babbling. "Not the most beautiful yard, I'm afraid. None of my guys are what you might call green-thumbed . . . if you know what I mean . . . anyway. I'll be in room three when you're ready."

"Thanks. I won't be long."

Lexi waited for the door to close. Grabbing one of the chairs, she dragged it over to the back of the garden. At first glance, the wall looked relatively low. But when Lexi stood on top of the chair, she realized that there was a good three feet between her outstretched fingertips and freedom. She'd have to jump for it.

Bending her knees, arms stretched upward, she leaped as high as she could. The chair slipped from beneath her feet, clattering loudly onto the concrete. Panicking, Lexi looked behind her at the station door.

Don't open. Please don't open.

Agonizing seconds passed. Nothing happened.

Hanging by her fingers from the top of the wall, Lexi could feel her hands sweating. *I'm slipping.* Her feet flailed in the air, desperately scrambling for some sort of hold, a protruding brick, a crack, anything. It was no good. The wall was like ice. She was losing her grip.

Oh God! I'm going to fall.

A warm, male hand clamped down over hers. Then another. Fingers tightened around Lexi's wrists. Someone was pulling her, so hard Lexi thought her shoulders were about to dislocate. Seconds later, she was flying headfirst over the top of the wall.

A garbage can broke her fall, but Lexi still landed hard, bruising her elbow and hip on the hard ground of the alleyway. She cried out in pain.

"Quiet."

Someone scooped her up off the ground like a rag doll. Bundling her into the back of a car, he took off at full speed. Lexi lay on the floor of the backseat, her heart pounding. Memories of her childhood kidnapping came flooding back to her. Only this time she knew where she was going.

After ten minutes, and numerous sharp turns, the car began to slow down. Lexi felt the bumps as they turned off the road. At last, the engine stopped.

"You okay?" Robbie's voice sounded shaky.

"I'm fine. Thanks. I didn't know if you'd make it."

Overwhelmed with relief, Lexi burst out laughing.

"I wouldn't celebrate just yet if I were you," said Robbie. "That was the easy part. Now we have to get you off the island."

"US Air flight twenty-eight to Providenciales, you may board the aircraft at this time."

Gabe and Greta were in the first-class departure lounge at Bangor International Airport. Maxine lay sleeping like a black-haired cherub in her nanny's arms. Two floors below, at the gate, an army of paparazzi was waiting, hoping for a picture of Lexi en route to her honeymoon. Baby Max would be an added bonus.

"You ready to go?"

"Yes, sir. Ready as I'll ever be."

"Good."

Gabe looked at his watch.

Come on, Lexi.

Lieutenant John Carey waited for five minutes. Then ten.

Should I go out there and get her?

What with Lexi being so unexpectedly forthcoming, he didn't want to look insensitive. He remembered his ex-wife when she was pregnant. Hormones out of control, like an angry hippo. You could tick a pregnant woman off just by breathing. *I need that confession.*

Fifteen minutes. *This is getting ridiculous. Maybe I should bring her a glass of water or something? Yeah. That's a good idea. Act like I'm concerned for her health.*

Three minutes later, Lieutenant Carey walked outside with a paper cup full of water. When the duty sergeant heard his boss's scream, he thought he was having a heart attack. He rushed outside.

"Don't just stand there!" Lieutenant Carey was apoplectic. "Put a call out to all units. The suspect has absconded. I want roadblocks. I want guys at the airport, the docks. I want helicopters."

"Yes, sir."

"And get me Sanchez and Shaw."

"Yes, sir. Should I call anyone else, sir?"

"Like who?"

"I don't know, sir. I thought maybe . . . the FBI?"

Lieutenant John Carey closed his eyes and watched his retirement condo on Kaanapali Beach crumble into dust. He glared at his sergeant.

"No. This stays within the department. Understand?"

"Yes, sir."

"She must still be on the island."

I'm gonna find that conniving little bitch if it's the last thing I do.

The flight attendant smiled at Gabe.

"I'll show you to your seat, sir. Right this way. My name's Catherine."

"Thanks, Catherine." He followed her to the front of the plane. Max had woken up a few minutes earlier and was now gurgling contentedly in his arms. The flight attendant thought: *How cute to see such a hands-on dad. Most fathers would give the baby to the nanny for the whole flight and open a newspaper.*

"Congratulations by the way, sir."

Gabe looked blank.

"It was today, wasn't it?"

"Oh! Yes. Thank you." *The wedding.* It felt like a lifetime ago already.

"Mrs. McGregor's not flying with us today?"

"No." He didn't elaborate. The flight attendant hoped she hadn't inadvertently put her foot in it.

"Well, anyway. I hope you'll both be very happy."

Gabe didn't know whether to laugh or cry.

So do I, Catherine. So do I.

It was so dark Lexi could barely see her hand in front of her face. She heard the lapping of the waves. Holding her brother's hand tightly, she inched along the dirt track toward the water.

"Danny!" Robbie hissed through the blackness. "You there?"

"Right here."

Illuminated by a handheld gas lamp, a familiar face jumped out of the gloom. "Hey, Lex. Long time."

"Oh my God. Danny French?" Lexi hugged him. "I don't believe it."

Lexi had known Daniel French since she was a little girl. They used to play together during summer vacations at Dark Harbor. Once, when Lexi was thirteen, they'd even kissed under the nets of his dad's trawler. She hadn't seen him in decades.

"Robbie told you?"

"He told me you were in trouble. That's good enough for me. Hop aboard."

Taking Lexi's arm, Danny walked her to the rotting jetty at the end of the track and helped her onto a small fishing boat. There was a makeshift hiding place beneath some nets and tarpaulin. It reeked of fish. Lexi couldn't have been more grateful if Danny had been showing her to her suite at the Ritz.

"Thank you." Her voice was choked with emotion. She'd never done anything for Danny French to deserve this kind of loyalty. *Danny should have been at my wedding, not a bunch of stupid senators. When will I learn?*

"You're welcome. I figured if anyone can work her way out of a jam, it's Lexi. When this is all over and you're stinking rich again, you can pay off my mortgage. Deal?"

Lexi grinned. "Deal."

Danny started the boat's engine.

Robbie Templeton watched from the shore until the darkness swallowed his sister completely. He had no idea when, or if, he would see her again.

THIRTY-TWO

"CAN I GET YOU ANYTHING ELSE BEFORE WE LAND, madam? A hot towel perhaps? Something to drink?"

Greta Sorensen shook her head. She gestured toward the tiny pink bundle strapped to her chest. "I don't want to disturb her."

"She's been good as gold, hasn't she?" The flight attendant smiled. "I don't think we've ever had an infant as quiet as that."

"She likes her sleep. Takes after her father."

Across the aisle, a pile of blankets heaved rhythmically up and down. The only sign that there was a human being underneath them was the tuft of white hair sticking out of the top.

"Bless him," said the flight attendant.

Lieutenant Carey was on the phone.

"What do you have for me?"

"They're booked into the honeymoon suite at the Amanyara. Turks and Caicos."

Detective Antonio Sanchez spoke quickly.

"Flights?"

"They were both booked on the nine-fifteen P.M. flight to Providenciales. But Gabe McGregor changed the reservation this afternoon, right after we came up to the house. He canceled his wife's reservation and had new tickets issued for the nanny and the little girl. He kept his own seat."

"He went on the honeymoon on his *own*? With his wife in the slammer?"

"Yes, sir. It would appear that way. He should be in the air right now."

"Hmm." Lieutenant Carey thought for a moment. "Anything else?"

"Yes, sir." A note of excitement crept into Detective Sanchez's voice. "Right after he changed the first reservation, he booked a third ticket. Also to Providenciales, on a private charter. That plane is due to leave Bangor at midnight tonight with twelve passengers."

Lieutenant Carey's heart skipped a beat.

"What name did he book it under?"

"That's the best part. The passenger name is Wilson. Jennifer Wilson."

Lieutenant Carey closed his eyes. The name rang a bell, but he couldn't quite place it . . . Finally, it came to him.

Of course! Jennifer Wilson. President of Cedar International. Chairman of DH Holdings. Lexi Templeton's trading alias.

Had Lexi honestly believed it would be that easy? That she could use a false name and join her husband on their honeymoon, as if nothing had happened? Perhaps she'd gotten away with so much for so long she believed she was untouchable. *Well, not this time, sweetheart. I've got your number.*

Lieutenant Carey hung up and looked at his watch.

He had to get to the airport.

The blond woman with the oversize sunglasses handed her passport to security.

"Would you please remove your sunglasses, ma'am. I need to see your face."

She did as she was asked. For a few tense moments, the man in the booth looked at her in silence. Then he smiled.

"Have a good flight, Ms. Wilson. Enjoy Turks and Caicos."

"Thank you. I will."

Gabe stared out of the plane window. The carpet of clouds below him looked soft and welcoming. *Peaceful.*

He thought about Lexi. Where was she right now? He hated not knowing. Gabe had played his part. But had Lexi played hers? Was she safe? Even if she was—even if, by some miracle, her plan had worked—what then? He wondered what the future would hold for them? What kind of life would it be for little Max, growing up as the daughter of a criminal on the run?

Make that two criminals. I'm up to my neck in this now. Too late to turn back.

Gabe thought about Eve Blackwell. How her hatred and bitterness had destroyed so many lives. Would his be one of them? Would his daughter's?

He heard his father's voice ringing in his ears, that familiar Scottish brogue: *The Blackwells ruined this family. Thieves, the lot of them, nothing but stinking thieves!*

"Are you all right, sir? Can I get you anything?"

Lexi's a thief. But I love her. I can't help it.

"No thanks. I'm fine."

Lieutenant Carey felt his blood pressure start to soar.

"What the hell is with this traffic? Put the sirens on."

His driver hesitated. "I thought you said we were doing this hush-hush, Chief?"

"Just put the damn sirens on and go already!"

Lieutenant Carey had decided to go to the airport himself. This was too important a job to trust to some minion. If word got out that Lexi Templeton had escaped from police custody—*his* custody—he'd be a laughingstock. He had to keep her from getting on that plane.

At last they arrived. Lieutenant Carey jumped out of the car before it had even stopped.

"It's gate sixty-two, boss." Detective Sanchez's voice crackled through his earpiece.

Lieutenant Carey was running. His cheeks burned, his crumpled suit pants chafed at the waist and his white shirt was soaked with sweat.

Midnight exactly. Had the plane gone already?

The screens were still flashing: GATE 62, CLOSING. A few late-night travelers were milling around. Lieutenant Carey elbowed them out of the way. *Hurry!*

He increased his speed, sprinting down the corridor.

Gate 46 . . . 52 . . . 58 . . . Gasping for breath, he turned a corner. There it was. Gate 62.

Shit.

Gate 62 was completely deserted.

THIRTY-THREE

THE BLOND WOMAN WITH THE BIG SUNGLASSES FELT THE rumble of the plane's engine as it prepared for takeoff. She gripped the side of her seat.

"Nervous flier?" asked the man sitting next to her.

"Not usually. I'm a little stressed tonight."

"Don't be. Just think, tomorrow you'll be lying on a beach under a palm tree without a care in the world."

The blond woman thought: *Without a care in the world? Wouldn't that be nice.*

A male steward appeared behind the desk. Lieutenant Carey flashed his badge. He was so breathless he could barely speak.

"I . . . Police . . . I need to get on that plane."

"I'm sorry, sir," the steward began. "I'm afraid it's impossible. The cabin crew has closed the doors."

"Don't give me that shit, Nancy Drew. Now you listen to me. You radio down there and you tell them to open the goddamn doors right now, or I'm personally gonna see to it that you spend the rest of your life wearing your balls as earrings."

The steward loved a macho man, especially a cop. Unfortunately *this* cop was old enough to be his dad, was fatter than Santa Claus and stank like an overripe Stilton cheese. Not that it would have mattered if he was George Clooney's twin brother. There was nothing he could do.

"I'm *sorry*, sir. It really is out of my hands."

He turned and looked out the window. Lieutenant Carey followed his gaze.

The twelve-seater jet was already speeding along the runway. Seconds later, its wings shuddered as it soared into the air.

Bad news travels fast. It took Lieutenant Carey a full minute to wave good-bye to his Hawaiian retirement fantasy. About the same amount of time it took the jet to disappear from sight, its taillights swallowed up by the blackness.

Then he was on the phone.

One hour later, a group of senior Interpol officers was being briefed across the West Indies. A deputation would be sent to meet first Gabe's flight, then Lexi's, at Providenciales Airport. Both of them would be arrested on landing and immediately repatriated to the United States. After that, they were the FBI's problem.

Lieutenant Carey felt the bitterness well up in his chest.

Happy honeymoon, Mrs. McGregor.

I hope they throw away the key.

THIRTY-FOUR
⚭

THE PASSENGERS OF US AIR FLIGHT 28 STREAMED INTO THE arrivals hall at Providenciales Airport in Turks and Caicos looking exhausted. It was almost two-thirty in the morning local time. Mothers with bags under their eyes as big as their suitcases cuddled fractious babies while their husbands struggled with the luggage. The Interpol officer studied them all. He was looking for one baby in particular.

"There they are."

Emerging through the double doors, the trio was instantly recognizable, despite the silk cravat that the man wore over his nose and mouth. The Interpol officer remembered his brief.

Swedish female, thirty-one, blond, with newborn infant. White-haired male, six foot one. (Someone had fucked up on that one. This guy couldn't have been more than five nine on a good day.) *Minimal luggage.*

Flanked by three colleagues, the officer stepped forward. He put a hand on Greta Sorensen's shoulder. Two other officers seized her companion, while a policewoman reached for the baby.

"Excuse me, miss. Sir. We'd like a word."

The man lowered his cravat to reveal a face crisscrossed with deep wrinkles. The guy must have been in his seventies at least. When he spoke, it was with a pronounced European accent.

"Is something the matter, Officer?"

"You're not Gabriel McGregor!"

Paolo Cozmici smiled. "Indeed I'm not. Didn't the airline tell you?"

"Tell us what?"

"That I'd be flying in Mr. McGregor's stead. It's quite aboveboard, I can assure you, Officer. It's the blasted paparazzi, you see. They follow Gabe and Lexi everywhere. It got so bad with the wedding that they decided to leak false honeymoon details to the press, to throw them off the scent."

"To throw the *press* off the scent?" The Interpol officer rolled his eyes. Was this guy for real?

"That's right. US Air was most helpful about it all." Paolo looked pleased with himself. "Greta and I are *decoys*! Isn't it fabulous?"

Oh yeah. It's fabulous, all right.

"Sir." The female officer tapped her boss on the shoulder.

"Not now, Linda." He turned back to Paolo. "So you're telling me if I called US Air's head office right now, they'd know all about this little scam of yours?"

"Absolutely." Paolo chuckled. "I thought it was rather ingenious."

"Sorry, sir," said the policewoman. "But I really think you should take a look at this." She passed him the swaddled bundle that Greta Sorensen had obligingly handed her a moment before. The Interpol officer's eyes widened. *Jesus Christ.*

There was no baby.

Inside the tightly wrapped pink blankets was a life-size plastic doll.

Gabe felt a sharp *bump* as the plane's landing gear hit the runway. In his arms, the real baby Max was screaming her head off.

"She'll be fine in a minute," said the attendant helpfully. Catherine Blake had only recently been hired to work on Gabe and Lexi's private jet. She wanted her new boss to like her. "I'll get her a bottle of something. Once she starts to swallow, her ears'll pop."

"Will they? Okay," Gabe shouted back over the din. "Let's give that a try."

Rocking his daughter in his arms, he wished Lexi were there. She'd know what to do.

"How long till we take off again?"

"Not long, sir. We should refuel in forty minutes or so. The pilot will let you know our next takeoff slot."

"Okay."

Gabe sighed. He just wanted this whole thing to be over.

When the second plane landed in Turks and Caicos an hour later, the Interpol officer was there to meet it.

"Jennifer Wilson?"

"Yes, sir?" The blond woman smiled politely.

"Would you take your dark glasses off, please, ma'am."

"Certainly."

She was pretty. Definitely a looker.

But she was no Lexi Templeton.

Nor was she a criminal mastermind. Jennifer Wilson was just a secretary who'd worked for Kruger-Brent for years. Lexi Templeton had picked a name she knew for her alias. But that was no big surprise. Most people did. The *original* Jennifer Wilson had no idea what she was getting into when she accepted Gabe's offer of a free, all-expenses-paid vacation. A reward for her long, loyal service.

"Am I in some sort of trouble?" Jennifer Wilson's face crumpled with anxiety. The policeman looked pissed

"No, ma'am." The Interpol officer sighed. "But someone sure as hell is."

Interpol blamed the local police. The local police blamed the FBI. *Why had nobody checked with the airline?* Everybody blamed John Carey, the schmuck in Maine who'd let Lexi slip through his fingers.

On a conference call in the early hours of the morning, the senior FBI agent in charge of the case mused aloud.

"You've just pulled off one of the biggest financial frauds in U.S. history. You have one of the most recognizable faces on the planet. You're on the run with your equally recognizable husband and your newborn baby. Where the hell do you go?"

From somewhere on the other side of the world, a lone voice echoed down the phone line.

"Somewhere that has no extradition treaty with the United States."

"Preferably with white-sand beaches, palm trees and a decent five-star hotel," piped up another joker. Everybody laughed.

The FBI agent was silent for a moment. Then he laughed, too. It was staring him in the face.

Of course.

I know exactly where they are.

THIRTY-FIVE
☞

24 Hours Later

SUNLIGHT FLOODED THE WHITEWASHED ROOM. GABE opened his eyes and quickly closed them again. "What time is it?"

"Almost noon. You've been asleep for hours."

Lexi was walking around the room naked, opening the wooden shutters. Outside, the Indian Ocean lapped at the sand. Their private beachfront villa had spectacular views of the ocean on one side and of the paradise island of Ihuru on the other. Lexi had bought the house years ago for a song, back when property in the Maldives had crashed. Now it was once again a valuable piece of real estate.

Not valuable. Priceless.

There were about fifty countries around the world that did not have extradition treaties with the United States. Unfortunately for Lexi, most of them were either impossible to get to, especially at short notice, or were the sort of backward, festering dumps that made the idea of a stretch in federal prison start to look appealing. Lexi had no intention of raising Maxine in a refugee camp in Cambodia, or winding up as an exotic item on the menu in Equatorial Guinea.

And why should I when I have the perfect honeymoon house sitting waiting for me?

"Where's Max?" Gabe sat bolt upright in bed. He was sweating. "The crib's empty! Someone's taken her!"

"Relax." Lexi came over and kissed him. "She's downstairs with the housekeeper. We're safe here, darling. We're together. You don't have to worry anymore." Pulling back the sheet, she slipped into bed beside him.

"Let's make love."

It was their first time as husband and wife and it was beautiful. By rights, Lexi should have felt tired. It had taken a day and a half to get there. Thirty-six hours in which she'd eaten nothing and not slept more than a few snatched minutes.

After Danny French sailed her safely to the mainland, he drove two hours into rural Maine to a friend's farm. From there, Lexi hitched a ride on a single-engine crop duster to a larger, private airfield where a jet was waiting to fly her to Le Touquet in northern France. Then it was on to London, switching planes again before the longest leg of the journey.

Gabe was already in the villa when Lexi arrived, passed out on the bed with one arm draped protectively over Max's crib. She touched his arm and he awoke, hugging her tight, his relief too profound for words. Seconds later, they were both deeply asleep.

Now, lying naked in Gabe's arms, their lovemaking over, Lexi felt more awake and more alive than she had ever felt in her life. There was so much to *do*. She sprang out of bed and opened the closet, looking for something to put on. None of the clothes looked familiar. She hadn't been to the house in years.

"What's your hurry?" Gabe yawned, watching her discard one dress after another. "You're supposed to be on a honeymoon, remember?"

"I know, honey. But I have a lunch meeting at the Angsana Resort. I can't show up for it naked." Settling on a plain brown sundress, Lexi slipped it over her head.

"A *lunch meeting? Here?* Are you serious? Who with, for God's sake?"

"With my lawyer, of course," said Lexi. "He checked into the hotel last night, just like we arranged. If anyone can prove my innocence, it's Mark Hambly."

"Darling," Gabe reminded her gently. "You *aren't* innocent."

Lexi looked at him reproachfully. "Whose side are you on?"

Mark Hambly sipped his chilled Chablis and handed Lexi the latest copy of the *Wall Street Journal*.

"Congratulations. You made the front page."

Lexi scanned the article impassively. As usual, the *Journal* was frighteningly accurate on the facts. She was more interested in the picture. Some bright young thing had gotten ahold of a shot of Lexi in her wedding dress. She looked stunning. *I was so right to go vintage.* She returned the paper.

"You have to get me off this, Mark."

"I'll do my best."

"I can't stay here, I'll go crazy. I have to get back to the States."

"Whoa, slow down a minute, would you? You only just got *out* of the States. And that wasn't easy."

"I want my company back."

Mark Hambly laughed. "One thing at a time, Lexi. Let's focus on keeping you out of jail, shall we?"

"What do you suggest?"

Mark explained the various possibilities for a defense: Eve Blackwell was known to be of unsound mind. Lieutenant Carey hadn't followed proper procedures.

"But your best bet, honestly, is to pin all this on Kolepp. I don't know how you'd feel about that."

Lexi shook her head. "Uh-uh. No way. I can't do that to Carl."

"Why not? The guy's in Paraguay, totally cashed out. He's happy as a clam."

"Even so . . ."

"Think about it. The feds can't touch him. And what does Kolepp need to go back for? Nothing. He's not married. His company's gone."

Lexi thought about it. Mark did have a point.

"Or . . ." The lawyer took another sip of his wine. "You could take a page out of Kolepp's book yourself."

Lexi frowned. "What do you mean?"

"I mean forget going home. Settle down here. Chill out. Retire. Make a life. I'm assuming you have offshore funds you can access?"

"Naturally."

"So, why not? There are worse places."

Lexi gazed out over the tranquil blue ocean. Twin sailboats bobbed on the horizon, bathed in pale butter-yellow sunlight. She thought about Gabe, still naked and asleep in their bed. And baby Maxine, content and sleepy in the housekeeper's arms. *I love them so much.* For a moment happiness flooded through her.

Then she thought about Eve Blackwell. Happiness turned to rage.

"No. I have to go back."

"Okay." Mark raised an eyebrow. "It's up to you. But, you know, even if I get you off the fraud charge, you're going to have a ton of civil suits against you. All your U.S. assets will be considered fair game. You'll be declared bankrupt. Gabe, too. I can't protect you from any of that."

"I know."

"You'll be poor, Lexi. You don't know *how* to be poor."

"I know. But Kruger-Brent . . ."

Mark said brutally: "Kruger-Brent is finished, Lexi. I'm sorry. But you have to face reality. There's no way back from this. Not this time."

You're wrong. There's a way. There's always a way.

Later that afternoon, Lexi walked alone along the beach. The seawater was as warm as a bath between her toes. A gentle breeze blew the hair back from her face.

It's so peaceful here.

Gabe and Maxi were back at the villa. Mark Hambly was already on a plane, on his way back to New York to face the music on Lexi's behalf. It wouldn't be long before word got out that she and Gabe were in the Maldives. When that happened, the sleepy island of Ihuru would turn into a war zone. The paparazzi would attack by land, air and sea. Lexi would retreat to the seclusion of the villa. It was beautiful, but it was still a prison. She had to savor her freedom while it lasted.

Sitting down on the sand, she unfolded a piece of paper. She'd only received it two days earlier, but already Eve's letter was worn thin with use. Now Lexi read it again for the last time. Her aunt's beautiful handwritten Palmer script leaped off the page.

> *425 5th Avenue*
> *New York*
>
> *October 12, 2025*
>
> *Dear Alexandra,*
>
> *May I call you Alexandra? Of course I may. If you're reading this, I have already gone to join my dear sister, your mother, in hell. The dead may do as they please.*
>
> *They all think I'm mad. But I'm not. I'm the only one in this family who has kept her head. I should have been running Kruger-Brent from the start. Then none of this would have happened.*

I know what you've done. I know everything. You were right to get rid of my son. Max was a fool, weak like his father. But did you really think you would get away with bankrupting my *company? You're a thief, Alexandra. You stole from shareholders and you stole from me, just like your mother. Thieves must be punished.*

The police are on their way. I've sent them another letter, detailing everything. You have no way out, Alexandra. Not this time. You and your friend Mr. Kolepp can reminisce about what might have been from the comfort of your jail cells. Jail is worse than you can possibly imagine, Alexandra. Take it from someone who knows.

May God curse you and your children, as He cursed me and mine.

Good-bye, Alexandra.

Your loving aunt,
Eve

With the letter still in her hands, fluttering in the tropical breeze, Lexi hitched up her skirt and waded into the ocean. She walked far enough for the water to reach the top of her thighs. Then slowly, deliberately, she began tearing the paper into tiny pieces, scattering them on the waves like confetti.

Good-bye, Aunt Eve.

Good riddance.

I may not have won the game. Not yet. But I'm still here. Still playing.

For Eve Blackwell, it was all over.

But for Lexi Templeton, the game went on.

AUTHOR'S NOTE

I have been a huge fan of Sidney Sheldon's writing since I first read *If Tomorrow Comes* at the age of fourteen. When I wrote my first novel, *Adored,* I actually sent Sidney a copy of it along with a letter telling him how much his work had inspired me. He wrote me a very kind and generous reply, which now hangs above my desk in London. Little did I imagine then that five years later I would have the honor of being approached to write a sequel to *Master of the Game,* Sheldon's epic family saga.

Sidney Sheldon was always known as the Master of the Unexpected. The hallmarks of his writing are suspense, excitement and, above all, a gripping and compelling story. His heroines are all strong, unforgettable women—I would go so far as to describe Sidney as a feminist, another of the factors that drew me and millions of women like me to his books. But Sidney's books do not appeal only to women. During his lifetime, he received hundreds of thousands of letters from men and women, from all walks of life, who felt compelled to let him know how much his books meant to them. Sheldon readers are as diverse as Sheldon characters: princesses and paupers, Mafia bosses and death-row prisoners, cancer patients and Greek shipping magnates. All were drawn to his storytelling. And those stories live on.

Writing *Mistress of the Game* has been more fun than any job has a right to be. It is my sincere hope that Sheldon fans everywhere will enjoy the book as much as they have enjoyed all of Sidney's wonderful stories, and that perhaps a new generation of readers will now be lucky enough to discover the magic of the incomparable Sidney Sheldon.

T. B., 2009

ACKNOWLEDGMENTS

My sincere thanks are due to everyone who has worked so hard to make this book a reality. First and foremost, to the entire Sheldon family for their trust in me and their generosity. Also to Mort and Luke Janklow, without whom none of this would have happened—I owe you both so much—and to everyone at Harper-Collins in New York and London, especially my editors Wayne Brookes and Carrie Feron. To my own family for their love and support, especially my parents and my husband, Robin. Finally, I would like to thank the late, great Sidney Sheldon for being an inspiration to me and to so many others. It's been an honor to follow in his footsteps.